Emma and her Daughter

Linda Mitchelmore

Book 3 in the Emma series

D1514369

Where heroes are like chocolate – irresistible!

Copyright © 2015 Linda Mitchelmore

Published 2015 by Choc Lit Limited
Penrose House, Crawley Drive, Camberley, Surrey GU15 2AB, UK
www.choc-lit.com

The right of Linda Mitchelmore to be identified as the Author of this Work
has been asserted by her in accordance with the Copyright, Designs and
Patents Act 1988

All characters and events in this publication, other than those clearly in
the public domain, are fictitious and any resemblance to actual persons,
living or dead, is purely coincidental

All rights reserved. No part of this publication may be reproduced,
stored in a retrieval system, or transmitted in any form or by any means,
electronic, mechanical, photocopying, recording or otherwise, without the
prior permission of the publisher or a licence permitting restricted copying.
In the UK such licences are issued by the Copyright Licensing Agency,
90 Tottenham Court Road, London, W1P 9HE

A CIP catalogue record for this book is available
from the British Library

ISBN 978-1-78189-272-5

FIFE COUNCIL LIBRARIES	
HJ442691	
Askews & Holts	11-Dec-2015
AF	£7.99
GEN	AB

Rog, this one's for you.
And in memory of my mother – the best
little dressmaker in town

Acknowledgements

Jan Wright and Jennie Bohnet have been with 'Emma' and me every step of the way. No journey is long with good company, so thanks for being there for me, girls.

Huge thanks to the Choc Lit Team, my fellow Chocliteers, and the Choc Lit Tasting panel (Olivia, Catherine, Robyn, Lynda M, Jo, Lisa, Betty, Liz and Caroline). Your support and encouragement knows no bounds.

I know I've given Ian Tomlinson, computer genius, more than a few headaches, so thanks, Ian, for never making me feel anything was my fault – even though it probably was!

And last, but by no means least, a massive thank you to my family – James, Elisabeth, Sarah, Alex, Emily, Eric and Sheila here in the UK, and David, Susan and Sharon in Canada. I love you all.

Chapter One

'A year, Fleur,' Emma said. 'We'll give it a year. A lot can happen in a year.'

'Yes, Ma. I could curl up and die in a place like *this* well within a year.'

'You don't have to be so dramatic,' Emma told her. Yes, she – and she alone – had made the decision to uproot Fleur from the only home she'd ever known and all her friends, so she was prepared to put up with a bit of petulance until the girl settled. But that thought did nothing to quell the ripple of unease under Emma's breastbone that she might have made a mistake leaving Canada and coming back to England. Might.

Fleur sighed heavily. 'I didn't want to come here.'

But I did. I never really liked the vastness of Canada. The perishing winter cold that meant the harbour froze and Seth's seine netters couldn't put to sea for weeks. I never really settled, or made friends. We were a unit of three, Seth and Fleur and me, but ...

'Well, we're here now. Our furniture and paintings and all the things we chose to bring have arrived. They're in storage at Pickfords until we need them. It will be exciting to see it all in a new situation, don't you think?'

'But, Ma, please, please tell me you're not going to live in *this*?' Fifteen-year-old Fleur's voice was thick with horror, as though it had been ladled on with a plasterer's trowel.

'We can't stay at the Grand Hotel forever,' Emma told her.

'Why not? Pa left you a mint. Didn't he?'

Emma couldn't argue with that. The Vancouver fishing

1

fleet Seth's uncle signed over to him had been far bigger than the one Seth had owned in Brixham. Far, far bigger. Huge boats with crews to match. Lots of money had been made and invested. But Emma would swap it all in a heartbeat to hear Seth's voice again, feel his lips on hers.

'Your pa left me well-provided for, yes. For the moment. But it won't last forever. I'll have to find some way of earning money and I won't be able to do it at the Grand Hotel.'

'I suppose. But *this*!' Fleur said, wrinkling her nose.

The *this* in question was Nase Head House, a grand building that used to be a thriving hotel, that overlooked Brixham harbour. Emma had worked – and lived – in Nase Head House between 1909 and 1911 and had been mostly happy there. At least she'd had a roof over her head and good food in her belly, even though she'd been a servant. She'd grown up there. She'd seen her sixteenth, seventeenth, and eighteenth birthdays in this house, turning from a girl – an orphaned waif – into a woman. What if Mr Smythe, the owner, *had* been grooming her to become his second wife after he'd been widowed? Emma had seen through his plan in time. And, with Seth's help, she'd escaped. Grown to love Seth as a woman and not with the calf love she'd had for him when she'd been younger. And she'd married him. And now she was his widow.

The estate agent from Haarer and Mott, standing discreetly behind Emma and Fleur, coughed. Rent it for goodness sake, it's cheap enough, that cough said, and ignore your daughter's horror at the thought.

'Could you leave us for half an hour?' Emma asked him.

So many memories were swirling around her just standing in the foyer that she felt faint with them. The last thing she wanted was to make a fool of herself if she did faint.

'I could make it forty-five minutes,' he replied.

'Perfect,' Emma said, and the man walked off across the foyer and out through the double doors, leaving them slightly ajar.

Emma waited until she heard his footsteps go down the curved steps. She peered from a window and watched as he walked to the gate and leaned against one of the stone pillars, lighting a cigarette.

She took a deep breath, holding it in for a few seconds to steady herself, then let it out slowly.

'It could be lovely again, Fleur. Really lovely. The rent is extremely reasonable and I'd have carte blanche to redecorate.'

'But, Ma, it's *filthy*! And it's enormous. It's far too big for the two of us.'

'I'll concede the last bit,' Emma said. 'It *is* big, but we could run a business. Open a small school, perhaps?'

'You have to be jesting with me, Ma, yes?' Fleur said. 'Lots of little brats peeing their pants all the time.' Fleur screwed up her nose at the thought, and Emma couldn't help but laugh.

'Perhaps not that,' she said. 'But something. It will be good to have a job of work to do again. I miss the time I worked alongside your pa.'

Within days of their arrival in Vancouver it became obvious that Seth wouldn't be able to do all the office work required for such a big business on his own. As well as the fishing fleet itself, his uncle also had shares in the fish market. A fast learner, Emma had soon picked up the rudiments of bookkeeping. Her original plan to start a dressmaking business had been put on hold – until now, perhaps. And so had begun the pattern of their days, until those days were cut short.

'I know. I wish you could still be working together. You and Pa.'

'Me, too,' Emma said. She put an arm around Fleur's

3

shoulder but Fleur was still spikier than a Scottish thistle and shrugged it off.

'Well, don't expect *me* to live here,' Fleur said.

'Don't be silly. Where I go, you go.'

'I could go back to Vancouver. Delia Gethin said her ma would take me in any time. We'd be like sisters. Actually, Ma, Mrs Gethin was planning to speak to you about just that very thing before we left—'

'She would have been wasting her breath if she had done so,' Emma cut in. 'You're a minor and will remain in my care until you reach your majority.'

'I could run away.'

'Stop being so melodramatic, Fleur. There's nowhere you could go without money.'

'I could if you weren't so mean about giving me an allowance. You could at least let me have *some* of what Pa left me.'

'You know I can't. It's in trust until your twenty-fifth birthday.'

'I'll be on the shelf by then. An old maid. No one will want me.'

'And your fortune will still be intact, not squandered away by some feckless fellow who might have wanted to marry you for your money and not for *you* when you were twenty-one. But enough, we're wasting time talking about all this when we should be talking about this house.'

'Which you're *not* going to rent, Ma. I ought to at least have some say in where I'll live – Pa would have wanted that.' Fleur stormed across the foyer, hit her hand against the wall. Then she marched back again and did the same to the other side. Dust swirled around her feet as she went, the sound of her stomping footfalls echoing in the large space. She put a hand to her brow. 'I'll just *die* if I have to live here.'

'You should be on the stage,' Emma said, the words

out of her mouth before she realised what she was saying, vocalising a secret from the past that Fleur didn't yet know. That Emma wasn't Fleur's birth mother – Caroline Prentiss was. Caroline Prentiss who *was* on the stage – or was it films? – albeit it under another name. Or she had been when last Emma had heard her name come up in conversation. Emma wasn't sure and cared even less. Both secrets she and Seth had kept from Fleur because they'd thought it the right thing to do. In many ways Emma did still think that, but she knew the day would come when Fleur would have to be told. But not yet, please not just yet.

'The stage,' Fleur said, twirling around on one foot. 'I might just do that. When I've shingled my hair.' She lifted her long, straight, ebony hair at the sides, visually shortening it to a fashionable bob.

Ever since Fleur had seen Louise Brooks in *Love 'Em and Leave 'Em*, she'd been going on and on about getting her hair cut. And every time she mentioned it Emma said that no, it would make her look too old. What Emma didn't add was that Fleur's looks might attract the wrong sort of attention from men, and that she was too young to cope with that. She was too inexperienced.

'No,' Emma said. 'Your hair is beautiful as it is.'

As if of its own volition, Emma's hand reached up to touch the hair on the top of her head. And it was as though she could feel lips there. Matthew Caunter's lips, the day he'd danced her around this room when she'd been just a girl still a few months short of her sixteenth birthday.

'Ma?' Fleur said, sounding alarmed. 'You've gone very pale. Are you—'

'I'm fine,' Emma said. 'It's just a shock being in here again.'

'Again?'

'I used to work here. Live here.'

Emma reached for Fleur's arm and pulled her towards

the circular carousel seat in the middle of the foyer. The leather – no longer scarlet, but now a faded cherry almost – had seen better days. There were one or two cigarette burns, and it was ripped in places. A vision of Seth sitting on that carousel with a present and flowers for her on her sixteenth birthday swam before Emma's eyes as though he was still in the room with her. Again she saw the shock and the sadness in his eyes as he'd seen her reach up and kiss Matthew Caunter on the cheek to thank him for a lovely day out in Torquay. A day when Matthew's wife, Annie, had been with them – except there had been no chance to tell Seth that as he'd stormed out.

'You never said,' Fleur muttered.

No. And there are a lot more things, Fleur, I've never said. And I have a feeling you are going to hate me when I do tell you. But that won't be just yet. I need time.

'Then I'll tell you. About the time I lived here. Let's sit down.' Emma patted the seat and a cloud of dust rose into the room.

'I'd rather stand,' Fleur said. She screwed up her nose and pointed to the carousel seat. 'That's *filthy*!'

As briefly as she could – because time was ticking away and the estate agent would be back, wanting her decision soon – Emma gave Fleur a resumé of her time at Nase Head House. She kept to what she had done there – the tutoring in French of Mr Smythe's motherless children; how she'd made crab tarts and tarte Tatin to be served in the restaurant; how she'd made friends with a girl called Ruby – the girl in the photograph that had been on their mantelpiece back in Vancouver. Emma was going to call on Ruby soon – very soon. She was impatient to see her old friend now, to surprise her with her return to England.

'Well, Ma,' Fleur said, when Emma finished her tale, 'all I can say is you must have been made of strong stuff because it's like an icebox in here.'

'Isn't it just,' Emma agreed.

'And it's seen better days.'

'Most of this country has,' Emma told her. 'France is just across the water there.' She waved an arm vaguely in the direction of France. 'And the Germans were getting closer. You heard the estate agent say that Nase Head House was used as a convalescent hospital for American officers.'

'And a bit of shooting practice.'

No one could have failed to notice the missing bits of masonry outside – like pockmarks on the face. *That would be first on her list of jobs to do*, Emma thought. Her mind became a swirl of colours for fabrics and wall coverings, furniture and fittings. Nase Head House had, in the estate agent's words, potential.

'They could have taken their beds with them when they left.' Fleur pointed to two old iron beds tipped on their sides in the corner of the foyer. She wrapped her arms across her stomach and shivered theatrically.

And put in some form of central heating that was better than the old boiler that had been down in the cellar in the days when she'd lived there, Emma decided. *It was cold in here, very cold.*

'This floor needs a good clean,' Fleur said.

Emma made a little circle in the dirt and the dust on the tiles with the toe of her shoe.

'But I don't know how to dance.'

'Then I'll show you.'

And then Emma was in Matthew's arms again as he taught her how to waltz. She heard again the words he'd sung so well, so softly, so close to her ear. Could words and experiences – emotions – stay in a room for all time?

She put her arms up in a dance hold and moved backwards around the room. Round and round she went. She leaned her head forward the way she'd done when she'd danced with Matthew a second time, two years later,

7

and it was as though he was there with her, kissing her hair. She could smell the soap he'd always used, and the delicate aroma of champagne on his breath.

Would she ever dance in Matthew Caunter's arms again? Would she?

Three more times Emma waltzed around the carousel – not wanting to let go of her memories – before flopping down onto it, the dust swirling up around her, making her eyes itch, and tickling her throat. But none of that mattered. She *had* been right to come back to England – this experience alone was enough to tell her that.

'Ma?' Fleur said, her voice a tremble of fear and disbelief all rolled up together. 'You look like you've seen a ghost.'

'No, Fleur, not a ghost.'

Seth was dead. He would always have a place in her heart, a very special place. But Matthew, where was he? Did he still have the amethyst necklace that had been her mama's and which she'd given him for safe keeping before she and Seth had left for Canada? She hoped so.

'Memories then?' Fleur said, surprising Emma with her insightful remark.

'Yes, Fleur, memories.' There were more memories here for Emma than there were in Canada; the happy life she'd lived with her parents and her brother, Johnnie, before their deaths. Her time here with Seth, and dear old Beattie Drew – who'd been like a mother to them both – Ruby. And Matthew. 'Memories which mean I won't be renting Nase Head House after all.'

And Emma knew with that one, short sentence that she'd been right to come back to be amongst those memories again.

Two days later Emma stood, a little anxiously if the butterflies fluttering in the pit of her stomach were anything to go by, on the doorstep of Shingle Cottage. She rapped the knocker, and stepped back a little. Ah, at last – footsteps. The butterflies in Emma's stomach were a frenzy of activity now. The door creaked open.

'Bleedin' 'ell, Em, what are *you* doin' 'ere?'

The tone of Ruby's voice and the look of horror in her eyes as she peered through the slimmest of cracks in the barely-open door, told Emma that her friend wished her anywhere but standing on the doorstep of Shingle Cottage.

'I've come to see you,' Emma said.

What else could she say? It was the truth. She'd been waiting years for just this moment. But now …

It was hard to meet Ruby's eyes because Emma didn't like what she saw in them. Their wonderful hazel colour had dimmed – as though there was a veil of something over it. And Ruby's curls – so thick and lustrous, like chestnuts the second they fall from the shell in Emma's memory – were thinner and straggly. Greasy, too. From where Emma stood she could smell days' old cooking.

'Oh, gawd, Em, you're the last person I want to see. If I blink can you bugger off again? Then I can believe I've imagined it. Go back where you belong. Canada, id'n it?'

'Vancouver,' Emma said, wanting this conversation to end yet unable to move from the spot. 'You know well enough where I've been living. But I can't go back.'

I can't go back because Seth is dead – has been for two, long years now – and there is nothing for me there now. But she didn't think Ruby would be able to dredge up a smidgeon of compassion for her if she told her.

'Well, you always were a stubborn bugger, Emma Jago, and I can see you id'n goin' to do as I ask. So, I've got a question fer yer. Fallen on 'ard times, 'ave yer? Come to take Seth's cottage back?'

'I'm not short of money, if that's what you mean,' Emma said, sadness making her voice sound different, even to her own ears. 'Shingle Cottage is mine now … now Seth's dead.'

Ruby was staring hard at her, making Emma feel uncomfortable. Emma searched for compassion in Ruby's eyes but saw nothing but hostility.

'Dead?' Ruby said. 'You never said. You're supposed to be my friend. All those letters we sent to one another back and forth across the bleedin' Atlantic. Why didn't you tell me somethin' as important as that before?'

Ruby's voice was accusatory. As though she now had a valid reason for not letting Emma in over what was, in law, her own doorstep.

'I couldn't bring myself to write the words to tell you. It made it seem too *real* to do that. Seth died two years ago. He jumped into the harbour and saved a woman from drowning. But his arm got caught up in some fishing gear and it was ripped off just above the elbow. Gangrene set in and—'

'Bleedin' 'ell, Em,' Ruby interrupted. She sounded, Emma thought, as though she didn't quite believe what she was hearing. 'You waited long enough to tell me. I imagine you're gettin' used to it by now. Anyway, 'e didn't die with a bullet in 'im like some did, did 'e? Escaped the war nicely, didn't 'e, doin' a spot of fishin' over in Canada?'

'Ruby! That's an unkind and very unfair thing to say. And the war's long over. Besides, fishing—'

'Don't give me no excuses, Em! 'E dodged the war by leavin' England when 'e did, knowin' there were rumours of war flyin' about like midges in May, and that's the truth of it. But I'll tell you one thing – since the bleedin' war some people 'as got a livin' death and I'm one of 'em.'

'I don't know what you mean,' Emma said.

'Well, I'll tell you. It's like this fer me now.' Ruby hissed the words out between clenched teeth. 'I've got company. So you can't come in 'ere. Understand?'

'Tom?' Emma said.

Tom was Ruby's husband. Emma had had their wedding

photograph on the mantelpiece beside her own for years now. In it Tom was smiling, so handsome, so in love with Ruby. And she with him. This scenario she had in front of her was wrong – all so very wrong. It was as though Emma had stepped into a nightmare.

'What do you think?' Ruby rolled her eyes heavenwards – and you're an idiot for even thinking that, Emma Jago, the gesture said.

'But I don't understand,' Emma said. 'In your letters you—'

'Look, Em, it took me years to learn to read and write but I learned pretty quick that you can't believe everythin' you read. Now, are you goin' to bugger off or am I goin' to 'ave to get Stephen out of that bed up there to come down and do it fer you?'

So, Ruby's letters had been all lies. The accounts of picnics in Battery Park with Tom and the children, Alice, Sarah and little Thomas – so like his father with his huge, almost coal-black eyes and his cheeky grin, Ruby had written in almost every letter – had been figments of Ruby's obviously well-honed imagination. And Tom, where was he if someone called Stephen was in Ruby's bed?

But was Emma any better than Ruby really? Hadn't Emma's letters to Ruby been all lies, too? Was not mentioning Seth after his death an omission of the truth just as much as a lie was?

It had taken her most of the time from the moment she'd seen Seth's coffin lowered into freezing Canadian earth for her to sell the fishing business. So many potential buyers had simply walked away when they discovered it was a woman selling it – as though she was a lesser form of life. But she'd persevered, for Fleur's sake as much as her own. In his will Seth had stipulated that money was to be put aside for Fleur to inherit on her twenty-fifth birthday and so Emma had done her best to make sure that was as much money as possible.

What would Ruby's children be inheriting she wondered now as she trudged up the hill towards the cliff top. Did Alice, and Sarah, and Thomas even exist? It was a Saturday. Surely the children should be somewhere around on a Saturday if they weren't at school?

After Seth died it had only been Ruby's letters that had kept Emma going. Ruby had even said in the letter Emma had received only a month ago that she'd been to the cemetery and laid flowers for Emma's parents and her brother Johnnie who were buried there. Would there be evidence of those flowers if Emma were to walk to St Mary's now? Emma didn't think she'd be able to bear the pain if Ruby had lied about that, too. She would go to the cemetery soon, but not just yet, because she was still in shock at the state Ruby was in. She didn't need to see the headstones to remember her parents and Johnnie, they were forever in her heart. She would leave a visit to the cemetery until she felt stronger in herself, until she felt more settled in her new life.

She wished with all her heart she'd told Ruby about Seth's death before having to blurt it out on the doorstep of Shingle Cottage. She might have had a more cordial welcome if she had. Might.

'Bleddy freezin' up there it is, missus. And a wind enough to rip a couple of layers of skin off.'

Emma, head bent as she picked her way carefully over puddles on the narrow, stony path, looked up. She hadn't heard anyone approaching, but then would she with this wind? The man didn't look threatening – or sound it – she decided, so she struggled to dredge up a smile in greeting.

'Good morning. And I agree, it is quite brisk,' she said, slowing her pace, not that she was going to stop and engage this man in conversation. She pushed her shoulders up nearer her ears and hunkered down into the beaver fur collar of her coat. 'For April.'

But it wasn't the coldness of the day so much that was chilling her. Ruby had seen to that.

'For any bleddy month, missus,' the man chortled, and Emma wondered if he might have been drinking.

'If you'll excuse me,' she said, having to step off the path, rough as it was, onto the grass to get past him. 'I need to get on.'

'Not from these parts, are you?' the man said, stepping sideways now to let Emma through. 'Accent like that? American, is it?'

'No,' Emma said.

She hurried on. *No* was as much as this stranger needed to know, and as much as she was prepared to divulge. But what a surprise he'd given her with his comment – she hadn't realised she was speaking differently these days; that she'd picked up the accent of those around her in Vancouver in the fourteen years she'd been there.

But she *had* been from 'these parts' for the first, almost, twenty years of her life. This place was as much a part of her as her eye and hair colour were. It was why she'd come back.

The man had been right. The wind was stronger now as she battled against it, past the fort on Berry Head built to keep Napoleon out, except he had never come this far. She was being buffeted on all sides now as the wind whipped in off the channel.

The sea – zinc bucket grey with scrappy, uneven strings of foam the colour of dirty dishwater – seemed to have a life of its own as it heaved and swelled and rolled and crashed noisily. The same sea that had claimed her parents and little Johnnie.

Emma, planting her booted feet down firmly with every step to stop being blown away, walked as near to the edge of the cliff as she dared.

How easy it would be to jump now, leave all her cares and heartbreak behind her. More than a few desperate people had jumped from this cliff top, but Emma wasn't going to be one of them, life was too precious to her for that, even though she knew the wind would take her breath – her scream as she fell perhaps – away. There would be no witnesses. There would be hardly a soul to mourn her either – except Fleur.

And Fleur was waiting for her back at the Grand Hotel in Torquay. She had to stay strong for her, because Fleur was still mourning her father. And something good had to come out of Emma's decision to return to the place that had shaped her, formed her; the place where she had fallen in love – not once, but twice.

Her first love had gone. But where, Emma wondered, as she turned and headed back towards the town and the railway station for the journey back, was her second love now?

'Matthew,' Emma whispered into the wind, letting it take the softness of the sound of his name, so that in a split second it was as though she'd not spoken at all.

'Bella, bella, bella.'

Fleur Jago was doing her best to ignore whoever it was who was repeating the same word, over and over. She didn't feel like being flirted with in the slightest, not now her ma had left her to her own devices while she was out gallivanting, catching up with an old friend. Hah! All right for Ma, wasn't it? She still had a friend. Fleur had had to leave all her friends behind in Vancouver, hadn't she?

'Bella, bella, bella.'

'Oh, shut it,' Fleur hissed, only a fraction above a whisper, through clenched teeth. 'Or speak English, for crying out loud.'

'Bella, bella, bella.'

'Oh, go tell it to Sweeney!' Fleur mumbled. Honestly, did he have no other word in his vocabulary? He was probably some wizened old man who thought he was God's gift to women. There were a few like it in the hotel. One had even winked at her across the dining table two nights ago. Ugh!

Fleur brought her book, *Tess of the D'Urbervilles* – which she was reading even though her mother had forbidden her to for some stupid reason – closer to her face. *She'd have to remember to hide it under the mattress before her mother got back, wouldn't she? Or there'd be an almighty telling-off.*

Whoever it was trying to engage her in conversation laughed.

'I still see you! You still *si bella*,' the voice said, and Fleur could hear his laughter in the words. And the voice was young, not old, wasn't it?

He wasn't in the least put out by her rudeness and he wasn't giving up, was he? Would it hurt to take a peek at him? Slowly, Fleur lowered the book, first so only her lashes rested on the top of it, but gradually getting lower so she had the speaker in her vision now.

Oh! Fleur made a perfect O of her mouth behind the book. She swallowed.

Well, this was a turn-up for the books. So far England, and Torquay, had been boring, boring, boring. This hotel – the Grand – was anything but in Fleur's opinion. It was filled with people who had to be, oh, at least fifty years old, sixty maybe.

But the boy standing grinning at her, leaning against the front bumper of a small van, was about the same age as she was. Perhaps a little older.

'You like read?' the boy said.

He moved away from the van's bumper, stood up and stretched – much like a cat does. A warm flicker of something made its way up Fleur's spine as she watched him. That flicker made her squirm slightly in her chair – but it was a pleasurable squirm; a new feeling. She rather liked it.

CASCARINI'S it said in green letters edged with gold on the side of his van. ITALIAN ICE CREAM.

Fleur licked her lips. She'd eaten a praline ice cream for dessert only the night before. Had this glorious boy delivered it? But it was too cold out here on the terrace, even wrapped in her ma's fur coat – better get it off and back in the wardrobe before she got back – to be eating ice cream now, even though the sun was bright in the sky.

'Shouldn't you be around the back with that van?' Fleur said. 'Tradesmen's entrance or something?'

'I finish deliver. I see you on way to tradesmen's door. I come back to see you.'

'Well, you've seen me now. Twice. You can go away again.'

Why was all this stuff coming out of her mouth? She didn't mean any of it. How glorious he was. Glossy, black curls that glistened in the April sunshine. A large, hooked sort of nose, but it gave his face life, accentuated his full lips somehow. And those eyes of his – like two, miniature, highly-polished coals in his tanned face – as he stood smiling at her, were mesmerising.

'I can, but I no want,' he said. 'I am Paolo.' Then he pointed to the name on the side of his van.

'Paolo Cascarini?' Fleur said, doing her level best to make some sort of Italian pronunciation of the name. She'd heard enough Italian spoken in Vancouver to know how the words should be pronounced. And Russian and Volga German and Yiddish for that matter, although she wouldn't care if she never heard any of them again.

'Sì. And you?'

Fleur shrugged. She knew what her ma would say if she were to be caught chatting to delivery men – not that she cared what her ma thought, not really.

Fleur hadn't wanted to come to England in the first place. And in April for goodness sake! Okay, so this was the English Riviera she'd been brought to – warmer than most other places in the country – but it wasn't Cannes, was it?

'I think,' Paolo said, 'you is pretty if you smile.'

'Do you now?'

'I good Italian boy. I no lie.'

His eyes held Fleur's and she felt her own widen and lift at the corners. As though they had a mind and a life of their own her lips parted and she smiled.

'I right,' Paolo said. '*Bella. Si bella.*'

'Oh, I bet you say that to all the girls!' Fleur laughed.

'Not here,' Paolo said, his face breaking into the broadest grin Fleur had ever seen as he waved an arm in an arc to the hotel behind her.

But you've said it to a few, no doubt, Fleur thought. *And would more than likely say it to a good few more in the future.*

Paolo began to walk towards her. Slow steps. As though waiting for her to tell him to go away or shout for a member of staff to do it for her. He had one foot on the bottom step of the terrace now.

'You holidays?'

Fleur thought to correct his English. But decided against it. His way of speaking had charm to it – it was warming her in a way even her mother's best fur coat wasn't.

'No,' Fleur said.

Paolo had both feet on the first step now. And still he was smiling at her.

'You no live *here*?' he said.

And Fleur thought she read fear in his voice that she might and that if she did, he'd stand not a single chance of talking to her again if the owner found out.

'Thank God, no,' Fleur said.

'I no understand,' Paolo replied.

He walked up the next two steps and sat himself down on the top one by Fleur's feet, turning his body sideways to look up into her face.

'I don't know why I'm telling you this,' Fleur said, 'but my pa died and my ma can't live in Canada any more without him, so she's come back to the place where she was born. Only I don't mean this hotel. And not Torquay either.' She pointed out across the bay. 'She's over there at the moment.'

Paolo's forehead became a mass of deep, tanned furrows. He hadn't understood all of that, had he?

'I so sorry about your papa,' Paolo said.

Ah, so he'd understood that much.

'And me,' Fleur said. 'He was the best pa a girl could ever have. And I miss him. I will always miss him.'

A lump rose in Fleur's throat which she thought might choke her. Her eyes welled with tears. She'd thought she was over that raw grief, but she obviously wasn't. And now here she was, making a complete fool of herself in front of a foreigner she'd only just met – albeit a very sympathetic and handsome one.

'I lose my mama,' Paolo said. 'In London. Big bomb. The whole road go. Papa and I were in café that day. The *guerra*. You understand *guerra*?'

Paolo mimed shooting a rifle, making bang, bang noises, then clutching his chest. His ma had been killed by the Germans, hadn't she?

'Yes. I understand the word. It means war.' The Italian word was very similar to the French for war – *guerre*. 'I'm sorry about your mama.'

Fleur folded her hands in her lap and stared down at them.

'So,' Paolo said, suddenly brightening. 'We are both sorry. We have both sad. But now we see one another we sad no more. For a little time? *Si*? I tell you my name, but you no tell me yours.' He looked pleadingly at Fleur, the way a puppy looks pleadingly for food. How could she deny telling him her name?

'My name's Fleur Jago. And ... oh my God!' Horrified, Fleur saw a taxi was pulling into the drive and she could see her mother was in the back of it. 'Got to go,' she said, leaping from her chair. 'My mother. My book. This coat. I ...'

Fleur fled from the terrace. Her ma would undoubtedly give her a telling-off for taking her coat without having asked first, if she were to find Fleur wearing it.

She raced into her mother's bedroom, shrugging off the coat as she went. She yanked out a wooden hanger, emblazoned with the hotel's name, rammed the coat onto it. Hung it up. Then she raced to the window.

Paolo was only just opening the door of his ice cream van. He looked up and waved – as though he'd known which window she would be looking out of.

Fleur waved back.

Well, well, well ... coming here might not have been such a rotten idea after all.

Chapter Two

'Exe Motors,' Matthew Caunter said, snatching at the telephone. The thing had rung at exactly the same moment a potential customer had walked onto the forecourt. And he couldn't see his mechanic, William, anywhere. Sloped off down the canal for a ciggy, no doubt, seeing as smoking was forbidden anywhere around engines, and oil, and petrol.

He glanced at himself in the mirror propped on the windowsill beside his desk, put there so he could give his hair the once-over and check for oily smudges – a necessary evil given his business. Grimacing, he ran a hand through his hair – once red-gold but now faded somewhat, and rapidly so now he was in his mid-forties. An ex-lover had, ingloriously, likened it to the rust on a tin bucket left out in all weathers. Yes, well, she hadn't lasted long and he wasn't proud of the fact he'd only wined and dined her a few times to fulfil a need he'd known she'd furnish.

'Good afternoon,' he barked.

God, but you can be a miserable bastard at times, he thought. It wouldn't have surprised him if the caller had slammed down the telephone. Some days he wouldn't have wanted to speak to himself either.

'Gosh, you *do* sound cross,' the voice on the end of the line said, but with humour. 'Am I calling at a bad time?'

'Ah, Stella. It's you,' Matthew said, his mood lifting and his face breaking into a smile at the sound of her voice. He'd been seeing Stella Martin for six months now. Growing closer to her each time he saw her. Stella was tall and slender with the fairest hair he'd ever seen that hadn't been enhanced with peroxide. Not quite as tall as Matthew was, but tall enough that he didn't get instant neck ache when he kissed her. And she was funny, and fun to be with. And not – usually – demanding. Being a nurse she understood that work often had to come before pleasure. And he and Stella had shared a fair bit of pleasure together of late although – unusually for him – he was taking things slowly, not rushing Stella into bed. What he felt for Stella was deeper than mere lust. And he hadn't expected to ever have those sort of feelings for someone again – not after he'd practically forced Emma Jago to walk out of his life – but now he had. 'Where are you?'

'At the hospital. Just finished my shift. I know it's late, but it's been a pig of a day. Two sudden deaths, a new mother off her head with grief, poor woman, after a stillbirth. Oh, and a whiskery old wino wanting to kiss me.'

'Did you let him?'

How could anyone not want to kiss Stella's pretty little Cupid's bow lips?

'What do you think?' Stella laughed. 'No. Matron was walking past at the time and she soon frog-marched him out of reception. So ... I'm wondering if I could see you?'

'Now?'

'Well, as soon as the train will get me there. If you're free, that is?'

'I can make myself free,' Matthew said. 'William's itching to be left in charge, so I'll let him for once.'

'Good. With luck, if I run, I'll catch the 4.15.'

'Then run.' Matthew laughed. 'Look, sorry, got to go. A potential customer's just come in and ...' *Ah, thank goodness. William was back and engaging the man in conversation.* 'I'll bring the Clyno to St Thomas station to meet you.'

And who knows, with luck maybe you'll stop the night and save me the drive back to Torquay, he thought. But then again he was playing it softly, softly with Stella. He didn't want to rush her because Stella might – just might –

be the one to make him consider walking down the aisle for a second time.

The White Horse was packed with diners. A trio was playing a slow jazz number discreetly on a dais at the far end of the room and Stella, sitting opposite Matthew at a small, round table, was tapping her foot to the rhythm – the movement of it making ripples of air flutter up Matthew's trouser leg. And she was nodding her head to a slightly different rhythm – slower, as though she was thinking.

'Penny for them?' Matthew asked, just as the waiter placed a plate of poached chicken in front of Stella and a steak and kidney pudding in front of him, in one deft movement.

Stella downed what was left of her glass of wine, swallowed. 'Sorry. Distracted. I can't get that poor mother out of my head, and goodness only knows I should be used to that sort of thing by now. But it was the way she was bundled out of maternity and rushed to women's surgical the second her baby died, as though she might bring bad luck to everyone else waiting to give birth.' Stella jiggled her shoulders at the discomfiting thought.

'Could you try?' Matthew said. 'To forget her for a moment. You can't carry the troubles of the world on your shoulders, you know.'

'I know. Sorry. I'll eat up like a good girl. Well, woman …' Stella's voice drifted away as she cut, very elegantly, a sliver of chicken and popped it into her mouth.

Everything about Stella was elegant. Matthew couldn't imagine her doing the job she did – all the bodily functions of the ill and infirm she dealt with every day. The blood, the gore, and the smells.

Matthew re-filled Stella's glass with Sancerre. Filled it to the brim. He had lashings of respect for what she did and the dignity with which she did it. He forked up a mouthful of steak and kidney pudding, the fatty smell of the suet pastry filling his nostrils – a not terribly pleasant aroma, although this hotel was known for its excellent cuisine. Certainly the pastry wasn't up to the standards Emma Jago had cooked up for him way back in 1909. Or Emma Le Goff as she'd been then.

And just why was she in his mind at this moment? Not that she was ever far from it, if he were honest with himself. Matthew prided himself on his honesty and so far he and Stella had been nothing less than totally honest in their answers to personal questions, although he'd purposely omitted to mention Emma and her place in his life. And Stella, who'd moved to Torquay from Bristol just three years previously, wouldn't know of Emma, and therefore wouldn't ask.

Matthew had learnt that Stella had been engaged to marry once but had called off the engagement because she knew in her heart that she wanted to nurse, and she wouldn't have been able to marry *and* nurse, the two together being against hospital rules. For his part, Matthew had told her about his marriage to Annie, and their son, Harry, who was now seventeen years old. And how Annie had left him for another woman. He had, he told her with total honesty, bedded a dozen or so women in the years since his divorce. Stella hadn't even raised an eyebrow at that. All she'd said was, 'Of course. You're a man.'

'Penny for them yourself, Matthew,' Stella said, wiping her mouth on the edge of the linen napkin.

Oh, some of those thoughts were worth far, far more than that! The ones of Emma and Harry, if not those of Annie.

'Ah, here's the waiter. Dessert, Stella?'

'A sorbet if they have it, please. Lemon would be good,' Stella said. She patted her pancake flat stomach, product of all the walking about she did at the hospital, up and down stairs all day long, walking the lengths of very long wards.

The waiter cleared their plates and Matthew requested a lemon sorbet for Stella and an apple crumble for himself.

'So,' Matthew said, as they waited for their desserts to arrive. 'Was there anything in particular you wanted to see me about today that warrants a run to the station after a long day's work?'

He said it as kindly as he could, but still the words came out as some sort of accusation – as though he had given up valuable time to be with Stella and that wasn't the case at all. But he'd never seen her so pensive, so withdrawn.

'Yes,' Stella said. 'This isn't going to be easy to say, Matthew, but I need to know where I stand. With you. In the long term. Whether marriage is on the cards for us, or not. I like you very much, Matthew. No, more than like ... I'm falling in love with you. We've been seeing one another regularly for six months now and I know enough about human nature to know how you feel about me, too. I'm not wrong, am I, in thinking you care for me rather more than the dozen or so lovers you've had? Am I making this clear enough?'

Stella's gaze held Matthew's and he thought – for a second – he could see the startled look he knew he had on his face reflected in her eyes.

'Perfectly clear.'

'Sorry. It blurted out quicker than I meant it to,' Stella said. Still she held his gaze.

'Is this a proposal?' Matthew quipped – wrong-footed as he might have been, he was used to thinking on his feet, or had been when he'd been a customs officer and then a private detective, and he rallied fast.

'It could be,' Stella said, smiling warmly at him. 'Since John, well, I've never found anyone I wanted to settle down with until I met you. Or anyone I'd consider giving up my career in nursing to marry. As it doesn't look as though I'll ever be promoted to ward sister, now seems a good time.'

A good time to what? Was he reading this correctly? Was Stella saying he was the next best option seeing as she'd gone as far in nursing as she could go?

'And there was me thinking you'd fallen for my handsome chops and my charismatic aura,' Matthew said.

Mercifully the waiter arrived with their desserts, putting a halt to this rather unsettling conversation. Matthew had never been proposed to before, and while he found it faintly amusing, he wasn't sure he liked it much.

'Anything else, sir? Madam?' the waiter asked.

'A brandy,' Matthew said – he was definitely going to need a brandy. *Yes, he liked Stella, liked her very much. But marriage? So soon? Was he ready for that?* 'Make it a double. Neat. Stella? Sweet white wine?'

'Nothing else for me, thank you,' Stella said.

She attacked her sorbet with a long-handled spoon, sucking in her cheeks with the tartness of it as she slipped a spoonful into her mouth. She licked her top lip and the action made something stir in Matthew's loins. Hmm, perhaps marriage with Stella wouldn't be such a bad idea.

'Actually,' Stella said, 'can I change my mind? This *is* rather sharp. A sweet white wine would be lovely.'

'Of course,' the waiter said, and left to get their drinks.

'We have to face facts, Matthew. Neither of us is getting any younger. Before we know it we could be facing a lonely old age.'

'Hey! I've had better compliments.' Matthew laughed.

And I can still do the necessary required of a husband, thank you very much.

'Sorry,' Stella said. 'My mouth got ahead of my brain there. It's not how I usually do things but, well—'

'Can we sleep on it?' Matthew interrupted, tilting his head to one side. *Let Stella work out what he meant by that.*

'We can,' Stella said. 'But separately tonight.' She leaned

across the table, and indicated for Matthew to lean forward. 'I'm ... how shall I put it? ... inexperienced,' she mouthed at him.

'Then you've come to the right man,' Matthew said. 'I'll be happy to increase your knowledge.'

'But not just yet.' Stella laughed. 'Ah, our drinks have arrived.'

Matthew took his brandy and knocked it back in one go. He had a lot of thinking to do. Stella was right, neither of them was getting any younger, not that he felt any older than, oh, twenty-seven, in his mind. He'd been twenty-seven years old when he'd first met Emma. Was he likely to ever see her again? He had her amethyst necklace for safe keeping but it looked as though time was running out for any sort of reunion with Emma. And sitting in front of him, asking him to marry her, was the very delectable Stella.

'Oh, Matthew, you should see your face! I've shocked you, haven't I? But this is 1927 and women are starting to take the lead. We'll get the vote soon, I'm sure of it. And besides, I'm used to making instant appraisals of people in my job and making decisions, and I knew the second I saw you that you were a very special sort of man indeed. So, will you? Marry me?'

Chapter Three

'Ma,' Fleur wailed. 'My feet *hurt*. How many more houses are we going to have to traipse around?'

Emma considered reminding Fleur that she was sitting on the number twelve tram, bowling along Torquay promenade in front of Torre Abbey, and that she'd been sitting there for the past fifteen minutes since they'd left Paignton. But perhaps not. Fleur had been in a funny mood all morning, barely answering Emma's questions, slouching from room to room in each of the three houses they'd looked over, her arms folded across her chest.

'None today. I think I like that last one, Romer Lodge, the best of all we've seen.'

'Well, why didn't you *say* when we were there?'

'Because it never does to show too much interest right away. Seth taught me that. We'd never have got Mapletop Ridge at the price we did if he'd said "yes" he wanted it, the second he saw it. He got it at a good price for his patience and I hope to get Romer Lodge at a lower rental than they're asking. Ah, here's our stop.' Emma sprang to her feet. 'Come on, Fleur, for goodness sake. You ...' Emma stopped herself from chivvying Fleur up. All this was strange to the girl, wasn't it? A new life in a new country without her pa and with new friends to be made at some stage.

The tram rattled to a halt and Emma and Fleur got off.

'But why have we got off here?' Fleur said, turning to look in the direction the tram had come from and pointing. 'The Grand Hotel's back *there*!'

'I know it is. But I thought we could find a draper's shop and get some material to make you a dress. Or two. The weather will be warming up soon and what was suitable in Vancouver won't be quite right for here. But, if you're feet hurt ...'

'Oh, they're not so bad now, Ma,' Fleur said quickly. 'Sitting on the tram has rested them.' Fleur linked her arm through Emma's. 'But I *am* hungry? We've missed lunch.' Fleur began to quicken her pace and Emma had no option but to quicken hers to match it.

After the huge breakfast you ate? Emma thought. She wondered where the girl put all her food but it seemed she had no problem keeping her slim figure however much she ate. Fleur's birth mother, Caroline Prentiss, had been whippet thin; certainly the last time Emma had seen her, she had been. She shook her head banishing Caroline Prentiss from it as best she could.

'So we have,' Emma said, although she wasn't in the least bit hungry herself. She had so much to think about and the next meal wasn't high on the list – besides, the food at the hotel was excellent, if becoming a bit samey now they'd been there a fortnight.

They were near the harbour now. There were plenty of cafés from which to choose – Godwins, and Macari's. And The Lanterns where once Emma had dined with Matthew Caunter and his wife, Annie, and where she'd embarrassed them both by saying she didn't think much to the puddings. Then she'd asked to speak to the manager and offered her own French pastries. Looking back she couldn't believe the audacity of it, given she'd been hardly any older than Fleur was now.

'Oh, look, Ma!' Fleur said, suddenly gripping Emma's arm more tightly, leaning into her. 'There's an Italian ice cream parlour over there!'

'So there is,' Emma said, smiling. She had fond memories of buying delicious bread from the Italian bakery on Draper Drive back in Vancouver. The people running it had been bright and noisy, their characters like a ray of sunshine – a tonic – on the coldest of Canadian winter days.

Emma was happy to allow herself to be dragged along the pavement. Coming back to Devon had to work out for Fleur as well as for herself. And if Fleur wanted to eat ice cream on a cold April afternoon, then she'd indulge the girl. The café had to serve coffee as well. And tea. And possibly hot chocolate. And cakes – yes, a cake would probably be enough before they had to face another three-course dinner at the Grand Hotel.

CASCARINI'S it said in gold-edged curly writing over the door.

Cascarini's? Emma had a vague memory of seeing the name somewhere before as Fleur pushed open the door and they went inside. Fleur plonked herself down at a table by the window, took off her gloves and placed them on the top. She had an ear to ear grin.

'Isn't it lovely, Ma?'

The proof of the pudding will be in the eating, Emma thought, but she sat down opposite Fleur without offering up her opinion and picked up the menu. Most of the things on it seemed to be ice cream.

A man with black hair that had random patches of silver in it had his back to them doing something with some bottles on a shelf behind the counter.

'Ahem,' Fleur said, with a throat-clearing, attention-seeking cough.

'Fleur!' Emma admonished her. 'The man will be over in a moment.'

There were, Emma noticed, no other customers. Well, who could blame anyone for not wanting to eat ice cream on such a cold day? Although there *had* been people on roller skates working up a sweat on the pier, gliding up and down, doing fantastic turns as they'd passed. *What*, Emma had wondered, *would it feel like to roller skate. Was she too old at thirty-four years old to learn?*

The man turned round then. He fixed his gaze on Emma and for a moment their eyes held. *How sad his eyes looked*, Emma thought. *How serious his face.* It was almost as though he didn't want customers – didn't want to see anyone. This, then, must be Signor Cascarini without a doubt, with that hair and those dark eyes and skin the colour of toffee. She wondered what might have happened to him to make him look so sad.

He turned towards an open door at the end of the counter and spoke in a volley of Italian to someone Emma couldn't see.

'*Si. Arriva!*' someone said – a woman's voice.

Rather impatient Emma thought.

A woman of about sixty or so came bustling out. She was wearing a flowery apron over a plain powder blue dress. Her feet – quite swollen – were encased in black leather shoes with a thin strap across the instep, and with a little heel. And those heels clicked noisily on the tiled floor of the café as she approached Emma and Fleur's table.

She pushed strands of silver hair back behind her ears, and smiled. '*Signora. Signorina,*' she said, with a little bow. She tapped the menu lying on the table. 'How you want?'

'Black coffee, please,' Emma said. She turned to Fleur. 'And you?'

'Pistachio ice cream. With extra nuts on the top. And a long spoon to eat it with. And I wouldn't say no to a wafer biscuit if you have one. Please.'

'*Scusi?*' the woman said. She put her hands across her mouth. Then she pulled her hair from behind her ears before pushing it back again. 'I no understand. *Uno momento.*'

The woman scurried across the room to the bar area and to the man who seemed to be doing his level best to ignore everyone, his back to them all.

'Why did you do that?' Emma scolded Fleur. 'I think you knew the poor woman wouldn't understand more than a basic request. You could have just said "ice cream" and pointed to it on the menu.' Emma picked the menu up off the table. It was written in English and Italian as she'd guessed it would be. 'It's never nice to make people feel discomfited.'

'I've gone right off it now anyway,' Fleur said. 'I'm not a child, you know, to be told off all the time.'

Oh, yes you are, if you warrant telling off.

The woman stood on tiptoe, and leaned her elbows on the bar. She began talking rapidly in her own language to the man who looked back at her over his shoulder but who continued to arrange the bottles on the shelves.

He shrugged. Then he left the arranging and leaned over to put his arms around the woman's neck. He spoke more rapidly to her than she had to him if that were possible. Then he kissed her cheek. Emma heard him say, 'Mama,' drawing out the first 'a' in a sad sort of sigh.

The woman scurried off, and Emma was left with a lump in her throat that she had no man – father, husband or son – to put his arms around her any more, or kiss her cheek.

'Paolo!' the man yelled.

And almost before the last syllable had left his lips a young lad appeared in the doorway. His concerned expression turned into the widest of grins. He was staring straight at Fleur who – Emma couldn't help but notice – was grinning just as widely back.

'Just as I thought,' Fleur whispered to Emma. 'I saw the van parked in the side alley.'

Of course. Emma remembered now. She'd seen the ice cream delivery van at the hotel. It was there the day she'd arrived back by taxi after her disastrous meeting with Ruby. So *that* was who Fleur had been looking out for daily!

These two had already met. That was evident now. But

this was the first time since that day, wasn't it? And Emma knew now why Fleur had been so grumpy – she'd been expecting to see Paolo again, but hadn't.

Paolo came to their table and with much flirting – Fleur – and flashing of chocolate button eyes – Paolo – their order for coffee and cake, and ice cream was given and delivered.

Paolo found a dozen reasons to return to their table and ask Fleur something; Did she like Torquay? Was the ice cream to her liking? Did she roller-skate? They were to, please, forgive his *nonna* for not understanding because she had much sadness. He even turned his charm on Emma and told her she looked too young to be Fleur's mother, which threw Emma momentarily, but she smiled and thanked him for his compliment with good grace. Paolo seemed as upbeat and full of joy as his father and grandmother were of doom and gloom.

'You scheming little madam,' Emma said, wiping cake crumbs from the corners of her mouth, but she smiled as she said it.

How well she remembered walking in a certain direction in the hope that Seth would be walking that way, too, when she was just the age Fleur was now. And what bittersweet memories the encounter between Fleur and Paolo was conjuring up. What emotional hurdles was she going to have to jump over before she found peace in her own heart again? And just where is this friendship going, she wondered, as she saw Paolo slip Fleur a note as they left Cascarini's?

Emma couldn't put it off any longer. She had to see Ruby again. She'd resisted while she was so busy with the negotiations to rent Romer Lodge, but now it was all agreed and hers to move into in two days' time. Although it was fully furnished there was still room for the few bits she had in storage with Pickfords: her writing desk, a favourite stool, her Victorian sewing box and, of course, all of Seth's paintings. She'd agreed to keep the garden tidy and the internal and external paintwork to the same standard as it was now for a reduction in the rent. And while she'd waited for all the paperwork to be completed she'd hired a sewing machine from Rockhey's, bought lengths of material – cotton and lawn, georgette and silk – and she'd made dresses for herself and Fleur. Sample dresses for future clients of her dressmaking business to see and admire – she hoped! From a junk shop on the corner of Avenue Road she'd bought a mannequin that only needed a good scrub to make it serviceable again. She'd been almost happy doing this. Almost. Ruby, and the state she'd been in when Emma had seen her a few weeks' ago, was never far from her mind.

And now here she was, about to knock on Ruby's door once more.

Taking a deep breath Emma picked up the knocker and let it drop just once against the wood. She crossed her fingers behind her back that Ruby was alone.

'Ma! There's someone at the door!'

A child's voice, hard to tell if it was a boy or a girl. But at least Ruby wouldn't be 'entertaining' a man in the bed that was hers and Tom's if there was a child in the house.

No, make that *three* children as the door opened and three startled pairs of eyes looked up at her. And Emma was pleased to see that the children were all clean and tidily dressed.

'Hello,' Emma said. 'You must be Alice, Sarah and Thomas. I've got your photograph in my valise.'

'Why's it in your valise?' the younger girl, Sarah, said.

'Because I haven't got a home of my own just yet to put it on the mantelpiece. But I will soon.'

Emma looked over the tops of the children's heads and saw Ruby coming down the stairs – stairs which she herself had walked down many times.

'Oh, it's you,' Ruby said, coming to stand behind her children. She placed her arms around them, resting her hands on Alice's and Thomas' shoulders in a protective gesture. 'I wondered when you'd be back.'

'Wonder no more,' Emma said. 'Can I come in?'

Ruby began to usher the children away from the door. 'You lot,' she said, 'find your coats. You can go and play in the garden until I come and call you.'

'Can we get dirty?' Thomas asked. 'Only you said we wasn't to get dirty in case your busybody friend came back. I—'

'Get your coats, and out!' Ruby stopped him.

The children went, shouting excitedly to one another so loudly that even the sound of gulls screeching overhead was drowned out by their chatter.

Emma remained standing on the doorstep of Shingle Cottage, wondering if everyone saw her as a busybody, as it seemed Ruby so obviously did. It wasn't a comfortable thought, sitting somewhere around her heart like indigestion.

'You took your time comin' back,' Ruby said, when, at last, the children were out of earshot. 'I thought, maybe, you'd seen enough and didn't want to see me no more.'

'Of course I want to see you,' Emma said. How she longed to throw her arms around her old friend as she'd done often when they were girls, but now ... well, now she'd wait for Ruby to make the first move.

'As Master Big Mouth let on, I've been keepin' 'em clean and tidy in case you did.'

Emma laughed. *Children did have a habit of letting the cat out of the bag. And you're a lot cleaner and tidier than when I last saw you, too.* Ruby's hair, Emma was pleased to see, looked freshly washed, and brushed. Her skin seemed less sallow, too. She was wearing a maroon wool skirt Emma remembered giving her back in 1913 just before she and Seth had left for Canada. It reached almost to Ruby's ankles. How old-fashioned Ruby looked wearing it. Emma had long since shortened all her clothes to just below the knee. Perhaps, if they could re-kindle their friendship, Ruby would accept Emma's offer to shorten the skirt for her. Or make her a new one.

'So, Ruby, can this busybody come in?'

Ruby laughed nervously. 'I don't know where that young tyke 'eard *that* word from.'

'Well,' Emma said. 'I'm prepared to forget he said it and to forget I heard it if I can come in. I've brought cakes. Not home-made I'm afraid because I expect the chef at the Grand Hotel would have taken a dim view of it if I'd asked to take over his kitchen.'

''E would an' all,' Ruby said. 'Not that I doubt fer a minute you wouldn't 'ave asked if you'd really wanted to make cakes.'

Emma dangled a cardboard box of chocolate éclairs, bought from May's Bakery near the railway station, from its paper string.

'The sun's getting stronger by the second,' Emma said. 'The chocolate on them will melt.'

'Won't be up to your standard, chocolate or no chocolate,' Ruby said. 'But I'll force meself.'

A smile played at the corners of Ruby's lips and the sight of it made Emma's heart flip with a frisson of hope and happiness that Ruby wasn't beyond saving as she'd said at their last meeting.

Ruby opened wide the door and ushered Emma inside.

'*Ti amo*,' Paolo whispered.

He had one hand on the back of Fleur's head and the other was edging up her side, getting closer and closer to her breast with each passing second.

The sign on the ice cream parlour door was turned to

CLOSED. Paolo's father was out the back, across a yard about twenty feet wide, churning a fresh batch of ice cream that had to be watched carefully and would take half an hour. And his grandmother was upstairs having a siesta. Paolo had let Fleur in through the back door, and they were pressed up against the wall in the tiny kitchen.

Ma would kill me if she knew I was here, Fleur thought. And somehow that thought – that her mother didn't know where she was – brought an extra thrill to the moment.

So this was what the start of sex was like. A tingle. And not just up her spine, either. Fleur could feel a dampness in her drawers. Was she wetting herself? No, not that.

'What—'

'Sssh,' Paolo took his hand from behind Fleur's head and put two fingers to her lips.

'I ...' Fleur began to mumble through his fingers. She poked her tongue through her lips and licked Paolo's fingers. He made a strange sort of low growling sound that rumbled through his chest and into Fleur's, almost.

Her first kiss was about to happen. She knew it. Her heart began to race and she felt the blood pumping past her ears.

'I ... I ...' she began again.

But Paolo stopped her flow of words by kissing her. He began to part her closed lips, gently, with his tongue. And then his tongue was in her mouth, moving slowly, sinuously. Oh my God! Thomas Hardy didn't explain the half of it in his book, did he?

'What does what you just said mean?' Fleur mouthed, barely a whisper, when at last Paolo decided the kiss was finished. This particular kiss because Fleur knew there would be others.

'It mean, I love you,' Paolo mouthed back, over emphasising his mouth movements as though he were speaking to someone totally deaf.

His hand – which hadn't quite reached her breast in the kissing, much to Fleur's disappointment, and even though her nipples had gone hard and she'd thrust them at him almost – was thumped hard into his chest and he knocked himself off balance, teetering sideways towards a pile of tins that toppled over.

'In here,' Paolo said, balling his fist up and thumping his chest again. 'I feel it. Like fire.'

But the words came out louder than he had probably intended them to. He hurriedly tried to right the tins.

Then they heard footsteps coming down the passage.

'Paolo!'

And then a volley of Italian Fleur didn't have a snowball's chance in hell of understanding although she knew beyond doubt Paolo's pa wasn't saying '*Ti amo,*' as he came rushing into the back kitchen.

She withered under the older man's gaze. He was looking at her as though she were a lesser form of life. Just for kissing his son? Fleur bridled. And besides, if anyone was going to take the blame then Paolo was, for letting her in the kitchen in the first place. The plan had been for Paolo to turn the sign on the door to OPEN and then for Fleur to be seated at a table, the first customer for the afternoon, when Signor Cascarini came back from his ice cream making, and Paolo's grandmother came down from her siesta. After the kissing.

But now the plan had backfired.

'Where your mama?' Signor Cascarini asked her.

'Well, she's not here, obviously,' Fleur said.

No way was this man going to make her feel guilty for kissing his son. She wasn't a child. The feelings she'd had weren't a child's feelings. She'd felt like a woman in Paolo's arms. And he'd told her he loved her. She wasn't some sort of good time girl, letting any man kiss her, was she?

'You bad girl,' Signor Cascarini said.

Well, that did it!

'So, it's all right for a man to kiss a girl in a kitchen in the middle of the afternoon but it's far from all right for that girl to want to be kissed and to kiss back, is it?' Fleur yelled at him.

Signor Cascarini shrugged. Because he thought all that, or because he didn't understand? Fleur didn't know which and she cared even less.

'You not good Italian girl.' Signor Cascarini seemed to have found his voice again.

'You're right about one thing – I'm not an Italian girl. Good or otherwise. Although I imagine Italian girls do get kissed in kitchens in the middle of the afternoon sometimes.'

'Fleur,' Paolo said. He put an arm around her shoulder and turned her towards the back door. 'I take you back to hotel now. My papa and—'

But Paolo's father grabbed Paolo roughly by the elbow and pulled him away.

Volumes and volumes of angry Italian filled the air. Paolo and his father seemed to get louder with every word. Fleur knew she could probably just leave and they'd never notice, but she was mesmerised by the passion in their voices, the musicality of the Italian language. She had to learn to speak it – she just had to.

All the noise must have woken Paolo's grandmother because she came bustling into the kitchen in very worn carpet slippers, her bare big toe peeping through the right one.

The men stopped their arguing and the old woman's eyes widened with surprise when she saw Fleur. She made a spitting sort of sound, although no spit came out, thank goodness.

'I'll say it before they do,' Fleur said. 'Paolo can translate, although I know his father understands English well enough. I was invited here by Paolo because we wanted to be alone.

We have walked out together a few times now. Along the seafront. In Torre Abbey gardens. In public. We are friends, Paolo and I – very good friends. And we are going to stay friends, whatever other ideas you two might have.' Fleur reached towards Paolo and grasped his left hand between both of hers. She raised it to her lips and kissed the backs of his fingers. 'It would have been nicer had we had our first kiss in better circumstances but I don't think I'm ever going to forget it. I don't want to. Now, I'm going. I can find my way back to the hotel, Paolo.'

It was obvious Signor Cascarini had understood the bulk of what Fleur had said because he opened the back door for her.

'No, not that way,' Fleur said. 'I made a mistake coming in that way. I'll leave by the front door.'

'And I come with you,' Paolo said. 'I am gentleman.'

He rushed forward to the front door and unlocked it. Fleur and Paolo left the ice cream parlour without looking back and without shutting the door behind them. A volley of Italian followed them, but Paolo didn't answer whatever it was his father and grandmother were shouting at him.

'What are they saying?' Fleur asked.

'Oh, that I am the big disappointment in the world to them. Papa is happy my mama dead not to see how I behave. Papa now do the deliveries I not doing. My grandmother must speak English which she hates doing because Papa not there at opening time. And you—'

'I'm a whore or whatever the Italian word is for it?'

'Is *puttana*. But you not that. But you in big trouble,' Paolo said. 'And I think you can, how you say, fight yourself.'

'Fight my corner,' Fleur said. 'Oh, yes, I can do that.'

Not that she was going to have to because Paolo had stood up to his father and grandmother and was seeing her home – like a gentleman should.

Paolo made a crook of his arm and Fleur slipped her hand through, held onto him.

'Not just me by the sound of it.' She laughed.

Paolo's father's voice was still within earshot, and he didn't sound as though he'd calmed down one little bit.

'Oh, it is expected an Italian man have many lovers before he marry. And after, too ...'

'Was that what I was about to become?' Fleur asked, outraged at the thought. 'Was I just minutes away from being another of the many lovers you expect to have before marriage?'

Fleur went to withdraw her arm from Paolo's but he second-guessed her and grasped her hand so she couldn't. He beamed down at her.

'No,' he said. 'On the life of Mary and all the saints, you would have been the first.'

'*Will* be the first,' Fleur said. 'One day. I expect ...'

But her words were drowned out by the Cascarini delivery van being driven past them and at high speed.

And in the direction of the Grand Hotel.

'Where's Fleur?' Ruby asked, pulling out a chair for Emma to sit at the kitchen table. She plonked a black teapot with bright blue forget-me-nots painted on it in the middle of the table. 'I thought you might 'ave brought 'er to see me.'

'I will, but not just yet.'

'Ashamed of me?' Ruby said. She let her gaze slide from Emma's and began fussing with the crockery, letting the cups bang so heavily on the saucers that Emma feared they might break.

'No,' Emma said. 'Any shame – if there is any – is yours. But I *am* concerned for you and the way you're ... well, living your life at the moment.'

It had to be said and that was the kindest way Emma could think of saying it.

Ruby looked up from pouring tea into a cup, the teapot held with both hands in mid-air.

'I'm doin' me best, Em,' she whispered. 'To be a better person. But it ain't easy. Where is 'er? Fleur, I mean.'

'At the lending library,' Emma told her. 'She's become very keen to learn Italian all of a sudden because she's met an Italian boy she's sweet on. Paolo. His father owns an ice cream parlour.'

'And you'm greener than grass if you think that's where she's to.' Ruby laughed. 'She's more 'n likely takin' advantage of you bein' 'ere and not there keepin' an eye on 'er.'

Ruby could well be right, but Emma hoped she wasn't. She had to trust Fleur to do the right thing – or at least not to do the wrong thing. *But who was she to moralise seeing as she and Seth had lived as man and wife for a good eighteen months before they'd made their union legal?*

'I'm not here to talk about Fleur,' Emma said.

'I know. Don't say it,' Ruby said. 'I'm a mess, ain't I?'

'Which do you want?' Emma asked, her heart beating faster than she'd expected it to – she'd never been nervous around Ruby before, but she was now. 'For me to say you are, or to deny it?'

Ruby shrugged. 'Same difference either way,' she said. 'Gawd but you gave me a shock turnin' up back along. What've you been doin' since you were 'ere last?'

'Renting a house,' Emma said. 'I've paid a year's rent in advance.'

'Just like that! Same as I buy 'alf a pint of milk and water it down to make it go further, I suppose?'

'Romer Lodge. I'm renting it fully furnished and it'll be all ready for me to move into next week. It's in Cleveland Road.'

Emma glanced around the kitchen of Shingle Cottage –

little had changed since she'd seen it last, if anything. That made her sad – for Ruby.

'Very swanky,' Ruby said. 'A *lodge*. Whatever that is when it's at 'ome.'

Ruby took one of the chocolate éclairs Emma had brought and bit into it, the cream oozing out onto her chin. She reached over and grabbed a tea towel from the draining board and wiped the cream away.

'Don't be jealous, Ruby,' Emma said. 'It's how different our lives have turned out. I'd give anything to be back in Vancouver with Seth but that can never happen now. At least you've got Tom.' She struggled to push to the back of her mind what it was Ruby had been doing to earn money to feed her family. 'If you'd written to me, about how things were here, then I'd have helped you out. Financially, I mean. Really I would.'

'I don't know as 'ow I'd want your charity, Em. Friendship, yes, but not charity. So ...' Ruby took a deep breath. 'And you might not even want that when I've told yer what it is I 'ave to tell.'

'Can I be the judge of that?' Emma said.

'Dare I try and stop you?' Ruby answered, and just for a moment Emma saw the spark of their old friendship in the devilment in Ruby's eyes and the way the corners of her mouth twitched up in the beginnings of a grin, and Emma's heart slowed to a comfortable rate.

'Tell,' Emma said. She reached for Ruby's hand and held it fast between her own. 'Just hanging on so you can't run off.'

A tear escaped the corner of Ruby's eye and slid down her cheek. Neither woman did anything to wipe it away.

'Like I told you in me letters, Tom and I were wed just after you and Seth left fer furrin' parts. 'Ad to, as it 'appens. You lettin' me 'ave this place before we wed meant we 'ad opportunity, Tom and me. So that was Alice.'

'She's beautiful,' Emma said. 'So if you're blaming me for getting in the family way, can I take the credit for her beauty?'

Emma was making light of it, but it stung that Ruby had fallen for a baby so quickly when she herself never had.

'The beauty's all Tom's side of the family,' Ruby said, looking serious. 'I never was a looker. But my Tom came 'ome from the war a broken man, Em. The first thing he said was that I wasn't to ask 'im no questions and 'e wasn't goin' to tell me of the 'ell 'e'd been in either. 'E were in Wipers, I know that.'

Emma had to bite her tongue not to correct Ruby's pronunciation of Ypres.

'I'm sorry. It must have been dreadful beyond belief.'

'Weren't it just! It were two years before Tom was a proper 'usband to me again, if you get my meanin'. And then when 'e were again, Sarah and Thomas 'appened fast. After Thomas was born my Tom said 'e thought that was enough of that business seein' as I falls fer 'em quicker than seagulls swoop on scraps. And 'e seemed to disappear inside 'imself, and the injuries 'e got from France began playin' up. 'Is leg and that. Doctor Shaw did the best 'e could with fixin' Tom's bones and gettin' 'im an operation up to Exeter to re-break his leg and set it again so 'e didn't limp so bad. And 'e organised some phsyio threropery to make 'im more mobile, seein' as 'ow Tom's shoulder 'ad 'ad a bucket load of shrapnel in it.'

Ruby took a swig of tea.

'Physiotherapy,' Emma said. 'That's the word.'

'Gawd but you don't change a bit, Emma Jago – ferever correctin' 'ow a body speaks!' Ruby said. 'No offence taken, though, 'cos it's like music to me ears, Em, to 'ear you doin' it. Like old times. Like the years between 'ave never been.'

Except they have. A chasm of them. Was it going to be possible to close a chasm? Emma thought.

'How is Doctor Shaw?' she asked. The man had been kindness itself to Emma, especially the time when Emma had been beaten unconscious by Margaret Phipps in the churchyard, and Fleur kidnapped – one of the reasons that had made Seth take the step to emigrate to Canada.

'Dead in the last influenza epidemic, God rest 'is soul. 'E might 'ave done wonders with Tom's leg but 'e couldn't mend Tom's mind. There was no Nase Head House fer Tom to be goin' back to work in once the war was over, seein' as Smythe upped sticks and left fer London with 'is new wife and little 'uns, and the Americans took it over as an 'ospital. 'Ave you seen the state it's in, Em?'

'I have. I looked round it. I thought about—'

'Buyin' it or rentin' it?'

'Renting,' Emma said. Although Emma had inherited Shingle Cottage from Seth and also his house in Canada, women still weren't allowed to buy property of their own. *Would that day ever come?*

'Some difference we've got between us in the bank balance department then, Em, if you can afford to rent a blimmin' 'otel! Don't tell me you've got a bleedin' car and all. Gawd, those larks we had in that great car of Seth's.'

'I haven't got a car,' Emma said. 'Yet.' But she was thinking of buying one. Something smaller than the Wolseley Seth had bought, and given to Olly Underwood when they left for Canada. She would have to see where she could get advice on what would be the best car to buy. 'Go on. About Tom.'

'Well, 'e did 'is best to find work. But all the big 'ouses 'ave reduced their staff since the war. 'E's good at 'is letters and 'e ain't bad with numbers, so 'e applied fer a few office jobs but they always go to them as 'ad better schoolin' than Tom 'ad. Besides, 'is right shoulder gives 'im the gyp and some days 'e ain't got the strength to 'old a pencil, never mind write wi' it. But we 'ad to eat, didn't we – us and those little varmints out there.' Ruby waved a hand in the direction of the back garden where the children could be heard playing a very noisy game of some sort. 'Better save them a few of these éclairs, eh?'

'Yes, *you* better had!' Emma said, grinning at her friend. Ruby had demolished two éclairs and had just picked up a third off the plate. It was as though the cakes were giving her strength to say what it was she had to say.

Ruby put the éclair down.

'Despite what this lousy government of ours says about 'elping those what fought for King and country, there ain't much reachin' us down 'ere. Tom 'ad to go and see two doctors over to Torquay and they said 'e was fit for work. 'E was found a job behind the counter in Annings, but when it came to liftin' the 'eavy ironmongery stuff, 'e couldn't do it. So 'e got 'is cards. But it isn't only the work, Em. Some nights 'e cries all through the night like a baby. And there's no comfortin' 'im – neither wi' cups of tea and a round of toast, or wi' me body, such as it is these days.'

Ruby paused, as though she was wanting Emma to say something.

'There's a bit less of you than when last I saw you but if money's been tight for food I can see why.'

'I've always fed the children first, Tom and his old mother second, and me last,' Ruby said. 'So I ain't *all* bad, am I?' She looked pleadingly at Emma, and her eyes welled with tears, but she blinked them away.

'No,' Emma said. 'You're far from all bad. You kept up your letters to me, and—'

'And they was all *lies,* Em. For *years* they were lies. I oughtn't to 'ave done it. It might 'ave been better if Tom 'adn't taught me to read and write.'

Ruby hung her head, but Emma reached over and with her forefinger tilted Ruby's chin up so she was forced to look at her.

'Who knows what any of us would do to save our children from starvation if we had to, Ruby?' Emma said gently. Her heart was breaking for her old friend, and she had to swallow back her sadness. Her tears wouldn't help Ruby, would they? 'Where's Tom now?'

'At 'is mother's place. Same as the children 'ave been while I've been doin' you-know-what to feed 'em. His mother's lovin' 'avin' her boy back with her, givin' 'im bits of meat off 'er own plate, and always a second 'elping of puddin', but *I* want 'im back, Em. 'E were a good 'usband before. And I think 'e could be a good 'usband again, but 'e needs 'elp. It's me what ain't been good. But 'onest to God, I couldn't see any other way of earnin' money when times were 'ard. You'd never believe who's come in over my door—'

'I probably wouldn't,' Emma interrupted, startled. She didn't want the full details, thank you very much. 'And don't even think about telling me, please.'

'But they ain't comin' in no more, Em, because seein' you again 'as shocked me into me senses – what little sense as I've got, that is. I watched you walkin' away down the road that day and I vowed then never to make you 'ave that look in your eye because of me. This is your 'ouse, and I'd best be rememberin' that. I'd turned it into a … a … brothel, 'adn't I? Could have been prosecuted, couldn't I? And you with me.' Ruby laughed nervously. 'When you told me about Seth dyin' and all it made me realise I was lucky to still 'ave Tom, whatever state the poor man is in.'

'So,' Emma said, struggling to find the right words to say. 'What are you going to do to earn money for your family from now on?'

'Search me. I ain't got that far yet.' Ruby drained the last of her tea. 'You was always the one with the wonderful ideas. 'Elp me, Em. 'Elp me. *Please.*'

Before Emma could think of a thing to say or come

up with an idea to help Ruby, one of the children started screaming out in the garden, and Ruby rolled her eyes heavenwards at Emma.

'Oh, gawd. Killin' one another again, I expect. I'd better go an' sort 'em out.'

She skittered across the kitchen and out the back door, and Emma took advantage of her absence to find two five pound notes in her purse and put them under the teapot, just the edges of the narrowest ends poking out. That was all she could think of for the moment that would bring Ruby immediate help. Emma had noticed there was little in the cubbyhole that was used as a larder in the corner of the kitchen – just two tins of fruit, and two plates with something that was probably leftovers in between. Was there a difference between charity and a gift? Emma wondered. Would Ruby throw it back in her face?

The screaming stopped, replaced by the previous happy yips and squeals of playing children and Ruby came back in.

'More tea?' she asked Emma. 'I might 'ave got a few leaves left I can ...' Her hand hovered over the handle of the teapot. She'd seen the money poking out. 'An' I might 'ave lied about not acceptin' charity but—'

'It's not charity. It's a gift,' Emma interrupted.

'Gawd, but did a body ever tell you 'ow much they love you, Em?' Ruby said. She swiped away a tear.

Emma swallowed the lump in her throat. Ruby was the best friend in the world, learning to read and write so she could correspond with Emma when she'd been in Canada, even if those letters had been mostly lies for years.

'I love you too, Ruby,' she said. She opened her handbag and found a piece of paper and a pencil and wrote her telephone number on it, glad of the diversion because she was too full up to speak for a moment. Ruby was the sister she'd never had, wasn't she? She had to help her. She handed

47

the piece of paper to Ruby. 'Telephone me if you need help. But I'll come and see you whenever I can, once I'm settled into Romer Lodge.'

'Just as well you were an old bossy boots and nagged me to read and write, then, idn' it?' Ruby said, with a watery smile. She slid the piece of paper under the teapot with the money.

'Isn't it just,' Emma said, her own voice more wobbly than a half set blancmange. 'And we'll get through this, Ruby. Together. Or my name's not Emma Jago.'

Emma had to know. Ruby had said in her letters that she'd put flowers on the graves of Emma's parents and her brother, Johnnie, but had she? Had the worry of Tom being traumatised by war, and what she'd had to do to earn money, made her forget? Or not care? What were a few flowers on the graves of people she wasn't related to anyway? Just half an hour ago in Ruby's kitchen she'd seen the old Ruby – the loyal and loving friend. But had she been so over the last few years?

Emma went to her papa's grave first.

'It's been a long time, Papa,' she said. 'But I'm back now.'

There was a jam jar half buried in the grass at the foot of the simple tablet Seth had had made. There was an inch or so of water in the bottom. Clean water. Rain water at a guess. Emma ran her fingers along the lettering. Guillaume Le Goff.

Emma had come here on impulse and she wished now she'd thought to buy some flowers on the way. But while there might not have been flowers in the jam jar, the memorial stone was clean, which wasn't the case for many of the gravestones as they had moss growing in the lettering, and seagull droppings smattered in brown and white streaks.

She walked on to her mama's and Johnnie's joint grave.

Rachel Le Goff, aged 39 years,
taken cruelly by the sea, 24th February, 1909
with her son, Johnnie, aged 7 years.
Together forever.

Oh. A jam jar was sunk into the grass here, too, and it was full of primroses. A few primrose leaves, too. And a twig of something with leaves beginning to burst open.

Emma bent and pulled out a primrose, held it to her nose. Such a delicate scent, hardly there at all and yet unmistakeable at the same time.

'Yer didn't believe me, did yer?'

Emma jumped, startled. She hadn't known Ruby had followed her – hadn't heard her footfalls on the gravel path. She must have walked across the grass. Slowly she turned to face her friend.

'I wanted to,' Emma said, truthfully. 'But I was afraid.'

'That I'd lied?'

'Yes. But I wouldn't have blamed you. Not now I know what's been happening in your life while I've been away. Tom ...'

'Stop talkin' rubbish. I ain't really got no excuses for what I've been up to, 'ave I? I can't go blamin' Tom's troubles on 'ow I be'ave forever, can I? An' I only 'ad time to put these 'ere flowers on your ma's grave when I came last. I've kept the stones clean an' all. Did yer notice?'

'Oh, Ruby,' Emma said. She held out her arms towards her friend. 'Of course I noticed. Come here.' Ruby stepped towards Emma, and Emma folded her into her embrace. 'Thank you.'

The two women stood, rocking together gently for a few moments, before Ruby pulled away.

'I guessed you'd come 'ere, Miss Bossy Boots,' Ruby said. 'You ain't changed a bit.'

Oh, but I have, Emma thought. *We both have*. But the

core of their friendship was still there. She couldn't think what to say that wouldn't sound trite, or condescending – show up the differences in their lives. It was so quiet here. Just the softness of their breathing, and somewhere, far in the distance, a robin's cry.

'What's up, Em? Cat got your tongue?'

'No,' Emma said. She poked out her tongue playfully. 'It's still in the same place.'

But Ruby looked serious, close to tears. 'Gawd, but I'm glad you'm back, Em.'

'I'm glad I'm back, too.'

'Well, now that's settled and we've agreed we're not goin' to kill one another, I'd better get back to my nippers. Mrs Coffin from next door is keepin' an eye on 'em fer me. Five minutes, I said.'

'Off you go, then,' Emma replied. 'And thank you ...'

'Will you close that silly mouth of yours? The thanks is all mine, Emma Jago, and we both know it.'

Emma swallowed the lump in her throat and watched her friend run back out of the cemetery.

Chapter Four

'Madam,' the reception desk clerk said with a nod of respect the second Emma arrived in the foyer of the Grand Hotel. He looked up at her anxiously. 'I have to tell you that there's a gentleman waiting for you. He says he knows you. I've asked him to wait in the breakfast room. He seems rather agitated.'

'Really?' Whoever could it be? Her solicitor about something to do with the rental agreement for Romer Lodge? Or perhaps it was the estate agent? He'd said he knew of a property that might suit Emma better, but it wasn't on the market yet. Maybe it was now? But it was too late for that – she'd already signed her part of the contract to rent Romer Lodge and she'd been told the owner had, too. 'I'd better see what he wants,' she said to the reception desk clerk.

But as she pushed open the door to the breakfast room her heart dropped like a stone when Signor Cascarini, his forehead furrowed and his eyes narrowed, came rushing towards her.

'Your daughter bad girl,' he said. 'She—'

'Don't you speak ill of my daughter to me, signor! And seeing as she's not here to defend herself I only have your version of events, whatever they might be. And until Fleur—'

'Your daughter in her room.'

'Suite,' Emma corrected him. 'We have a suite. With a sea view.'

There, best let him know just who he was dealing with – a woman who could afford a hotel suite, rather than single rooms at the back with only the outlook over the railway line to look at.

'Sweet?' Signor Cascarini said. '*Zucchero*?' He looked genuinely puzzled and it was all Emma could do not to laugh. Something had got lost in translation there and she didn't think she'd be able to sort out the confusion. So she wasn't going to bother.

'I know Fleur and your son have been seeing one another, Signor Cascarini. And I've told Fleur I'm happy for her to have made a friend so soon after arriving from Canada. I know they've met and walked along the seafront a time or two, and in the grounds of Torre Abbey, because Fleur has told me as much. A friendship between two young people isn't a bad thing.'

Yes, she knew she was on the defensive, and she'd been caught on the back foot as well. It seemed as though Ruby's instincts had been correct and that Fleur hadn't been at the lending library as she'd said she would be while Emma was out.

'Is not only friendship. It is, how you say? ... Intercourse.'

Emma gulped. She only had this man's word for whatever it was Fleur had been up to. Her brain seemed to take on a life of its own and all she could see was Fleur with her head hung low, saying she was 'so sorry, Ma' and that she was pregnant. And how was Emma going to cope with all that? *But how could she moralise?* She and Seth had lived as man and wife long before they'd married. No babies had come along for them though ...

'Were they in bed?' Emma asked. 'Did you disturb them there?'

'No!' Signor Cascarini looked genuinely shocked at her question. 'In kitchen. I just in time—'

'Well.' Emma smiled. 'Well.' Nothing had happened, had it? Certainly not what Signor Cascarini was implying.

'Is not well. My wife, she want big, big *matrimonio* for Paolo. Good Italian *ragazza*. Many *bambini*. *Una Cattolica*. If only my wife ...'

Signor Cascarini slumped down into a chair. He put his head in his hands and, to Emma's horror, he sobbed. Loud and wracking sobs shook his shoulders. He twisted his hands over and over in his lap. Emma had seen Seth cry a few times but there had always been a very deep and moving reason for it. And she'd seen tears in Matthew Caunter's eyes when she and he had said their last goodbyes, but he'd held them back. She'd never seen a man cry like this and so suddenly and over what, to Emma, seemed such a trivial matter – his son and her daughter doing what the young do, walking out together, holding hands in all probability. Stealing a kiss or two perhaps? *It must be the Italian in him! Didn't the world know they wore their emotions on their sleeves?*

Emma sighed. First Ruby needing her emotional support – as well as financial it seemed – and now Signor Cascarini. He couldn't have the first idea whether Fleur was a Catholic or not, unless she'd been asked – which Emma doubted. He was making assumptions, just as Ruby had assumed Emma would think of something to help her. Whatever was in the air today?

Emma sat down on the chair beside Signor Cascarini's. She patted his shoulder a couple of times, then his arm.

'Has something happened to your wife? Is she ill perhaps?'

'She dead,' Signor Cascarini said between sobs. 'Big bomb. In London. Half the road dead. I wish I dead, too.' He looked up and brushed an arm across his face to rid it of tears.

'Dead? Oh, I'm so sorry. My husband is also dead. Being a parent on your own isn't easy, is it?'

A waiter came in then and Emma ordered tea. And a whisky. She had no idea if Italians drank whisky but Seth had always had a glass if he was upset about something.

'Not easy,' Signor Cascarini said. 'And now kissing.' He practically spat the word out.

'Only kissing?'

Signor Cascarini shrugged, took a deep breath and let it out in a long, sad sigh.

Only kissing as far as Signor Cascarini knew? Was that what the shrug meant? She would have a word with Fleur later. Not that she expected Fleur to tell her the whole truth if she had done more than kiss Paolo.

'And where is Paolo?' Emma didn't think for a moment he was up in her suite or in Fleur's bedroom, but ... well, weren't there at least two couples in this hotel who weren't married, Emma was sure of it, even if the management pretended not to notice? She'd seen the names on the register when she'd signed her and Fleur in. Mr and Mrs Smith indeed! 'He's not up in my suite with Fleur, is he?'

Signor Cascarini's eyebrows shot up in alarm at her question. 'He not! He at work. Paolo good boy. He must serve peoples. My *suocerà* no good in *inglese*.'

And she's not the only one whose English isn't very good, Emma thought. She made a wild guess that the woman she'd seen in the ice cream parlour wasn't this man's mother and that *suocerà* more than likely meant mother-in-law. The poor man had taken on the responsibility of looking after his mother-in-law now his wife was dead, hadn't he? Well, didn't *she* know all about responsibility?

'I wonder, Signor Cascarini,' Emma said on impulse, 'if you and Paolo would like to join Fleur and me for dinner this evening?'

She had a feeling this man was lonely since his wife's tragic death. And possibly it was the Italian hot-bloodedness in him that had made him react to a bit of kissing the way he had. It was *her* daughter who had added to this man's distress and Emma wanted to ease the situation a little for him if she could. And if the four of them were to sit around a table and share food, talk, laugh – it would be the semblance of a family for all of them once again, wouldn't it?

'Dinner? You mean *cena*?' Signor Cascarini mimed using

a knife and fork to cut up something. '*Mangare*? This night?'

'Seven-thirty?' Emma said.

'No here,' Signor Cascarini said, standing up. 'I no like big place. I cook for you. In my *ristorante*. Good Italian food.'

And he beamed at Emma, all his tears over the loss of his wife gone. How handsome he was when he smiled – an only slightly older version of the very good-looking Paolo with his black hair and his ebony eyes. Olive skin. Taller than Paolo was, too, when he pulled himself up to his full height. There were more crinkles at the sides of Signor Cascarini's eyes, but yes – he was still a very handsome man.

He seemed to be pulling himself together in front of Emma. Stomach in, chest out. He ran a hand through his silvering hair. How old? Forty? A little older? Or had his loss aged him? The war had ended in 1918 so he'd had at least nine years to get used to the idea of widowhood. Emma had had only two years as a widow, but already she was realising that life had to go on, even though Seth would be in her heart forever.

'I think that's a lovely idea,' Emma said. 'Thank you.'

Goodness, there had to be something in the air today – she'd just asked a man to dine with her.

'I expected better of you, Fleur,' her ma said.

'It was only a kiss or two, Ma,' Fleur replied.

Signor Cascarini had put a stop to anything else – which Fleur was never going to admit to her ma was probably just as well really. She had no idea how you stopped babies coming although she knew well enough how you made them. And she didn't want a baby – not now, and probably never.

'I said I believed your explanation of things. And I would have expected you to steal a kiss or two at your age. What's upsetting me is that you lied. You said you were going to the library and that's where I expected you to be.'

'I was going to go there afterwards,' Fleur said.

After what? After sex with Paolo if his pa hadn't interrupted us?

Her ma gave her a funny look – nose wrinkled up towards her furrowed brow; it made her look like a chipmunk or something, chewing nuts.

'Come on now,' her ma said. 'Stop looking at that frock and get it on. We're going to be late. You do like it, don't you?'

Fleur looked at the dress as though seeing it for the first time, even though she'd had to get in and out of it at least a dozen times while her ma stuck pins in to find where to put the darts, and take up the hem. It was a lovely frock and her ma knew it.

Fleur risked a teensy shrug, but her ma saw it.

'You don't have to wear it.'

'It might look better on me if I cut my hair. I'd look more grown-up. Louise Brooks's hair is the same colour as mine. It looks ace on her.'

'We can't all turn into film stars, Fleur. And, trust me, when you look old, you'll wish you looked younger,' her ma said. 'Your hair's beautiful as it is. I'd really rather you didn't cut it just yet.'

'*Yours* is bobbed, Ma,' Fleur said with a smile, even though she knew she was stating the obvious. 'It looks really nice on you.'

Even though there are a few grey hairs peeping through. Not that she was going to tell her ma *that*! She'd scupper her chances of being given the money to go to a hairdresser, wouldn't she? Up until now her ma had always trimmed her hair, but even her clever, good-at-everything ma, would probably fall short at styling a bob.

'Thank you. And you don't fool me for a moment. All this talk is putting off the necessary. Now, into that frock.'

'Oh, Ma! We're not really going, are we? Tell me it's a joke.'

The last person she wanted to see was Signor Cascarini, although she wouldn't mind seeing Paolo, especially as he'd been a hero and stood up for her against his pa and walked her home, and kissed her – on the lips – in the hotel garden and told her again that he loved her, in Italian, before going back to face the music with his pa. Fleur's heart had stilled for a moment or two when she'd entered the foyer to see one of the waiters escorting Signor Cascarini to the breakfast room. She'd breathed in quickly because she'd come over a little faint, and the breath caught in her throat and made her cough. Signor Cascarini turned around then and saw her. He'd given her a withering look. But, head held high, Fleur walked past him and up the wide staircase to her room.

'I can't. Because it's *not* a joke. We're eating with Signor Cascarini and Paolo tonight. At his *ristorante*, as he put it, although I seem to remember the name over the door saying it was an ice cream parlour.'

'But I *can't* go!' Fleur wailed. How could her mother have arranged this? Didn't she know she didn't want to set foot in that place? Not after what Paolo's pa had said to her, implying she was nothing but a whore for kissing his son. And she'd told her ma what he'd said, too! How could she? 'Not after what he called me.'

'Yes, you can. We all say things in the heat of the moment and I'm sure Signor Cascarini only said what he did because he was surprised to find you in his *kitchen*.'

Her ma put a little emphasis on the word 'kitchen'. *When you were supposed to be at the library and weren't* was what her ma meant, but if there was one thing she admired her ma for it was that she didn't go on and on and on about a misdemeanour – once she'd said her piece that was it, she let it drop. Thank goodness.

'Sorry, Ma,' Fleur said. 'About not being at the library.'

'Apology accepted. Now, let's put this all behind us. I really don't mind you having Paolo as a friend but you must consider that his father is having a bit of a hard time of it since his wife's death. We can understand how that is, can't we?'

'Yes,' Fleur said. She wondered what her pa might have said about her being found kissing Paolo – and almost doing something else – if he'd been alive. She doubted he'd have been as understanding as her ma was being about it. 'Paolo told me about his ma. A bomb ... I can't imagine it.'

'And we haven't had to, for which we must be grateful.'

Her ma fixed the pearl earrings she always wore for best in her ears. Then she dabbed some perfume on her wrists. She smiled at herself in the mirror and then twisted this way and that. How slim her ma was, how young she still looked even though she was well over thirty now – almost forty for goodness sake.

And then it hit her – her ma was getting all dressed up because she fancied Paolo's pa, wasn't she? This was nothing about healing the bad feeling between Signor Cascarini and her and Paolo, was it?

Eurggh. Something bitter rose in Fleur's throat. Bile? Distaste? Her shoulders shuddered at the thought of her ma kissing Paolo's pa. Her ma was spoiling everything, wasn't she? Taking over. Taking charge. If only her pa were here then none of this would be happening. She was going to die of embarrassment in front of Paolo, wasn't she, if her ma was making cods' eyes at his pa all night?

'Ma,' Fleur said, picking up the dress from the bed. She stepped into it and wriggled it up over her hips. The dress was made of fine jersey, almost like silk to the touch. A Chanel copy, so her ma had said. She slid her arms in and fastened the asymmetrical buttons. 'I miss Pa. I wish we weren't here. I wouldn't even mind not having met Paolo if I could have Pa back.' Her voice was a whisper.

Surely her ma wouldn't make her go out if she was grieving so.

'I know,' her ma said. 'I miss him, too. But this is our life now and we have to make the best of it. Besides, I'm rather hoping Signor Cascarini will be able to advise me where I can buy a car.'

Emma had never eaten spaghetti before. Or any sort of pasta for that matter. She wasn't sure she liked it. It felt heavy in her mouth and slippery with oil at the same time.

But Signor Cascarini had made it for her. When she and Fleur had arrived it was to see curtains on poles had been placed a little over halfway up the windows – to stop people looking in no doubt. And most of the tables and chairs had been placed to the edges of the room and there was just one big table in the centre with five chairs placed around it. It had a red and white checked cloth on it, and a vase of tulips – brilliant purple ones – in the centre. Wine glasses sparkled under the overhead light. How bright and welcoming it all looked.

But dinner had been far from ready. Signor Cascarini had insisted Emma and Fleur join him in the kitchen. And there, Emma had been surprised to see him tip flour – almost yellow in appearance – from a small bag with Italian writing on it into a bowl, add olive oil, and turn it into a very elastic dough, which he kneaded quickly before putting it through, what looked to her like a mini-mangle.

A big saucepan of something that smelled heady with herbs was bubbling on a hob.

Signor Cascarini's mother-in-law sat on a chair in the corner, arms folded across her chest, muttering under her breath. Now and again she shouted out something in her own language to which Signor Cascarini shrugged. She did it again now.

'She no like I cook,' Signor Cascarini said, with a slight jerk of his head towards his mother-in-law. 'She think only women should cook.'

Emma didn't know what to say to that. She'd been used to a male chef in the kitchen when she'd worked at Nase Head House even if he hadn't been the best cook in the world.

'Pah,' the old woman said.

And Emma was left wondering if she understood more English than she let on.

'Is ready,' Signor Cascarini said. 'Paolo, help your *nonna* to the table.'

'*Si.*'

Emma smiled – she liked that this was a united family, if sad now Paolo's mother was no longer alive.

'You like?' Signor Cascarini asked now that they were all, at last, sitting down. Emma knew she'd had rather too many aperitifs while they all waited for dinner to be ready. It had been hard to refuse. And after the rather trying day she'd had, she didn't know that she wanted to.

Signor Cascarini tipped his head to one side and glanced at his plate of food.

'The sauce is delicious,' Emma said. 'But I'm not going to be able to do that as long as I live.'

She pointed to the spaghetti wound around Signor Cascarini's fork like so many twisting, writhing worms. Fleur, she noticed, was getting on wonderfully well with Paolo's assistance, happy to have his hand around hers as he helped her to twist the spaghetti onto her fork and then stir it into the sauce. *How nice it would be to have someone hold her hand,* Emma thought. *Was this man who had gone to so much trouble to feed her and Fleur – and who seemed to have forgotten completely how angry he'd been at his son and Fleur found kissing in his kitchen what was mere hours ago – the man to hold it?*

'It need practice,' Signor Cascarini said. 'I show you.'

He reached for Emma's hand but she whisked it away before he could touch her. She wasn't ready for that sort of personal contact just yet.

'I'll just have to try harder,' Emma said. 'If Fleur can do it I'm sure I'll master it in time.'

But possibly not before it's all gone cold. There was no meat in the sauce, Emma realised now – at least none that she could taste.

Everything about this was a new experience for Emma. She'd only ever dined with two men in her life. Firstly with Matthew Caunter up at Nase Head House before the war, and secondly with Seth. On each of her birthdays when they'd lived in Vancouver Seth had taken her to a hotel for dinner. While fish might have featured heavily on the menu it had all been delicious. The puddings, too. And there had been lots of wine – lots and lots of wine. But despite her being very relaxed after it, and she and Seth had made love most of the night, no babies came along.

'You come here many times,' Signor Cascarini said. 'You will be *perfetta.*'

He leapt up and crossed the room, went behind his counter and came back with a bottle of wine. From his pocket he pulled out a folding corkscrew and while Emma tried to get a huge forkful of spaghetti and sauce into her mouth in something resembling an elegant fashion, he opened the bottle.

Her mouth too full of food to refuse, Emma could only watch as he filled the wine glasses with wine the colour of blood.

'Chianti,' Signor Cascarini said. 'The best *vino* in the world.'

Emma swallowed her food.

'Just one glass,' she said. 'I've a busy day tomorrow. I'm renting a house, you see, and I have to find someone to take our luggage from the hotel to Cleveland Road in Paignton. Do you know any taxi drivers, Signor?'

'I, Eduardo, *bella donna*. Eduardo. Eduardo take luggages. No pay. Is gift for you, *bella donna.*'

A torrent of rapid Italian filled the air. Eduardo's mother-in-law's cheeks were pink and she glared first at Eduardo and then at Emma. What was she saying?

Emma thought she could guess.

'I'm sure the hotel will be able to find a taxi for me,' Emma said. 'I don't want to upset your mother-in-law. I—'

'She say I have ice cream to make, cupboards to paint, new cloths to buy for the tables.' Eduardo laughed. 'She wrong, *bella donna*.'

Emma wondered just how many aperitifs and glasses of wine Eduardo might have drunk before she got there. Dutch courage, perhaps? Well, she could understand that, although he didn't look or sound in the slightest bit drunk. *Perhaps he was used to drinking alcohol?*

'*Bella donna?*' Fleur said, looking quizzically at Emma.

'He call your mama "beautiful lady",' Paolo told her.

'Then I think,' Fleur said, taking a huge swallow of wine, 'your pa needs to see an optician.' But she giggled as she said it and Emma giggled with her.

'*Op, op?*' Eduardo said. 'What is *optishoo*? Is like sneeze, yes?'

'Nothing like it, Papa,' Paolo said, and everyone laughed.

He leaned over for the bottle of wine and topped up Fleur's glass and Emma did nothing to stop him. Fleur needed to relax a little too – not too much wine, but a little more wouldn't hurt for now.

This whole evening was surreal almost.

Emma couldn't wait to be in her own home now. She felt she'd made a friend in Eduardo Cascarini, although she realised it could get awkward if Fleur were to fall out with Paolo. First love seldom lasts, although it had for her and Seth. And there was his mother-in-law to consider, too, because from what Emma had seen so far around the table, she had a feeling she wouldn't be happy about another woman taking her daughter's place. Not happy at all.

Goodness, what was getting into her tonight? Even thinking about Eduardo being a permanent fixture in her life! She looked up and caught Eduardo's eye and he wrinkled his nose at her and smiled broadly. And then he winked.

Winked. Would she ever be able to see a man wink and not think of Matthew whose wink had often told her what words couldn't? Although Eduardo's wink had been friendly enough and probably something he did all the time, she wished he hadn't done it. For her a wink meant Matthew. And even though she didn't know if she would ever see him again, there was something fluttering around her heart, and something making colour rush up to the sides of her neck, that told her she wanted to – really, really, wanted – to see him again. But would she?

'I happy you like my *ristorante, bella donna*,' Eduardo said. He patted the side of his neck to let Emma know he'd seen the flush on it.

She flushed some more. He was totally misinterpreting the reason for it.

'Emma. Please call me Emma, Eduardo.'

'Emma, my *mama*.' Fleur giggled.

No, I'm not. Not really. Suddenly the fun had gone out of the evening for Emma. Is this how it was always going to be, harbouring her secret? Fleur needed to know who her real mother was – she should have been told before. When they were settled at Romer Lodge and Emma's dressmaking business was up and running, she'd tell her then. She had to.

'If you could help me with my luggage that would be wonderful, Eduardo. Thank you,' she said. 'And if you could tell me where I might buy a car of my own, then that would be wonderful, too.'

Chapter Five

'An opal,' Stella said. 'I think I'd rather have an opal than a diamond if it's all the same to you, Matthew.'

The salesman in Jamieson's Jewellers in Gandy Street looked up sharply at Stella's words. He looked from Stella to Matthew, and back again to Stella.

'An opal, madam. Are you sure?'

Oh for goodness sake, let the woman have what she wants, Matthew thought. For his part he was finding it quite touching and rather humbling that Stella wasn't going for the most expensive ring on display. They'd looked in three jewellers' shops before lunch. Then they'd enjoyed a good and leisurely plate of lamb chops with mint sauce and roast potatoes in the Beaufort Hotel, washed down with a bottle of red wine between them, and they'd been in two more jewellers afterwards. So far Stella hadn't seen the perfect engagement ring for her. But now it seemed she had, and some stuffed-shirt was questioning her.

'Quite sure,' Stella said. She turned to smile at Matthew, and the smile told him she meant she was sure about her choice of stone, and also sure about marrying him. 'The one on the middle shelf in the cabinet over there, second from the right.'

She waggled the fingers of her left hand in the air. How slim her fingers were – like the rest of her. Sometimes, when Matthew held her in his arms, he was afraid he'd break a bone somewhere – a collarbone perhaps. Or a rib. It amazed him to think that she had to lift heavy and often unconscious patients about, day in, day out, and sometimes through the night, too. *Would she miss all that when they married*? he wondered. *Had she thought the whole thing through about giving up a career for marriage?*

'If madam is sure,' the salesman said.

Matthew couldn't help himself: 'Madam is,' he snapped.

The assistant blinked in shock at his sharpness but rallied quickly. He leaned towards Matthew, turning his head away slightly from Stella.

'Opals, sir, have an element of bad luck about them,' he said, his voice barely above a whisper. 'They're considered *unlucky* as a betrothal stone.'

Before Matthew could think of a retort, Stella laughed loudly.

'I consider myself the luckiest woman in the world at the moment, that Matthew's said yes to my proposal!'

'*She* proposed to *you*, sir?'

'I most certainly did,' Stella said, flushing. Her eyes shone. She had had, Matthew thought, perhaps just a little too much wine at lunch, seeing as she had told him she'd skipped breakfast so as not to miss the train from Torquay. 'And in case no one's told you,' she continued with a giggle, '*she* is the cat's mother. Now, the opal, if you please.'

'That's my girl,' Matthew said as the assistant walked – like a man going to the gallows, Matthew couldn't help thinking – to fetch the ring of Stella's choice. Stella had spirit and he liked a woman with spirit. Emma had had spirit. He hoped she still did have. Wherever she was. Oh, he knew he would be able to find her if he really wanted to – or had to if he ever learnt that her life was in danger, as it once had been – but it wasn't his intention to meddle in her life. She'd chosen Seth over him back in 1913 and he had to leave it at that, even though she'd never left his heart. And he hoped against hope that he would be the sort of husband Stella deserved because always in the back of his mind would be Emma. '*And if the day comes when you are a free man and I am a free woman you can put my amethyst necklace around my neck for me,'* she'd said. What a bittersweet moment that had been – and how he'd relived it in his mind a million times over. It seemed disrespectful to the good-natured and trusting Stella to be thinking of Emma. Especially right at this moment.

'You're not having second thoughts, are you?' Stella said, standing on tiptoe to whisper in his ear.

Matthew tensed.

The assistant seemed to be taking an age unlocking the cabinet and Matthew placed a finger under Stella's chin and tilted her face up. Kissed her lightly on her wine-scented lips. Yes, she'd definitely had a bit too much to drink at lunch. He hoped the kiss would answer her question.

'Phew!' Stella said, her arm threaded so loosely through Matthew's that he had to put a hand on her wrist to check she was still there, as they made their way over cobbled Gandy Street towards the city centre. 'He was a hard nut to crack! He certainly didn't want me to have this!'

She waved her left hand in the air, twisting it this way and that, admiring her opal. It was catching the light from the shop windows and it seemed, to Matthew, as though all the colours of the rainbow were trapped in it, the way oil spilled on water brings rainbow colours to it. Sometimes it seemed he was walking through a rainbow when the forecourt of his garage business was puddled after a downpour. He thought about finding a telephone box so he could ring William to check there were no problems at Exe Motors but decided against it – Stella might think his mind was on his business and not on her. He didn't want to be the one to take the wonderful smile off her face and the joy from her voice.

'Any ideas when you want me to put the plain band one on to go with it?'

'Gosh, no,' Stella said, leaning into him. 'I want to enjoy this stage of the whole proceedings first. I won't be able to wear my lovely opal on the wards, of course. Well, not on my finger, but I've got a thin gold chain I could put it on and wear it around my neck. Matron might not see – if I'm lucky! And besides, I'll need to think about a dress and shoes and all the other things. I'll have to start looking at wedding dress patterns and material and see if I can find a good dressmaker to make it for me. No immediate rush. Maybe September. I love autumn. Or February. I love the cold, crisp days of February and the way the sun is low in the sky deepening colours. Snowdrops. I could carry snowdrops, perhaps?'

'Venue?' Matthew asked, happy for Stella that she was indulging herself in some fantasy. 'I'm a divorced man so ...'

'I know. The church won't marry you, although I've heard the vicar at Cockington often turns a deaf ear and a blind eye. I don't mind. Really, I don't. It's the marriage that's important, not the fancy ceremony. Perhaps a chapel would marry us? I don't know. If not, then a registry office will suit me fine. I've hardly anyone to ask to a wedding anyway. Have you?'

They'd reached the main street now and Matthew steered Stella towards South Street. They turned the corner, going down the hill, back towards the quay where Matthew had his business beside the canal.

'My son, if he wants to come, William who works for me and I dare say he could rustle up a girlfriend to bring along. That's about it.'

'Tell me about your son,' Stella said.

'Harry?'

'Unless you have another one you haven't told me about!' Stella laughed.

They crossed the road and began walking down the steep hill to the quay. Matthew pulled Stella closer because the path was slippery from a recent shower.

'Harry's coming up for eighteen. He wants to go to

university. He has a fancy to be a scientist. Goodness only knows where he got that notion from. Not me.'

Matthew had already told Stella about his wife – well, ex-wife now – Annie, and how she'd left him for another woman. They were still together, Annie and Patricia. What a strange life it must have been for Harry with, effectively, two mothers bringing him up. Sometimes Matthew regretted moving back to England from America which had meant he saw little of Harry – once a year at the most if he could get away and if it suited Annie for him to see his son.

'Oxford? Cambridge?' Stella asked, her voice still a bubble of happiness.

'No. Somewhere in America. Yale or Harvard. I'm not too up on American universities but everyone's heard of those. We've not discussed it. He'll write to me when he's decided where. And I'll send him a wad of cash, I suspect.'

'As is right for a father to do, of course,' Stella said. 'I'm looking forward to meeting him. But do you know something, Matthew Caunter, although I know you have a garage business and you drive a Clyno, and that you have a Norton motorcycle and a big house in Polsloe Road, I don't know what you did before all that.'

I was responsible for sending men to the gallows. Two of them Jagos – Carter and Miles. I know every spying trick in the book. I've risked my life more than a few times but, so far, got away with it. I've been paid to spy on husbands with their lovers, and the other way around. I've been in places you don't want to know about in the pursuance of my quarry.

'HM Customs,' was what Matthew chose to say. 'Or HM Customs and Excise as it is now. I was in covert surveillance. Then, when I went to America, I ran a private detection agency. A lot of people hated me for both occupations, but I have no regrets whatsoever about anything I've done.'

Stella turned to look at him with a surprised look on her

face. And then she smiled her wonderful, accepting smile. 'I'd better watch my step then, and not go flirting with anyone I shouldn't once we're married!'

Matthew laughed, if a little uneasily. Sometimes he woke in the night wondering if someone would come after him; if someone was, right at that moment – as he listened to the night sounds and the sound of his own breathing – outside and about to break in. He'd fitted good locks to all his doors – window locks, too – but he could never be sure.

'You will,' he said. 'As, I think, will I. A girl like you knows what to poison a man with, I should think.'

'Oh, yes.' Stella giggled. 'A needle in your buttocks while you sleep – you wouldn't feel a thing!'

It began to rain then. Sharp spits of it that stung Matthew's face. He prised Stella's arm from his and put his arm around her shoulder.

'Come on. Run. We're going to get soaked. Tea and cake at the Swan's Nest and then I'll drive you to the station. Unless you want to stop the night?'

Stella brushed raindrops from her eyelashes. She slid an arm around the back of Matthew's waist and leaned her head against his shoulder.

'And you don't think you've given me enough pleasure today? Lunch? The ring? Indulging me in my wedding planning?'

Her voice was teasing, and yet there was a tremor of something running through her because Matthew could feel it where their bodies touched.

'A girl can't have too much pleasure,' he said.

It had been a while since he'd made love but hell, it was like breathing, wasn't it – while the heart was beating you never forget how to do it.

'But not just yet.' Stella laughed. She waggled her fingers, kissed her engagement ring.

Bugger, Matthew thought. *Bugger.* But he was a patient man – he could wait a while longer.

Chapter Six

Emma didn't know when she'd last been so busy. May had flown by and now June was coming to a close. Eduardo Cascarini had been as good as his word and turned up at the Grand Hotel to take Emma's and Fleur's luggage to Romer Lodge. He'd even pitched in and helped Emma give the tiles in the hall a good scrub. And it had been a great help having him there to move heavy furniture about.

What else could she have done but accept his invitation to dine with him? He seemed to have forgotten he'd said he didn't like eating in grand places because he'd taken her to the Imperial Hotel and paid a small fortune for food which Emma thought was way below the standard of the meal Eduardo had cooked for her in his *ristorante*. And she'd told him so which put a grin on his face, like a child in a toyshop, for the rest of the evening. When he'd kissed her goodnight – one feather-light touch of his lips on each cheek – and asked if she would like to take a drive with him along the coast on Sunday afternoon, after church, she'd said 'yes'.

Eduardo's disgust that Fleur wasn't Catholic, and his implication that she wouldn't make a proper wife for Paolo, didn't apply to himself it seemed. He hadn't asked Emma her religion and she hadn't told him. But, whatever those differences between them might be, she found herself enjoying Eduardo Cascarini's company more each time she saw him. He'd promised to look for the telephone number of the garage he used in Exeter where he had bought his van and had the signage for the ice cream business painted on.

'He good man,' Eduardo had said. 'No charge *fortuna*. He know I not rich.'

And he'd laughed. Emma had laughed with him because it was obvious from the quality of his leather shoes, the gold fob watch in his waistcoat pocket, and the cut of his suit that Eduardo Cascarini was far from poor.

'Hmm, I must remember to ask him for that telephone number,' Emma said out loud now as she busied herself in her atelier. She had set aside a room in Romer Lodge for her sewing with a large table for cutting out, and a chest of drawers – brought down from one of the bedrooms – in which to keep all her sewing notions; the pins and the scissors and a selection of threads. Somewhere she could bring her clients, to measure them, and to talk through their requirements for dresses and blouses, skirts and coats. She'd been buying *Vogue* magazine for weeks now and had a little pile of them on a small table in the corner for clients to look through. She'd even put a small chaise longue against one wall – somewhere for clients to sit. Doing that had brought back memories of Seth. There'd been one in the house Seth had been gifted by his father, and it was as though it was yesterday that she'd escaped from Nase Head House to Hilltop. Mrs Drew, Seth's housekeeper, had let her in and they'd waited half the night it seemed for Seth to come home. And when he had, he'd been bloodied and bruised and half-unconscious. Emma always thought that was the moment she really fell in love with him – the fear of losing him heightening her feelings.

She'd opened an account with Beares, the haberdashers, in Victoria Street, where the manageress had said they could deliver if needed. Emma needed. Well, until she got around to buying a car, that is. She missed driving. Back in 1923, in Vancouver, Seth had bought a Buick Sedan as different from his Wolseley, that Emma had driven in England before they'd left for Canada, as it was possible for a car to be. It was a huge thing, the colour of morello cherries, with running boards. It had leather seats and a little window flap on the windscreen to let in fresh air in the summer. Emma had enjoyed driving it even though some of the roads had been rougher than rough over there. But she didn't need anything quite that large in Devon. Just something big enough for her and Fleur – a two-seater would do – as long as there was a decent-sized boot to carry things.

'Ma! Where are you?' Fleur's yell jolted Emma back to the present.

'In here. In my atelier.'

Fleur peered around the edge of the half-open door. 'I'm going out,' she said.

'Oh! Where?'

Fleur sighed theatrically. 'For a walk. With Paolo. Well, actually, we're going roller-skating.'

'But you haven't got any roller-skates. If you—'

'Ever heard of hiring things, Ma?' Fleur interrupted.

Well, of *course* she had. Hadn't she hired a sewing machine when they'd been staying at the Grand Hotel – a hand-operated one. She'd sent that back now, though, and had her deposit back, and was now the proud owner of the latest Singer sewing machine to come on the market – it came with its own wooden base with a motor and boasted a foot-operated control. Not quite an industrial model but it would cope with thicknesses as well as doing the finest of stitches. And it was a far cry from the treadle machine her mama had used at the beginning of the century.

'You don't have to be so snippy,' Emma said. 'I was going to say that if you like roller-skating then I could buy you some for your birthday next month.'

Fleur sighed again. 'I *know* when my birthday is, Ma. Same as you do. Neither of us is likely to forget, are we?'

Emma's blood chilled in her veins. A ripple of unease snaked up her spine and the hairs on the back of her neck stood on end. She knew she'd have to sit Fleur down and tell her as gently as she could, that she hadn't given birth to her. Another woman had. And that woman was Caroline Prentiss – someone Emma hoped with all her heart she'd never set eyes on again. Fleur ought to have been told before. Seth said he was going to do it – he'd know the moment, so he'd said. But for Seth that moment had never come. And now Emma would have to do it. She would have to dredge up the courage from somewhere but, like Seth, she hoped she'd know when the right time to say what she had to presented itself.

'No, no we're not likely to forget,' she managed to say.

'Well, then,' Fleur said. 'Can I go now? Please?'

'If you can do something for me on the way, yes.'

Emma reached for a sheet of paper on the edge of the table. She'd drafted out an advertisement for her business, with her name and address, and telephone number on it and the name of her business written in a swirly hand in the centre. *Femme.* The French for woman and wife. She'd drawn two figures – one in a dropped-waist dress with an asymmetric hem, and the other in a fitted costume, on either side of the word.

'What?' Fleur said.

'Could you drop this into Partington the Printers and ask them to print six the same size as this piece of paper, or thereabouts, and one hundred at calling card size? Please?'

The large ones, Emma intended to place in newsagents' windows to advertise her business, and the little cards she would hand to each client she garnered from that, with the request they pass it on to anyone else who might be interested in Emma making things for them.

Fleur huffed. 'You're making me late,' she whined.

'Well, you're worth waiting for, aren't you?' Emma said, with a smile. Fleur was getting more beautiful by the day and would be more beautiful still if only she'd smile more. Emma knew Fleur's lack of smiles was because she was having trouble settling in England. She hoped this budding friendship with Paolo would bring the smile back to Fleur's face soon. 'If Paolo thinks enough of you, he'll wait.'

Seth had waited for her, oh how he'd waited. He'd given her the time to make up her mind – make her choice, him or Matthew Caunter? To go to Canada with Seth, or not? Emma had made her choice, and she hadn't regretted it for a moment.

Why then, over the years, had Matthew Caunter, and the kiss he'd stolen from her up at Nase Head House on the night of Rupert and Joanna Smythe's wedding, come to her in dreams ever since?

'He might,' Fleur said. 'And he might not.' She made patterns with the toe of her shoe on the wooden floor and folded her arms in front of her at waist level.

Ah, Emma thought, *things aren't going so well with Paolo.*

'You don't have to go if you don't want to,' Emma said. 'But you do have to let him know you're not coming.'

'Yes, ma'am,' Fleur said, and she said it with a Canadian accent.

Back in Vancouver Fleur had had to say ma'am and sir to just about anyone older than she was when she met them, and when she said goodbye. Was saying it now letting Emma know she was homesick for Canada and the only life she'd known?

Now she was looking at her properly, and not with half an eye on things that needed doing in her atelier, Emma could see Fleur looked a little pale, with dark patches under her eyes.

'Fleur,' she said, 'you can stay here and help me if you really don't want to meet Paolo. We need to talk about what you're going to do at some stage and today might be a good opportunity. A study course of some sort? Accounting? Shorthand and typing? Teaching?'

'Ma, stop!' Fleur said. 'Who said anything about all that

accounting and teaching stuff? I said I was going *out*.' Fleur took a few steps into the room and snatched up the piece of paper from the table. 'I'll take this with me.'

'Thank you. Can you tell them I'll call in a day or two to see if they're ready?'

But we do need to talk, and soon – about everything. You can't just do nothing. It's not good for you.

'Uh?' Fleur said, and for a moment Emma wondered if she'd said the words out loud instead of thinking them. 'What did you say?'

'Never mind. Six large ones and one hundred calling card size. Can you remember that?'

Fleur rolled her eyes heavenwards but Emma effected not to notice. She didn't want, or need, an argument with Fleur. Eduardo had invited her to a concert at the Pavilion. She wondered if she would have enough time to make a dress to wear to it. Something in lace, perhaps? And long. Although she wore her day clothes much shorter these days, as was the fashion, sometimes she missed the swish of fabric around her ankles and the longer, leaner line a full-length dress gave her. She reached for the latest copy of *Vogue* – she'd seen a photograph of Coco Chanel wearing a lace dress with a bolero. She could copy it, she knew she could. But she'd have to limit her outings with Eduardo – or anyone else for that matter – because she had a business to start, and make a success of.

And she would – or her name wasn't Emma Jago.

'Fleur!' Paolo came running towards her, his hair dishevelled and his face rather pink. 'I sorry I late. My papa he make me do strawberry ice cream and then he make me wash floor in kitchen. *Mia nonna*, she not well.' Paolo pulled a sad face and Fleur couldn't be sure if it was because he'd been made to make ice cream and scrub a floor, or that his grandmother was ill.

'It doesn't matter,' she said. 'I'm late, too. I've only just arrived myself. Ma made me do an errand.'

She pulled a face. What a dump the printing shop had been. There'd been ink on just about everything – the counter, the chair in front of it where she'd had to wait a few minutes for the customer in front of her to be served and on which she hadn't sat, and the door handle. She'd had to spit on her fingers to get ink off them after touching it. Eurghh.

'We must,' Paolo said. 'Is duty to help *genitori*.'

'Jen ... what?' Fleur asked.

'Mama and papa.'

'Oh, you mean "parents",' she said.

Every time she met Paolo they spent the first half hour or so trying to understand one another. She'd found it endearing to begin with but now she was becoming irritated by it – why couldn't he speak English properly, for goodness sake? He'd been born in London! Or so he'd said.

'*Si*. Parents. For me is only papa. And for you is only mama.'

Yes, and what a pain she is at times. How does she think she is going to find people in this dump to make fancy couture clothes for? Well, she hadn't met up with Paolo to talk about her *mama*, had she?

'At the *momento*,' Paolo said, grinning at her as though he had a secret.

'What does *that* mean?' Fleur asked – and she didn't mean the Italian word, she meant the implication of his comment.

'That my papa like your mama. He like very much.'

'Well, he didn't like *me* much a few weeks ago when he caught us kissing in his kitchen.'

Paolo shrugged. 'He not meet your mama then properly. He sing in house now. *La bohème. Così fan tutte. Don Giovanni*. He know all the parts, all the words. He ask me if I like your mama, and he point to *dito matrimonio*.' Paolo pointed to the wedding finger of his left hand.

What? Was the man mad? People got married to have families and her ma was far too old to have another baby, wasn't she? If she'd wanted one of those she'd have had one before now, wouldn't she? *A brother or sister for me.*

Time to change the subject!

'Are we still going roller-skating?' Fleur asked, tapping her wristwatch to let Paolo know time was whizzing by as he only had two hours from ice cream delivery duties to see her. But it looked as though they might not be able to roller-skate after all, because the pier was full of figures roller-skating with various degrees of success, and there were no skates left for hire in the rack. They would have to wait their turn, but for how long? She'd only said she would try roller-skating so she could hang onto Paolo's arm and she wasn't sure she wanted to do that now. She'd had a sudden vision of the future in which she'd seen herself playing nursemaid to an ageing Ma and she hadn't liked the picture of that one little bit. And she knew that Paolo was already in dutiful son mode, wasn't he?

'It looks very busy and it's getting very hot,' she said. 'We'd only get hotter roller-skating.'

Paolo shrugged. 'I no mind,' he said. 'I happy only that I with you. We can walk.' He held out his hand towards Fleur and she placed hers in it.

'We can,' she said. 'We could go to Beacon Cove.'

It was secluded there. Paolo had taken her once before and they'd kissed and kissed and Paolo's kisses had made her body ache for something else. She'd felt Paolo's 'thing' hard against her stomach when he was lying on top of her. He'd reached down and had begun to pull her skirt up when they'd been disturbed by a man with a large dog coming down the rough steps towards them.

'We go,' Paolo said. He quickened his pace as though he

couldn't wait to get there and start kissing her. Fleur liked that. She speeded up to keep alongside him.

Hmm, perhaps today they wouldn't be disturbed? She liked Paolo's kisses and the way they made her body feel. Womanly. And not the kid her ma still thought she was, telling her she'd have to find something to do for heaven's sake! As though she didn't know that herself! Well, whatever it was it would be her choice and not her ma's. And then an idea came to her.

'I think, before we go to Beacon Cove, that I'd like to get my hair cut. Washing and drying this ...' with her free hand she lifted the heavy curtain of her hair up and let it flop down again, '... takes up too much time. And it makes me look like a little girl.'

'You no *little* girl,' Paolo said, laughing. 'You beautiful *donna* now. You cut hair for *movimento femminista*?'

Movimento femminista? Oh, Fleur could just about make out what Paolo was saying – feminist movement.

'No,' she said, feeling defiant. 'I'm doing this for me. Besides, getting my hair bobbed is really going to get my ma's goat.'

'Emma? Is that you?'

Emma had to hold the earpiece about a foot away from her ear because the person on the other end was shouting so loudly. She knew the voice. Ruby. And she also knew she hadn't given a thought yet to how she was going to help Ruby. Yes, she'd left two five pound notes under the teapot on Ruby's kitchen table. And she knew Ruby had seen it before she'd left, all thoughts of not accepting Emma's charity thrown out of the window at the sight of them. Not that Emma minded that. But she knew it might be best not to ask if the money had run out and was that why Ruby was calling.

'Yes, it's me. But you don't have to shout, Ruby,' she said. 'You're deafening me.'

'Well, I don't know 'ow to use these things, do I?' Ruby said, speaking normally now. 'Not like some as I can mention. Your turn to speak. I've just been told I've got to say that.'

'Whose telephone are you using?'

Emma didn't think for a minute that Ruby had used the money she'd given her to get a telephone installed in Shingle Cottage.

'The doctor's. The new one where Dr Shaw used to be. It's a woman, Em. Dr Howard. 'Er's got a receptionist an' all. An' there's a nurse 'ere for the women's private bits. Did you ever?'

Emma waited for Ruby to tell her why she was calling from Dr Howard's surgery, and her heart plummeted with dread. Was something wrong with Ruby? Something terrible like the canker that had killed her beloved Mrs Drew? Or Tom? Had Tom succumbed to his troubled mind? And then she realised Ruby was waiting for a response from her. When nothing more from Ruby was forthcoming, Emma said, 'Ladies can be doctors, Ruby. Is something wrong? If you're seeing a doctor?'

Guilt enveloped her, uncomfortable and making her squirm a little, like a rough woollen garment against the skin. She ought to have gone back to see Ruby before now, to see how she was managing, and to let her friend know she still wanted to see her and that she was proud of her for making the break from her old life.

'It id'n me what's ill, Em. It's my Alice. 'Er's been proper poorly. Doctor thinks it's some sort of fever 'er's 'ad. I should've brought 'er before but I didn't 'ave the money. And now I 'ave brought 'er I still 'aven't got the money to pay. What you left me went on feedin' my little varmints, an' I'm grateful for it seein' as I wasn't doing the other to earn money. But, I were wonderin', could I come and do a bit of cleanin' or summat in that 'ouse you've got. And can

79

I tell this woman 'ere I'll 'ave the money soon to pay the bill? Please, Em.'

I could, Emma thought. And I will. The way Ruby was chattering on like her old self warmed Emma's heart and she guessed whatever fever it was Alice had had it wasn't life-threatening, and thank heaven for that.

'Did you 'ear any of that, Em, only you ain't said anythin' yet.'

'I heard,' Emma said. 'And I'm really sorry to hear about Alice.'

'Me an' all, Em. I thought I was goin' to lose her one night back along, that's for sure.'

Emma heard Ruby gulp – swallowing back tears no doubt. Fleur had been ill more than a few times, especially when they'd first gone to Canada and her little body had had trouble acclimatising to the cold the first winter they were there. Emma had sat up through the night many a time, willing Fleur to breathe. To live.

But the last thing Emma wanted was for Ruby to be working for her to earn money for doctor's bills for Alice – it would change their friendship, wouldn't it? But Tom? Might it help him if he were to feel useful again? The garden had been left unattended for a good six months before Emma had become the tenant at Romer Lodge and Tom had been a gardener up at Nase Head House before the war.

'Yes, of course I'll let you have the money, Ruby. How much?' Emma said.

'Two guineas,' Ruby said. 'Oh gawd, I'm goin' to wear me knees out scrubbin' your floors to earn that much. Oh, and I've got somethin' else to tell you, but that can wait. Your turn to speak.'

'Goodbye,' Emma said.

Well, someone had to let the doctor's receptionist have her telephone back.

* * *

'I love it even though I know Ma will hate it,' Fleur said to herself as she caught her reflection in the window of the conservatory. She put the backs of her hands by her ears and lifted the sides of her bob up and let them fall again. She had a chill feeling on the back of her neck now there was no longer a yard of hair covering it but she was certain she'd get used to it.

She'd been so long in the hairdresser's that there hadn't been time to go to Beacon Cove after all. Paolo had had to go back to work. Oh well, as her ma had said earlier she was worth waiting for, and if Paolo wanted her, he'd wait.

Fleur took a deep breath and turned the huge brass knob on the front door.

She sent up a silent prayer that her ma had had a good afternoon poking about in her atelier, as she liked to call it. And she had her trump card – or one hundred calling cards and posters to be exact – up her sleeve. Her ma wouldn't be expecting her to have those already but the printer had said if she could call back around six o'clock then her order should be ready. It was.

'Ma!' she called cheerily. 'I'm back.'

Chapter Seven

Emma wasted no time getting her notices put in shop windows. Fleur had happily gone with her, and Emma knew that was because she hadn't read her the riot act over the haircut. Remembering how Fleur had stood in the doorway of the atelier, one hand showing off her bob, the other holding out the calling cards and posters, brought a smile to Emma's face whenever she thought of it.

'I take it all back, Fleur,' Emma had said immediately, not giving Fleur a second to throw in some sort of defence for having gone against her wishes. 'A bob suits you, and probably better than it does me. And thank you for doing that.' She took the posters and cards from Fleur, and quickly checked the wording was correct. 'We're in business now!'

Far from making Fleur look like a film star – Louise Brooks or Clara Bow – it made her look young and fresh and modern. A bright young thing indeed, although Emma sent up a silent prayer that Fleur wouldn't be embarking on the cigarette smoking, and the drinking of exotic cocktails, as the newspapers reported bright young things got up to on a regular basis.

She asked the newsagent next door to the Pavilion in Torquay if she could put a poster in his window and already she'd had two enquiries from it. The newsagent said he had a sister nursing up at the hospital and if Emma had a spare poster then he would let her have it for the nurses' common room. Emma had given him one and thanked him profusely for his foresight in thinking of it. Lots of women worked at the hospital – domestic as well as nursing staff. Emma had had a flutter of excitement in her stomach at the possibilities of it all.

The manageress in Beares, the haberdashers, said she would happily put one in the window because wasn't she sick to death of customers asking where they could find a good dressmaker.

'If you made that, Mrs Jago,' the manageress had said, looking admiringly at Emma's Chanel copy dropped waist jersey dress and matching edge-to-edge jacket, 'then you're a wonderful walking advertisement for your skills.'

And now she had someone calling to see her at eleven o'clock. About a wedding dress. A nurse. A Miss Martin. She'd sounded very nice and also very young and giggly on the telephone but perhaps that was what having a wedding dress made for you did. Emma had made her own when she'd married Seth. She still had it packed in tissue in the bottom of the trunk she'd got Eduardo Cascarini to put down in the cellar of Romer Lodge for her. She doubted she would ever wear it again but she hadn't been able to part with it, as old-fashioned as it was now.

Someone rang the front doorbell – a huge bronze thing on a chain that Emma was certain anyone with perfect hearing would be able to hear down on the harbour-side every time the thing was pulled.

'I'll go, Ma,' Fleur shouted from the hallway.

'Thanks!' Emma called back.

She hurriedly tidied then re-tidied the pile of magazines on the small table in the corner by the couch. She re-arranged the roses she'd picked that morning from the garden – a climbing rose that scrambled up the wall at the side of the house. It had no thorns, was a deep magenta, and smelled divine. What it was called Emma had no idea but she'd see if she could find someone to ask.

And then Fleur was back. With Miss Martin.

'This is Miss Martin, Ma,' Fleur said. 'About a wedding dress?'

There was just the hint of a question at the end of Fleur's

sentence and Miss Martin said, 'That's right.' And she dropped her head just a little as though embarrassed to be wanting a wedding dress. And anxious – Emma thought she looked anxious.

Far from being a young woman as Emma had thought when speaking to her on the telephone, Miss Martin had to be the same age as Emma was – thirty-four – or thereabouts. Possibly older. Just for a second she reminded Emma of Caroline Prentiss with her blonde hair piled on top of her head in a loose sort of bun and her slimmer-than-slim figure.

Brushing off all thoughts of Caroline Prentiss the way one would brush off dirt, Emma walked towards Miss Martin her hand held out in greeting.

'I'm very pleased to meet you, Miss Martin. I'm Emma Jago,' she said.

'And I'm Fleur,' Fleur said, offering Miss Martin her hand.

'Pleased to meet you both,' Miss Martin said.

'But not for long,' Fleur said. 'I'm off, Ma.'

You little minx, Emma thought. *Presenting me with a fait accompli in front of a client knowing I can't challenge you. Hmm.*

'To the library,' Fleur said. 'In case you were wondering.'

She beamed at her mother – *gosh, how beautiful she was, her eyes flashing like dark coals* – nodded respectfully at Miss Martin, then turned to go.

Emma heard the rapid click-clack of Fleur's heels on the tiles of the hall floor and wondered if the *library* was a euphemism for *seeing Paolo* as it had been once before.

'Don't rush back,' Emma called after her. 'Miss Martin and I will probably have lots to discuss.'

But the thud of the front door shutting told her Fleur had already left.

'You have a beautiful daughter, Mrs Jago,' Miss Martin said.

'Thank you. She takes after her father for looks.'

And then she realised what she'd said and laughed. Miss Martin put a hand over her mouth to stifle her own laugh, but failed miserably.

'Gosh, that came out all wrong, didn't it?' Emma said.

'It did rather,' Miss Martin said. 'I shouldn't have laughed but I couldn't help it. And we all need a laugh sometimes, don't we?'

'We do,' Emma agreed. But it was true – Fleur was a Jago, through and through. And thank goodness for that. Although sometimes her sharp ways reminded Emma too much of Caroline Prentiss and she did her best to smooth off the rough edges of Fleur's character. 'Now then, shall we look through these?'

Emma had selected the magazines with pictures of wedding dresses in them and opened them at the relevant pages. They were spread across the cutting-out table. She'd had the foresight to ask in Beare's for some sample fabrics telling the manageress she had some future brides coming for consultations. A little white lie there with the brides, plural, when it was only the one – Miss Martin – for the moment, but she had to start somewhere. And if she made a good job of Miss Martin's dress then other brides would flock to her door, wouldn't they?

Well, thank goodness Ma has got something else to think about other than pestering me to do something, Fleur thought.

She neared the pier and on a whim decided to go on it. Paignton pier was nothing more than a few sheds on stilts, with a row of one-armed bandits down one side, and was nothing like the elegant one over in Torquay, but it would be something to do. She had a few pennies in her purse and would play the machines for a while. Her ma would go crazy if she knew she was doing that. Gambling was a sin, wasn't it? Well, that's what all the notices outside the churches said, although her ma had never told her as much. And what's more, her ma never set foot inside a church. Fleur remembered asking her once, back in Vancouver when she'd been ten or something like that, why they didn't go to church on Sundays like everyone else and her ma had replied that she'd fallen out with the church over an issue many years before and she saw no reason to fall back in with it. And that had been the end of that conversation. Not that Fleur minded really. Although she'd seen some very good-looking young men coming out of St Andrews Church in Sands Road last Sunday with their parents. Hmm. Paolo had asked her if she'd like to go with him to church one Sunday for Mass but she'd declined. Why would a woman want to wear a bit of lace over her head to go and pray? And they had incense in Catholic churches, didn't they? And from what she could remember, girls who were Catholics at her school in Vancouver had told her every darned thing was a mortal sin and you needed to confess it. She and Paolo had done a few things that if she'd been a Catholic she'd need to confess but why the heck would she want to tell some old bloke who'd never married sitting the other side of a little grille thing in a wooden box what she'd done?

But she would have to do something to fill her time, she knew that. She was getting bored. But what?

'A course of some kind?' her ma had said the night before at dinner. 'Shorthand and typing, perhaps? Accountancy? Your father was very good with figures.'

And he was very good at gutting fish as well, Fleur had answered whippet-fast, which had brought tears to her ma's eyes. She regretted that. Her ma was her ma and, she knew, a lot less strict than some. She didn't make her put her hat on to go out, for one thing. And before she'd had her hair shingled, her ma had let her wear her hair loose, not coiled up and rolled up and stuck underneath a hat. *How Paolo had loved to run his hands through her hair! And how tingly it had made her feel when he did.* But her hair was shorter now and she'd discovered that Paolo could do other things to make her feel tingly.

Fleur put a penny in the slot of the machine and pulled the handle. The little barrels with pictures of fruit spun round, going faster and faster so that the colours spun out to a whiteness. When they eventually stopped there weren't three of anything in a row.

'Lost again,' she said. Well, that was six pennies she might as well have thrown down the drain. The church might not be right in thinking gambling was a sin but it *was* a fool's game. She wasn't going to waste another single penny on it.

She walked out through the double plate glass doors onto the open end of the pier and walked over to a railing, resting her elbows on it.

France was over there somewhere – home of her grandfather, Guillaume Le Goff. A little place called Benodet in Brittany so her ma had said. Not for the first time she wondered why her ma didn't go to France, if only for a holiday. There were three large yachts moored in the bay and Fleur daydreamed about what it might be like to sail. Her pa had suffered from seasickness, she knew that. He'd been happy enough to work in the office of his shipping business, though. And he'd loved painting even more – God how she missed him.

Tears began to well thinking about her pa and how she'd loved to stand beside him while he painted at the easel – not talking, just watching. She had at least four portraits he'd done of her growing up, and she wasn't going to get another one now, was she? Fleur gulped in an attempt to swallow her tears, but one escaped and slid down her cheek anyway.

'You look like you could use a cigarette.' A man's voice somewhere behind her, but close.

A cigarette? In a holder? Fleur had seen Mary Pickford in the film, *Rosita*, smoking a cigarette. The thought of smoking thrilled her and frightened her in equal measure. *But did she want to smoke just because a stranger was offering her a cigarette?* Paolo smoked and she wasn't sure she liked the taste of nicotine on his lips, or the smell of it in his hair.

Fleur shook her head.

'I'm not offering to push you off the end of the pier,' the man said, with a hint of a smile in his voice. He sounded kindly enough. Fleur turned to look at the speaker. He had to be at least thirty if he was a day. Very dapper. He was wearing white flannels and a short-sleeved shirt with a V-neck sleeveless pullover. His dark hair was so shiny, with a precise parting on the left-hand side that Fleur wondered if he might have polished it. He raised his eyebrows at her in a do-you-want-a-cigarette-or-not? sort of way. He had a moustache she thought would probably tickle if he tried to kiss her. Not that she was going to give him the chance.

He took a packet of cigarettes from his pocket. And a lighter. He leaned onto the rail beside Fleur, shuffled closer.

'One won't hurt,' he said, and Fleur could smell alcohol on his breath. Spirits. There'd been enough men with spirits on their breath at the Grand Hotel for Fleur to know what it was.

'You could be right,' Fleur said. 'But I don't want one. Thank you.'

'You sure?' the man asked. 'Plenty of women smoke. Bright women. Smart women.' He looked at Fleur from head to foot as he spoke, as though he was appraising something he was thinking of buying. The look made Fleur shiver, despite the warmth from the sun.

'Do they?' Fleur asked. She'd never had a man force his

attention on her before and she didn't know how to deal with it, apart from running off.

'Sure do,' he told her.

Fleur scanned the pier for women smoking. Yes, there was one on the other side, leaning against the rail, a cigarette dangling from long fingers. She was wearing a large hat with the brim almost covering her face. And then, as though sensing Fleur looking at her, the woman pulled the brim of her hat even further down, turned sharply, looking out to sea.

The man began to draw a cigarette from the packet. 'Beautiful girl like you should be welcoming new experiences.'

Fleur thought she detected an accent in his voice that wasn't English. Not Canadian though. American, perhaps? Well, she certainly wasn't going to ask him. And this was an experience she could have done without.

She turned and ran back down the pier, conscious that the man's eyes were on her. She should have gone to the library like she'd told her ma she was going to. What a jerk that bloke was! What had he taken her for? A floozy? Well, she was far from that.

But, God, growing up was hard to do!

It was as though Emma had known Stella all her life. Within minutes of Fleur leaving Stella asked Emma to stop saying 'Miss Martin' every other word and to call her Stella, because goodness not many people called her by that name any more. At the hospital all the patients called her Nurse, and she was Miss Martin to just about everyone else from the woman behind the counter in the dairy to matron and everyone in between. It was as though the making of the dress had already been agreed upon between them.

'Except my fiancé,' Stella said. 'He calls me by my Christian name, of course.'

'Stella's a lovely name,' Emma said. 'And you must call me Emma.'

She wasn't sure if it was etiquette for a client to be so informal but what did it matter, really, as long as there was respect there.

An hour flew by as they looked at magazines and Stella told Emma what sort of dress she'd been thinking of. Emma could see that Stella would need something designed just for her, and not made from a Butterick or a McCall pattern. Certainly nothing in the magazines she'd shown Stella was quite right.

'I could design something for you,' Emma had said. Could she? She'd never really done that before but she'd adapted patterns many times so it couldn't be too hard, could it?

'Gosh,' Stella said. 'You're making me feel like a rich film star.'

'It needn't cost any more than a paper pattern would,' Emma told her. 'I can cut a pattern from just about anything – brown paper, newspaper, tissue paper, whatever I can lay my hands on.'

That much was true – she could, and she had. And she was good at drawing. Seth had told her she had a natural flair but he'd given her some tips on perspective so she was fairly certain she could make a good fist of a design for a wedding dress for Stella Martin.

'Gosh, can you? How clever. Where did you learn to do that?'

'I think I absorbed it through some sort of osmosis,' Emma said with a laugh. She reached for a sheet of foolscap paper on the dresser, found a pencil and began a quick sketch. 'My maternal grandfather was a tailor and he taught my mama. She wanted to be apprenticed to him so she could learn tailoring but it wasn't allowed. But my grandpapa taught her anyway. He was dead before I was born.'

'I'm sorry.'

'Don't be,' Emma said. 'It's how things are. My mama began teaching me from when I was old enough to thread a needle. I hated it then. I was a very grumpy, reluctant student at times but ...' Emma shrugged her shoulders and concentrated on her pencil drawing. 'Something like that?' She slid her lightning sketch across the table to Stella before snatching it back again. 'No wait. That neckline will need jewellery.'

Quickly she drew a head and shoulders into her design and pencilled a chain and a pendant at the neck. *Her mama's amethyst necklace. The necklace Matthew had hunted down after it had been stolen, not once, but twice.* How easily she remembered the shape of it. How easily she drew the leaf and rosebud tooling on the gold mount around the stone. She wondered for a moment where it might be now, where Matthew might be in whose safe keeping she had left it.

'Well, I'm very glad your mother persevered with you,' Stella said. 'Very glad.'

And so am I now.

'That pendant,' Stella asked. 'What stone is it?'

'An amethyst. As dark as blackberry juice and as plumped up as a goose feather pillow.'

'It sounds as though it's precious to you.'

'It is. It was my mama's.'

'Then I won't ask to borrow it for my "something borrowed" for good luck.'

'I don't have it at the moment,' Emma told her. 'I left it in the safe keeping of a friend when I went to Canada and ... and I haven't got around to asking for it back yet.'

Emma crossed her fingers behind her back that Matthew – wherever he might be – still had it and that he would return it to her one day.

'I wouldn't *dream* of asking to borrow something

so precious,' Stella said. 'Honestly. And did you know amethysts were worn in amulets by the Greeks to ward off drunkenness?'

Emma laughed. 'Really? I've no need of that!'

'I could use it sometimes up at the hospital on a Saturday night,' Stella said, laughing with her. 'More than a few drunks wander in for the warmth and mistake me for a long lost lover!'

How good it felt to Emma to share laughter.

'What I've done,' Emma told her, stabbing her forefinger onto the photo of a model in a copy of *Vogue* wearing a boat-necked dress, 'is I've taken the neckline from that one and the skirt from something else I saw in another magazine. You need fullness.'

'Because I'm so thin!' Stella laughed. 'My fiancé is always telling me he's afraid I'm going to break when he hugs me! He should see me lifting fifteen stone men about! All the running up and down the wards keeps me thin, not that we're really allowed to run.'

'No,' Emma said. 'I've heard nurses aren't allowed to run, even in an emergency.'

What would it be like to have a man, a fiancé, to hug her? Would she ever feel a man's arms about her again?

Emma sketched and Stella chatted on.

'I hope people won't laugh when they see me getting married in a white dress.'

'Why would they?' Emma asked.

'Well, at my age, I mean.'

Emma didn't know quite what to say now as 'how old are you?' didn't quite fit the bill. And wasn't there a saying that you should never ask a lady her age? Or was that just that men shouldn't ask a lady her age?

'I'll be forty next birthday.' Stella helpfully provided the information. 'But I'm hoping to marry while I'm still in my thirties. Have a baby … sorry, I'm being indiscreet.'

Emma still hoped in her own heart that she would have a baby of her own, although she realised it would disrupt her life – and Fleur's – quite considerably if she did. But she would face that when the time came – *if* it came. Was time running out for her, too, as Stella was implying it might be for her?

'Have you set a date? For the wedding, I mean, not for the making of babies ... oh, my, there I go again thinking out loud. I'm sorry, I ought not to have said that.'

Stella laughed. 'No, no date set yet for the wedding, and my birthday's not until February, so plenty of time to make the dress ... and anything else.' Stella grinned at Emma. 'Virginal white for my wedding dress,' she said. 'Very appropriate.'

Well, there was nothing Emma could bring to that piece of information so she didn't. She was enjoying Stella's company enormously – inappropriate information being shared, or not. She hoped she'd made a friend in Stella. She needed her friends. She made a mental note to call on Ruby and ask Tom if he would like to garden for her, and soon – then she would hold, perhaps, an afternoon tea. She could invite Eduardo and Paolo, and now Stella and her fiancé. Her social circle was beginning to widen, wasn't it? And thank goodness for that.

'I'm hoping to marry at Cockington Church,' Stella said as Emma carried on making lightning sketches, doing her best to create something suitable for Stella. 'It's part of the Mallock estate but open for worship to parishioners. The hospital is in the parish so I'm rather hoping that as I live in nurses' accommodation I'll be allowed to marry there. My fiancé ... oh ...' Stella picked up the piece of paper that Emma had just discarded. 'I like that. But I'm not sure about a veil.'

'A cloche close-fitting cap would look better with that design anyway,' Emma said. 'Crochet perhaps. I'm useless

93

with any needle that's not for sewing, but I'm sure we can find someone who could make what you need.'

'I'm sure we can,' Stella said. 'Honestly, Emma, this is the best fun I've had in a long while. Nursing can be very sad at times.'

'I'm sure it can,' Emma said, and with her words Beattie Drew and how she'd died holding Emma's hand in the cottage hospital in Paignton came to mind. The smells, the sounds, the pallor of poor Beattie's skin. Time then, to change the subject. For Stella as well as for herself. 'Your fiancé,' she said. 'What does he do?'

'He owns a garage. Cars, commercial vans, that sort of thing. And he's got a motorcycle!' Stella gave a mock-shudder at the thought, but Emma could only think, how exciting! She had a fancy to sit on the pillion of a motorcycle on a flapper bracket with her hair blowing free.

'A garage, you say. I want to buy a car. I used to drive in Canada. And here, before the war.'

'I'll write the number down for you before I go,' Stella said. 'But back to wedding dresses, yes?'

'Yes,' Emma said, smiling. Things were moving forward nicely for her again.

Ruby panicked when Emma went to Shingle Cottage and invited her, Tom, and the children to afternoon tea, telling her there would be other guests.

'No!' Ruby said. 'I don't think Tom could cope with that. Not yet. People 'e doesn't know. Sometimes the 'orror of what 'e went through comes back to 'im in waves from things people say, or the way someone looks. Only the other day 'e saw a fisherman down on the 'arbour with a burn on 'is arm and Tom simply ran back 'ome.'

'Just your family, then,' Emma said.

'And Fleur.'

'Yes, I'll try and make sure that she's not out and about

with Paolo. But if you think it would still be too much for Tom coming over to Romer Lodge then we can postpone to another time ...'

''Ere! You're not soundin' so keen now, milady. You sure you didn't come 'ere just to check up on me? Makin' sure I've cleaned up this place and meself with it?'

'Of course not! How could you think that?'

Ruby had struck a nerve, hadn't she? Because Emma had been looking and been heartened to see that everything was very much cleaner, and fresher-smelling than it had been on her previous visits. But no, she hadn't been checking up on her, not really.

'Because your eyes 'ave been everywhere since you sat in that chair, that's 'ow.'

'So that's me told off!' Emma laughed, doing her best to diffuse the situation. 'So will you come or not?'

'We will as long as you make that tatty tart you used to make up at Nase Head House. And maybe some chocolate éclairs. 'Ome-made ones, mind, not those shop bought ones you brought last time you visited. Remember we 'ad them just before you were leavin' for Canada, only you wouldn't tell me where you were goin'?'

'I remember,' Emma told her. Everything. I remember everything. How I'd asked Matthew to kiss me before I left only he refused, saying one kiss would never be enough for him. *How could I have done that, loving Seth?* 'And it's *tarte Tatin*.'

'I know it is. But I loves 'ow you come over all superior correctin' me. Oh, Em, isn't it wonderful? We're almost back to 'ow we were, aren't we?'

The tea party for Ruby and her family was a happy, relaxed success, and making éclairs and *tarte Tatin* seemed to revive Emma's love of cooking again, something she'd lost ever since Seth had died. The children had been on their best behaviour and said 'please' and 'thank you' without being prompted – well, most of the time. Tom had been very quiet and Emma had left him to his thoughts, merely making sure he had cake on his plate and tea in his cup at all times. Ruby had been disappointed not to see Fleur but Emma promised that they would meet again soon.

So, on the strength of that, Emma decided to invite some of her neighbours in for drinks. She didn't know their names yet but she never would unless she called on them and introduced herself. With a handful of business cards she walked out into Cleveland Road. Croy Lodge, opposite her own home, was very large. She imagined there would be an army of servants inside.

As well as her business cards, Emma had handwritten some invitations to a drinks party. 6 pm to 7.30 pm in two days' time.

She rang the bell of Croy Lodge and almost immediately a young, uniformed servant answered. Emma introduced herself, and the thought that not so many years ago she had been that servant girl made her smile. How far she had come!

'Madam's not—' the girl began but a woman, who was most obviously the mistress of the house, came sailing down the corridor, putting a stop to her words.

'I'll deal with it, Maria,' the woman said.

'Very well, ma'am.'

Maria turned and crossed the hallway and disappeared.

'I know you,' the woman said, and Emma's heart began to sink. Did she know her as a Jago, wife of a man whose father had died in prison and whose two brothers were hanged? 'Well, not by name,' the woman went on, 'but I've seen you. You've taken Romer Lodge, haven't you?'

'Yes. I'm Emma Jago.' Emma extended a hand.

'Myrna Passmore. And I've been dying to meet you. I've seen you walking along the promenade into town and I've admired your beautiful clothes. Do tell me where you get them? Not around here, that's for sure. But I'm forgetting my manners. Come in, come in.'

Myrna Passmore ushered Emma inside and into the front parlour.

'I'll get Maria to bring coffee or tea or whatever else you would like in a moment, but I am just so glad you called. Now sit down, do.'

Gosh, but the words were fairly tumbling out of Myrna Passmore's mouth, weren't they? Like a little stream that had burst its banks after heavy rain.

Emma sat.

'Now. Your wonderful clothes. Do let me in on your secret. And please don't tell me you go over to Paris to get them or I will go quite, quite green with envy. I can't leave Mr Passmore, you see.'

She pointed a finger towards the ceiling indicating that Mr Passmore was up there somewhere and couldn't be left. Emma would wait to be told why not.

'No, not Paris,' Emma said. 'Although the designs are from there. I make all my own clothes and ...' Emma handed over one of her business cards. 'These are my details should you, or anyone else you know, want to get in touch.'

'I'll take them all,' Myrna Passmore said. And then she burst out laughing. 'But I won't be handing them out to my friends because I want to keep you a little secret all to myself. Just because I don't travel very far on account of Mr Passmore doesn't mean I don't want to be well-dressed.'

Emma knew Myrna Passmore would do no such thing because while it was obvious there was something seriously wrong with her husband she was very good-humoured – as her own mama would have said ... Mr Passmore has the right wife.

'And I've brought this,' Emma said, handing Myrna Passmore an invitation to her drinks party. 'A getting to know my neighbours event,' she explained. 'Do say you'll come. If you can leave Mr Passmore for an hour or so.'

'I most certainly can. Maria is wonderful with him in my absence. And it's been on those little absences that I've seen you, and always looking so beautifully dressed.'

'Thank you,' Emma said. 'So, you'll come? To my drinks party?'

'I most certainly will. But only if you promise to put me first on your list of new clients.'

'Promise,' Emma said.

Maria was called and instructed to bring sherry with which to toast a new professional liaison. Emma couldn't help but notice that Mrs Passmore didn't include 'friendship' in the toast but she let it pass because she and Myrna Passmore chatted easily enough together. As Emma was leaving, the good woman gave Emma the names of all the near neighbours so that when Emma knocked on the door with her invitations and her calling cards she would have a name to address.

Things were getting better and better. She might even have to rope Fleur in to help with the straight sewing if she got lots of new clients.

'And your husband?' Mrs Groves at Seaspray House asked, Emma's invitation in her hand. 'What does he do?'

Mrs Groves had told her that Myrna Passmore had telephoned to let her know Emma would be calling and Mrs Groves had invited Emma in readily enough.

They were seated in a large conservatory on the side of the house, the room smelling strongly of geraniums – a rather medicinal scent, a bit like cough mixture, Emma always thought, but they were cheerful enough. And she needed cheer now.

She took a deep breath. 'My husband is dead,' Emma said. 'He dived into a freezing harbour to rescue a woman.

His arm got ripped off in fishing gear. Gangrene set in. Then pneumonia. And he died. Two years ago now.' Emma spoke the words staccato fashion, as though she was reading from a medical report. Clinical. It was the only way she could say it – and each time she did it didn't get any easier.

'A hero, then,' Mrs Groves said, and her previous smile of welcome slid a little. 'But a dead one. And you're a widow?'

Mrs Groves glanced at Emma's ring finger, on which sat the beautiful diamond ring Seth had had made for her – an exact copy of her mama's that had been lost, either stolen or taken by the sea when her mama had drowned.

'I am. I have a daughter. Fleur. She'll be sixteen years old in a couple of week's time.'

'I see,' Mrs Groves said. 'And I'm sure you'll understand that as you are without a husband it won't be possible for me and Mr Groves to accept your invitation.'

I see perfectly well. You are terrified that I will get my claws into your husband seeing as I have no husband of my own to stop me. Or that Fleur will.

But Emma could only feel sadness for Mr Groves who was married to such a sour-faced woman.

'That's your decision,' Emma said. She stood up to leave.

'But I'd like to avail myself of your sewing skills. Mrs Passmore has been singing your praises and—'

'And I'm afraid my client list is full, Mrs Groves. Good afternoon.'

Hmm, Emma thought, as she walked back to Romer Lodge. Making friends – and customers – of her neighbours wasn't going to be as easy as she'd thought it would be.

But she wasn't beaten yet.

Chapter Eight

EARLY JULY 1927

Emma had at last got around to making herself a dress to go to the theatre in Palace Avenue with Eduardo; a simple sheath in the palest dog-rose pink with fringing just a few shades darker in diagonal bands from shoulder to hem. It barely covered her knees – the shortest thing she'd ever worn. It was last year's style, copied from an illustration in *Vogue* magazine, but Emma didn't think anyone in the small, provincial theatre would notice. Not that it would bother her much if they did. She'd bought a shawl the colour of rosehips with white peonies embroidered on it from Rossiter's department store to wear around her shoulders.

'What do you think?' she asked Fleur as she twirled round in front of the cheval glass in her room.

'It looks like something you should be dancing in, not wearing in the dark in a theatre.'

'Oh,' Emma said, the wind taken out of her sails completely by Fleur's remark although there'd been no spite in her voice as she said it. She had, Emma thought, sounded sad if anything.

'Like you should have a cigarette in a holder held at an affected angle like the woman in the illustration in the magazine you copied it from.'

'Oh,' Emma said again.

Fleur had been rather quiet lately – more serious, perhaps, as though she was thinking deeply about something she didn't want to talk to Emma about. Trying to put her finger on it now as they got ready to go out with Eduardo and Paolo, Emma realised the change in Fleur had happened round about the time Stella Martin had called about her wedding dress. Emma had ordered the fabric Stella had picked out from the samples from Beare's the haberdasher's, and bought the threads to sew it with. On a whim, she also bought some crystals to sew onto it discreetly. If the wedding was to be a winter wedding then the dress would need something with which to catch what little light there was at that time of year.

'And it shows your knees,' Fleur said.

'I know. I think I've got rather nice knees, why not show them off?'

Emma slid a gold bangle up her arm, past her elbow, and gently pushed it into the softer flesh of her upper arm.

'And you definitely need a cigarette with *that* look,' Fleur said, tapping the bangle on Emma's arm with a forefinger.

'I don't think so,' Emma said.

She wrinkled her nose because suddenly the smell of the strong cigarettes Eduardo smoked seemed to be in her nostrils. The smoke made her eyes water sometimes especially if they were in a small space. She imagined lots of people in the theatre would smoke in the interval, if not during the performance too. That thought didn't cheer her much, although until the start of this rather stilted conversation with Fleur she'd been looking forward to going to the theatre.

'A man offered me a cigarette on the pier,' Fleur said.

'And did you take it?'

'No!' Fleur sounded angry now. 'Don't you care that a strange man offered me a cigarette?'

Gosh but Fleur's moods were all over the place, weren't they? Was it the time of the month for her? Was that what it was? And then a chill seemed to freeze Emma's body – *has her monthly not arrived when it should have done? Was she pregnant? By Paolo, or... or the man who offered her a cigarette?*

'You didn't say he was strange. Was he drunk? In the middle of the day?'

'No. Not drunk. He did smell a bit of drink, though. He was rather good-looking, actually. But ancient. He must have been, oh, about forty or something. He pointed out that women smoked and that they were smart if they did. There was a woman on the pier with a cigarette in her hand but I didn't see her put it to her lips. He was a bit persistent, this man. He spoke funny, too.'

'Funny?'

'He had an accent I couldn't place. American perhaps but that maybe he'd spoken another language, like Russian or something, before he learned English.'

A tear slid down Fleur's cheek, and Emma shuddered – what else was Fleur about to reveal? Had she refused the cigarette but accepted something else?

'Sit down,' Emma said. 'On the edge of my bed. Is there anything else you want to tell me?'

Fleur sat, tucking her hands under her thighs, palms down on the cover, her chin practically on her chest. 'But we'll be late,' she muttered. 'Paolo said—'

'Paolo and his father will wait for us. It won't matter if we miss a little bit at the beginning.'

'It's an Agatha Christie, Ma! If you miss one sentence you might as well not bother. Although why Paolo and his pa wanted to go to see it I don't know because they're not going to understand everything, are they?'

No, they're not, Emma thought, admiring Fleur's reasoning.

'Possibly not but it will be fun to watch all the same. If we miss something we'll catch up easily, I'm sure. Now what's wrong?' Emma sat down beside Fleur and slid an arm around her back, placing a hand on her daughter's shoulder. 'You look gorgeous in that dress, by the way. Red really suits your colouring.'

Emma had made Fleur a dropped-waist dress in pillar-box red jersey with a white Peter Pan collar, and white cuffs on the elbow-length sleeves. She'd enthused about it excitedly when Emma had shown her what she intended to make. But now Fleur looked as though she was about to go to the gallows, poor girl.

'But Pa's not going to see me in it, is he?'

This was the moment when Emma would have liked to have been able to say, 'You never know, he might. He might be looking down from heaven.' But she couldn't say that because she didn't believe it. It must, she thought, be wonderful to have that faith and to get that comfort in the unknown, from some heavenly power, but it hadn't worked for her when she'd lost her parents and her brother, Johnnie. And it hadn't brought a crumb of comfort when she'd lost Seth – she'd seen the light go out of him as she'd held his hand as he'd breathed his last breath.

'No, he's not,' she said now. 'But if he were here I know he'd be proud.'

'If he were here, Ma, you wouldn't be going to the theatre with Signor Cascarini. And he wouldn't be making cods eyes at you all night. And ... oh, Ma, you can't marry him, you just *can't*.'

Fleur shrugged Emma's arm off and put her head in her hands. Her shoulders juddered up and down with loud, wracking sobs.

Cods eyes? Did Eduardo look at her like that? She'd only dined with him a handful of times. They were simply two widowed adults enjoying one another's company, weren't they?

And he was now more than likely on his way in his ice cream delivery van to pick her and Fleur up to take them to the theatre.

'It's never entered my head to marry him, Fleur,' Emma said.

Eduardo is lonely, I'm lonely if I am honest enough to admit it to myself – not the best scenario for a romance for either of us. But she could hardly tell Fleur that because it would sound as though she was using Eduardo, which wasn't the case. She genuinely liked the man and admired him for his care of his mother-in-law and the way he put his all into his ice cream making business.

'Besides,' Emma carried on. 'We've only dined together a handful of times, and he hasn't asked me to marry him.'

Fleur took her hands from her face and sat up straight. She turned to look at Emma. 'Well, he's told Paolo he's thinking about asking. And if you were to marry him that would make Paolo my stepbrother and it wouldn't be right. You're making things very difficult for Paolo and me.'

Ah, so that was the crux of Fleur's problem – she didn't like Emma seeing Paolo's father. All the talk about being offered a cigarette by a stranger on the pier was the run-up to this, and of no consequence? Emma wondered what it was Eduardo might have said to his son about marrying her but did she really want to know?

'Unintentionally,' Emma said. 'I think you're reading more into my friendship with Eduardo than there is. But I don't know that I should stop seeing him because you want me to.' And then, in a very quiet voice, Emma added: 'Seth and I talked about the possibility of one of us being widowed and we both said we hoped the other would find happiness, and love, again.'

'I know, Ma,' Fleur said. 'I was watching Pa paint a portrait of you just before he died and I don't know if he must have had a premonition or something, but he told me then that if anything happened to him I was to welcome any man you wanted to marry, and be respectful to him.'

Had Seth said that? What a generous thing to say – but then Seth had always been generous. With his money, with his time, and with his love.

'But it won't be with Signor Cascarini, Fleur,' Emma said. 'I can promise you that.'

But all the same, Emma wanted that sparkle in her eyes that Stella Martin had had. And the excitement of planning a future with someone; someone to watch sunsets with, someone to grow old with.

Was there any harm in wanting that?

'That was fun, Eduardo,' Emma said. 'Thank you for asking me. And Fleur. I think, despite her protests that she didn't want to come tonight, that she's enjoyed it after all.'

'And Paolo, he like whatever Fleur like,' Eduardo said with a chuckle, his shoulders rising and falling. 'Is the way of the young. And,' he reached for Emma's hand, 'the not so young.'

Quickly Emma withdrew it and began scrabbling in her handbag for something, nothing, anything at all – anything so Fleur, who was walking arm in arm with Paolo towards them, wouldn't see.

Ah, she'd found something. The slip of paper with the telephone number of the garage owned by Stella's fiancé. A recommendation might be a safer way of buying a car, rather than risk some underhand deal with someone she didn't know.

'I want to buy a car, Eduardo,' she said quickly. 'A client has given me this telephone number. Do you know it?'

She showed Eduardo the piece of paper. EXE MOTORS. Exeter 297.

'I no believe!' Eduardo said. 'Is like Agatha Christie mystery, no? Is the garage that do the CASCARINI on my ice cream delivery van! And sell me van, of course! And mend them when Paolo hit wall with them!' He laughed loudly, slapping a hand down on the table. 'I take you! We go!'

Goodness, Emma could almost see the exclamation marks dancing in the air like daggers on the ends of Eduardo's sentences. But, what luck. A double recommendation.

'Thank you,' Emma said. 'That will be lovely.'

'We will go on a Saturday,' Eduardo said. 'Is always quiet for ice cream sales on Saturday afternoons. I will telefono. Is good to go when boss man is there. He know me. He give you good deal. Is good?'

'Very good,' Emma said. 'Thank you.'

And it was left that Eduardo would let Emma know which Saturday would be best. But knowing nothing about the purchase of cars, only how to drive them and needing one, she hoped it would be soon.

'What would you like for your birthday, Fleur?' Emma asked the next morning at breakfast.

'I haven't thought,' Fleur replied. 'But if you're pushing me, I've seen a wristwatch in Conroy and Couch's that is the biz. Paolo and me saw it in the window and we went inside to ask the price.'

Fleur had been looking in jewellers' shops? With Paolo?

'Paolo and *I*, Fleur,' Emma corrected her.

'Oh, forget the stupid wristwatch,' Fleur snapped. 'You're *always* correcting me.'

'I'm not *always* correcting you. But you know I don't like sloppy grammar,' Emma said. 'It's important you speak properly. If you're going to be in a position somewhere, working for someone, then it will be important.'

'Who says I'm going to be working for someone? There's nothing to do in this place anyway except serve tables in some crummy hotel.'

'Then you could get some qualifications of some kind to get yourself out of it.'

Fleur jerked her head backwards, forehead furrowed, and stared in wonderment at Emma.

'Is something wrong, Ma? One minute you're asking me what I want for my birthday and the next you're reading me the riot act about grammar and suggesting I leave home. I've come down to breakfast washed and dressed and I've cleaned my teeth and brushed my hair and I'm not talking with my mouth full, so what have I done wrong?'

Emma couldn't help but smile at Fleur's remark. Hadn't she always, when Fleur had been little, repeated the mantra *'wash your face, clean your teeth, brush your hair'* until Fleur did those things without having to be reminded or sent back upstairs to do them? And she'd been an absolute dragon about Fleur not talking with food in her mouth, she knew that.

'Sorry,' Emma said. 'You haven't done anything wrong. It's me, I'm a little out of sorts.'

She had a lot on her mind. Driving back from the theatre with Fleur and Paolo in the back she'd turned around to say something to Fleur and seen Paolo place his hand on her knee. She'd seen Fleur push it away, but was that only because she'd known her mother had noticed? Unable to say anything at the time she was wondering if she should mention it now. And what was more, Eduardo had laid a hand on her knee while he was driving – no, not laid, it had been more of a grip that Emma hadn't been able to fend off without making a fuss. And with Fleur in the back.

She wasn't looking forward to driving to Exe Motors with him now, but she'd said she'd go, and how else was she going to get there? Train and then taxi was a possibility. Hmm … perhaps that might be best. But Eduardo said he would make the appointment and she'd said she'd go and Emma didn't renege on her promises. All she could do was wait to be told when.

Stella Martin was coming for her first fitting this afternoon. Emma had made up the design in very cheap cotton fabric just to be certain the size was right and that the shape suited Stella before she cut into the very expensive wedding dress material. Stella had said there was no rush for the dress but Emma wanted to get it done and then, hopefully, Stella would tell all her friends how much she loved it and Emma's business would start to boom.

But first there was Tom to see. He and Ruby were coming over for lunch, on their own. Tom's mother was looking after the children. Ruby had giggled that it would be like being on a date with Tom, going out for the day without the children. Emma was going to show Tom the garden and tell him what she wanted him to do – if he wanted to do it, and *if* he felt up to doing it. It would be easier to talk about these things without the children who had been with Ruby and Tom the first time they'd visited Romer Lodge. Emma was looking forward to seeing Ruby again – each time she saw her now, her friend looked happier, healthier. But she hoped that Tom wouldn't feel under any pressure from her about the garden.

'Ma?' Fleur said. 'You're miles away. Are you sure you're okay? Are you thinking about Pa?'

About Seth? No she hadn't been thinking about Seth. A strange sort of guilt flooded through her that she hadn't been.

'Not at this very moment, I wasn't, no,' Emma said. She thought quickly. 'I was wondering if you'd like a tea party for your birthday? Here. In the garden. We could carry some tables outside and lay them prettily with the best china. And flowers. We could ask Paolo and Eduardo. And Ruby and her family? And we'll go into town and I'll buy you the watch at Conroy and Couch. How will that be?'

It frightened Emma sometimes how fast she could think of things, make things up, and bend the truth. She'd had to do it many times when she'd been an orphaned fifteen-year-old, and she'd done it even more times after she and Seth had begun living together at Mulberry House, before they'd married. And somehow the habit had stuck. It wasn't a very nice habit to have but it was useful. As now.

'Expensive!' Fleur laughed.

'I can do expensive,' Emma said, laughing with her. 'And the tea party? Would you like that?'

Five adults, Fleur, and three small children hardly constituted a party but it might be fun. She could think up some games for the children to play – blind man's buff or something. And get some champagne in for the grown-ups – and Fleur – to drink.

And Stella? Should she ask Stella and her fiancé to come? Her social circle needed widening and Stella might be the person to help her to do that, mightn't she?

Fleur finished her toast and washed it down with the last of the coffee.

'Can I go now?' she asked. 'Only Paolo's *nonna* is ill and can't be in the ice cream parlour. Paolo's got to go out on deliveries and his pa's got a big batch of ice cream to make for the Imperial Hotel. Paolo's going to show me how to work the coffee machine. It shouldn't be too hard, should it? I said I'd help out. That's all right, isn't it?'

She smiled winningly and Emma wondered for how long Fleur had been rehearsing that little speech in her head.

'It's not what I want to do for ever and ever, Ma, but I can do it for now, can't I?'

'You certainly can. It's nice to help people out. But just so I know, what do you want to do for "ever and ever" as you put it?'

'Paint maybe,' Fleur said, quickly. 'Like Pa. He showed me lots of tricks about perspective and depth and how to mix colours and how when you're doing watercolours you don't put white paint on, you just don't paint the paper at all so it stays white.'

'Well, we'll look at courses, shall we?'

'There aren't any around here.' Fleur pulled a face. 'Only amateur groups.'

'Exeter, then?' Emma said.

'Look, Ma, can we have this conversation some other time? And can I look for my own course?'

'Yes, indeed. I'm only trying to help.'

My fault there, Emma thought, that Fleur had snapped at her. Being a mother was such a hard job – but it never seemed the right time to say anything to Fleur these days.

'I'm going to be late now,' Fleur said.

'Then you'd better hurry along,' she said. 'We Jagos don't break our promises, do we?'

Stella Martin seemed at least a stone thinner standing in front of Emma in her underthings – as though she never ate, or if she did she just picked at things. She had no bosoms to speak of and Emma made a mental note to add a bit of padding to the bust part of the petticoat and to adjust the other dress accordingly.

To Emma's joy, what she'd run up was a perfect fit. But somehow, it made Stella look like a rather large six year old. Well, all that could change soon once Stella was married and became pregnant and Emma wished with all her heart that Stella's fiancé – when he became her husband if not before – would take her to the giddy, sexual heights that Seth had taken her. And Matthew's kiss had done the same, but without the sex. What would sex with *him* be like?

'What are you thinking?' Stella asked. 'Only there's a flush creeping up the side of your neck?'

On instinct Emma clapped her hand to her neck. Yes. Rather warm there. She flushed some more.

'I was thinking, Stella, that you will make a beautiful bride and I'm also pleased that this mock-up is such a good fit. I can get on with putting my scissors to that very beautiful material you've chosen. I didn't want to make a mistake, although I'd have replaced the material if I had. At my cost, of course.'

'Hmm,' Stella said with a giggle. 'But there was something else causing that flush but I'm not going to push you! As a nurse I'm used to *hearing* what a person *doesn't* say as often as what they *do* say.'

Stella's words made Emma feel transparent – the way Matthew's words often had. *Now why had he popped into her head again?* She decided to change the subject.

'Stella, I'm holding a tea party for Fleur's sixteenth birthday. It's on the sixteenth – the week after next. A Saturday. Would you like to come? And you can bring your fiancé if you'd like to. If you *can* make it, and if you can come a little earlier, then I should have your dress tacked together to try on by then.'

Emma knew she was sounding rather desperate that Stella joined them. *It makes me sound totally friendless.* And she was, apart from Ruby. And Tom. Although when she herself had worked at Nase Head House Tom hadn't been there. She'd only seen him a couple of times before she'd emigrated to Canada with Seth and Fleur.

'I'll just check my diary,' Stella said. 'Can I get out of this thing first? Only it looks rather like a shroud.'

'It does rather,' Emma said, but she knew it was always wise to make up the pattern out of something cheap when expensive material was going to be used for the real thing. Her mama had done the same. *You taught me well, Mama, even though I was a very reluctant student at the time.*

She unpinned Stella and helped her off with the mock-up dress.

'Actually,' Stella said, 'I hope you won't think this is too forward of me seeing as I've only met you once before but, well, I was wondering if your lovely daughter would be my bridesmaid?'

'Bridesmaid?' Emma said.

'Well, yes. I've no nieces or nephews to ask, and if I were to ask someone I work with at the hospital, someone else is bound to have their nose put out of joint because I haven't asked *them*. Minefield!'

'I'll bet,' Emma said.

Her mind wandered back to March 1913 and the RMS *Royal Edward* and the captain marrying her and Seth in his cabin. She'd carried a bunch of stocks wrapped in cellophane she'd bought from a florist's on the quay at Bristol before boarding the ship. Fleur – a toddler then – had dozed on Seth's shoulder all the way through the ceremony. Emma had put a couple of blossoms in Fleur's hair and she'd made her a special white velvet dress to wear, seeing as she'd planned the whole thing in her head before departure. The dress hadn't stayed white for long!

'So,' Stella said. 'Do you think she will? I won't be offended if she doesn't want to. She hardly knows me.'

'I'll ask,' Emma said. She knew better than to present Fleur with a fait accompli – Fleur hated that as much as Emma did, although Fleur had presented her with one only that morning. 'She's out at the moment.'

'No rush,' Stella said. 'I haven't been able to pin my fiancé down to coming to look at the church yet!'

And then the conversation turned to men in general and then shoes and handbags and hats, and then it was time for Stella to leave.

'Perhaps,' Emma said, 'you and I could meet for lunch in town one day? On your day off. You do have a day off?'

Stella laughed. 'Half days are usually as much as I manage! My fiancé's become quite used to me cancelling things at the last minute if there's an emergency and I have to work on, or take on a shift for someone who's gone sick. But to answer your question – yes, I'd love to meet for lunch some time. Shall I telephone you with a suggested date when I have one?'

'Perfect,' Emma said. She could plan her day around Stella more easily than the other way around. 'I'll look forward to it.'

'But don't be offended if it isn't soon.' Stella laughed. 'It won't be because I don't want to.' She held out a hand to

Emma and the two women shook hands – how good it felt, another hand holding hers in friendship.

Well, that's nice, Emma thought as she watched Stella walk down the drive to the gate. *The sum of my female friends has increased one hundred per cent to a massive two!*

She sang all the way down the passage to the kitchen to get on with preparing lunch for Ruby and Tom.

'You look like the cat what got the cream,' Ruby said, kissing Emma on the cheek. 'More colour in yer face.'

'I could say the same for you.' Emma laughed. 'Hello, Tom.'

She was unsure whether to kiss him, or not.

'Go on, you daft bugger,' Ruby said, making the decision for her. 'Give my Tom a kiss. 'E don't bite. Well, not often!'

'Ruby!' Emma said, embarrassed for Tom although she realised he was probably more than used to Ruby's ways. But she did as she was told.

'I could get used to bein' 'ere,' Ruby said. 'You should 'ave 'eard our three when we told 'em they wouldn't be comin' over today!'

'They can come another time. But I've got a proposition for Tom.'

Tom visibly blanched. Took a step backwards. Emma could have bitten off her tongue for speaking so forcefully. Gently, gently, with Tom – Ruby had told her that.

'And what sort of proposition would that be?' Ruby asked. She linked her arm through Tom's, leaned her head against his shoulder. He's mine, the gesture said. 'Not that I think you've got designs on 'im, Mrs Jago.'

Emma breathed more easily – Ruby had diffused the situation.

'The garden. I've been wondering if you'd like to come and work for me, Tom. The garden mostly but on wet days

I'm sure there'll be something I can find for you to do in the house.'

'I ...' Ruby began, but Tom stopped her.

'If it's all right with Ruby,' Tom said. 'It'll mean she's got more to do for my old ma.'

'Nothin' I can't sort,' Ruby said, her voice thick with emotion.

Ruby smiled at Emma, tears in her eyes. Tom willing, and able, to take on a job of work again was a step in the right direction, wasn't it?

'We'll shake on it,' Emma said, offering Tom her hand. 'We can talk payment some other time. But now lunch. I've made crab soup with soda bread. And a bacon and egg tart with herbs. For pudding there's strawberry meringue if you've got room.'

'Bleedin' 'ell,' Ruby said. ''Ow the other 'alf lives, eh? Lead me to it before you changes your mind fer me cheek!'

Chapter Nine

Oh bugger – the telephone. Matthew cursed again under his breath – but a stronger word than 'bugger' which he hoped William, standing by the door with the mudguard of a motorcycle in his hand, hadn't heard. Two minutes later and he'd have been gone.

Stella had said three o'clock at the latest. She'd found a vicar who was willing to marry them in church even though Matthew had been divorced. It would take at least forty-five minutes to drive to Torquay. He prayed he wouldn't get caught behind a tractor going slowly up Telegraph Hill. He'd had it in mind to go to Bobby's on the Strand in Torquay before meeting up with Stella and look for some leather luggage for their honeymoon. He assumed Stella would want a honeymoon, although they hadn't discussed that yet. Italy maybe? Somewhere far from his office and the bloody telephone anyway.

'Telephone, boss?' William said, just the hint of question in his voice.

Double bugger, Matthew thought. Had William not been there he could have ignored the ringing.

'Yeah, yeah,' Matthew said. 'I'd get you to answer it only I'd never get the oil off it – look at your hands!'

William shrugged. Matthew had told him more than a few times to wipe his hands before coming into the office but the lad never listened. He was a good worker, though. Keen to learn. He came from the worst end of town but he was honest and cheerful. Matthew had decided to give him a chance.

He snatched at the telephone. 'Exe Motors.'

'Ah, is you Signor Caunter? Is me, Eduardo Cascarini.'

'Good afternoon, Signor Cascarini,' he said looking at

William. William raised his eyes heavenwards and grinned. Then he left the office, shutting the door behind him. They both knew a conversation with Signor Cascarini could go on a long time with misunderstandings to sort out.

Matthew swallowed back his irritation. Eduardo Cascarini was a good customer. The man was on his third van for his ice cream business now, all bought from him and then traded in for something newer. Matthew's firm had done the signwriting on the sides, too. And they'd repaired the damage Eduardo's son had done to it – playing at being Bentley or d'Erlanger on the Le Mans circuit, around the hills and bends of Torquay without a doubt – more than a few times. This could take some time.

'What can I do for you?' Matthew asked.

'Is not me who want a car. Is my ... how you say ... friend *donna*?'

Matthew thought fast. *Donna*? The Italian for woman or wife? Had the widowed Signor Cascarini got himself a new wife? Or did he have an English friend called Donna?

'Donna wants to buy a car?'

'No, not she. She Emma. Emma want car.'

At the sound of the name from the past that never failed to stab him in the heart, Matthew drew on his rationale and told himself there must be hundreds of women in Torquay called Emma. Besides, *his* Emma – the only one he wanted to see – was in Canada, wasn't she? And married. On instinct, he put his hand in the pocket of his trousers and his fingers immediately found Emma's amethyst on the gold chain he always kept there.

'When would Emma like to come and see about a car?' Matthew said.

'In one hour. I drive her in my *gelato* delivery van. You open still?'

And I bet she's going to love that, Matthew thought, sitting amongst the returned ice cream containers and the boxes of wafers, although he knew there was a removable seat for use for back seat passengers should Signor Cascarini have some.

'Yes, the garage will be open,' Matthew said.

'And you there?'

'Well, I ...'

'Signor, I say to *donna* you be there. You give her deal.'

But I won't be here. He couldn't let Stella down. He'd already cancelled two meetings with the vicar of St George and St Mary at Cockington through pressure of work. He couldn't do it to her again.

'William will be here,' Matthew said. 'He can show you anything you're interested in. I have to go out. To meet my fiancée. In Torquay.'

He didn't know why he was giving it, chapter and verse, to Signor Cascarini. All his life he'd been conservative with his personal information. It had been part of who he was. When he'd first met Emma he hadn't lied exactly about what he did for a living, except perhaps when he'd told her he couldn't read and write. Goodness, but she'd been cross when she'd found out that he could. There was a fire in her he'd wanted to tame with his lips. Emma. Just the name spoken a few seconds ago by a customer and Matthew was committing adultery against Stella in his mind. This would never do.

'But not just yet. Please, *signor*. I drive very fast.'

Matthew checked his watch. He'd given himself more than enough time for the detour to Bobby's before driving on to Cockington, assuming there would be no hold ups.

'I'll have to leave just after two o' clock at the latest,' Matthew said.

A potential sale, was a potential sale.

'*Grazie. Grazie. Arriverderci,*' Signor Cascarini said.

The line went dead. Matthew hung the telephone back on its rest. Drumming his fingers on the desk he thought about what he could do while he waited. But he'd leave just after two, Signor Cascarini and the mysterious Emma or not.

Paperwork. Wasn't there always a mountain of paperwork to sort out? He'd been to the barber's for a shave, had a bath, and was in his best clothes ready for the meeting at the church. No way was he going to get oil on anything. He would do paperwork while he waited.

Half an hour passed. Another twenty minutes. The clock seemed to be ticking more noisily than usual. He heard William banging on metal out in the yard – like gunfire. But still no Signor Cascarini. The minute hand clicked upright. Two o'clock. He'd give it another ten minutes then he'd have to go.

Matthew checked he had money – coins and notes. A handkerchief. His cheque book. He slipped his hand into his trouser pocket and brought out Emma's amethyst necklace. He didn't like going anywhere without it, but he didn't want to risk it slipping out and for Stella to see it, start asking questions. *Why are you carrying another woman's necklace? Who is she? What is she to you?*

He opened the drawer of his desk, put the necklace underneath a sheaf of papers and turned the key in the lock, put that in his pocket instead.

But now he would have to go. He'd waited as long as he could.

'William!' he called, opening the door to the yard.

'Boss!' William yelled back. He closed the bonnet of the car he'd been working on and came running.

'You've just been promoted. Signor Cascarini is bringing someone to buy a car. A woman. Name of Emma. But remember to call her madam. Make a sale and I'll give you five per cent. Give her a wink,' Matthew said with a laugh, 'and it'll close the deal.'

'Hah!' William said, running his oily hands down the sides of his overalls. 'I'll do my best.'

Wink? Why had he said that? Winking at a woman had been Matthew's stock in trade once. But not any more. Not since Emma – and the effect his winks had had on her.

Matthew ran to his car, found the starting handle and deployed it. The engine turned over, backfired, then began to purr. Good. Throwing the starting handle in the footwell in front of the passenger seat, Matthew got behind the wheel.

There were no other cars and Matthew reached the junction with the main road in minutes. Under the railway arch and on towards Pennsylvania.

And then he saw it. Signor Cascarini's ice cream van. He jerked his head sideways in the hope he wouldn't be seen and drove on.

'I've found someone to make me a dress,' Stella said. 'There was an advertisement on the noticeboard in the nurses' rest room up at the hospital.'

Their fingers were linked as they walked back down the drive of Cockington Court and Stella leaned into Matthew, and laid her head against his shoulder. He liked the weight of it there, the closeness, the way Stella was unafraid to show her feelings for him in public. Another couple walking towards them were arm in arm but that was the only parts of their bodies touching. And they didn't seem to be talking to one another. The woman certainly didn't look as happy as Stella had been when she'd made her way up to the church to arrange the wedding. But the couple rustled up a smile each and nodded politely as they passed.

'I hope it will be well-lined, then,' Matthew said. 'February.' He gave a mock-shiver.

If it had surprised him when the vicar had asked what date they would like for their wedding that Stella had chosen the eleventh of February, Matthew had reined it in. A Saturday. But he'd agreed that that would suit him fine. He was rarely busy with the garage that month and could easily close it on the day of the ceremony and for a week or two afterwards for a honeymoon with no great loss of trade. He'd need to try and boost business a bit between now and then, to give himself a cushion of finance to see him through the closure. If William made a sale today then that would be a start. To the Emma who wasn't the Emma he wanted to see. To hold. To give that kiss he'd so wanted to the last time he'd seen her but hadn't dared – one kiss wouldn't have been enough and they'd both known it. He hoped *his* Emma was happy with Seth Jago in Canada. After Emma and Seth had first left he'd kept tabs on them through his contacts from his old surveillance days. But he'd also been kept busy tracking down Seth's villainous brother, Miles, for the authorities. While Matthew couldn't say it had been a pleasure seeing Miles hang for his murderous ways, the world was most definitely a better place without him. He'd seen Emma was safe in letting her go. He hoped she still was. It had seemed an intrusion to keep himself aware of her whereabouts at all times, so he'd stopped. But it had hurt like hell, the not knowing.

'It will be,' Stella said, and for a moment Matthew had lost the thread of the conversation, and must have been too long in coming up with something to say because Stella added, 'My dress. It *will* be lined. And I'll have a cape of sorts to wear over my shoulders. But that's as much as I'm telling you because it's bad luck to let the groom see the dress before the wedding. I'm not even going to tell you who's making it or where.'

'I'm hardly likely to be visiting a dressmaker,' Matthew said.

He supposed he would need to visit a tailor though, and get a new suit made. He'd been wearing the suit he'd given his evidence in court against Miles Jago in as his garage business suit. It had most definitely seen better days. Today he was wearing flannels and a sports jacket. And an open-necked shirt. Neither outfit would do for a wedding, would it? It had been on the day that he'd given his evidence against Miles Jago that he'd decided to change career – he was done with surveillance and subterfuge and the danger it put him in; the danger it had put Emma in. All that had cost him Emma, he was sure of it. Not that he was in the habit of stealing another man's woman but ... what was the phrase? – all's fair in love and war?

Stella took her head from his shoulder.

'Matthew?' she said. 'Is something wrong? Only I'm not sure you're with me today? Are you not well?' She tightened her grip on Matthew's fingers.

'Sorry,' he said. 'I was thinking of something.'

Someone. Was it fair to be arranging a marriage with Stella who was so lovely, so kind, so caring, so perfect in so many ways – except that she wasn't Emma?

'Such as?'

'Well ...' Matthew took a deep breath, making a little time while he thought of a quick retort. He'd been good at that once – had had to be for the work he did – but he was getting slack, selling cars and motorcycles for a living. 'I was wondering why you don't want to get married sooner. February seems a long way away. My house is all ready for you to move into—'

'It's not that,' Stella stopped him. 'I promised matron I'd stay until Christmas. So I'll honour my promise. It will give her time to find someone to replace me and get her trained up. But ... oh, Matthew, I've been waiting half my life for this and now the hospital board have asked me to take some exams. This morning! They're considering promoting me from staff nurse to sister. Can you believe it?'

Stella sounded as though she couldn't believe it herself, although there was no regret in her voice that she would be turning it down to marry Matthew. They both knew that she couldn't be a nurse of whatever rank and be a married woman. Stella was giving a lot up for him, and now it looked as though she was going to be giving up, potentially, a whole lot more.

They'd reached the bottom of the drive now.

'Would you like to go somewhere and talk it through? This promotion?'

'No, don't be silly. I've made up my mind ...' Stella's voice faded away and Matthew thought, for a second, that perhaps she was about to change it. She let go of his hand as they neared his car. 'I asked you to marry me, and I'm not withdrawing that request.' She laughed. 'So, that's you brought up to date with all that's going on in my life. We could go somewhere to eat, though. What do you think? I only had time for an apple at lunchtime up at the hospital and I'm starving. You can tell me all about your life before you started selling cars. I know all about Annie and Harry, but not what you did to support them.'

'I've told you,' Matthew said. 'I worked for His Majesty's Customs. Now His Majesty's Custom and Excise. And I was a private detective in America.'

'Yes,' Stella said. 'I know you have. But I want to know everything about it. The people you met, the dangers you were in because I'm sure there must have been danger.'

'There was then, but not now. Selling cars hardly counts as a dangerous occupation.'

Stella laughed. 'I know! But if we're to be married, I need to know *everything*.' Stella made it sound as though she really, really, wanted to know every little part of him, and that she was prepared to hear anything. 'I've heard a lot of confessions in my time from patients and their families, and from medical staff, too. Nothing much shocks me these days. So, what *did* you do?'

Put men in prison. Sent some of them to the gallows. Spied. Lied to get information I needed and wanted. Used people without their knowledge to find out what I needed to know, although I never caused any harm to them in the using. And I wasn't beyond doing an underhand, illegal deal myself to get that information. He'd done just that to get Emma her amethyst back.

'We'll eat first,' Matthew said. He opened the passenger door for Stella and settled her inside.

You might not have much appetite for food if I tell you before we eat.

'You what?' Matthew said.

He didn't want to believe what William had just told him – he'd allowed Signor Cascarini's lady friend to drive one hundred and ninety-nine pounds and ten shillings' worth of brand new eleven horsepower Clyno Saloon off the forecourt and away. William had accepted a cheque. As if cheques were as good as cash!

'That's far too big a car for a woman to be driving. What possessed you?'

'Well, you did say to make a sale, boss. She saw the car and said, "That's the one" and the deal was done. She said she'd been driving for years, boss,' William said.

'And you believed her?'

'I sat beside her while she drove up and down the quay a few times the way you always do with new buyers. She could reverse well enough. Didn't end up in the canal anyway when she did a three-point turn.'

'And that makes it all right? There are such things as con-women as well as con-men, William. You know it's cash on sale if a car is driven away immediately, or wait for a cheque to be cleared.'

Matthew wasn't at all sure now that William knew that. Well, he did now.

'Con-women?'

William looked puzzled, as though the thought of a con-woman was a new one on him. 'She didn't look in the least bit criminal, boss. Her shoes were polished. And her clothes were clean and that. I remember you saying once when that man bought the Model T Tudor Sedan that he looked like money. Smelled of it. Well *she* did as well.'

'Go on,' Matthew said. 'Why don't you give me a blow by blow account of what she looked like while you're at it?' He knew sarcasm didn't become him, but ...

'If that's what you want, boss. Glossy dark hair that was escaping her hat. One of those new-fangled cloche things all the ladies are wearing. Reddy sort of brown colour. Large brown eyes. Good legs, slim ankles. Oh, and she was wearing earrings.'

'*That* should help me pick her out in a crowd,' Matthew grumbled, his sarcasm dripping thicker than engine oil this time.

'I'm sorry, boss, but I thought, seeing as you know the Cascarini chap, that—'

'But that's just it – you didn't think! This cheque might not be honoured for all we know.'

'You know where Mr Cascarini lives so you could go and sort it out with him, couldn't you?'

'Let's hope it doesn't run to that. What plates were on it?'

'The ones you put there, boss,' William said. 'Registered ones. I did check that before I let her drive it away. You did tell me if I made a sale you'd give me five per cent, so I did.'

Be grateful for small mercies, Matthew told himself. At least the car was insured under his name should this woman have lied about her ability to drive and was at that moment wrapping just under two hundred pounds worth of car around a tree on Telegraph Hill.

'Did she give you an address?'

'No, boss. But you know where that Cascarini chap lives, so—'

'Yes, yes, so you've just said. She could be conning him as well!' Matthew shouted. 'Ever thought of that, William?'

William's eyes went wide with fright. They were glassy

with tears. The lad was only nineteen years old – a pup yet. Matthew knew he was being hard on him, and that he should never have left him in charge of something so important. If this woman was indeed a fraudster of some sort then he only had himself to blame really. And he'd been in worse scrapes in his life with a criminal or two – no make that something like a hundred or two. He'd get out of this if necessary. He still knew how to track a person down if that person needed to be tracked.

'Cheque?' he said, holding his hand out, palm upwards.

'It's underneath the blotter,' William said, pointing at it. 'The top drawer was locked, boss,' William said. 'Do I come in on Monday or not? Only my ma will kill me if I lose my job. No money for her fags and booze, see.'

Matthew lifted up the blotter. A large cheque written in a flamboyant hand, face up. He checked the date. Not post-dated – good; that was an old trick he was more than wise to. Words and figures tallied.

E. Jago. His heart stilled for a second. Two. He recognised that writing now, every loop and tail, every dot and comma. Emma's handwriting. She'd replied to just one of the many letters he'd written her from America, not knowing she and Seth were man and wife. It had been a letter of condolence of a sort – her sadness at the death of his marriage and that he would be seeing less of his son. He still had that letter, safely filed with all his important and precious papers. Matthew gulped in air which made him cough. He was conscious of his heart rate increasing. Something like joy, pure joy, flooded through him. *E Jago.* This *had* to be her. *His* Emma. But Seth. Where was he? Why had Signor Cascarini brought Emma to buy a car? He'd just have to find out, wouldn't he?

'Boss?' William said. 'Put me out of my misery. Have I still got a job or not?'

Matthew laughed, placed a hand on William's shoulder.

'Oh, you won't be losing your job, William. Seven o'clock sharp, Monday morning.' The smile on Matthew's face grew wider with each word. Emma Jago. All he had to do now was find out where she lived. And Signor Cascarini was the conduit to that.

But not just yet. Stella would need to know Emma was back.

The line was bad. Matthew rang the number for the nurses' living quarters. Someone who wasn't Stella answered and said she would go and knock on the door of her room, and that he was to hang on.

He'd been hanging on for ages. Emma's face drifted in and out of his mind. He wondered if she still wore rose-scented perfume. She'd been wearing it the last time he'd seen her. Or was she buying something more expensive these days? Chanel No 5 perhaps? And if Emma was back, did that mean Seth was back as well? Or ... he hung onto the hope she was back on her own, especially as it had been Signor Cascarini who had brought her over to Exeter.

He caught sight of himself in the mirror – he had a huge grin on his face and it was in danger of making his facial muscles ache.

'Matthew? Is something wrong?'

Stella. At last. Kind, caring Stella who was sounding as though she really hoped there was nothing wrong with him and that if there was she'd make him better.

Nothing could cure what was troubling him. Love. Only not for Stella. Not the sort of love that Stella deserved.

'I need to talk to you,' he said. 'Face to face.'

'But, Matthew, we did that today. I'm not likely to cancel the wedding because of what you've told me. I'm a nurse. I've heard worse. But it's late, and—'

'I know. I'm sorry if I woke you from your beauty sleep. Not that you need any.'

God, what a crass remark. Not him at all. But then he wasn't feeling the same as he had when he'd been in the Imperial Hotel giving Stella chapter and verse of his life. He'd told Stella that a young and homeless girl had been his housekeeper way back before the war, but not her name. But now that girl was a woman, and older. And not homeless any more. And, hopefully, back in his life. A friend of Signor Cascarini's. Well, as he'd said before, all's fair in love and war and Signor Cascarini was going to have a fight on his hands.

'Thank you, kind sir.' Stella laughed. Her voice was higher-pitched and rather crackly over the telephone system. 'But I'd like to get back to that sleep soon. I'm on the very early shift in the morning. Oh, there's something I forgot to mention this afternoon. I think I might have found a bridesmaid. The daughter of the lady who's making my dress. She's a beautiful girl – very dark hair, almost black. Her mother is going to ask her. That will be all right, won't it? There's no one on your side you want to ask. Or is there?'

Stella's voice was full of excitement at her plans and it only served to make him feel a bigger heel than ever over what he was going to have to do.

'No, no one.'

He knew for certain Harry wouldn't want to be a bridesmaid although he had, tentatively, asked his son if he would be his groomsman when he'd last written to him. So far he'd had no reply.

'You'll have a chance to meet her on the sixteenth because we've been invited to her birthday party. Four o'clock. It's next Saturday. The garage is always quiet on a Saturday afternoon, isn't it? That's if you can make it and want to come. You don't have to.'

And now, Matthew thought, I don't think I can. But the sixteenth was a week away yet. It would buy him time.

'But if you want to meet me to tell me whatever it is you

forgot to tell me this afternoon,' Stella prattled on, happily enough, 'then I'm off duty … hang on …'

Matthew could hear the scraping sound of pages being turned. There was a book with the duty rota beside the telephone at all times – Stella had told him that.

'Oh, gosh, this is going to be difficult. If you can come over on, say, Wednesday, at around two o'clock, I'll have an hour. I could meet you in the park at Shiphay. I'll probably need a breath of fresh air by then but the thing is, I've said I'll cover for Mavis. Her mother's ill so I'll be doing double shifts.'

'Then I'll let you get back to bed,' Matthew said. 'I've kept you from it long enough. I'll try and get there for Wednesday, but if I can't—'

'Then it will keep, I hope,' Stella finished for him, although perhaps not the exact words he had in mind. He heard her yawn loudly.

Whether he told Stella what he had to now, or later, was one and the same thing – Stella's happy world of plans and dreams was going to be completely shattered.

'Sleep well,' Matthew said.

Stella made kissing noises down the line. But this time Matthew didn't return them.

'Goodnight,' Stella said. 'I love you.'

'Goodnight,' Matthew said.

But he couldn't say '*I love you*' back as he usually did. Because while he did love Stella in the way anyone would love a dear, kind and compassionate friend, it wasn't the sort of love he still had in his heart for Emma. He picked up Emma's cheque. Her hands had touched it, and he laid it against his cheek wanting to get closer to her.

You always did court trouble, Emma Jago, but this time you've handed me the baton.

And he wasn't going to bank her cheque. Not yet. Not until he'd found out exactly what the situation was between her and Signor Cascarini.

Chapter Ten

'Happy birthday, Fleur,' Emma said. She held out the wrapped wristwatch that Fleur had coveted in Conroy and Couch's. She'd also bought her a cream leather handbag from Trownson's with crocheted summer gloves to match. And she'd put twenty pounds inside so that Fleur could choose something for herself.

She could well afford it and she loved buying presents for her daughter. Emma's dressmaking business had kept her very busy since Stella Martin had become her first client. In just two weeks she'd made three dresses for three different women to wear to the Mayor's Ball. Thank heaven for Coco Chanel and her simplicity of design which meant the dresses were quickly made. And Emma was reaping the benefit of her foresight to make things for herself and Fleur to show prospective clients. All had been impressed and now they were giving recommendations to their friends. Sometimes Emma had to pinch herself because she found it hard to believe how much she'd achieved since her arrival in England back in April. Never go back, people had said to her in Canada, because it's never the same. But then, they didn't have the memories Emma had to be going back to.

'Thanks, Ma,' Fleur said, taking the proffered parcel, and reading the gift tag.

Emma had felt a real pang of sorrow writing 'With love from Ma' on it. Somehow it had accentuated her aloneness not being able to write 'and Pa'. But she'd swallowed it back. This was her new life. *Their* new life. Fleur seemed a lot happier since the night they'd all been to the theatre with Paolo and his father. She was still seeing Paolo, but not as much. And Emma had had a genuine reason for not being able to accept Eduardo's invitations to the cinema, or the theatre, or for him to cook her a meal in his *ristorante* after closing hours. She was busy. She'd had to sew until well after midnight some nights. Not that she minded. But in her heart she knew she was holding back from seeing Eduardo in the hope he would notice her coolness and end things between them. Emma had never in her life had to tell someone she didn't want them for a friend any more. She didn't know that she could do it.

Thank goodness she had the car now which was cutting the time she had been taking to pick up material and sewing notions from Beare's. She was going to use it later to go and fetch Ruby and the children, after she'd been to put flowers on her mama's and Johnnie's grave, and her papa's. And some on the grave of Seth's ma, too. She made a mental note to remember to take the lawn cotton dresses she'd made for Ruby's daughters to wear at the party – simple shifts that had taken no time at all to run up on her Singer. For Thomas she'd made some trousers out of an off-cut of linen she'd had leftover from a jacket she'd made for Fleur. And she'd given Ruby the money to buy Thomas a shirt to go with it. Ruby, being Ruby, had grumbled and said weren't they smart enough to come to Fleur's party as they were? But she'd laughed as she'd said it and she'd been effusive in her thanks for the dress Emma had loaned her to wear. Tom was coming over on the train before the rest of his family.

Emma checked the time on the clock on the mantelpiece. He should be here any minute. She had any number of instructions for him about what she wanted done, and where, in the garden. Thank goodness the weather had been hot and dry and the lawns were now in good order, watered daily by the sprinkler she'd bought. She added 'mow the lawns just one more time' to the list in her head.

'There's Tom,' Fleur said. She pointed to the gateway

where Emma could now see that it was indeed Tom walking slowly, as though each step was an effort. He was wearing his good clothes. Emma recognised the suit he had on – it had been Seth's. It hung off Tom now. There were working clothes in a cupboard in the hall for Tom to change into for gardening, but Emma was pleased to see he'd worn his best clothes over on the train.

'God, but is that man ever going to cheer up?' Fleur sighed theatrically. 'He's misery on a plate. I don't know how his wife puts up with it.'

'She puts up with it, Fleur,' Emma said, 'because she loves him. And I have to tell you he's been through a terrible experience. I thought you liked Tom?'

'I do. Sort of. He doesn't say much. But you didn't have to play at being his psychiatrist to make him well, Ma,' Fleur said.

'I'm not *playing* at anything,' Emma said sharply. 'Tom and Ruby need money and I've got it, but it will be better for Tom – well, for all of them really – if he feels he's earned it, rather than me giving it to them.'

And so far, Tom was indeed earning his money. He worked well and Emma had to insist at midday that he come into the house for some lunch and to put his feet up for half an hour. And she had to practically push him out of the gate again at five o'clock to go home again. '*Just this one bit of clipping, then I'll go,*' was what he invariably said, although he never met Emma's eye when he said it. He was doing wonders with the garden, if not with his mental health problems. The shrubs had all been cut back and some of them had started sprouting fresh green leaves already. The lawn edges were now all neat and straight again. Emma had bought some terracotta urns from Ireland's and Tom had planted three boxes of scarlet geraniums and some trailing ivy in them.

'Well, all I can say is, Ma, that I hope his wife has got a bit more life in her than Tom has.'

'That will be an understatement!' Emma laughed. She realised now that she ought to have taken Fleur to see Ruby – goodness, Ruby had asked her to enough times – but there'd never been the time or the opportunity. 'But no more. Tom will hear us.'

'Mornin', Emma. Fleur,' Tom said, knocking and coming into the breakfast room simultaneously through the door that led out onto the terrace.

Emma had said she didn't want to think of Tom as a servant of any kind. He was and always had been, and always would be, a friend – the husband of her dearest friend, Ruby.

'Good morning, Tom,' Emma said. She gave Fleur a look – say good morning to Tom, the look said.

Fleur pulled at the ribbons to undo her parcel and said, 'Good morning, Tom,' without looking up.

''Appy birthday, Fleur,' Tom said. 'And lots more of 'em.'

Fleur looked up then. 'I hope so,' she said.

'Ruby said I 'ad to say that,' Tom said, looking at Emma. And he was smiling. The first time Emma had seen him smile.

'Very Ruby.' Emma laughed.

'Isn't it just,' Tom said. ''Er said 'er'll be ready fer the time you said.'

'Two o'clock.'

She had lots to do before then. She'd already made the crab tarts and a *tarte Tatin*. And she'd got up early this morning and made a sponge cake so that it would be fresh and not starting to go solid as it would if she'd made it the day before. She planned to fill it with whipped cream and strawberries, when she'd been to Dey's to buy them. *Mental note to self – get Tom to prepare a strawberry bed so we can pick our own for Fleur's next birthday.* Then there would only be the sandwiches – cucumber, egg and cress, and some tinned salmon with capers and mayonnaise – to make an hour or so before Stella arrived for her wedding dress fitting. Stella was unsure, she'd said when she telephoned Emma to confirm that she'd be calling for her dress fitting, whether her fiancé would be with her or not. Emma loved the way Stella always said, '*my fiancé*', giving the words gravitas. It had been on the tip of Emma's tongue to ask what his name was a couple of times but it seemed a crime to deprive Stella of the pleasure of saying the words.

Much to Emma's surprise Fleur had been thrilled at the idea of being Stella's bridesmaid and was looking forward to talking to her about what colour dress she might have. Emma had promised to buy her some high-heeled shoes – her very first – for the occasion.

'Oh, Ma,' Fleur said, fastening the wristwatch on. 'This is beautiful. It really is. Thank you. And I love the bag and gloves.'

'Good,' Emma said. 'And I think you might like the bag even more if you open it!'

Fleur grinned at her – how good that felt.

Fleur did as suggested and waved the five pound notes in the air. 'Rockhey's here I come,' she said.

'Yes, but first we've all got work to do.'

'Lead me to it,' Tom said. 'It's goin' to be a beautiful day. Proper 'an'some.'

Two hours seemed to fly by, and it was only the position of the sun in the sky that told Emma it was now mid-morning.

They'd all helped carry tables onto the big lawn, setting them up under the Ginkgo biloba tree. Emma loved the pretty shape of the leaves ... like cockle shells almost. And such a beautiful shade of green, fresh and cooling.

Fleur was detailed to lay linen cloths on the tables – done without grumbling Emma was pleased to see. Emma found six old fish paste jars in the shed, washed them out, and filled them with small posies of flowers – roses and honeysuckle, and Mrs Sinkins' pinks which were actually white and smelled divine. They reminded her of her old home – Shingle Cottage.

'Us 'ave got they in the garden,' Tom said, picking up a bloom and inhaling the scent.

'Good, I'm glad they haven't died from age or neglect,' Emma said, and then she realised what she'd said. 'Oh, I'm sorry, Tom. I didn't mean you weren't looking after my property and garden. I ...' Best shut up now before she said too much, dug herself into a deeper hole.

'I 'aven't been,' Tom said, solemnly. He didn't elaborate. He pushed the flower back into the makeshift vase and slid it to the centre of the table. But the tone of his voice and the way he held Emma's gaze as he spoke said volumes ... he was on the mend.

'We'll stop for lunch soon,' Emma said. 'Not that we'll want much.'

She'd made some fresh tomato soup and bought a loaf of bread from May's Bakery the day before which she'd sprinkle with water and then warm through in the oven to freshen it up. And then she'd have to leave Tom and Fleur to do a final tidy up while she went to Tolchard's for some birthday champagne.

Champagne. Matthew. His name would forever be linked to champagne in Emma's mind. Her first taste of it had been at Nase Head House with Matthew, and when she'd said that it tickled her nose because there were bubbles in it Matthew had said, 'Champagne usually does have bubbles, Emma'. Seth had bought her lots of champagne but none of it had tasted the same as that first bottle – the sheer delight of it.

'What will the children drink, Tom?' Emma asked, hoping that guilt wasn't showing in her voice that she'd been thinking of a man who wasn't her husband. 'Lemonade?'

'They gets water mostly. A drop of milk if there's any spare.'

'I know!' Fleur joined the discussion. 'Why not ring Paolo's pa and ask him to bring some ice cream. We could get some soda from Dey's and then we could give the children ice cream sodas. And maybe some straws? They'd love that, I'm sure.'

'I'm certain they would. But Signor Cascarini might have things to do.' Emma wasn't sure now that she wanted to be beholden to Eduardo for anything. He'd been kindness itself, but ...

'Ma? Paolo's pa has gallons and gallons of ice cream. It's not as if he's got to stop and make it fresh!'

'No, but I don't think they sell soda in England yet.' Emma knew she was sounding like a damp squib, spoiling Fleur's excitement, throwing cold water on her bright idea. 'But lemonade would probably be just as good,' she said, trying to sound more enthusiastic for the idea because in her heart she was thrilled that Fleur was now embracing her birthday treat and wanting to please Tom and Ruby's children, whom she hadn't yet met. 'You ring him, will you? Oh, I've just remembered,' Emma went on before Fleur could answer although she knew the girl wouldn't give up a chance to talk and bill and coo down the telephone to Paolo, 'I've made some bunting out of fabric scraps. It's on the table in my atelier. I thought it might look good strung between the trees either side of the drive. I'll just go and get it.'

Then I'll see about lunch and after I've eaten I'll have to be off.

Fleur changed into her new dress the second her ma had left the house. She went into her ma's bedroom and drenched herself in her ma's Chanel No 5. Heavenly! She'd have to wander about the garden for a while to dilute the scent of it a bit or her ma would notice. Maybe she'd spend her birthday money on some perfume? She twisted her arm this way and that admiring her new wristwatch, and the way the sunlight streaming in the large bay window caught the light and made the diamonds sparkle like a whole night sky of stars.

'Fleur!'

Tom's voice. What did he want? She thought he'd said he was going to rake the gravel on the drive and then give the stone gateposts a brush to rid them of any spiderwebs, before he put up the bunting.

She checked the time on her watch. Her ma should be back by three because Stella Martin was coming for a fitting for her wedding dress. Fleur didn't think she'd ever seen anything so beautiful. Not that she wanted to get married. Well, not yet. Not for ages and ages, although Paolo was always going on about it. His cousin, Marianna, back in Naples, had married at fourteen years old and had a baby nine months later. No thank you!

Perhaps Stella Martin had arrived early. She'd have to go downstairs and see. No hardship because they could discuss what colour dress Fleur was going to have as a bridesmaid's dress. Anything but green!

'Coming!' she yelled and skittered down the stairs.

Tom was dressed in his best clothes, his hair brushed and slicked with Brylcreem.

'I've strung up the buntin' like your ma asked but now I need to go into town,' he told her. 'Everythin' your ma 'ad on the list is done as well. Looks proper 'an'some out there it does.'

'Thank you, Tom,' Fleur said.

No reason for Tom going into town was forthcoming and Fleur didn't ask. She knew her ma had paid him earlier so perhaps he had things to buy in town – like a present for her.

'You'll be all right on your own while I'm gone, will you?'

Of *course* she'd be all right.

'I won't be on my own for long,' she said checking the time on her birthday wristwatch. 'Ma will be back with your wife and the children soon and Miss Martin should be here in a few minutes.'

Paolo and his pa weren't due to arrive until four o'clock. They'd asked if *nonna* could come with them, and Fleur's ma had said that of course she could. Fleur wasn't so sure about that. The old woman spent most of her time sniffing and crying when she wasn't forced to serve customers it was obvious she didn't want to serve. She'd rung about the ice cream and the straws but it had been Paolo's *nonna* who had answered and Fleur couldn't be sure Paolo's pa would get the right message even though she'd said ice cream in Italian – *gelato*. The old woman had said, '*Si, si*' to everything Fleur had said. Out of devilment, Fleur had said, 'I think it's going to rain later.' And *nonna* had said, '*Si. Bene.*' Which had made Fleur laugh and *nonna* had laughed with her, which made Fleur wonder if she was getting over the death of her daughter at last, and that a birthday tea was just what the woman needed. And at best, Fleur would get an extra present, wouldn't she?

'Oh, and the postman gave me these for you,' Tom said.

He handed Fleur a small bundle of cards. Two had Canadian stamps on. Delia would have sent one, she knew that. And maybe Delia's ma. One envelope was in her ma's large and loopy handwriting, and one had been written in the smallest upper case. The postman must have strained his eyes reading it.

'Ruby's bringin' 'er card with 'er,' Tom said. 'I'm off.'

And he was gone.

Fleur wandered out into the garden, leaving the front door open so she'd hear the telephone should anyone ring: Paolo or his pa, or maybe Stella Martin saying she'd be late. Or her ma to say the car had broken down. Oh, no, why had she thought that? Everything about today was perfect. Well almost ... her pa wasn't here in person, although he was in her heart, always.

Fleur counted the number of guests on her fingers. Eleven. There were eleven chairs around the tables but what if Stella Martin's fiancé, whatever he was called, came after all? It would look very unwelcoming not to have a chair for him, wouldn't it? She'd have to go and find another one.

Then she heard a car pull up in the road outside and voices. Then the car began to pull away again. Stella Martin arriving by taxi probably. Fleur walked towards the drive.

But it wasn't Stella. A woman who looked as though she'd stepped straight out of a Hollywood film was walking towards her. Gosh, how glamorous! What clothes! What a brilliant shade of scarlet lipstick! What presence she had! But who was she? And why was she here?

Well, her ma would kill her if she didn't make her welcome, wouldn't she? She might be a client come to call to ask her ma to make her an outfit or two. So Fleur walked towards the woman, a smile on her face. Now she was closer, Fleur could see that the woman wasn't as young as she appeared from a distance. Older than Ma, but she had style, and she was tall – holding herself erect as though there was a rod of iron sewn into her corsets. Her face was made-up and her skin looked matt, not healthy and glowing as her ma's did. But she had perfect teeth when she smiled. She oozed money.

But before Fleur could greet her, the woman said in an American accent, 'Were you expecting me?' and grinned. 'All this bunting!'

'No,' Fleur said. 'At least, I don't think so. The only person I'm expecting is Miss Martin and I know you're not her. And the bunting's for my birthday tea. At four o'clock.'

The woman's smile slipped for a moment. She fiddled with the cuffs of her gloves.

'If you've come about having a dress made, I'm afraid my ma's not here but—'

'I haven't. But how interesting. A little dressmaker, you say?'

A little dressmaker? Although Fleur had never told her ma as much, she was more than a little dressmaker. She could make just about anything – dresses, jackets, coats. Hats even. There wasn't a thing her ma couldn't make.

Fleur wasn't sure she liked this woman now. Her voice had turned to ice.

'The *little dressmaker*, as you put it, made me this. And it's as good as anything you can buy in Paris. But if you haven't come about having something made, why are you here?'

'To see you. You're the image of your father. And I'm your mother.'

Chapter Eleven

'Pipe down you lot!' Ruby shouted to her children sitting on the back seat of Emma's car, wriggling like a whole can of worms. All were talking excitedly at once.

'Faster, Mrs Jago!' Thomas yelled. 'Faster!'

'Didn't you 'ear?' Ruby said. She sat with her hands clasped tight over her knees, staring straight ahead, and Emma knew she wasn't as happy and excited as her children who were having their first ride in a motor car.

'Probably not,' Emma told her. She patted the backs of Ruby's hands. 'Not with all the din they're making. Leave them. They're excited and we're nearly there. Don't you remember how excited you were that first time I drove you in Seth's Wolseley?'

'Yeah. And it were a darned sight bigger than this rattle-trap. It's makin' me feel a bit queasy in 'ere.'

'Rattle-trap?' Emma said, laughing. 'This cost me just a few pennies short of two hundred pounds, I'll have you know.'

But the second the words were out of her mouth she regretted them because Ruby turned sharply to look at her.

'So you said,' she mumbled. 'More than once.'

'The Fair! The Fair!' Sarah screamed from the back seat, crawling over her brother to get closer to the window so she could see, and Emma was glad of the diversion.

She and Ruby were almost back to the friendship they'd had before she and Seth went to Canada, but not quite. The difference in how their lives had turned out was as wide as the ocean sometimes.

The Fair had arrived on the seafront the night before. Emma had woken at around three o'clock to the rumble of wheels. There had been lights on the road that ran between the green and the beach. And now Emma could see the big wheel going around and steam from the engines that powered the rides billowing into the bluest of blue skies. A perfect day for Fleur's birthday.

'I'll take you all later,' Emma said. 'After Fleur's party. A treat for being good.' She hoped that might cover her faux pas about the cost of her car in Ruby's eyes.

'*If* they're bleedin' good an' eat all the crusts on their sandwiches and don't talk with their mouths full,' Ruby said. 'My girls look like angels in those frocks but—'

'Don't say it,' Emma stopped her. 'Don't tempt fate.'

'No, miss!' Ruby giggled. 'Canada didn't knock the bossy out of you, then?'

Emma chose not to answer that because she had to negotiate the tight turn into Cleveland Road. A taxi was making a three-point turn in the road outside her house.

'Oh, heck,' Emma said. 'It looks as though Stella Martin is a bit early. I did say three. This doesn't look very professional, does it?'

'Gawd, girl, but you ain't perfect. None of us is. Say you got caught behind Farmer Treeby leadin' his cows along the road at Churston, or summat.'

Lie? Emma had thought she'd left all that behind her when she'd sailed from Bristol with Seth for their new life. She'd had to do it when she'd been a young girl to save her skin, to keep a roof over her head and food in her belly, but she had those things now.

'An' if you ask me, Em, the woman will more 'n likely be so excited about the beautiful weddin' dress you're makin' for 'er to be cross about you bein' a few minutes late. If what you're makin' is anythin' like *this* what you've loaned me.' Ruby fingered the hem of her borrowed dress – it was putty-coloured with white trim on the cap sleeves and the collar. A band of white ran down the centre of the dress and Emma had made a white belt to wear, slung low, on the hip. Ruby looked a treat in it. 'An' what those two little madams are gettin' all creased up back there.'

Emma slowed, changed into first gear and drove carefully between the pillars into the drive. Oh, good, Tom had hung up the bunting.

'Good,' Emma said. 'Tom's given the pillars a going over with a brush. And cut the overhanging branches back a bit. They were almost touching the roof of the car when I left.'

'Thanks for, you know,' Ruby said, lowering her voice. She jerked her head slightly towards the children and Emma knew Ruby didn't want to mention their father's problems. ''E's come back to me a bit, if you know what I mean?'

Emma wrinkled her brow.

'In the bedroom department,' Ruby whispered. 'We're goin' to try for another one. I expect it'll 'appen as fast as the others. As soon as 'e 'angs 'is trousers on the bedpost ... ' Ruby gave a contented sigh at the thought of it.

Emma's heart froze. She was happy for Ruby, of course she was, but another baby ... when she herself had never known what it was like to be pregnant, and give birth, and hold a child of her own in her arms. She swallowed back tears of regret. And longing. A baby wasn't going to happen for her now, was it? But she had Fleur. And maybe one day Fleur would have a child of her own and Emma would know the feeling of cradling a newborn baby.

'Penny for 'em, Em,' Ruby said. 'Or maybe in your case that should be a pound.'

'Don't. Don't be jealous, Ruby. There's nothing to be jealous of.'

But I am. I'm surprised Ruby can't see me going green.

Emma drove on down the drive, past the front of the house to where she always parked the car under a tree, to keep it shaded from the sun when it was hot. The leather seats burned like crazy through her clothes if she didn't.

'Right, out you get, you lot,' Ruby said. 'And no runnin' off until Mrs Jago tells you where it is you can run to.'

'Anywhere,' Emma said. 'The lawn might be a good place to start.'

The children scampered away and Emma got out of the car and closed the door. Ruby came around to her side and linked her arm through Emma's.

'I'm lookin' forward to seein' that girl of yours,' Ruby said.

'And she, you. She gets on well with Tom.'

'I know. 'E's forever tellin' me she makes the best cup of tea in the world. And 'ow beautiful she is. Not that I'm jealous. 'E'll get 'is tea 'ow I makes it or go without.' Ruby leaned into Emma. 'My, but it's so good us all bein' together again.'

Emma hurried up the drive, pulling Ruby with her. 'You can get to know one another, you and Fleur, while I'm fitting Stella Martin into her dress.'

But as they rounded the corner of the house and the lawn came into view Emma could see it wasn't Stella sitting with Fleur. Fleur had her legs crossed and her arms folded over her chest and a thunderous look on her face.

Emma froze and pulled Ruby back.

'Oh, bleedin' 'ell, Em,' Ruby said, gripping Emma's arm tight. 'Caroline bleedin' Prentiss.'

'Shush, Ruby. Keep your voice down.'

''Er's 'ardly likely to 'ear me from 'ere unless 'er's got ears what can 'ear a gnat fart at an 'undred paces.' Ruby wheeled round so her back was to the party on Emma's lawn.

'I 'eard rumours, Em, as 'er's Caroline Jago now. 'Er married Miles over in America before 'e was 'anged. Well, of course it would 'ave been before 'e was 'anged and not after, wouldn't it?' Ruby prattled on, nervously. ''Er's been back 'ere for a while lookin' after her sick ma, although if you ask me it was only so as others didn't get any of 'er ma's money and jewels and that. But now the old girl's gone and died. There'll be a funeral soon if there ain't been already. I should 'ave told you 'er was back.'

'Yes,' Emma said, disentangling Ruby's arm from hers. 'I think you should. How many times have you seen her?'

'Two or three. The last time 'er 'ad a man with 'er. Tall. 'E were wearin' one of they long coats like Mr Smythe used to wear when 'e were goin' somewhere important when us used to work for 'im.'

'What did he look like?'

Ruby shrugged. "E 'ad an 'at down over 'is eyes, didn't 'e? Gurt big thing it were.'

'I get the picture. Come on. We'll have to go. You can tell me anything else you remember afterwards.'

But if Caroline, with whatever surname she was going by these days, thought she could spoil Fleur's birthday tea and stop Emma from seeing to her client, and building up a dressmaking business, then she'd got on the wrong boat!

She and Fleur had a good relationship – most of the time – and they'd see this through. They had to.

Emma marched across the lawn, Ruby scurrying along beside her, her shorter legs struggling to keep up but being there for Emma – solidarity between friends. Emma's mouth was scarily dry with nerves and she ran a tongue over her lips to moisten them.

'Where's Tom?' Ruby asked.

Fleur shrugged. Without looking at Ruby but staring with blatant hostility at Emma, she said, 'He got all dressed up then he said he had to go into town for something. He said he wouldn't be long.'

'Let's 'ope not,' Ruby said. 'Just like a man to bugger off when you need 'im. Sorry, Em, but—'

Emma laid a hand on Ruby's forearm. 'I'll deal with this,' she said.

Caroline was staring at her with a sneer of a grin on her face – I've upset the applecart here, haven't I? that grin said. It was all Emma could do not to swipe it off her face for her.

'And you can wait there, Caroline,' she said. 'Or you

can go. The choice is yours. You might have come into my garden unasked but you're not entering my house until I invite you. *If* I ever do.'

'Not the first time I've entered your premises uninvited, is it?' Caroline said, a sickly sweet, false smile on her face.

No. No it wasn't. Just before Christmas 1911 Caroline had been waiting for Emma in her own bakery, with baby Fleur in her arms – although she'd been called Rose then. And she'd left her there. Dumped her on the table as though she was worth less than a sack of rotting potatoes.

But Emma wasn't going to answer her question. She turned to Fleur.

'I'll explain everything. Inside. Just you and me. I'm so sorry it's happened like this but—'

'*You're* sorry?' Fleur said. She looked, Emma thought, as though she wanted to spit in her face.

''Ere, miss,' Ruby butted in. 'I might not 'ave seen you since you were knee 'igh to a grass'opper, but I know Emma's been the best ma in the world to you so you just go and listen to what 'er 'as to say, or you'll 'ave me to answer to.'

Fleur looked startled for a second at Ruby's command, but she leapt to her feet and ran for the house.

Emma ran after her.

'I don't know that I can believe anything you tell me, Ma,' Fleur said, throwing herself down into the armchair in the sitting room. No way was she going to sit on the couch and have her ma sit beside her and put her arm around her to comfort her. Not any more. 'Or should I call you, *Emma*?'

'Don't, Fleur. I'm still your ma.'

Her ma went over to the windows and pulled down the sashes. Huh! They all knew what had happened – even Ruby, it seemed, knew that Emma wasn't her real ma by what she'd said. What difference would it make shutting in their voices now?

'But you're *not!*' Fleur waved the birth certificate at her. The first thing her ma had done when they went in the house was to get the certificate from the bureau. At least she hadn't lied about it, denied it. 'It says here under *mother* – Caroline Florence Prentiss. Thank God it says Seth Jago under *father.*'

She didn't know what she'd have done if it hadn't said that. All the portraits her pa had painted of her when she was a little girl would have meant nothing, wouldn't they? He'd done them as a sort of diary of her growing up. She had the one he'd painted of her when she was eight years old – leaning up against a maple tree in the garden of their house in Vancouver reading a book – on the wall beside her bed. Fleur hadn't known he'd been sketching her, ready to transfer that sketch to an oil painting in his studio at the top of the house. Her pa had used paints and brushes the way other people used a camera to catch magic moments. All the other portraits her pa had done of her where in boxes in the loft. *Well, ma could just get them out again, couldn't she, should she want to remind herself of what she looked like. There was a room in Delia Gethin's house ready for whenever she wanted to go back. Just as soon as this conversation with her ma was over she'd telephone and tell Delia and her mother she was coming back.* She didn't know that she wanted to be here any more.

'Sweetheart—'

'Don't call me that. Pa used to call me sweetheart. My name's Fleur. Or is it? It says Rose on this birth certificate. Rose! Why did you change my name?'

'We both changed it and it's a long story, Fleur. We need to be alone, you and me, when I tell you and without a garden full of people waiting for us to join them. Your pa always said he would do the telling because he'd know when the time was right to do it, except that time never came for him, did it?'

'I've only got your word for that.'

146

Although she was biting the insides of her cheeks to stop herself crying, and screwing up her eyes so any tears that escaped wouldn't fall, Fleur began to sob. Her tears, hot and salty, slid down her cheeks and around the sides of her neck. She did nothing to wipe them away. And they were no comfort whatsoever.

'Did Caroline tell you anything before I got back?'

'Only that she was my mother! And she wasn't married to Pa! And he wouldn't let her keep me! Isn't that enough?' She knew her voice was raised and they'd probably heard her outside but she didn't care. 'I put my hands over my ears and told her I didn't want to hear any more until you got back. She'd only been her five minutes before you returned.'

'That's not true,' her ma said. 'The bit about your pa not letting her keep you.'

Fleur shrugged. 'No?' she asked.

'No, but what I don't understand, Fleur,' her ma said slowly, 'is why you are instantly believing what Caroline says and yet dismissing my words.'

Fleur grabbed the antimacassar off the back of the chair and wiped her wet face with it. She sniffed back more tears. 'I said I didn't want to hear what else she said. That's not instantly believing her, is it?'

'No.'

'But it's completely wrecked my birthday tea.'

'We'll still be having your birthday tea. Mark my words.'

Fleur unstrapped her wristwatch, took it off, and slammed it down on the side table. 'I don't know that I want to wear this any more. It's buying me off, isn't it?'

'No, Fleur. Never that.'

'Huh! And this dress—'

'—is beautiful. And *you* are beautiful. And I have been proud to be your ma. I still am.'

'Perhaps,' Fleur said, 'if we hadn't come back to England I'd still be living in ignorance about my existence.'

'Not forever. I would have told you.'

'That's what you say.' Fleur stood up. 'I'm going to telephone Paolo and tell him the tea is cancelled. And then I'm going to my room.'

'No. Don't do that, please? There are three little children out there all expecting a tea party and none of this is their fault. I don't suppose they've ever been to a tea party in their lives. And the girls have never had such pretty dresses before either. Couldn't we at least give them a happy time, if only for an hour? I'll ask Caroline to go. She can come back tomorrow and by then I'll have told you everything. Caroline, of course, will have her version of it, but I've never not told you the truth, Fleur.'

'Except the most important truth of all! Who my mother actually *is*! Oh God, that's Stella Martin arriving, Ma,' Fleur said as she saw her walk past the window. The front doorbell rang. 'I expect you're going to put her before me as well now and do her fitting.'

'You will always be first in my heart, Fleur, but sometimes we have to be aware of other people's sensibilities. Ruby and her family, and Stella Martin, and a little later on Paolo and his family, are those people at the moment. Please, Fleur, give me two minutes to go and ask Mrs Prentiss to leave —'

'*Mrs* Prentiss? She was married to someone else when she and Pa —'

'Widowed.'

And then to Fleur's utter astonishment her ma wrapped her arms around her and hugged her close. 'I love you more than words can say and my life would have been far, far emptier had you not come into it,' she whispered. 'And should you leave it now, it will be the saddest day of my life.'

'Even sadder than the day Pa died?' Fleur sobbed against her ma's shoulder.

Her ma didn't answer for a moment and then she said, 'Yes, it would be, because you are all I have of him now.'

'Oh, Ma …' Fleur said. Her mind was telling her to stop calling her ma and say Emma, but she knew her pa wouldn't want that.

The doorbell rang again, for longer and louder this time.

'Go and put some cold water on your face while I let Stella Martin in. By the time you've done that Caroline will have left.'

'But you'll let her come back?'

'Yes,' her ma said, and walked to the door. 'I promise. I owe you that.'

Tom was back when Emma returned to the garden. He was standing by the chair Ruby was sitting in, a hand on her shoulder, and he'd placed himself, protectively, between Ruby and Caroline. The children were around because Emma could hear their excited voices although she couldn't see them.

Emma wondered just how much of anything Ruby had told Tom about Fleur and how she'd come into her and Seth's lives. She knew Ruby hadn't believed the story Emma had told her that Fleur had been Seth's cousin Frank's child, and that Frank's wife had died in childbirth – no, not for a minute had Ruby believed that although she'd gone along with the lie and hadn't asked any questions. She had, though, told Emma that Caroline had been seen in Victoria Park talking to Seth and with a baby in her arms, and just weeks before Caroline had turned up in Emma's bakery with Fleur.

Caroline still had a smug smile on her face, but her eyes were closed and her head turned up to the sun, the hat she'd been wearing placed on the table in front of her, as though she intended to remain there awhile. Emma regretted saying she could stay if she wanted to.

'Tom and I will be over there with the children, if you want us,' Ruby said, standing up as Emma reached them. 'Just give Tom a shout and 'e'll throw 'er out, 'ook, line, and bleedin' sinker.'

'That won't be necessary,' Emma said with a smile for her friend. 'But I'll bear it in mind.'

Goodness only knows what Caroline was likely to say. To do. But she wasn't going to sit down to let Caroline do it. She'd remain standing.

'I should never 'ave left Fleur on 'er own,' Tom said. 'I wouldn't 'ave let *'er* in otherwise.'

'It's not your fault,' Emma told him. 'But if you could both leave Caroline and me alone for a few minutes …?'

'We're gone,' Ruby said, and she grabbed Tom's hand and pulled him across the lawn with her towards the children.

'And now,' Emma said when she was sure Tom and Ruby were out of earshot, 'I'm going to have to ask you to leave my premises. I take back what I said about giving you the choice to stay or go now I've had time to think about it. I have a client waiting for a dress fitting, and friends expecting a tea party for Fleur's birthday, and that is what I am going to give them all. Were he here, Seth would tell you the same thing. So, you have two minutes in which to get yourself out through that front gate. You can come back tomorrow. At two o'clock.'

That should give me enough time to tell Fleur everything I know and, hopefully, begin to repair bridges between us. Seek legal advice. The look Caroline was giving her was telling Emma that Caroline Prentiss – or Jago, if what Ruby had said was true – wasn't simply going to sail back out of their lives again the way she'd sailed back into it half an hour ago. She was here to make trouble.

'Where is Seth?'

'In a grave on Vancouver Island. He died two years ago. Not that I have to tell you anything.'

'You always were a mouthy one,' Caroline said.

Which, Emma thought, *isn't meant as a compliment.* But she was going to take it as one – she'd unnerved Caroline by what she'd said, she knew she had, because Caroline had picked up her hat and was fiddling with the rim of it.

Caroline stood up.

She put her hat back on, taking an age to do it, as though she was looking in an invisible mirror as she tilted her head this way and that, getting the angle of it on her hair just right. Vain was the word that sprang immediately to Emma's mind, followed swiftly by self-centred, scheming and calculating. To say nothing of down right criminal seeing as Caroline and Miles Jago had sailed on the *Titanic* under false names.

'Two o'clock, you say?'

Emma nodded. She couldn't trust herself to say another word to this odious woman for fear of saying too much.

'I'll be here, Emma. But brace yourself. You don't know the half of it yet, although I know you think you do. You've got a surprise coming, mark my words. Both of you.'

Emma watched Caroline go, walking slowly and with very careful steps across the grass on her high heels. As she reached the corner of the house she turned and raised a hand in farewell towards Emma.

Emma didn't respond. She just stood as still as a statue while her mind raced. She'd deal with whatever Caroline had to tell her tomorrow.

She heard a car approaching and the squeal of brakes immediately outside her gate. A car door creaked opened, and then a few seconds later it was banged shut again. Had a car been waiting for Caroline? Emma struggled to remember how wealthy Caroline's parents had been. Her pa had been a builder before he'd bought Seth's fishing fleet. Wealthy enough for a chauffeur although she didn't remember Caroline's pa employing one. But it had all been a long time ago.

Right now she had a very lovely woman waiting for her in her drawing room. *Thank goodness someone has a clear and happy vision of her future*, Emma thought, as she hurried back indoors.

Chapter Twelve

To Emma's relief the tea party for Fleur had been a happy enough event given the circumstances. The children had seen to that. They'd swarmed around Fleur as though she was some sort of fairy tale princess, much to Fleur's amusement.

Eduardo and Paolo and *nonna* – as both men called her, but whose name was actually Lucia – came bearing gifts. A leather purse from Paolo with an Italian coin in it. He'd handed it to Fleur and said he hoped to be able to take her to Italy one day so she could spend it. Emma had gulped back her emotions at the romance of it – would Fleur want to do that now, once she had heard whatever else it was Caroline had to say? *Nonna* gave Fleur a pretty silk scarf which Emma thought might have been her daughter's because while it was pure silk and obviously expensive, it wasn't new. Fleur had accepted it with good grace – or possibly in total shock still that Caroline had turned up – and immediately placed it loosely around her neck.

Eduardo brought ice cream for the children – *nonna* had remembered to pass on the message – much to their delight and they made ice cream sodas with lemonade. And Eduardo had brought Fleur an Italian cake he'd made himself – a cake normally given at Christmas called *panforte*, which had been absolutely delicious eaten with a glass of champagne. But it was a huge cake and there had been loads left which Emma gave to Ruby to take home for the children after they'd all been to the Fair for an hour and made themselves g iddy on the rides.

Ruby had said the Fair could wait for another time, given

what had happened but Emma had insisted she honour her promise to the children. It had come as a welcome relief to be carefree amidst the noise and the smell and the fun of the Fair if only for a short while.

Tom's visit into town had been to buy flowers for Fleur for her birthday. He'd handed the small posy of roses over with a shy look and Ruby had said, 'Where's mine then, you tight-fisted whatsit, 'cos you've never given me any flowers.' But she'd said it with a big grin on her face and she'd given Tom a kiss on the cheek to let him know she was only joking. Ruby had been pleased Tom was thinking about someone else now, and not just himself and the horrors he'd been through in the war and the love that shone from her for her husband had told Emma that.

Stella's fiancé hadn't turned up. While Emma thought Stella had been upset that he hadn't, Stella hadn't shown her feelings. 'I expect something's happened at the garage that he's had to deal with,' she'd said. And Emma had told her to let him know how happy she was with the car he'd sold her. Stella promised that she would. But Stella hadn't stopped long. Just long enough to drink one glass of champagne and nibble at an egg and cress sandwich. She had, she said, to keep her figure for February because Emma wouldn't want to be letting the dress out all the time, would she?

'I know you probably think I'm well in hand having a wedding dress made now for a February wedding, but winter, when there's so much influenza about which often turns to pneumonia and death, is always the busiest time in a hospital and I've been known to do double shifts for months and months with little spare time for dress fittings,' was what Stella had said.

Emma agreed. 'More time to find shoes and sort the flowers and everything. And plan your trousseau.'

More work for Emma, hopefully, making things for Stella to wear on her honeymoon.

Next time Stella called, Emma would try to remember to ask her what her fiancé was called although, in her heart, Emma knew Stella was still finding it a novelty that she had a fiancé. She'd confessed she'd done the proposing. 'How wanton of me!' she'd said. That the much longed for fiancé owned Exe Motors, Emma knew, but the lad who had dealt with the purchase of her car had called him 'the boss', and very proudly, too, so she still hadn't found out what he was called. Eduardo hadn't been forthcoming with a name either, and she hadn't thought, at the time, to ask.

Emma had suggested a tiara might be best for Stella, rather than a veil. Neither had said, '*at her age*' but the words had been there in the air between them. Or a crystal covered bandeau? Yes, that could look good, too. Almost like a hat but not quite. More glamorous.

But now, Emma had everything ready for Caroline's visit. Fleur's birth certificate was in the top drawer of the bureau. And the drawer was locked. Emma had written down everything Seth had told her about his time with Caroline. Well, not all the personal things about the conception, but everyone knew how that happened, didn't they?

Except it never has for me.

After breakfast, Fleur had demanded to be told, again, everything Emma knew about how Caroline had abandoned her. It was as though Fleur was checking Emma said exactly the same thing each time, almost as though she was trying to trip her up. But there was only the truth and Emma could repeat that accurately until the cows came home, as the saying had it.

'I don't know that I can take much more in,' Fleur said. 'Yesterday was such a horrible shock and yet a good day, too. Do I have to be here when she comes?'

'Not if you don't want to. It might be best if you're not.'

'But you'll tell me everything she says?'

Emma had swallowed. It would depend on what Caroline

had to say and she would use her own discretion as to what she would report back to Fleur.

For answer Emma had smiled warmly at her and Fleur had given her an unexpected hug, assuming Emma was saying that yes, she would tell her everything.

And now Fleur had gone to the ice cream parlour for the afternoon and she'd gone readily enough and not put up any objection as Emma had thought she might. Perhaps the romance of the purse with the Italian coin in it was pride of place in Fleur's mind. Fleur liked serving up ice cream sundaes to people, so she said. And she was learning Italian. Emma hoped with all her heart that Fleur's youth would mean she could accept her new circumstances more easily.

'*My Italian's better than nonna's English!*' Fleur had laughed at the tea party the day before when she'd had to translate something *nonna* had said to Ruby in her mother tongue. How good that laugh had sounded.

Emma had told Fleur she would drive over to Torquay and pick her up in the car when Caroline had gone. Seven o' clock at the very latest, she'd said. That should give her and Caroline enough time to say what needed to be said to one another, shouldn't it?

Ah, here was Caroline now. And dressed more glamorously than the day before if that were possible. Like a film star. And then Emma remembered that Caroline had told Seth she was going to America to break into films. Perhaps she had.

Emma hurried out into the hall, ready to open the door before Caroline's knock. A last minute check on her hair and to see that her petticoat wasn't hanging down below the hem of her skirt and Emma was ready for anything.

'Caroline,' she said, opening the door with a nod. She did not offer her hand. This could hardly be called 'greeting' could it? To greet implied one was happy to see the other person. *Dancing with the devil had to be better entertainment!*

She ushered Caroline inside.

'Some place you have here,' Caroline said. 'Fishing must have been good in Canada.'

'Legal fishing,' Emma said, turning her back on Caroline to lead the way into the drawing room. *Digest that*, she thought, because she knew what Caroline had implied with her reference to the profitability of fishing. Seth's pa and brothers had smuggled other things onto their boats apart from fish and been gaoled for their practices. 'Follow me,' she called back over her shoulder. 'Take a seat.'

Emma waved an arm over the two couches and the two single armchairs. Take your pick, the gesture said. Caroline chose the single chair with her back to the window, and sat down.

Emma had to be in control of this, if control could be the word with the entire forest of butterflies she had fluttering inside her was anything to go by. She'd made a pot of tea, guessing that Caroline would be on time. She had been.

'Milk?' Emma asked.

'Yes, but after the tea goes in, not before.'

No *please* Emma noted. And there was no *thank you* either when Emma handed her the cup and saucer which Caroline placed on the side table.

'So, why are you here?' Emma asked.

'To see Fleur.'

'Not today. It's just you and me today.'

'Where is she?'

'I prefer not to tell you that for the moment. But not being here was her choice. That I *can* tell you.'

'I only have your word for that.'

Fleur had said those very words to Emma the day before, and a shiver ran through her remembering. There was something in the way Fleur had looked at her then, and the same look was in Caroline's eyes now.

Caroline crossed her legs at the ankles, and then placed

her handbag, which had been on her lap, on the floor by her feet. She took off her hat and placed it beside the cup of tea on the side table.

As though she intends to stay for some while. She'll be lucky!

'I'm afraid that's all you have. My word. How did you find us?'

Us, not me. Let her know we are a family, Fleur and I.

'Dear old Bettesworth.'

'The solicitor?'

'Of course the solicitor. I was there dealing with my mother's estate and he said, "Well, this is a coincidence, Mrs Jago. The second Mrs Jago to pass through my hands, as it were, recently."'

So what Ruby had heard was true. Caroline had married Miles. And it sounded as though she hadn't married again after his death – by hanging after he was run to ground by Matthew Caunter. *Oh, Matthew, where are you? I need you now as much as ever. If only thoughts could conjure you up, like a magician's rabbit out of a hat.*

'That was very unprofessional of him.'

Bettesworth hadn't acted for Emma, but she knew he'd acted for the owner of Romer Lodge. Damn and blast the man. He knew about Fleur's parentage, too, because Seth had gone to him to get Fleur's name changed from Rose by deed poll.

She felt sick. Had Bettesworth said anything to Caroline about Fleur? She desperately wanted to know but she couldn't ask. She'd wait to be told. Everything. However unpleasant that everything might be. She'd deal with it. She had to.

'Be that as it may. But I think it just slipped out. "Romer Lodge," he said. "Lovely house." So I came over yesterday to see for myself if it was you or another Mrs Jago. Fleur – as you seem to have called her – looks just like her father. I'd have known her anywhere.'

The thought that Caroline might have seen Fleur out in town, or walking along the seafront, sent a chill through Emma. She'd been living in Romer Lodge for months – Caroline might have known that for months, too. What might she have said, or done, if she had met Fleur somewhere? Recognised her and made herself known? How shocking that would have been for Fleur.

'Tell me why you've come,' Emma snapped. While what she said might be true she hadn't bothered with Fleur before – not even a card or a present on her birthday or at Christmas. Had she done that, then Emma – or Seth – would have been forced into telling Fleur about her birth. 'Say your piece and go.'

'Curiosity. It seemed like fate when Bettesworth mentioned your name.'

No burning desire to see your daughter, then? And there's no way on this earth I'm going to ask when that was, show any fear.

'Curiosity isn't good enough,' Emma told her. 'Fleur's emotions are at risk here. Anything else? Before you get out of our lives again.'

'Just one thing. Seth wasn't Fleur's father. His brother, my late husband Miles, was.'

'Does she have to sit there all the time?' Fleur asked.

She jerked her head towards *nonna* sitting in the kitchen of the ice cream parlour, her arms crossed in front of her leaning on the table, peering through the open doorway into the café. Watching. Watching Fleur and Paolo as they served customers. A run of them today in the heat. All the tables were in use, every seat taken. Thank goodness it would be closing time soon. Six o'clock. She could tell Paolo about Caroline then. She still couldn't believe what she'd been told. It was all a horrible dream. Except it wasn't. And right now her birth mother would be at

Romer Lodge with her ... Emma. Fleur had carefully avoided saying 'Ma' at breakfast, or when she'd asked Fleur to sit down while she told her the whole story about how Caroline had turned up one day and left her, Fleur, on the table in the bakery. How could that be true? What sort of mother would do that?

'Si. *Nonna* live here,' Paolo said.

Well, she knew that, didn't she? What Fleur wasn't liking was *nonna*'s eyes boring into her, following her around the room as she made coffees, and served up the ice cream sundaes. As though she didn't trust Fleur not to take money from the cash register. Or that she'd eat half the produce or something. Steal a cup of coffee without paying for it. There'd been no time for that this afternoon. Paolo's pa was out in what he called his ice cream *fabbrica* churning cream and adding fruit and nuts to make replacements for tomorrow, and it seemed most of Torquay had come in the shop, all wanting the most complex of ice cream sundaes made.

Fleur chopped angrily at a cherry and dropped the pieces onto the top of the sundae she was making. She drizzled cherry juice over the top. Another customer came to the counter and placed orders. There was to be no let up yet. It seemed busier than ever. And she knew if trade was good that Paolo's pa would stay open longer.'What would happen if your pa married again?' Fleur asked. 'Would she still live with him?'

'*Si*. Or with me.' Paolo ran water into the sink underneath the counter and put half a dozen dirty sundae dishes in it. He reached for the washing soda and tipped in a generous amount. Swirled his hands in the water to dissolve the powder. 'It's what Italian's do. Is family. Always family.'

Fleur felt herself welling up. Family. Did she have one any more?

'All right for some,' she said, sniffing back tears.

Paolo looked at her sharply. He took his hands from the water and wiped them down the sides of his apron. Then he laid a hand on top of Fleur's.

'You not happy today,' he said. 'You no smile. You no like being with me?'

Paolo pulled a mock-sad face, and ran his hands through his mop of black curls.

Only a cadaver wouldn't want to be with him. Especially when he smiled.

'Of *course* I like being with you. Why else would I be doing *this*?' She slammed a long-handled spoon into the sundae ready to serve it.

What I don't like is not knowing who I really am. And I don't like that nonna could be part of my future with her sour expression and her constant crying. God, she could live forever!

'At the moment,' Fleur said, as her anger gave way to sadness, 'you're the only thing that's still real in my life.'

'I no understand,' Paolo said. He took the ice cream sundae from her. 'I serve this. You wipe tears and you tell me what made you sad later. Troubles soon over.' He gave Fleur a quick kiss on the cheek and hurried across to the waiting customer.

'Over?' Fleur said, knowing Paolo wouldn't hear her. Besides, he meant the service in the café for the day, didn't he? 'For me, it's only just begun.'

'Tell me ... that's ... not true,' Emma said. She seemed to be gasping for air to breathe.

Her legs had gone weak, and her head seemed to be spinning. All the colours in front of her were meshing into one. Caroline's face was going in and out of focus. Seth had adored Fleur, and she him. What would it do to Fleur to know Seth hadn't fathered her? She had already been devastated enough to learn that Emma wasn't her mother.

Caroline could be here simply to stir up trouble, and she was making everything up. Too much time in the film industry, if that is where she had been and that wasn't all made up too.

'I could, but that would be a lie.'

Emma picked up the sugar tongs and put a lump of sugar in her tea, even though she never took sugar. Slowly she replaced the tongs in the bowl. Even more slowly she took the teaspoon from her saucer and stirred the sugar, watching the bubbles rise and break on the surface of the liquid. Buying herself time.

'And Fleur wasn't born on July the sixteenth either.'

'Go on,' Emma said. This was becoming more farcical the more Caroline said.

'The birth certificate you have and which I am sure you've now shown Fleur, is a forgery.'

'Of course.'

Sarcasm, her mama had told her often, is a poor form of wit. But her voice had dripped with it with those two words, hadn't it?

But she'd wait until Caroline told her when it was exactly that Fleur had been born. A shiver rippled up her spine as she waited because she could remember Beattie Drew saying, the first time she'd seen Fleur, that she was a bit small for a baby that was five months old. All Beattie's babies had been twice that weight at that age. Well, Emma hadn't queried it at the time. All babies were different anyway, weren't they?

Except her own – the one she'd never had.

'Fleur was born on September the twenty-second. In Plymouth. I have the laying in bill.'

'I'm sure you have,' Emma said. She'd play along with this for the moment. Sound calm, look calm, even though she was alternating between boiling hot and freezing cold with anger and anxiety inside.

She folded her hands in her lap and waited for the next instalment.

Caroline was taking her time, too, sipping at her tea now, dabbing the sides of her mouth with a handkerchief she took from her jacket pocket.

'Have you had enough time to do the mathematics?'

'Never my strong subject,' Emma said. 'You tell me.'

Most babies were born nine months after conception, give or take the 'honeymoon' baby of those who rushed to the altar.

'Miles was, as I'm sure you've worked out by now, in prison at the time of Fleur's conception. But gaolors can be bought off. Miles's was. I'd been seeing Miles before I took up with Seth, and then when Seth finished our relationship because of you, I took up with Miles again. Seth never was a good lover.'

Oh, yes, he was. Tender, caring, considerate. And Emma didn't like him and his character being laid out before her like a slab of meat in the butcher that she might or might not want.

'You do realise don't you, Caroline, that in telling me all this I could go to the authorities. It might be an old offence but—'

'But you won't. Go to the authorities. Because then Fleur would have to know who her father really was. And you don't want that, do you?'

No. Not if I can prevent her knowing.

'You know I don't. I can't bear to think how she'd feel knowing her birth father was hanged for murder.'

Caroline smirked at her, as though she didn't give a toss about her husband having been hanged. Where and when Caroline had married Miles, Emma didn't care and certainly wasn't going to ask.

'There's no need for her ever to know. That means, of course, that I want something from you now I've found you.'

Caroline waved an arm around the room. 'Lovely silver. Beautiful furniture. Wonderfully soft carpets.' Caroline slid her foot from side to side on the best Axminster money could buy. 'Nice portraits. They must have cost a small fortune.'

'Seth painted them.'

Emma's portrait was on the left hand side of the large marble fireplace and Fleur's was on the right. In Emma's portrait she was looking sideways out of the window, at their garden back in Vancouver, a tiny landscape of its own in the background. Fleur had been ten years old when Seth had painted that particular portrait – she had at least a dozen others packed away carefully in the loft and Fleur had one in her bedroom.

'Good to know he had one talent,' Caroline said.

'Let's just cut this chit-chat, Caroline, shall we?' Emma said. 'How much – to get out of our lives again?'

Even if it means I have to give you every penny that I have, then I will. I've been poor in the monetary sense before and I could be poor again. It wouldn't kill me.

'Oh, I don't want your money. I've made quite enough of my own. Before Miles's death, and after it, although – if you ask me – half of everything *you've* got should have gone to him. And then there might not have been the need to falsify Fleur's birth certificate to make sure she wasn't denied her inheritance. The film industry pays well.'

The term 'casting couch' came to mind. Caroline was venomous trash wrapped up in expensive clothes. And the sooner Emma – and Fleur – saw the back of her the better.

'What *do* you want, then?'

'Fleur,' Caroline said, a sickly sweet smile on her face. 'I want Fleur. I want her to come back to America with me. I want her to see the life I have there. I only get given the dowager duchess parts these days, but Fleur—'

'Over my dead body,' Emma stopped her.

Caroline's smile vanished in an instant. *What an actress!*

'Miles didn't get his revenge back in 1913, or his share of his pa's fishing fleet, he—'

'It wasn't his pa's. It had been signed over to Seth.'

'Can I go on?' Caroline curled her lip in displeasure at having been interrupted. Emma gestured with the tiniest wave of a hand for her to continue

'Miles didn't get his revenge in 1913 because that interfering bastard, Matthew Caunter, got wind of his intentions. But that doesn't mean I'd fail at the same task. And trust me, I'd apply myself to it.' Caroline leaned forward in her chair and glared at Emma. Then she laughed. 'Not right at this moment. Goodness, you're shaking something dreadful, Emma.'

Well, who wouldn't be?

'Before we carry on with this conversation, Caroline, can you tell me why you want Fleur now, when you haven't so much as sent her a birthday or Christmas card before?'

'Because she's young. Because she's beautiful. Because I can see a film career stretching ahead for her. I have contacts. Contacts who can pull strings if strings need pulling. And because she is *my* daughter. Are those enough reasons for you?'

Because your own career in films is washed up, no matter how much make-up they pile on you, however much they dye your hair.

'She's a minor,' Emma reminded her.

'Tut, tut, Emma, I had you down as far more perceptive than that. If you don't agree to her coming back with me then I might just have to let slip that Seth wasn't her father. Because, you see, there are no witnesses to our conversation here today. But I can quite easily burn that laying-in bill if I have to. I am very good at setting fire to things. And besides, who's going to believe you if you go to the authorities and tell them what I've said?'

Setting fire to things? So it had been Caroline who'd

torched her bakery, hadn't it? And with that one short sentence – 'I am very good at setting fire to things' – Caroline was letting Emma know she'd done it once and she could do it again. Burn Romer Lodge to the ground and probably with her and Fleur in it.

Emma's blood seemed to freeze in her veins. This woman sitting in front of her in her fine clothes and her leather shoes, with hair expensively coiffed, putting on airs and oozing confidence was bad, mad, and very dangerous. And Emma was frightened of her. But she'd walk over hot coals and parade naked through the streets before she'd show it.

She knew now that everything Caroline was saying was more than likely true. 'Aren't we forgetting the most important person in all this?' Emma said, coolly, although where that coolness was coming from she had no idea. It was as though some other force was helping her. 'Fleur. I'll tell her you've asked to take her to America. And why. It will be up to Fleur if she decides to take you up on the film offer though.' Emma stood up.

'I'm sure she could be persuaded.'

Caroline wanted the last word, didn't she? Well, Emma wasn't going to let her have it.

'We'll have to wait and see about that. But now I'm going to have to ask you to go. I have things to do. If you give me a telephone number to ring I'll call you when I've spoken to her. But I'll leave the decision to her.'

Caroline – for now – was dismissed.

'Stella?'

'Yes,' Stella was saying in her ear. 'I did say I'd let you know if and when I had a moment for us to meet. Is this not a good time?'

Emma stared at the mouthpiece in her hand. Yes, she'd wanted to develop a friendship with Stella and had instigated the idea. But now?

'Are you still there?' Stella asked.

'Yes ... yes, I am. Sorry, it's just that I've had a bit of a shock.'

And that was the understatement of the year. Her legs had gone from under her the second she'd closed the door on Caroline. She'd fallen against the chair by the hall table and then the telephone had rung. Her thigh was still pressed painfully against the arm of the chair and she knew she'd have a bruise on it later.

'A shock? Can I help? I'm in Paignton unexpectedly free at the moment. I thought we might meet.'

Stella had stopped speaking and Emma put the mouthpiece to her lips.

Seeing Stella might be just what she needed. But not here. There seemed to be a bad feeling in the house now, as though she needed to open the windows and rid it of Caroline's evilness.

'Where are you?'

'In Torbay Road. Dellers is open I notice. We could meet there, or I could get a taxi to Romer Lodge.'

'No. I'll meet you. I can be there in ten minutes if I hurry.'

The two women shook hands and then, on impulse, Emma leaned forward and kissed Stella's cheek.

'I'm so glad you telephoned,' she told her.

'You do look a bit pale,' Stella said. 'I thought I detected a sadness around you yesterday. An atmosphere. Shall we sit?'

Am I that transparent? Emma thought as they busied themselves pulling out seats, getting comfortable. The action was giving Emma time to think about what she was going to say to Stella about what had just happened, and if she was going to say anything at all.

A waitress came to the table and they ordered tea.

'And some sandwiches,' Stella said. 'And a selection of cakes, please.'

'Of course, madam,' the waitress said, scribbling on her notebook before walking off.

'Tea and something sweet is good for shock,' Stella said, 'even though we might not feel like eating. Has something happened to your daughter? You don't have to tell me anything, of course, but ...'

'Yes. Fleur. In a way.'

Emma halted. She wasn't at all sure she should share such a serious confidence with Stella so soon in their friendship. Perhaps she should have taken the train to Brixham to see Ruby. But Ruby had her family around her and it might not have been convenient and here was Stella, unexpectedly free as she'd said. Perhaps it was meant to be.

'A nurse can be like a priest,' Stella said. 'Patients often tell us things they've never told their families, or even the doctor treating them. We don't break those confidences unless we consider the patient's life at risk.' She touched Emma lightly on her forearm.

'Thank you. I understand what you're saying.'

The waitress arrived then with a silver tray piled with cups and saucers, tea plates, a teapot, sugar bowl, and milk jug.

'I'll be back with the rest of it shortly,' she said, and hurried away again.

'I'll be mum,' Stella said. 'I hope! One day.'

Me too, Emma thought, too full up to respond immediately. She was relieved when Stella left her to her silence and set out the cups, turning the handles so they'd be easily picked up, pouring tea, adding milk.

'Fleur,' Emma said, gathering all her mental strength, 'is my stepdaughter.'

'Ah,' Stella said. 'I did wonder. You have very different looks. I hope I didn't upset you when I first came to see you and, well, we had that embarrassing conversation.'

'When you said how beautiful she is and I said she takes after her father?'

167

'Yes,' Stella said.

And that, Emma realised now, was what had made her warm to Stella. She knew now, beyond doubt, that anything she said to Stella would stay with her. She also knew that if she didn't let out all the things that were in her head then she might burst with it.

'You didn't upset me in the slightest. But her birth mother turned up yesterday. Just before you did. She was in the garden when I got back from fetching Ruby and the children from Brixham.'

Now the words had been said Emma felt better, much as a body feels better after they've been sick from eating food that's too rich, or gone off.

All the same, Emma was glad that the waitress chose that moment to return with the cakes and the sandwiches. This was a story that needed to be told, almost like a book, chapter by chapter. No, not a book, maybe just a synopsis. There would be things she couldn't tell Stella. Not yet. If ever. About how she and Seth had lived as man and wife even though it had been years before they'd married. And how she'd kept more of Matthew in her heart than it was right for a married woman to keep.

'And am I guessing correctly if I say this woman hadn't been expected? And that, perhaps, Fleur had been kept in ignorance of —'

'Yes,' Emma butted in quickly. 'It was wrong of me. Us. Seth always said he would tell her when the time was right but he died and it was left to me and I just didn't know how. But I would have.'

'You'd be surprised how many people don't know the truth of their entry into the world until they marry and need a birth certificate before they can have a marriage licence.'

'That doesn't take any guilt off me.'

'Rubbish!' Stella placed a cucumber sandwich on Emma's plate. 'As I said, I guessed something was wrong yesterday but I've also had a lot of experience of people and I'll stick my neck out here and say, given what she'd just been told, Fleur coped magnificently and in a very mature way for her age. She was wonderful with Ruby's children, wasn't she? She behaved as though she didn't have a care in the world – just a girl enjoying her sixteenth birthday tea.'

'Thank you.'

As they ate their way through the sandwiches and cakes – or rather Stella did while Emma nibbled at things, her usual excellent appetite gone for the moment – and drank cup of tea after cup of tea, Emma told Stella how Fleur had come into her life and how much she loved her. She told her how Caroline wanted to take Fleur back to America with her, get her into the film industry. And how she didn't want her to go. Stella didn't offer advice, but simply listened.

Talking had made Emma's mouth go dry, despite copious cups of tea. They ordered another pot.

'That's enough about me and my woes, I think,' Emma said. 'You said you were unexpectedly free today. And you didn't want to spend it with your fiancé?'

'I did,' Stella said. She pulled a mock-sad face. 'I telephoned him to let him know I'd swapped duties with my friend Mavis. Her mother is ill and being transferred to the Royal Devon and Exeter Hospital tomorrow and she wants to go with her. Goodness, but you don't want to know all this ...'

'I do, if we're to be friends. Go on.'

'Well, my fiancé said he had a car to deliver to Earl something or other at Powderham Castle. When people of that order want something on a Sunday they get it on a Sunday. We hardly see one another, what with my duties at the hospital and his business.'

'Then more fool him,' Emma said. 'But wait until he sees you in that wedding dress!'

'And trousseau! I'll need clothes for the honeymoon which I hope you'll have time to make for me. But it seems frivolous talking about such things given your shock today. And yesterday.'

'Not at all. I can't change anything. What's happened has happened. Talking to you has helped me think more clearly. Thank you.' Emma checked the time on her wristwatch. 'Oh my. Is that the time? I'll have to get back very soon.'

The visit from Caroline and now the unexpected meeting with Stella had put her behind with her jobs for the day. She'd need to get at least some of them done before going to fetch Fleur. She knew that Fleur would be able to stay with the Cascarinis until she was collected but it didn't pay to impose on people, did it? And in the light of Caroline turning up, and the shock revelation for Fleur, her letting Eduardo down – telling him she didn't want to go to the theatre or the cinema or out to dinner with him again – was going to be the easier option, wasn't it? And it had to be done. But perhaps not today.

'But we can meet up again?' Stella said.

'I certainly hope so.'

'If we can get our diaries to synchronise!' Stella laughed.

And then they got ready to go, split the bill, agreed that it would be easier for Emma to accommodate Stella's duties so they could meet up again, and said their goodbyes.

Her heart just a little lighter, Emma hurried back to Romer Lodge.

'But your mama, she come,' Paolo said. 'We no can go out. She say she come in car for you. She speak to Papa and she say.'

'She'll wait,' Fleur told him. 'Trust me, she'll wait.'

The second the last customer had gone and all the dirty dishes washed and put away, Fleur had told Paolo she wanted to walk down to Torre Abbey beach. She hadn't given him a chance to refuse because she'd grabbed her jacket and run for the door.

Paolo had followed but he was still protesting that they ought to have stayed and waited for her ma to collect her.

Past the entrance to the pier, Fleur hurried around little groups of people who stood chatting, or simply leaning on the railings looking out to sea, admiring the view – as though they had all the time in the world to do such things. She was holding tightly to Paolo's hand and almost dragging him along behind her.

'Is problem?' Paolo asked as at last they ran down the slope to the beach. The tide was out and the sand firm beneath their feet.

Fleur kicked off her shoes. Then she reached up inside her skirt and unfastened her suspenders. First the left leg, then the right. She rolled her stockings down to her ankles, and took them off.

'Problem? You could say that,' Fleur said. She knew she ought not to be quite so snappy with Paolo but she couldn't help it. She wasn't herself at the moment. *If* she knew what *self* that was!

Thank goodness the beach was emptying. Everyone leaving, with bags and deckchairs tucked under their arms, all going back to their hotels or their boarding houses. A small white dog with a large fluffy tail yipped excitedly at a seagull which flew off squawking.

'Your mama no like you have bare legs,' Paolo said.

'Well, she's not here to see me, is she?' was Fleur's retort. *Whichever mama that might be.*

'You have good birthday?' Paolo asked. He took Fleur's shoes and stockings from her and carried them. Had he noticed an atmosphere yesterday, if only for a little while before Ruby's children had run riot, insisting she join them in their games?

'In part,' Fleur said. 'I liked your present. No ... I *loved* your present. Thank you.'

Her pa would want her to remember her manners. *If*

he were here. She still couldn't quite believe that he hadn't thought it important enough not to tell her who had actually given birth to her!

'Is good Italian leather. And good Italian *lire*.' Paolo laughed. He put an arm around Fleur's shoulder and pulled her close.

Fleur liked that closeness. At the moment that was the only truism in her life – Paolo and the fact he wanted to be with her all the time, sometimes more often than she wanted to be with him.

'Can we walk around the edge of the cliff?' Fleur asked. 'Across the rocks.'

'We can. But your feet …'

'Good. Come on.' Fleur raced along the beach not caring how unladylike it might look to anyone watching. Who knew her here anyway?

'Sit down,' Fleur said, once they'd scrambled over the rocks and rounded the cliff. She dropped down onto a flat red rock. Sandstone her ma had said it was called. She'd never seen rock that colour before. 'I've got something to tell you.'

Paolo sat. He nibbled at the side of her neck.

Fleur shrugged him off, but reached for his hand to show him she still cared, still wanted him near her.

'Do you like my ma?' she asked him.

'*Si*. But perhaps not as much as my papa like her. Is right answer, no?'

'Probably not. What would you say if I told you she was the biggest liar on this earth?'

'Liar? You mean, *bugiarda*?'

I don't know, do I? Although she'd hazard a guess *bugiarda* was the Italian for liar. Paolo understood more than he let on he did sometimes, she was sure of that.

'She tell you one thing but is another?' he added.

'Yes. Exactly that. I'm going to tell you something and I

don't want you to tell another living person. Not even your pa.' Fleur slid her feet up towards her over the warm, flat rock and hugged her knees. 'She's not my ma. Yesterday, before you and your pa arrived at my birthday tea, another woman turned up and told me she was my ma.'

'This other woman, she lie. She burn and die in hell's fire.'

'No. Ma admitted it. She showed me my birth certificate. Only that's a lie as well because my *real* mother, Caroline, called me Rose. Pa changed it. I ... I ...'

And then the tears came as Fleur told Paolo as much as she'd been told.

Paolo held her while she cried and talked. The sun started to sink in the sky and the few clouds around were tinged with pink. It might have been beautiful and romantic if not for ... this!

He kissed her hair, and ran a hand soothingly up and down her back.

'*Cara mia*,' he said, over and over. And then, when at last Fleur had run out of things to say and had stopped crying, he said, 'What you do now?'

For answer, Fleur kissed him. Long and hard. His tongue slid into her mouth and the kiss deepened. Since the time Paolo's pa had disturbed them in the kitchen they hadn't had the opportunity to be alone much. But now? Well, now, there was no one to see them, tucked into the cliff wall with only sea in front of them, although should anyone decide to clamber over the rocks then they would be seen.

Her ma would go mad if she knew what a public spectacle she was so close to making of herself.

All that grief her ma had given her about taking a college course, or getting a job, making something of her life. Well, if she knew *who* she was she might be able to think about those things. She'd listen to what Caroline had to say – somehow she couldn't quite think of her as her mother just yet – and then she'd decide.

But right now, she'd give herself up to Paolo and his kisses. That would be a start to her finding herself, wouldn't it?

I'll call the reason for my visit a follow-up service on the car if it's not my Emma, Matthew told himself as he drove far too fast towards Paignton. The delivery of a car to Powderham Castle hadn't taken as long as he'd thought it would, and no driving instruction had been required. He had the cheque Emma had left with William in his inside jacket pocket. He had no intention of banking it until he'd made certain for himself that the Emma Jago who had signed the cheque with such familiar-to-him handwriting was *his* Emma Jago. It wasn't beyond the realms of possibility that there was another Emma Jago somewhere with similar handwriting, he knew that. He'd once spent weeks trailing a cheating husband called Ernest Spencer, who had thick fair hair, green eyes and an Irish accent, only to find he'd been trailing the wrong Ernest Spencer entirely. He'd got his man in the end, though.

Finding out where a Mrs Emma Jago was living in the Torbay area hadn't been too hard. He'd considered telephoning Eduardo Cascarini under some pretext that the cheque had been incorrectly made out and he needed to get in touch with Mrs Jago immediately. But that was underhand.

'Underhand?' Matthew laughed out loud. All his working life, until he'd bought the garage business, had been about finding things out about people by whatever means. But none of it had been done with malice – all had needed to be found for some reason; murder, fraud, infidelity, rape, smuggling. A telephone call to the rates office purporting to be a clerk at a rates office in another area had done the trick. A forwarding address for Mrs Emma Jago had been given readily enough. Romer Lodge. Cleveland Road. Mrs Jago was head of the household. One minor living with her. No servants. So far, so good. It looked as though this Mrs Emma Jago was a widow. Or, possibly, divorced. More and more women were filing for divorce these days.

Had Emma rung to ask why her cheque hadn't been banked yet he would have said he was far too busy to go into town to the bank. True enough. He *had* been busy. He'd had to pull out of escorting Stella to some birthday tea for the daughter of her dressmaker. As if that was his idea of a fun afternoon out with his fiancée? He hadn't been entirely sure that Stella had believed him when he said the Earl of Devon wanted his new car delivered the following day and there was oil to check, and the brakes to test, and all manner of things before he could release the vehicle. But it was the truth and she hadn't made a huge fuss about it. But again, that was Stella. And there had been many times she'd had to cancel lunch out, or dinner, or a drive along the coast to Plymouth because of something that had happened at the hospital.

As Matthew bowled along the road, the sun streaming through the window, the steering wheel getting hotter and hotter by the second, he amused himself by seeing how many cars he passed that he recognised because he'd sold them. Summer was always a good time for sales. A week of fine weather and people began to think how nice it would be to drive themselves up onto Dartmoor for a picnic, see the ponies, have lunch in Widecombe or Princetown without having to be tied to the timetables of the train or the omnibus or the tram. He always dropped his prices by twenty pounds or so in summer to draw customers in.

And then, *if* the Emma Jago who had written and signed the cheque in his pocket was the Emma Jago he'd never forgotten, and dreamed of frequently, he'd call on Stella on the way back to Exeter and break it to her as gently as he could that he couldn't accept her proposal of marriage after all. He would pay her for any expenses already incurred, of course – the dress, so she'd told him, was well in hand. And material had been bought for a bridesmaid dress. He didn't think Stella had put a deposit at a hotel for a wedding breakfast yet but he'd ask – and if she had then he'd pay that back, too.

No, correct that. He'd call on Stella anyway and somehow break it to her that he couldn't go through with the wedding. It wasn't fair on her that he was having the feelings he was for Emma – stronger feelings than he had for Stella. Feelings he knew he would leave a relationship, a marriage for. Stella was far too lovely a woman to have to be second best to anyone.

Ah, the Fair was on the green. He could see flags fluttering on the tops of tents as he drove down over Barcombe Heights. At Manor Road a policeman waved him across the junction and within seconds he was turning right, skirting the Tembani Hotel, past the Redcliffe, and onto the promenade. He had to drive more slowly now. There were excited children running back and forth between the beach and the green where the Fair was in full swing. He could hear the screams of people coming down the helter-skelter. The big wheel turned in a cloudless sky.

Perhaps I'll take Emma there later. After I've told Stella what it is I have to tell.

Not far now. Past the Gentlemen's Club and into Sands Road. Belle Vue Road. Turn left ...

'Christ!' Matthew had to slam on the brakes as a car shot out of a driveway. He recognised that car. He'd sold it. And the woman driving – who seemed totally oblivious to having been inches away from an accident – was definitely *his* Emma Jago. Alone.

Matthew hit the horn with his fist. He *had* to get her attention. His heart was racing madly and it was nothing to do with the near accident. It was Emma. How she affected him. How she'd always affected him.

But Emma was staring resolutely ahead, racing on down the road to the junction. Matthew almost cricked his neck turning his head to watch her go. She hadn't even stopped at the junction either although she had slowed a little. It was as though the hounds of hell were after her. Emma had always been headstrong, but he'd never known her put her life at risk. And now the lives of others were at risk with nearly two hundred pounds worth of potential killing machine in her pretty little hands.

As fast as he could, Matthew affected a three-point turn. But his car was big and with a lousy turning circle. Emma's Clyno was much nippier. By the time he got to the junction Emma's car had disappeared. Had she turned left or right into Sands Road? There were so many cars and bicycles, and even a couple of horses and drays that it was impossible to spot Emma amongst them.

'Damn and blast. Damn, damn, damn.'

He'd seen her now. He knew what he had to do. He turned left up towards the railway line and a different route back to Torquay purposely bypassing the Fair. The Fair with all its jollity and promise of happiness would do nothing to lift his mood about what he had to say to Stella and how he was going to say it. But perhaps not today.

Emma banged on the glass of the front door of Eduardo's ice cream parlour. The door was locked and there was no one inside. She ought to have kept an eye on the time. Emma knew she'd said she would collect Fleur by seven o'clock at the latest, but it was barely that now.

No answer. So she banged again, louder this time.

'He's never worth it,' a woman passing by said.

Emma turned to look at her sharply. '*She. She*'s worth it.'

Ah, *nonna* at last. The old lady plodded her way to the door and turned the key in the lock. Emma burst in.

'Where's Fleur?' she asked. *Had Caroline found Fleur*

after leaving Romer Lodge? Told her what she herself had just been told? Emma wriggled her shoulders, shrugging off unwelcome thoughts.

Nonna spread her arms wide and shrugged her shoulders. 'I no know. They here before. Eduardo make *gelato*.'

Emma had never been out the back but she soon found her way, through the kitchen, out the back door, across a yard to a long, low shed with a sagging roof. The door was open and Emma could hear Eduardo singing something – opera probably. He had a good voice. If only she had time to appreciate it. There was a strong scent of vanilla and Emma realised now that Eduardo always had that smell about him. She'd thought it was the soap he used but no, it had to be the vanilla.

'Emma!' Eduardo said as she raced in the door, knocking over a couple of empty cans that rattled noisily on the terracotta-tiled floor. He wiped his hands down the sides of his apron. 'Is big surprise.'

Eduardo kissed her on both cheeks.

'I've come to collect Fleur,' she said as calmly as she could, although goodness only knows her entrance had been rather dramatic. 'She knew I was coming. I'm only a tiny bit late. Only she doesn't seem to be here. Or Paolo.'

Eduardo's brow furrowed.

'Fleur, she not here. I think you early. Take her home early and I not see you. I no expect to see you, but now you here and I happy.'

Emma sighed. Eduardo's halting English had been quite endearing in the beginning but now it had become irritating, and that was hardly his fault. Caroline's re-appearance had changed everything. For all of them.

'*Nonna* doesn't know where they are,' Emma said, eager to get back to the issue in hand. 'I've asked her.'

'I no surprise. She sleep all time. She no think about her daughter if she sleep.'

Sad as that was to hear, she couldn't take on *nonna*'s problems, could she? 'I really need to find Fleur,' Emma said.

She was regretting spending so much time with Stella now, as helpful as the meeting had been. It had made her later than she should have been coming to collect Fleur.

'And Paolo,' Eduardo said.

He took Emma by the elbow and guided her back to the ice cream parlour and she was glad to be guided. Uppermost in her mind was that Caroline had somehow found Fleur and told her ... goodness knows what. And if she'd told Fleur that Seth wasn't her father – even if that was a lie, as Emma hoped with all her heart it was – then what would Fleur make of that? What would she do?

'I hope they haven't run away,' Emma said, shocked to realise she had actually spoken the words, not just thought them.

'And me. I no run my *ristorante* and make the *gelato* without Paolo. He come back soon. Sit, please.'

Eduardo pulled out a chair and helped Emma down into it. 'We can only wait,' he said. 'And if you want say why you so *inquieta*, I listen. If no, I make cup of good English tea, even is I Italian and coffee is the best.'

'Thank you,' Emma said. 'Tea will be lovely.' She placed her hands, palms down, on the table in front of her, steadying herself. *Stop going off into flights of fancy. Worry about things when they've happened, not before.*

Nonna seemed to have disappeared upstairs to the sleeping quarters and Emma was glad of that. Eduardo began to sing again in his native tongue. Something slow, almost like a lullaby.

Emma closed her eyes. She saw herself with Fleur as a baby in her arms, the night Caroline had dumped her in the bakery. She'd sung to Fleur then in French. À la claire fontaine ...

Eduardo brought her tea. And a slice of cake. It smelled of almonds. She didn't think she'd be able to eat another thing, even though she'd only nibbled at the sandwiches and cakes in the café with Stella. But she'd have a little taste at the very least because Eduardo was being kind.

'*Olio d'oliva*,' he said. 'And, how you say, *mandoria*?'

'Almonds,' Emma said. That had to be what he meant. She pulled off a few crumbs and put them in her mouth. Yes, definitely almonds. How good and kind Eduardo was. He would be a wonderful husband for someone. Kind and loving. Handsome, too.

'We go cinema? You and me? Dinner at Imperial?'

'I can't think about that right now,' Emma said. 'I'm sorry.'

Perhaps it had been a mistake inviting him to Fleur's birthday party. A family event. Had he had it in his mind to combine the two families? The way Eduardo was looking at her now told her he more than likely was.

'I understand. Things that are *bella* are worth to wait. I wait. For you I wait.'

No not for me. I'll have to tell him. Now?

But then the door opened and Fleur and Paolo were filling the space, Fleur looking rather dishevelled Emma thought. The fabric of her dress was creased and Emma didn't want to begin to imagine how that had happened, because the overriding feeling she had was relief – relief that Fleur had returned.

'Ah, there you are,' Emma said.

'I'm not that late,' Fleur said. 'You said seven.'

'And it's gone half past now,' Emma told her. She knew her voice had come out sharper than she had meant it to. 'I was concerned for you. For your —'

'Are you going to be checking up on me all the time now?' Fleur snapped at her.

'No. But, in the light of yesterday and today, I—'

'Come in, come in,' Eduardo butted in. He rushed forward, pulling the two young people into the room and Emma was glad of the diversion.

Emma stood up, ready to go.

'I've told Paolo,' Fleur said. 'What I know so far. Does *he* know?' She jerked her head towards Eduardo, and folded her arms across her chest, tucking her hands in under her armpits.

She looked so frightened, and yet angry at the same time. *To go to her and envelop her in her arms or not? Would that embarrass her further?* As though sensing Fleur's distress, Paolo put an arm around her shoulders.

'Eduardo and I haven't been talking about you, no,' Emma said. 'But we must go now, you and I.'

'I no understanding,' Eduardo said.

'You go with your mama now,' Paolo said. 'I tell my papa what is happen. You must do what your mama say.'

Fleur's shoulders shuddered. She leaned her head against Paolo's shoulder and then took it away again. She slipped out from under his protective arm.

Emma went to her then.

'Don't hug me,' Fleur hissed at her under her breath. 'I might cry.'

And so, Emma thought, might I. But this wasn't the place to be airing their private business. Home, Romer Lodge, was the place for that. But even then she'd have to think very carefully about what she was going to tell Fleur about what Caroline had said.

Chapter Thirteen

'You can't come in, Mr Caunter,' the nursing sister blocking the doorway to the house Stella shared with four other nurses said. 'No men allowed.'

'I don't want to come in. I merely asked if I might see Staff Nurse Stella Martin.'

Matthew had put off calling to see Stella but he couldn't drag his feet over the matter any longer. And he was here now and no one was going to turn him away.

'And I, I'm afraid, have said you can't.'

The sister folded her arms across her skinny chest but held them, sharp elbows sticking out in front of her, like a shield. Formidable was the word that sprang to mind.

Matthew didn't think for a second that Stella might have told the sister to turn him away should he turn up, although he realised now that was what he would deserve.

A nurse came down the corridor towards the front door and the sister was forced to step to one side to let her go past, cape swinging, hair piled inside her starched cap. She smiled at Matthew as she passed, but Matthew struggled to smile back.

'Nurse Martin is off duty,' Matthew said. 'I know that. She gave me a list with her days off on it, although I know that can change. She is off duty, isn't she?'

'Yes.'

'And in?'

'Yes.'

'Then I'd like to see her.'

'She's resting.'

'Is she ill?'

'She's indisposed. But it's not hospital policy to divulge to anyone other than close relatives why that should be.'

'And if I'm a doctor ...'

'Which you're not. Nurse Martin has told me you own a garage business. And I do hope you realise you are depriving the nursing world of a most excellent nurse in marrying her.'

Which I'm not going to be now. Whether Emma wanted him or not wasn't the issue here. Stella was a thoroughly decent woman and while he was going to tell her what she probably didn't want to hear, he had to – she deserved a husband's full love and not a portion of it.

'I wasn't aware I had to ask your permission,' Matthew said. He'd met some cold-hearted, immovable people in his time and this woman was up there with the worst of them.

'Sister!' someone yelled down the stairs. 'Can you come. It's Stella, she—'

The sister turned to look towards the voice, and Matthew took advantage of her distraction. He raced past her and up the stairs. While he might not love Stella as a fiancé should, he did care for her deeply. The alarm in the voice calling for the sister told him something was seriously wrong.

'In here,' the nurse at the top of the stairs said, ushering him into a room that had two single beds in it. Stella, her face scarlet, her hair wet with perspiration, lay in one, groaning and writhing. She'd kicked off the cover and her nightdress had ridden up almost to her waist, exposing naked flesh. Her legs were juddering as though there was an electric current pulsing through them at intervals.

'Are you the new doctor?' the nurse said.

'No, he isn't,' the sister answered for him. 'Cover Nurse Martin, nurse,' she instructed.

'I can do it,' Matthew said.

How thin Stella was. Did she get enough to eat in this godforsaken place? How loveless it must be if the sister was an example of the human nature she was amongst. He reached for the cotton sheet and covered Stella's modesty. But she kicked it off again.

'Go for Dr Taylor, nurse.' The sister barked her orders. 'And you can go with her,' she said, turning to Matthew.

'I don't think so,' Matthew said. He'd never forgive himself if he left now and Stella were to die with this harridan of a sister to hold her hand – or not – in her dying moments, if that was what Stella was having. Her moans were animal-like in their depth and intensity now and a shiver of real fear went through him. He'd seen plenty of people die, or dead, but he'd not been close to any of them, and this felt very different. 'I'll stay until the doctor arrives and I'm told what is wrong.'

'Sister …?' the nurse began.

'Go!' Matthew said. 'Please.'

The nurse did as she was told.

'What's wrong with her?' Matthew asked.

'A fever of some sort,' the sister said.

'Well, ten out of ten for perspicacity,' Matthew said. A facetious remark but what the hell, this woman hadn't so much as laid a finger of comfort on Stella or spoken to her.

'She's very thin,' the sister said.

Stating the obvious. Some people were naturally thin and he believed Stella was one of them – certainly, if the amount of food she ate when he took her out for a meal was anything to go by.

'Then she can't afford to sweat off any more flesh, can she?'

There was a basin in the corner of the room and Matthew marched over to it, swiped a towel hanging from a rail on the side and ran it under the tap. He wrung it out slightly.

'Don't meddle,' the sister said, when Matthew returned to the bed and began to tap the damp cloth gently on Stella's forehead.

'Don't try and stop me,' Matthew barked at her.

The action of the towel pressed to her forehead quietened Stella, and the moaning stopped. The shock of the cold water? Matthew neither knew nor cared because at least he had got a reaction from her. Holding the damp towel to her forehead with one hand, he placed his other hand on Stella's wrist. She had a pulse, fast and flickering, but there.

Everything happened fast then. The doctor arrived, the nurse who'd fetched him following in his wake. If the doctor was surprised to see Matthew in the nurses' quarters he didn't show it.

Stella's eyelids fluttered and for a second Matthew thought she might be opening her eyes so he leaned over her.

'I'm here,' he said. 'Matthew. We'll get you well.'

And then what? I'll make you feel like hell all over again when I tell you I'm breaking off our engagement?

'Sister?' the doctor said. 'A moment.'

'Certainly, doctor,' came the reply.

The doctor and sister walked away from Stella's bed towards the window. They turned their backs on Matthew and even though his hearing was pin-sharp he couldn't catch a word of what they were saying. It was probably all medical information anyway.

The young nurse pulled up a chair and sat on the opposite side of the bed to Matthew, her back to the window.

'I'm Betty,' she whispered. 'Stella's been out of sorts for a couple of days now. She was made to do a double shift and was nearing the end of it when she started to shake. Like she was having a fit,' she said, her voice louder now.

'That will do, nurse!' the sister said. 'You may go down into the nurses' sitting room and wait there.'

'Yes, sister.' She stood up scraping her chair on the bare boards, and Matthew wondered if she might have done it on purpose to make a noise so as to rouse Stella.

'And do it quietly.'

Betty gave Matthew the briefest of smiles. 'Yes, sister,' she said. And then she scurried out the door.

A fit? Matthew had seen people fitting before but usually they simply slept after it. He'd never known a fitting person to have a fever afterwards.

'And you are?' the doctor asked, not looking at Matthew. He took Stella's pulse, put his stethoscope to her chest. Then he opened her mouth and put two fingers in, sliding his fingers this way and that. He took a thermometer from his jacket pocket, took it from its case and placed it under Stella's armpit.

'Matthew Caunter. Stella and I are engaged.'

'Then, perhaps, Mr Caunter, you could go and join Nurse Donnelly downstairs in the nurses' sitting room.' He smiled at Matthew as he spoke and his voice was kindly enough. Good at gauging people's character, Matthew knew a good man when he saw one. 'I'll speak to you before I go.'

'Doctor, I don't think—' the sister began.

Doctor Taylor silenced her. 'I doubt very much whether Nurse Donnelly's honour will be at stake in the circumstances, do you, sister?' He turned to Matthew and laid a hand on his shoulder. 'I need to do a few more intimate checks, Mr Caunter. But I think Nurse Martin is going to be on the receiving end of hospital care, not the giver of it, tonight. And possibly for some little while to come.'

And God help her if this sister is doing the caring, Matthew thought.

'I feel as though I'm two people at the moment,' Fleur said. 'No, make that three.'

She and Emma were sitting across from one another at the table in the kitchen. Fleur had her hands clasped around her second cup of hot cocoa, even though the July night was warm, and hardly cocoa weather. But it was comforting, and Fleur had asked for it. Emma had been happy to oblige, especially as she'd added, 'Please, Ma,' on the end of her sentence.

'Three?' Emma asked. Two she could understand – the Fleur who thought she, Emma, was her mother and the Fleur who now knew that Caroline was.

'I'm a daughter, a stepdaughter, and a girlfriend. And I don't know which of those I like best.'

'You're still Fleur.'

'Am I? Aren't I really called Rose?'

'Legally, yes. But your pa didn't get given a chance to know Caroline was expecting you and he didn't get a chance to choose your name either. So when Caroline decided she didn't want to bring you up, your pa heard me say "Fleur" when I was rocking you to sleep, and he liked the sound of it. So he had your name changed.'

'I like Fleur better than Rose,' Fleur said. '*If* Pa was the one who chose that.'

'He was. But it's getting late. We ought to be getting to bed. I've got lots of sewing work tomorrow and—'

'And that's more important than *me!*'

'No. You know that's not true, Fleur. You know I'd give it up in a heartbeat for you if that was what is needed.'

Emma yawned. She couldn't stop herself. She was physically and emotionally spent now. It seemed that she and Fleur were having the same conversations day in, and day out – and often late into the night, as now – about Caroline's visit. Although Emma knew she couldn't tell Fleur all that Caroline had said about Miles being her father, not Seth. It could all be a lie. She hoped it was. But she had told Fleur on the drive back from the ice cream parlour to Romer Lodge that Caroline was waiting for a telephone call to let her know when Fleur was ready to see her. Fleur had said she would let Emma know when she was. So far she hadn't. But it was early days.

'You haven't asked why I was late getting back to the ice cream parlour.' Fleur's voice was challenging now. 'Don't you want to know?'

But that was days ago, although obviously Fleur was still disturbed about it for some reason.

'You were with Paolo. You came back safely. I think, Fleur, that's as much as I need to know.'

No, it's not. Not really. I want to know if you made love, but it's not my place to ask.

'Suit yourself,' Fleur said, but her eyes glittered with tears in the light from the lamp on the kitchen dresser.

'If you want to tell me, you can,' Emma said. 'And if you want to see Caroline then I'll telephone her and let her know.'

'No! Not yet. I'm going to bed now.' Fleur took her cup to the sink, rinsed it out and upended it. 'I'm not ready for that yet.'

And neither am I.

'Goodnight, Ma,' Fleur said, and then before Emma could respond she fled from the room.

Ma. She'd said Ma. No kiss goodnight as she had almost every night of her life, but the bonds between them were still there, weren't they? Not severed yet.

But there was one thread, if not a bond exactly, in her life that Emma was going to have to cut. And very soon.

Chapter Fourteen

'I'm sorry, Eduardo,' Emma said again. She had her hands clasped over her handbag on her lap. She'd felt the way she imagined a judge might feel sending a man – or a woman – to the gallows when she'd told Eduardo she didn't want to see him any more. He'd not taken it kindly. She'd been putting off this encounter but she had to do what she knew in her heart was the right thing. She felt much as she imagined her papa had felt when their cat had had kittens and none of the neighbours wanted one, and he'd had to drown them. He'd put it off and put if off, but the deed had had to be done in the end.

'Tell me is a funny,' Eduardo said.

A funny? Ah, he meant a joke.

'No, it's not a joke,' Emma told him. 'I've been thinking about this for a while now. I don't want you to think that we – you and I – might have a future together, based only on a few visits to the theatre and the cinema, and dinner out in hotels a few times.'

'But you no husband and me no *donna*.'

Emma, despite the sadness of the occasion – for Eduardo at least – was finding it hard not to laugh at his less than mastery of the English language.

'That's hardly the basis for a marriage. I like you, Eduardo, very much. But I don't love you. And I know, deep in my heart, I will never love you the way a wife should love a husband.'

A future husband. Because Matthew fills that space in my head and my heart.

Eduardo's eyes filled with tears. He looked, Emma thought, like a baby fawn – all dark eyes in a small head.

'Fleur she need man. Man who be like papa to her. I be that papa.'

'No. Fleur had the best papa in the world. She doesn't need another. His love and guidance of her will be with her always.'

And may that be true now Caroline is back in the picture.

Eduardo shrugged. 'I do many things for you.'

'I've never asked you to do anything for me. You offered. I'm not beholden.'

Gosh, this was harder than she'd ever imagined it would be. It wasn't as though they had even kissed – apart from the double-cheek kiss of greeting – or held hands, or shown any passion for one another, was it?

'I no understand. Be what? I no hold anything that is yours.'

Emma took a deep breath. 'That isn't important. And I must go now. I didn't want to telephone you to tell you, but please, from now on when and if we see one another it will only be because our children are friends. Nothing more.'

Emma spoke slowly and clearly. She didn't think she could rustle up the energy to explain it all over again. She stood up. She considered shaking hands to say goodbye, if only out of manners, but decided against it. In her head she saw a scenario where Eduardo pulled her towards him, wrapped her in his arms, kissed her. Begged her not to end their friendship.

'Goodbye, Eduardo.' She headed for the door of the ice cream parlour, opened it, closed it behind her.

And she didn't look back.

For two days Matthew was allowed to sit by Stella's bed for half an hour, twice a day, but that was all. Influenza had been suspected as it was rife in the area, and he'd been advised not to visit but he'd ignored the advice. He'd spent half a lifetime in areas swimming with typhoid and worse and he'd never picked up a thing. Stella's fitting had been put down to her high temperature. Most of the childhood diseases – chickenpox, measles, German measles – had been considered as a reason for Stella's malaise and all had been discounted. Whatever was causing Stella to be so ill had opened up an avenue for pneumonia to set in.

Matthew didn't go far from the hospital, booking himself into a hotel so he could be reached should Stella take a turn for the worse, although how much worse she could get without dying he couldn't imagine. He left William in charge of the garage but instructed him not to make any more sales in his absence. He told William he could take a deposit and then Matthew would follow up the possible sale once Stella was conscious.

The sister who'd been in the nurses' accommodation the day Stella had been taken ill, treated him with indifference. She could barely bring herself to be civil to him – it was as though she blamed him for whatever was wrong with Stella. Well, that suited Matthew – she was never going to be his bosom buddy, was she? As long as she was professional and cared for Stella as she should that was as much as they needed to be in one another's lives.

Oh God, there the dragon of a sister was, standing at the top of the steps in the open doorway of the hospital entrance. As though she'd been waiting for him. She'd have known he would arrive for two o'clock, and his allotted half hour.

'In my office,' she barked at him as he reached her.

Silently Matthew followed her down the corridor. The smell of antiseptic stung his nostrils – how did medical people ever get used to it? They both had to squeeze against the wall as a porter pushed a bed with a very large woman on it towards them. A nurse scurried past holding a bedpan covered with a cloth at arm's length. The sister said something he didn't catch – possibly not to him anyway.

Besides what was there to say to her? The expression on her face had been angry rather than sad when she'd spoken to him, and Matthew knew the difference.

'Close the door behind you,' she snapped at him.

Matthew did it as slowly and as quietly as he could. Then he sat before being asked to do so.

'I take it you have news of Stella for me,' he said. His heart speeded up a little but a couple of deep breaths sorted it. He'd been in worse situations.

'Nurse Martin has insisted I tell you. She was operated on today. You could have *killed* her.'

'Killed her? How?'

'Don't come the innocent with me, Mr Caunter. You and Nurse Martin are engaged. She goes to Exeter to visit you. She—'

'What, exactly, are you implying?'

He had an inkling that whatever was wrong with Stella related in some way to her womb but if she was pregnant, or had had a miscarriage, then it was some other man who was responsible, not him.

'Nurse Martin has been under too much pressure, by you, to marry,' the sister continued through pursed lips. 'That pressure has encouraged an underlying disorder to manifest itself. There has been a rupture and haemorrhage. We are lucky to still have Nurse Martin with us.'

The sister couldn't meet Matthew's eye and instead shuffled bits of paper around on her desk.

'So, she came through the operation,' Matthew said, knowing he was stating the obvious.

'Yes. She's regained consciousness but has pneumonia. Pleurisy is also suspected. She can barely breathe without chronic pain.'

'But she's alive. That's a good starting point. She's of strong spirit. She'll pull through.'

'Excellent nursing care pulled Nurse Martin through.'

'I'd like to see Stella now,' he said. 'And that is not a question. I'm not asking you if I may. I will see her regardless of whether or not you want me to.'

'Don't you think you've done her enough harm? Nurse Martin is going to take months to get over this. Months. Her parents have been informed. They'll be here to see their daughter ...' the sister checked the watch pinned to her uniform. ' ... in about ten minutes if the train is on time.'

'Well then, if Stella is well enough to see her parents, she's well enough to see me. I'll see myself out. I know the way.'

Stella's eyes opened as Matthew touched his lips lightly to her forehead.

'Have you been here all the time?' she asked. Her voice sounded hoarse. And God, her skin ... like alabaster. Her eyes seemed to have sunk into her head, and her lips were almost white.

'Not all the time,' he said. 'Dragon sister only let me sit with you for half an hour twice a day when you were in and out of consciousness. But I've been staying in a hotel in Avenue Road.'

'Oh,' Stella said, her voice weak. 'The garage—'

'Is in William's capable hands.'

'Oh,' Stella said again.

Her hands were underneath the thin coverlet and Matthew wondered if he ought to fish one out and hold it. If that was what she was expecting of him. He'd been in some strange and frightening situations but never this. A woman who loved him, but whom he didn't love enough to marry had almost died. Soon – very soon – he was going to have to ask to be released from their engagement. It would serve him right if she took him to the highest court in the land for breach of promise.

Matthew cocked his head to one side to see if he could

hear the sister coming down the corridor – somehow her heels clicked louder than anyone else's, and more rapidly. But all he could hear was rain beating against the window – it suited his mood. And a door banging somewhere. Someone screamed out in agony not far away.

'I'll need to put on a bit of weight before my wedding dress will fit,' Stella said, her voice barely above a whisper.

'Oh.' Matthew's turn to use that one little word that could convey so much depending on how it was spoken.

A tear escaped from the corner of Stella's eye. She let it fall, not taking her hands from under the coverlet to wipe it away.

Matthew felt in the pocket of his trousers for a handkerchief, pulled it out. And with it came Emma's necklace, the chain caught around his middle finger.

In all the years he'd been carrying it around this had never happened before. Why now? *Why the hell hadn't he left it locked away in the top drawer of his desk?* No, he knew the answer to that. He'd hoped, beyond hope almost, that Emma would welcome him with open arms and then he'd place the amethyst around her neck as he'd promised, back in 1913, he would one day. Had she not come hurtling out of her drive when she had it could have been around her neck at this moment. Except it wasn't. And Stella's eyes were on it, just as his were.

He saw her gulp. She squeezed her eyes shut as though she was in pain, then opened them again. Her eyes on Matthew now.

'I'd like to think that beautiful necklace might be for me, but I don't think it is, is it?'

'What makes you think that?' he asked quickly.

His sharp thinking was back – it hadn't deserted him while he'd been doing a safer job selling cars.

'It would be in a box, surely, if it were a gift?'

Her voice, Matthew thought, was stronger now. She was

no longer in need of a handkerchief to wipe her eyes either. What could he read into that, if anything?

'It belonged to … my … mother,' he said, merely mouthing the word 'my'. 'She was a wonderful woman. It keeps me close to her having this to hand.'

Lies, lies, all lies. But were they? Wasn't he simply laying a smoke trail? And Stella would never guess that it was Emma who was a wonderful woman to him, would she?

'Then hadn't you better put it away?'

Matthew unwound the chain from his finger, cupped the necklace in the palm of his hand and slid it back into his pocket.

'The operation I had,' Stella said with a sad smile. 'The influenza was a lucky accident for me. It threw up other things.' She placed the palm of her hand over where Matthew imagined her stomach to be. 'I'd always hoped that I would have a family of my own but now that is going to be impossible. If it's what you want, then …'

Another gulp. A forced bright smile. *How stoic she is*, Matthew thought.

'You do understand what I am saying, Matthew?'

'I've never considered it, either way, until now.'

That much at least was true.

'Then perhaps we ought to have spoken about it before. And perhaps now is the time to think about it?' She gave Matthew a sweet smile. 'Oh, no. Here's sister coming.'

'I heard the clacking heels,' Matthew said. His salvation. He never thought he'd be pleased to see the woman but he was now. This wasn't the place or the time to tell Stella that their relationship was over. *What sort of a rat would do that!* But he wasn't in love with her. He was certain of that now. One glimpse of Emma Jago and her beautiful features set in concentration racing down the hill had told him that.

'That's quite enough time with Nurse Martin in the

circumstances,' the sister said. 'Her parents are waiting in the corridor outside.'

'Then I won't make them wait a second longer,' Matthew said. He leaned down to kiss Stella on the forehead again.

'You can go back to Exeter now,' Stella told him. 'I'm going to live.'

But not with me. God, but he was hating himself more by the second. Whipping and flogging would be too kind.

Still her hands were under the coverlet.

'I think I must,' Matthew said. 'I'll come again—'

'At authorised visiting hours,' the sister snapped. 'And only if I consider Nurse Martin fit to see visitors.'

'Get well, sweet Stella,' Matthew said, with a quick, contemptuous glance at the sister – I'll visit with or without your permission that glance said. He dropped another kiss on Stella's forehead. 'Get well.'

He wished her nothing less.

Chapter Fifteen

AUGUST 1927

Although it was now a fortnight since Fleur had gone missing with Paolo, Emma was still uneasy when she was out of her sight. She remembered waiting anxiously for Fleur to return to the Cascarini ice cream parlour and now felt a dreadful fear every time Fleur went out that she would never come back.

'Ma! The telephone?' Fleur shouted from upstairs.

Had she been so deep in thought she hadn't heard it? Almost always, the second it rang, Emma raced to it to snatch it from its cradle in case it was Caroline. So far Emma hadn't rung Caroline to arrange a meeting between her and Fleur. Fleur wasn't – in Emma's opinion – ready for that yet and had said as much herself. Since Caroline's surprise, and rather shocking, visit, Emma had told Fleur over and over as much as she knew about Seth's and Caroline's time together. Fleur had also walked out with Paolo and talked it all through with him over and over again, so she'd said. Fleur admitted that with each telling she was beginning to believe it a little bit more. What Paolo thought of it all and what advice he'd given Fleur, Emma couldn't guess at and didn't like to ask.

Caroline hadn't rung Emma either, not that Emma had given her her number, but if Bettesworth had been so unprofessional as to give Caroline Emma's address he would probably have no guilt at giving out her telephone number as well, or finding it from somewhere.

'Shall I answer it?' Fleur asked, coming into the kitchen, wrapped in a dressing gown that had once been Emma's – pink shantung with apple-green embroidery on the lapels. How young she looked, how beautiful. And how vulnerable.

The telephone was in the hallway down the end of the corridor.

'Ma, are you all right?'

No, not really. When it began to get dark and you weren't at the ice cream parlour as I'd expected you to be, it was like the time you'd been snatched from me as a baby in the churchyard of St Mary's. The night Margaret Phipps beat me black and blue and for which she'd been incarcerated in an asylum, deemed too mad to face charges of abduction and assault and battery.

Still the telephone rang on – and still only seven-thirty in the morning.

Emma shook her head to banish the bad thoughts.

'I'll answer it,' she said. 'It might be Tom calling to say he can't come in today.'

Tom had been wonderful about protecting Emma as much as he could. And Ruby had caught the train over twice and called in to check that Emma was all right. She'd come on the pretext of buying things for the children for school from Rossiters but Emma had known that it was just so she could see for herself that her friend was fine. Tom was almost always at Romer Lodge about now. Emma had bought him a bicycle so he could cycle over in fine weather. If it was wet, he'd get the train. Today was fine. Yes, it might be Tom seeing as he wasn't here yet.

Emma hurried down the passageway to the hall. She snatched up the telephone. 'Hello. Emma Jago.'

'And about time, too.'

Caroline Prentiss – or Jago, as she now claimed. Emma resisted the urge to slam the telephone back on its rest.

'Time is mine to do with as I choose,' Emma said. She wondered how Caroline had got hold of her telephone number but wasn't going to waste breath asking. She could even have seen it on one of Emma's advertisements for her dressmaking business, she knew that.

'Then perhaps you could choose to let me speak to my daughter.'

'In person, not on the telephone,' Emma said. 'And I will be present.' The first time at least. After that it would be up to Fleur, but Emma owed it to Seth to protect her. 'And I will require evidence. If I say *September* you will know what I mean.'

'Ah, little ears are listening, since you are speaking in code?'

'Fleur is here, yes.'

Although not standing next to me. Emma could hear Fleur crashing about in the kitchen doing something with pots and pans. A cupboard door was slammed shut.

'So, when?'

'This afternoon. At the Cliff Hotel. Three o'clock,' Emma said, the words coming to her as though she was reading from a script, or someone else was putting them into her mouth.

But now she'd said them, she knew it would be best to have the conversation they were going to have in a public place.

'Don't be late.'

Emma winced as Caroline slammed the telephone down. She'd had the last word. *Well, let her – she isn't going to get her daughter back if I've got anything to do with it.*

The post shot through the letterbox then and Emma bent to pick up half a dozen letters or so. One from the bank. She put that on the top and went into the sitting room, found the paper knife and slit open the envelope.

What? The balance was higher than it should have been, given she'd paid for lots of fabrics and notions in Beare's and bought a car from Exe Motors.

Emma scanned the bank statement. Exe Motors hadn't banked her cheque yet. She would have to ring and ask why not. How could she keep an eye on her finances if others were so slapdash about presenting cheques?

Something else to deal with. But small fry in the scheme of things considering what might come out in conversation this afternoon.

Emma fixed a smile on her face and went back to the kitchen.

'That was Caroline, Fleur,' she said. 'She wants to meet you.'

'When?'

Fleur didn't sound frightened at the thought, which gave Emma encouragement to present her with the fait accompli, although she would cancel the meeting if Fleur was dead against it.

'This afternoon. Are you ready for that?'

'I can't put it off forever, can I?'

'No, *we* can't. I've said I'll be there with you.'

'All right,' Fleur said, although Emma thought she sounded as though it was anything but really.

'So,' Emma said. 'I've got a lot of sewing jobs to do before I can go out anywhere, I'd better get on.'

She wasn't going to let her business suffer because of this.

Caroline was already waiting at the Cliff Hotel when Emma and Fleur arrived. Emma gave their names to the receptionist and ordered tea for three, and he pointed them in the direction of the conservatory.

'Mrs Jago is through there, Mrs Jago,' he said, and the strangeness of the sentence brought a smile to his face. He sucked in his cheeks in an effort, Emma guessed, to stop himself laughing.

'That sounds a bit odd,' Fleur said.

The whole situation is odd. Emma had woken in the night, every night, since Caroline had turned up, finding it hard to get back to sleep each time. Not for the first time she wondered if Caroline would have come looking for her daughter had Mr Bettesworth not been indiscreet in his professional dealings.

Caroline rose from the wicker couch on which she was sitting, back to the window, the second she saw Emma and Fleur – as though she was holding court.

'Just about on time,' she said.

Emma chose not to comment. She was a couple of minutes in hand and they both knew it. She waited for Caroline to offer a hand in greeting, but the gesture didn't come. Well, Emma certainly wasn't going to instigate the niceties.

'I have a present for you, darling,' Caroline said, bending to pick up an elaborately wrapped package from the floor. 'I've had to guess your size.'

Darling? Obviously the endearment's not directed at me, Emma thought. But 'guess the size' – what could Caroline have bought Fleur?

'Shall we sit?' Emma said, when Fleur seemed reluctant to step forward and take the present. It wasn't quite a question – more an informed suggestion.

'Present first,' Caroline said.

A waiter came in with the tea and his presence galvanized Fleur into action. She took a few steps forward and reached out to take the present from Caroline's outstretched arms.

'Thank you,' Fleur said.

'Open it,' Caroline ordered.

'I'd like to do it in private,' Fleur replied. She turned and put the present down on a chair.

That's my girl! Don't let her start ordering you about, even if she is your mother. A bit late in the day for that!

Emma sat, hoping Caroline would follow her lead. She set the cups upright on the saucers and began to pour the tea.

'Milk in second,' she said, looking up at Caroline.

See, I've remembered. I've remembered you told me that a fortnight ago. Always try and make a friend of your aggressor – Matthew Caunter had told her that once, many years ago now. And he ought to know – he'd had enough aggressors in his time through his work for His Majesty's Customs.

Emma tried to smile but the smile wouldn't come. She was terrified of Caroline and her potential for danger. Criminal deeds. Murder even.

Emma handed Caroline a cup of tea. She took it without thanks or acknowledgement, and Emma hoped that Fleur would notice the lack of manners.

'I'd like to ask you some questions,' Fleur said as Caroline sipped at her tea.

Hah! She's wrong-footed you, Emma thought, seeing the surprise in Caroline's eyes. A mouth full of tea, she could hardly protest, could she?

'Why, when you turned up at our house on my birthday, didn't you bring me a present then? Seeing as you knew it was my birthday.'

Emma almost stopped breathing. What would Caroline say? The truth – that it wasn't actually Fleur's birthday? She was born in September? That the birth certificate Seth had been given was a forgery?

'I wanted to see you first. See how you'd grown. If you were as tall as I am. Your colouring.' Caroline's words came out pat. If she'd made them all up on the spur of the moment then she was a better actress than Emma had given her credit for. 'I see you have your father's colouring, not mine. But you're tall. Like *me*.'

And taller than I am. After Seth's death Fleur had started to grow like a weed. Emma had been forever letting down hems of dresses and coats, or making new ones. Fleur had often joked that she was going to be at least a foot taller than Emma and Emma's response had always been, 'I wouldn't be at all surprised. Your pa was tall.' Fleur had been happy with that. Until now.

'And another thing I want to know,' Fleur said, 'is why you never sent me anything for all my other birthdays. Not even a card on July the sixteenth before now.'

'I didn't know where you were living,' Caroline said. 'Your father moved and left no forwarding address with anyone.'

Yes, and you were the reason for that. You and Miles. Only Seth's trusted friend, Olly Underwood, and the bank manager – Seth had kept an account in England to collect the peppercorn rent for Shingle Cottage – had known how to contact him. And Ruby – Ruby had known.

'Ma says you dumped me on a table amongst all the cooking things. Is that true?'

Ma, not Emma. She's still thinking of me as her mother. Emma's heart thumped in her chest – anxiety mixed with excitement at Fleur calling her Ma still.

'Yes. I didn't know what else to do at the time.'

Caroline glanced at Emma as she spoke – just for the briefest of moments – before making eye contact with Fleur again.

'I don't know how a mother could leave her child with another woman,' Fleur said. 'Do you, Ma?'

Fleur wants me on her side! Emma could barely breathe now. Or speak.

'Your ma, as you call her, has never had a child to know whether she would or wouldn't leave that child,' Caroline said, before Emma could find her voice.

Emma winced at her words. Caroline was only guessing that Emma had never had a child – she couldn't have known for certain. And what if Emma had had a child and lost it? How cruel her words would have been then.

But not for the want of trying to have a child, Emma thought.

'Pa always said I was everything to him. He didn't need another child.'

Yes, Seth had said that. It was one of the things she and Seth had agreed upon to say when Fleur got old enough to question why she had no brothers and sisters. Emma was heartened now that Fleur had remembered his words and was – in a roundabout way even if she didn't realise it herself – letting Caroline know she'd been loved and cared for.

Emma's heart was in her mouth now. Was Caroline about to tell Fleur that Seth wasn't her father – Miles was?

'You *are* very special,' Caroline said.

The creep!

'So special,' Caroline went on, 'that I'd like to take you back to America with me. I want to show you off to all my friends so they can see what a beautiful daughter I have. I'll be sailing on the eighteenth of August. From Liverpool. Do say you'll come. And I hope you will because I've already booked your passage.'

Once Caroline got Fleur to America what would she tell her then, without Emma around to cushion the blow? *How long will it take for Caroline to poison Fleur against me?*

And then, as though sealing the deal, Caroline said, 'I'm in films. Wouldn't you want to be part of all that?'

'Films?' Fleur replied. 'Like Clara Bow, and … oh, how exciting!' Fleur clapped her hands together. But then she looked serious again. 'I don't know anything about acting.'

'Neither did I to begin with,' Caroline told her. 'But I met a director at a party and he took me under his wing. He paid for me to go to classes to learn the rudiments of acting. And dancing. He—'

'Dancing?' Fleur interrupted.

She shot Emma a glance – don't tell me off for interrupting like you usually do, please, the glance said. Emma was desperate to warn Fleur against being influenced by Caroline's words – true or false. But all Emma could do was resign herself to listening to Caroline bragging – and possibly lying – about her film career. And she hoped with all her heart that Fleur wouldn't be seduced by it all.

Not now. Not ever.

'A holiday, Ma. It could be like a holiday.'

Fleur unwrapped Caroline's present to her the second they got back to Romer Lodge. Underwear. Lots and lots of very expensive, very frilly underwear. Fleur was delighted with it although Emma knew it wasn't new because there were no price tags or makers' labels hanging from it. Caroline's cast-offs without a doubt. '*Tarts' underwear*' had been the words on Emma's lips but she'd dared not voice them.

'I doubt Caroline would see it like that. She would want you to earn your keep sooner or later.'

'Films? Didn't you hear her mentioning that?' Fleur's voice oozed sarcasm, which Emma chose to ignore.

Oh, yes, I heard.

'Fleur, I know it all sounds like a dream but I doubt you'll be given the role of leading lady right away.'

'Stop pouring cold water on the idea, Ma. I want to go.'

And I don't want you to. And your pa wouldn't have wanted you to either.

Emma reached for the *Western Morning News* on the arm of the couch. She'd bought it with the idea of putting an advertisement in for her dressmaking business.

Quickly she turned the pages.

'Here. Look. Dartington Hall. It's a college. Music, art, and drama. Enrolment—'

'Dartington Hall? Where's that? In England I suppose?'

'Of course, England. It's just outside Totnes. You said yourself you know nothing about acting and if you were to take this course you could see whether or not you like it.

And then there's art. There are some photographs here of students' art work. Your pa—'

'That's blackmail, Ma. Saying Pa would want me to take art.'

'You might at least show some respect and consider it. And I might remind you that you're a minor, Fleur. You can't go to America without my permission.'

Which wasn't strictly true. Emma had never officially adopted Fleur as her daughter. If Caroline took legal advice then in all probability she would be allowed to take Fleur to America. And Emma only had Caroline's word for it that the birth certificate she'd left the day she'd dumped baby Fleur was a forgery. Caroline had yet to come up with the *real* one, if indeed it existed.

And Fleur did not – yet – know any of this.

'Well, I'm going to meet her again,' Fleur said. 'There's a note here. See.'

Fleur waggled a scrap of paper at Emma. But when Emma went to take it, Fleur clutched it to her. 'I'm old enough to decide whether I want to do that.'

Yes. She was. Emma herself had made a lot of life-changing decisions before her seventeenth birthday – almost all of them had been for the good.

'What does it say?' Emma asked. Her mouth had gone dry but she had a smile fixed to her face so firmly her jaw ached with the effort of it. She ran her tongue around her lips to moisten them.

'Wednesday. In Torre Abbey Gardens. Four o'clock. There's a café nearby and ... oh ...' Fleur had discarded the note and was scrabbling about in the bottom of the box. 'She's put in some magazines. Film magazines, Ma.' Fleur picked one up and began to flick through it. 'I wonder if she's in one of them?'

Emma would have bet her last halfpenny that she was and that that's why she'd put them in the box with the underwear. Another little carrot to dangle in front of Fleur to get her to go to America with her.

But uppermost in Emma's mind was Wednesday. How could she engineer to be in Torre Abbey Gardens on Wednesday? At four o'clock. Her list of friends and acquaintances was still so small. Ruby? Ruby would go in arms flailing ready to kill on Emma's behalf if Caroline did anything to hurt Fleur, Emma knew that. But she'd have to bring the children with her because Tom's mother wasn't well and wouldn't be able to look after them. No, she'd have to discount Ruby as an accomplice. Stella Martin, then? She could fabricate a visit to the haberdasher to look at fastenings and fixings for the headdress, couldn't she? If Stella was off duty. Emma prayed that she would be.

Stop panicking, she told herself firmly. Torre Abbey Gardens was a public place. It would be daytime. What could happen? The worst thing, in Emma's thinking, was that Caroline would tell Fleur that Seth wasn't her father and then Fleur would really have something to hate Emma for – she'd never believe that Emma didn't know that, would she?

'Oh, there's something else in here, Ma,' Fleur said.

Oh, is there? It's like Pandora's flaming box, isn't it?

'And another note.'

Emma watched as Fleur read the note and then began peeling back layers of tissue with the tips of her fingers as though she were unpeeling an onion, layer by layer, so as not to make her eyes water.

'It's a dress. And ... and ... the note says *"I don't see why you should have to wear home-made things. I never have. This is cooture"*. Only she's spelled couture wrongly – she's put two o's. I expect she wrote it in a hurry.'

Well, I don't. She's uneducated. And I'm turning into a snob. Memories of chastising Ruby for every little grammatical error were coming back to haunt her. She'd been privileged to have been born half French and to know two languages and to have been good at her lessons.

Fleur pulled the dress from its wrapping and shook out the creases and then held it against herself.

Cobalt blue fabric caught the mid-summer sun streaming in the window. Silk at a guess. Expensive. From where Emma was standing she couldn't see a seller's label on it. More than likely there wasn't one because it was one Caroline herself had worn – if only once. A second-hand dress – albeit couture, which Emma could see this one most definitely was. *Who*, she wondered, *had paid for it?* Which lover?

And why am I being so spitefully suspicious of every motive?

Although, in her heart, Emma knew exactly what Caroline was doing – she was buying Fleur off. She was saying she could show Fleur a more elegant, a richer, a more exciting life than the one she had now.

And it's my job to keep you safe. For you. For Seth. And for me.

Emma left Fleur sitting on the couch entranced by her presents and went through to her atelier to find Stella Martin's telephone number – the one at the nurses' home where she shared a room with a girl called Betty.

'Can I speak to Stella Martin if she's there, please? If not, can I leave a message to be passed on?' Emma said the second the telephone was answered.

'Who's calling?' the female voice on the other end of the telephone said.

'Emma Jago. I'm a … a friend of Stella's.'

'Oh, yes, I remember Stella talking about you. You're the lady who's making her wedding dress, aren't you?'

'Yes, I am.'

'Well, Mrs Jago, I'm Betty, and I'm afraid I've got some bad news for you. Stella was taken ill a week or so ago. She's still in hospital. As a patient.'

'Ill? What's wrong with her?'

And to be still in hospital all this time?

'I'm afraid I can't tell you that.'

'No, no, of course not. I understand. But can I visit Stella?'

'You can. Visiting is from two until half past. She's on Singer Ward.'

'Will you tell her I've called? And that I'll see her as soon as I can? Tomorrow, hopefully,' Emma said.

She knew what it was like to be ill. She'd spent months recovering from pleurisy as a young girl in the home of the odious Mrs Phipps, her illness drawn out, no doubt, by Mrs Phipps's lack of care and appropriating the food good, kind Dr Shaw had had sent for Emma's recovery.

'Of course I will. But I've really got to go now, Mrs Jago. I'm on duty in ...' there was pause and Emma guessed she was checking the time, ' ... fifteen minutes.

Goodbye,' Betty said, and the telephone line died.

What luck to have caught Betty before she left the nurses' home. Emma's mind was a flurry of all the things she had to do now before going to visit Stella tomorrow. She had a hem to take up for a lady who lived further down Cleveland Road. And supper to prepare for her and Fleur before she went out. Then she'd need to leave early so she could buy something to take to Stella – flowers and fruit, and maybe something lovely for her bath if she was allowed to have one. Emma hurried back to the kitchen to prepare some vegetables for the following day.

But one thing was certain, she wouldn't be able to ask Stella to meet her in Torre Abbey Gardens on Wednesday as cover for her covert spying on Fleur. But thinking about it now, spying on Fleur wasn't such a good idea. If Fleur were to see her it could drive the wedge that was starting to push into their relationship, even further in.

And then the telephone rang.

'Can you answer that?' Emma called out to Fleur, hoping she was somewhere within earshot.

'Will do,' Fleur answered loudly and cheerfully, obviously still over the moon with her dress from Caroline and all the fashion magazines.

Emma heard the echo of Fleur's heels clicking on the hall tiles as she ran to answer the telephone. The ringing stopped as Fleur picked it up, but she was too far away for Emma to hear what she was saying.

But she heard Fleur laugh. And why shouldn't she? She strained to catch even a word of Fleur's side of the conversation so she could try and guess who she was speaking to. She prayed it wasn't Caroline. Perhaps she ought to have wiped her hands and taken the call herself? But what with the news of Stella and the presents Caroline had given Fleur, Emma's mind was in a whirl.

As soon as these potatoes are peeled, I'll go and see who Fleur was laughing with on the telephone. Damn! She caught her thumb on the sharp point of the potato peeler. Just a nick. She stuck her thumb in her mouth and sucked hard on the globule of blood. But it did little to stem the flow, so she ran her thumb under the cold tap and at last the bleeding stopped.

'Fleur?' Emma called.

'In here.'

Fleur's voice was coming from the sitting room and Emma found her perched on the arm of a chair flicking through one of the fashion magazines that Caroline had given her. She didn't look up when Emma came into the room and Emma tried not to mind because wasn't there a big pile of magazines in her atelier for Fleur to look at if she wanted to?

'Ma? What have you done? You're dripping blood everywhere!'

Emma stared at her thumb. The exertion of walking from

the kitchen to the sitting room must have started it bleeding again.

'So I am. I cut my thumb peeling potatoes. Who was on the telephone?' Emma asked, knowing her voice had risen with her question.

'Not Caroline, if that's what you're thinking.'

Good. Although I think I'm in danger of becoming paranoid every time the telephone rings.

'I wasn't thinking any such thing,' Emma said, pressing hard against her cut with the forefinger of her other hand. 'I was just asking. It could have been a client wanting to make an appointment.'

'Well, it wasn't. It was Paolo.'

Paolo. Good. Not Caroline.

'That's nice. Are you seeing him?'

'Yes. His pa wants me to help in the ice cream parlour while Paolo does deliveries. Tomorrow afternoon. He's going to pay me. I'll be earning money. Aren't you pleased?'

Pleased? Well, of course Emma was pleased that Fleur realised money had to be earned.

'And I'm invited to supper,' Fleur said, when Emma was slow to answer her question.

'Oh, that's nice.' Emma was more than happy that Fleur had Paolo to talk to about the appearance of Caroline in her life if she needed to. 'I'll come and collect you.'

But not go in. It would be too awkward having to make conversation with Eduardo now she'd told him there was no chance of them becoming a couple. And there was the danger he might think she'd changed her mind about their relationship and was open to invitations to go out somewhere if she were to go in.

A slow smile spread across Fleur's face. 'Yes,' she said. 'Why not?'

Good. That will mean I won't have to rush back from seeing Stella and can look around the shops in Torquay.

And I'll know where Fleur is. With Paolo. In the ice cream parlour.

One more day when she could be certain where Fleur was – safe. But after that – what then?

'Oh, and ...' Fleur said. 'I'm not sure what I should be calling you now.' She waved a hand over the dress and the underwear Caroline had given her. 'After all *this*. Ma? Emma? What do I call you? I'm confused. But it doesn't seem right after I've been given all these gifts by my real mother to be calling you Ma, does it?'

Doesn't it?

'I'm going to have to leave that decision up to you, Fleur,' Emma said. 'But whatever happens, you will always be my daughter.'

And then, before she broke down completely with the emotion of it all she left the room.

'Stella?' Emma's voice was a whisper and she didn't want to believe that the woman lying, eyes closed, looking so grey, so ill, was who the nurse who'd shown her into the private room had said she was.

Stella's eyes opened slowly.

'Oh, hello, Emma.' Stella smiled and Emma was heartened to see there was brightness in her eyes. 'I'm in a mess, aren't I?'

'But you'll be well soon, I know it.'

'How's Fleur?' Stella asked. 'Is she coming to terms with the news about her birth?'

'I like to think so. But it's early days. She's meeting Caroline alone for the first time tomorrow.' A shiver of unease snaked its way up Emma's spine at the thought.

'And you're anxious about that?' Stella said.

'Yes. But I haven't come here to talk about my concerns or Fleur's.'

Talking to Stella for a while would take her mind off Fleur. And Caroline. And ...

'You can, you know. I'll be happy to listen. It will take my mind off other things.'

Stella reached for Emma's hand. How thin her hand was. Claw-like – all bone and raised blue veins, like rivers on a map. Were they feeding her in here? Emma wished she'd brought something more substantial than a few grapes and a small bar of Cadbury's milk chocolate now. And the flowers she'd brought – purple stocks – were hardly likely to help Stella put on weight, were they?

'So, that's both of us in the same boat?' Emma smiled. 'Things we should be talking about and thinking about but don't want to for the moment. When I spoke to your friend in the nurses' home she wouldn't tell me what was wrong. You don't have to tell me if it's, well … women's things.'

'Why shouldn't I tell you? You're a woman. We have the same things.'

Without even a smidgeon of self-pity Stella told Emma how influenza had turned to pneumonia, and how – at the beginning – the doctors had been unsure what exactly was wrong with her. How they'd suspected she might be pregnant and had examined her. Found things in her womb that shouldn't have been there and she'd been given a hysterectomy.

What trust she's putting in me, telling me all this, Emma thought.

'So,' Stella finished. 'My dream of becoming a mother has flown out of the window.'

Emma clapped a hand in front of her mouth even though, again, there was no self-pity in Stella's voice – it was almost clinical. Only a few minutes ago Stella had said – '*Why shouldn't I tell you? You're a woman. We have the same things.*' She couldn't have known how accurate that statement was and how much they had both dreamed of having a child of their own one day.

'I'm sorry,' Emma said. 'Truly sorry.'

To break down now in front of Stella and tell her about her own dreams of having a child of her own would do Stella no good at all. Emma turned and walked towards the window. Stella's room was on the third floor looking out over Torquay's grand Victorian villas down towards the sea – a strip of pewter merging with a slate sky on the horizon today. She bit the insides of her cheeks to stop her tears coming, a trick which usually worked, but which was taking longer now. She swallowed. She couldn't stay here forever staring out of the window.

'I'm sorry,' Emma said. 'That was rude of me.'

'I don't think so. I think you have a sadness, too. I know now that Fleur isn't your child. I assumed you and your husband wanted one together? Yes?'

'Very much. Despite our best efforts it didn't happen.'

'Best efforts can be good.' Stella smiled. And then the smile slipped. 'So I'm told.'

'Is there something else?'

Stella pulled herself to a sitting position, struggling to set the pillows more comfortably behind her, so Emma helped, then pulled a chair closer to the bed and sat down.

'My fiancé seems to have got cold feet. He's hardly visited at all. I know his business is flourishing and he has to make the deliveries himself until the lad who works for him is proficient enough at driving to do it. I expect he's busy but ...' Stella stopped speaking. Shrugged her shoulders, the boniness of them poking through the shawl she had draped over them.

'Running a business by oneself is time-consuming,' Emma said. 'I ran a bakery before I went to Canada and now my dressmaking business here and I know how hard it can be. He could be telling the truth.'

Emma had no idea why she was defending a man she didn't know and who wasn't visiting his sick fiancée as he ought. He should be making time for that, shouldn't he?

Stella twisted her engagement ring around and around her finger.

'This is in danger of falling off,' she said. 'The jeweller it was bought from said opals are considered bad luck as a betrothal ring and I'm beginning to think he might be right.'

'No!' Emma said. 'Don't think like that. Men can be very thoughtless around illness. When my mama had her miscarriages my papa used to go for long walks by himself when really all she wanted was for him to put his arms around her and hold her.'

'Well, I'm not going to have one of those now, am I?' Stella said.

'No. I'm sorry. Not that I'd wish a miscarriage on anyone but you know what I mean.'

'I do.' Stella smiled. 'Have you ever thought of marrying again?'

Emma flinched, surprised at Stella's question.

'Are you seeing someone?' Stella went on.

'There was someone – an Italian, Eduardo Cascarini – who had hopes that we might marry,' Emma said quickly, wondering why Stella seemed so eager to know. 'You met him at Fleur's birthday tea. He was very kind but I don't love him. I've told him I don't want to see him any more. We don't have the same vision for our futures.'

'But if you met someone and fell in love? Might you marry again?'

Only with Matthew. And he's hardly likely to materialise out of thin air if I snap my fingers, is he?

Should she confide in Stella about Matthew? Should she? A bell rang somewhere not far away.

'End of visiting time,' Stella said.

'I'll come again as soon as I can. We can talk trousseau. I'll get some fabric samples to show you. It will be something to look forward to. When you're well.'

Emma knew she was gabbling, trying to say as much as

she could in the few seconds they had left together before she was shown the door.

'I like to think so,' Stella said.

'I do, too,' Emma said. 'And not just because it will earn me money making it. I hope your fiancé comes to see you soon.' She bent to kiss Stella on the cheek. 'I'm glad we're friends.'

'I hope we always will be,' Stella said.

Chapter Sixteen

Fleur wore the dress Caroline had given her for her birthday to go and meet her ... mother. *How odd it felt, thinking of Caroline as her mother*. The dress fitted like a glove. She'd changed into it after her ma had left to go and see Stella Martin at the hospital. And how easy that had been, telling her ma that it was Paolo who had telephoned yesterday, when it hadn't been. It was Caroline who had rung. Usually her ma could tell when she was lying – although Fleur didn't have the first idea how – but she hadn't this time. And what a gift she'd given Fleur by asking if she was seeing Paolo. *Yes. Why not?* Which wasn't the truth but it wasn't exactly a lie either – she would be seeing Paolo sometime. Just not today.

How, Fleur wondered, had she not questioned the fact that she was taller than Emma by a good four inches, and was finer-boned? Well ... she had questioned it a time or two back in Canada after her pa had died, but her ma had always said that her pa had been tall. *But built like a tree! And I'm fine-boned*. Like Caroline, she realised. Even now Fleur could remember how it felt to climb up into a chair and sit on her pa's lap, have him wrap his arms around her and hold her tight. She remembered remarking once – she'd have been about seven or eight years old at the time – that her pa's forearm was bigger around than her thigh. And he'd laughed. Sometimes, before she fell asleep when she lay there thinking about her life with her pa, about Canada and all the friends she'd left behind there, and about Caroline now making a re-appearance in it, she could hear that laugh in her head. And see his coal black hair. At least she had that of him.

She didn't like the thought that her pa had taken someone

else into his bed before he'd married Emma. But she had to accept that he had. And that *she* was the result. She'd had a few weeks to think about it now. She'd talked it all over with Paolo and he was of the opinion that she should be grateful for the life that Emma had given her if Caroline had dumped her – as she'd admitted she had – on the table in Emma's bakery.

Emma had kissed her goodbye not ten minutes ago as she'd left to go and visit Stella Martin. And now Fleur was on her way to meet Caroline – without Emma playing chaperone. How powerful it had felt to say yes she would meet her, or no she wouldn't. And at what time. And where.

Fleur had suggested Victoria Park for her first meeting – alone – with Caroline. There was a bandstand with seats in it and a little stream running along in front. Behind, across an expanse of grass, there was a large ornamental pond with a bridge running across the middle. After they'd talked, it was Fleur's plan to suggest going to the Igloo, an ice cream parlour in Torbay Road that wasn't a patch on Paolo's father's over in Torquay, but she wanted to see if Caroline would agree readily to pay for the most expensive ice cream sundae on the menu. Emma wouldn't, she knew that.

Fleur pushed open the double iron gates into the park and then closed them behind her. She could see Caroline waiting and she hurried towards her. So far she'd not seen Caroline in the same outfit twice and today was no exception. She was wearing a finely pleated skirt that stopped just below the knee with a blouse that had a scallop trim at the hemline and around the cuffs and collar. White. And with it she was wearing a red cloche hat the same shade as rosehips. She was wearing it pulled down further over one eye than the other and there was a silver brooch – like a bent leaf – pinned on the side.

And it will fit me!

'Déjà vu,' Caroline said, standing up. She wasn't looking exactly pleased to see her, Fleur thought.

Should she shake hands? Offer Caroline a cheek to kiss? What was the form with a mother you hardly knew? Fleur had no idea. But what could Caroline mean by her greeting? Fleur knew her forehead was creasing up with little furrows.

'I'd have thought you would know what that means,' Caroline said. 'Or did Emma not teach you any French?'

Fleur wasn't sure she liked the tone of Caroline's voice. Of course Emma had taught her French. And in Vancouver just about every other person had been French so she'd spoken it on a regular basis.

'I know what déjà vu means in French although there's no real English translation – only the literal one,' Fleur said. 'I'm puzzled as to why you've said it. Here.'

'Sit, and I'll tell you.' Caroline sat down again and patted the seat beside her.

Fleur ran the palm of her hand over the seat to check it wasn't wet or greasy with the remains of someone's picnic. Usually there were people picnicking in little groups on the grass, or even in the bandstand, but today there was no one. Just her and Caroline. Fleur sat.

'A little closer,' Caroline said. 'I don't bite.'

Fleur slid an inch or two along the wooden seat although she wasn't very comfortable in doing so. Was that alcohol she could smell? Or some sort of strong perfume?

'That's better.' Caroline laid a hand on Fleur's knee then took it away again. 'It was here that Seth first saw you. A tiny, red-faced, screaming bundle you were, too.'

Fleur bridled. Caroline seemed different today than she had in the Cliff Hotel. She was beginning to regret suggesting this place now. While the day was hot, it was cooler here on the north side of the park. Colder.

'I expect most of us were tiny, red-faced, screaming bundles when we were babies,' Fleur said.

Emma would have said something like that. Perhaps she was more like Emma than she thought she was. Wanted to be?

Caroline laughed. 'You've got spirit, I'll give you that. And you've got acting skills. You're a little apprehensive today, but you're hiding it well.'

Fleur felt something cold run down the back of her neck, her spine. Her breathing quickened. She wasn't much liking being seen through as though she were a pane of glass.

'You'd be wonderful in films,' Caroline said.

'You mean like Clara Bow and ...?' She couldn't think of any other film stars offhand. *Me? Wonderful in films? If she agreed to go back to America with her could Caroline really get her into films?*

'Clara Bow has a reputation for being a very naughty girl. But it gets her places, if you know what I mean.'

Yes, Fleur did know. Who hadn't heard of the casting couch, for goodness sake? But if Caroline thought she was going to sleep with men just to get a part in films then she had another think coming. Was that what *she'd* done? Before or after she'd married Miles Jago? Miles was dead, Fleur knew that. Her pa had had another brother, Carter, who was dead, too. And now her pa was dead. The Jago men didn't make it to old age it seemed.

'You could make a lot of money in films,' Caroline went on. 'A lot of money. Wouldn't you like that?'

Well, who wouldn't? But Emma wasn't exactly poor and now with more and more clients for her dressmaking business she was making even more money. Fleur had secretly started drawing dresses – designing them, not copying them from the pages of *Vogue*. She'd thought about showing Emma who, she knew, didn't need a pattern bought from a shop to make something. She hadn't got around to it yet though. What would be the point if she was going to go to America? Paolo didn't want her to go

– he'd said as much when she'd told him Caroline lived in America and would be going back there. They'd fallen out a bit about that. He'd called her ungrateful for not appreciating everything Emma had done for her. Well, what did he know? He'd always known who his real mother was, hadn't he? Even if she was dead now he still had a truthful childhood to look back on.

Unlike me.

'Well?' Caroline prompted her. 'Wouldn't you?'

'I don't know. Ma … Emma … was telling me about a college course I could take here. Art, music and drama. I—'

'You don't want to even waste time thinking about that in that pretty little head of yours. You're a natural. I know it.'

'I can't make such a big decision on the spur of the moment.'

'Oh, for goodness sake!' Caroline said, with a giggle. But Fleur thought she sounded exasperated all the same.

'I won't earn much money to begin with, will I? I'd have to have money to pay rent and buy food.'

Caroline laughed loudly this time. 'Whatever makes you think that? I'm your mother. You can stay with me in my apartment. All the presents I've bought you were expensive things bought with money earned from films. Where else did you think the money came from?'

She's trying to buy me off, Fleur thought. And she was frightened. But a little part of her was fizzing with excitement at the thought. *Oh, what to do?*

'I've bought your passage, you know that. I thought you would have been grateful I've turned up to take you away from this dump.' Caroline waved one hand in an arc across the park, and with the other she clasped Fleur firmly at the wrist.

'Stop it,' Fleur said. She tried to wriggle her wrist free but Caroline had caught her by surprise and it was as though she'd frozen, like Vancouver harbour had for months on end.

'I think it's time you started packing for our journey, don't you?' Caroline leaned in close and it was definitely alcohol Fleur could smell on her breath now. But she let go of Fleur's wrist, much to Fleur's relief. 'But first I have something to tell you.'

'Tell me, then,' Fleur said.

'Do you know your mother also had a lover?'

'When Ma was married to Pa?'

'Yes.'

'I don't believe you. Ma would never do that.'

'Goodness, what a little innocent you are. His name is Matthew Caunter. Ever heard that name?'

'No.'

'Well, let me tell you it's a name that's caused me more grief than is right and proper. Matthew Caunter was responsible for sending your two uncles to the gallows. Did you know that?'

To the gallows? What had they done? Well, she wasn't going to ask. It could be the alcohol she'd obviously been drinking that was making Caroline say these things. Back in Vancouver, around the harbour area, there had almost always been men, as drunk as skunks, shouting out all sorts of rubbish at passers-by.

'No.'

'Emma hasn't told you anything of this, has she?'

Why would she if it wasn't true?

'I think you can guess she hasn't.' Fleur didn't know what to think now. If it were true then why hadn't her pa told her, if not Emma?

'I thought not. It was a while ago now. Trumped up charges for the murder of the Jago housemaid against Carter – a silly woman who didn't know which side her bread was buttered. Miles, God rest his soul, came back to

England to fetch you because I knew I'd done the wrong thing leaving you with Seth and *her*—'

'Emma. She's called Emma.'

And I want you now, Ma. Oh, how I want you now. If only to ask why you've kept all this from me.

'Don't interrupt. Has no one ever told you it's rude to interrupt when your elders are speaking?' When Fleur nodded, meaning yes, of course I know it's rude, Caroline went on: 'And Matthew Caunter prevented that. Miles had been wrongly imprisoned before we went to America, but he'd escaped. A warder got in the way.'

You mean Miles killed him in his escape.

A plane droned overhead. Fleur inhaled deeply in an attempt to steady herself, slow down her heartbeat. But it was going faster than the steam engine pistons on the hurdy-gurdy at the Fair.

'You're frightening me,' Fleur said. 'And I don't think mothers should frighten their daughters.'

'Don't you, then?' Caroline said. She threw back her head and laughed loudly. 'But I'll say this for you, you're spirited. Have I told you that already? You'll need spirit in the film industry.' Caroline fiddled with her necklace and then began primping her hair with her fingers. She took out a compact and powdered her nose and cheeks, and then found a lipstick and applied it with more vigour than accuracy.

Fleur thought it made her look like a clown but hell would freeze over before she told her so. Emma would never, ever, have powdered her nose in public. Come to think of it, Fleur had never seen Emma wear powder anyway.

'Who says I'm going to go into the film industry?' Fleur replied. 'Miss Baxter wouldn't let me have a part in the Nativity when I was six years old. I had to be a shepherd with the boys because I was so tall for my age.'

Keep talking. But agree to nothing. Fleur hardly knew the

223

woman really. But what she did know was that something wasn't right.

'And I've got a terrible memory,' Fleur said. 'I had the most terrific trouble learning my times tables, and as for Keats and Shakespeare, which I had to learn verses and verses of and recite to our stupid English teacher, Miss Bannister, I never could see the point in it. She rapped my knuckles more than a few times for not doing it properly.' Fleur struggled to think of something else to say. 'I ... I ...'

'You've got the most beautiful speaking voice. Talkies are the new thing. You'll be such an asset in Hollywood.'

If I go. If smelling of drink is expected of you in the middle of the day I don't know I want to be part of that. I shouldn't have come.

'Thank you for telling me what you have. I'd like to go home now and ask Emma why she's kept what you've just told me from me all these years.'

'You can. But not just yet. I've got a treat lined up for you today. I have a friend arriving soon ... oh, there he is now.'

Caroline waved an arm vigorously up and down to get the attention of a man who had just come through the park gates. He was tall, but not as tall as her pa had been. And he was wearing a long overcoat. An overcoat on such a humid, August afternoon! 'And my friend will tell you how perfect you are.'

Only because he thinks he might be able to make money out of me.

Fleur placed her hands together, prayer fashion, and slid them between her knees. She did not want to shake the hand of the man walking slowly towards them as though he owned the park, or indeed the whole country and the whole world. He was wearing a huge hat – a bit like a cowboy hat only white – covering half his face. And spats.

Again, Caroline threw back her head and laughed loudly

at Fleur's expression. 'You are a one! Part of me wishes I'd tried to find you before now, but another part tells me this is the perfect time. I've avoided all the diaper-changing, and the childhood illnesses I'd have had to cope with if I'd found you earlier. Goody-two-shoes *Emma* did all that for me.' Caroline made the word Emma sound as though it was something best left in the gutter.

Nothing to do with loving the child you gave birth to, then?

'Archie, this is Fleur,' Caroline said, standing up as the man took the steps up into the bandstand two at a time. She put her arms on Archie's shoulders and kissed his cheeks.

Fleur shivered. She recognised him now. He was the man who'd offered her a cigarette on the pier, wasn't he? And ... oh, had that been Caroline with a cigarette in her fingers on the opposite side of the pier that day? She'd barely registered the woman then, but now ...

'Hi, Fleur,' Archie said. 'We meet again. Pretty name for an even prettier girl.'

'How do you do,' Fleur said, looking at her feet. 'But I'm going to have to go now. My ma—'

She didn't know what was going on here but she was frightened and the sooner she could get away from these two the better it would be.

'But *I'm* your ma,' Caroline said. 'Although you'll have to learn to call me Mom in America.'

'Who says I'm going to America?'

Fleur saw Caroline glance at Archie and raise her eyebrows.

'See, I told you she'd be perfect,' Caroline said. 'Didn't I?'

'Perfect,' Archie said. 'Such drama!'

This is surreal. This conversation is not happening. There was no one else in the park except the three of them. Should she make a run for it now? No, there were two chances of being apprehended before she could make the gates and the road beyond. Or she could talk her way out of it.

'Have you been following me? That day on the pier …?'

'Bright, too,' Archie said. 'I'll let your mother explain.' He patted Caroline's hand.

'Archie is a film director—'

'Then why isn't he in America directing them?'

Caroline sighed heavily. Interrupting again, the sigh said. 'Because he's here. He was due a holiday and came here to see me. Even film directors have holidays, Fleur. I asked Archie to check you out.'

'Check me out?'

'I didn't want to mention the possibility of you being in films if Archie thought you weren't suitable. That would have been unkind.'

'Check out I'm not rat ugly, is that what you mean? I don't know if I can believe a word of this?'

'I rather guessed you might put up some resistance. I have a film magazine here with Archie's name in it. I can show it you.' Caroline reached in her bag for the magazine. 'And I've also got a newspaper with mention of Miles's court case – the one that Matthew Caunter—'

'I don't want to see them, thank you.'

If Caroline had brought evidence that her ma's friend – lover? – had sent her uncle Miles to the gallows then it had to be true. And all the film stuff, too. Fleur felt tears welling and squeezed her eyes shut to blink them away. But one escaped, sliding slowly down her chin. Nothing was real any more. Who could she trust to speak the truth?

'Tears on tap, Caroline,' Archie said. 'Even better than I thought. I repeat, such drama.'

'And talking of drama,' Caroline said. 'As I said, I've lined up a little treat for you. *Rolled Stockings* is showing at the Odeon in Torquay and—'

'*Rolled Stockings*?' Fleur said. Louise Brooks was in that.

226

And Nancy Phillips. And she'd had her hair bobbed like Louise Brooks! She gave it a little pat with the palm of her hand.

'Ah, I can see you are interested.' Caroline laughed. 'Paramount are the producers. And someone not a million miles away from you has worked for Paramount. And someone else not a million miles away from you got her that part. So, what do you say, Fleur, to a visit to the cinema so you can see what sort of world you could be living in soon?'

'Yes, honey, why not?' Archie said, and he slid an arm around Fleur's shoulder. She ducked out from under it and slid along the bench seat away from him.

She was tempted. But Archie ... she didn't trust him.

'I can't. I don't think I've got time.'

'Sure you have, honey,' Archie said, grinning at her.

And I'd rather swallow carpet tacks without the aid of a glass of water to get them down than have you touch me again. And that was another expression Emma used when she had to do something she really, really, didn't want to do. Fleur was, she was fast realising, more like Emma than she ever would be like Caroline.

'You can't say you don't want to be in films until you've tried it,' Caroline said. 'An hour and a half to see something both Archie and I are part of – how could that hurt?'

Fleur thought fast. She'd told her ma she'd be with Paolo and stopping for supper and that she'd telephone from there when she was ready for her ma to fetch her. Perhaps Caroline had a point. Oh, her thoughts were all over the place!

'Live a little dangerously,' Caroline said. 'And this dump could, sure as hell is hot, do with some life in it.'

Fleur took a deep breath. 'The cinema,' she said. 'Gosh, how exciting.'

* * *

Archie hadn't taken the quickest route, which was along the coast road, but had driven up hill and down dale, Caroline and Archie whispering to one another in the front seats so that Fleur hadn't been able to hear what they were talking about. But they were here now. There was a small queue of people outside the cinema – about twenty of them – and Archie pulled up sharply at the kerb. He leapt out of the driving seat and ran around the front of the car to open the passenger door for Caroline. Fleur slid swiftly across the leather seat, eager to get out of the car.

'Impatient little miss, isn't she?' Caroline said.

'I don't need a man to open doors for me,' Fleur said, straightening her skirt once she was on the pavement. She looked up at the billboard and Louise Brooks's eyes met hers, as though inviting her in. An hour or so watching a film couldn't hurt, could it?

'You don't suppose Louise Brooks got to star in a film without letting a man or two open a door for her, do you?' Caroline pointed a gloved finger at Louise Brooks.

Archie offered an arm to Caroline and she took it. He offered the other one to Fleur but she swiftly skipped around the back of him to walk beside Caroline.

No thanks!

Fleur had been to cinemas in Vancouver with Delia Gethin and her mother, but none of them had been as grand as this one. The foyer was as big as a ballroom and chandeliers hung low from very ornate ceilings. Everything seemed to have been dipped in gold – the backs of chairs, the frames of all the pictures of film stars lining the walls, and the pedestal on which a huge palm in a pot balanced, somewhat precariously, Fleur thought.

'Amazing, isn't it? Caroline said. 'And you can be part of it. From the inside, as it were. And now, if you'll excuse me. I need the powder room.'

And with that Caroline glided elegantly across the foyer,

slipping in through a door to the right of the desk. 'Left luggage' it said in thick black lettering at the top of the door. Perhaps that's where the powder room, or the 'Ladies' was, too – Fleur wouldn't know because she'd never been in a cinema like this one before. She couldn't think of a single thing to say to Archie, and now he was without Caroline, he seemed to have lost the art of conversation, too. He was looking anxiously across the foyer as though willing Caroline to come back soon. Ah, there she was coming out of the door – thank goodness for that. But no … it must have been the wrong door after all because Caroline scurried off and in through another door, too far away for Fleur to see to read the lettering on it.

Caroline seemed to take an age to come back.

And she was the one hurrying me up just now.

Ah, there she was, clutching her bag to her in both hands. Thank goodness for that because the film was about to start any minute. And they hadn't got any tickets yet!

'Mission accomplished,' Caroline said to Archie and he reached out a hand and put his fingers to her cheek.

'My little peach,' he said.

'No problem, you teddy bear, you,' Caroline said.

This was cringe-worthily embarrassing. But something to tell Delia about when she telephoned her. How Delia would giggle over it, especially if Fleur were to mimic their accents. Fleur sent up a silent prayer her ma wouldn't query the cost of the telephone bill when it arrived – all those transatlantic calls she'd been making to Delia would probably cost a mint.

'Ticket time, I think,' Archie said, dragging Fleur's thoughts back to the here and now.

He took off his coat and draped it over one arm, then he walked towards the desk to buy the tickets. He seemed a little unsteady on his feet because he kept bumping into people as he went, as though he wasn't nimble enough to skirt around them. Fleur saw one man turn round swiftly and glare at him as he made the return journey.

He wasn't a pickpocket, was he? Surely not. A shiver of unease rippled across Fleur's shoulder blades. But how would she know? Pickpockets were, Fleur could only assume, skilled at what they did, and she would never have seen one doing what he did, would she?

Archie came back with not only the tickets but a huge box of chocolates tied with a purple ribbon, too.

How bad could it be with a box of chocolates to share? Fleur's ma was forever going on about not eating too much sugary stuff and how it was bad for her teeth. Well, she wasn't here and she wasn't going to know, was she? But ...

'How long is the film?' Fleur asked anxiously. The last thing she wanted was for her ma to ring Signor Cascarini to say she was coming over to pick her up and take her home, even though she'd said *she* would be the one making the call.

'Stop fretting, little one,' Archie said, patting Fleur's arm. She jerked it away.

'Long enough.' Caroline laughed.

And what's that supposed to mean?

And then Fleur saw him. Paolo. With a girl with long fair hair, hanging onto his arm. They were looking at one another and laughing. Fleur went cold inside and then hot again. She wanted the ground to open up and swallow her whole. She knew her eyes had gone round and wide with the shock of it and she couldn't take them off Paolo. She doubted he would sense her looking at him, though, because he only had eyes for the girl he was with. She turned her back so Paolo wouldn't see her if he did turn around, but she was shaking, she knew she was. The rat! All her instincts told her to run over and confront him, call him a two-timing so-and-so but she could hardly do that seeing as she'd lied to her ma about being with him, when she wasn't – well, not exactly not being with him, because they were in the same cinema now, weren't they? She was in a fix, wasn't she? She'd have to find a public telephone to call her ma the second the film was over and then walk down to the seafront and wait outside the ice cream parlour. She couldn't risk Caroline and Archie taking her home.

'Darling, you look like you've seen a ghost,' Caroline said. 'You need a little snifter to settle you.' Caroline tapped her capacious bag hanging from her arm. 'This is all a new experience to you, isn't it?'

A snifter? She meant alcohol. Spirits. Was her bag full of alcohol? It did seem to be pretty full. Her ma would go mad if she went home stinking of drink, she knew she would. Well, not mad because her ma didn't lay down the law too much or shout and scream but she had a way of letting Fleur know when she wasn't best pleased with her.

Well, she'll be pleased I refused a single drop of alcohol, when I tell her I've been offered it, won't she?

'A box, ladies,' Archie said. 'We've got a box. No expense spared for our little miss here, eh?'

What was he talking about? The chocolates?

'You always did spoil me,' Caroline simpered and giggled. And then she reached for Fleur's arm and spun her round. Fleur expected to come face to face with Paolo but she didn't. He must have hurried on into the cinema. And now Caroline was propelling Fleur across the foyer and up a wide set of marble stairs. Dress circle, it said in very ornate letters. Gold-edged. An usherette greeted them at the top of the stairs and guided them along a narrow corridor with lots of doors on one side. She opened one of them.

'Enjoy the film,' she said. 'I'll be back in the interval to take your orders for refreshment.'

Interval? This was going to take hours. Even with the promise of seeing Louise Brooks on the screen, and a box of chocolates to eat, Fleur was beginning to regret not making a fuss about coming now. Caroline seemed to be two people – kind and caring one second, hostile and very scary the next. And then there was the fact she'd seen Paolo ... hmm, maybe it was just as well she knew now he was two-timing her rather than later. But still it wasn't a very nice feeling. How could he do that? How could he prefer that silly girl who was hanging onto his arm over her?

The 'box' turned out to be a balcony way up in the roof space of the cinema. There were just four seats in it. Red velvet seats with very ornately carved backs. The light was dim but Fleur just knew they would be gilded.

'You sit here, Fleur,' Caroline said, indicating an end seat. 'You'll be a little nearer the screen there.'

'Thank you.'

As Fleur settled in her seat, Archie sat in the one next to it, with Caroline on his other side.

'A rose between two thorns,' Archie said, with an affected laugh. He put an arm around the back of Fleur's seat, but not touching.

And you'll find I scratch if you so much as dare to touch me.

The lights dimmed – the sign that the film was about to start. An organ began to play down in the orchestra pit. The sound seemed to go right through Fleur's stomach. She had a feeling she'd got herself into something and was digging herself in deeper every second.

'Haven't you forgotten something, Archie?' Caroline asked.

'The key?'

'Yes.'

'I have it here,' Archie said, taking a key from his pocket and waggling it at Caroline. 'Sleight of hand!'

'Ssh,' Caroline said.

Fleur felt sick. She didn't need to be a genius to know that the key in Archie's hand was the key to the balcony door and that they were locked in.

'What if I need to go to the Ladies?' Fleur asked.

'She's a bright one!' Archie said. 'Well, little darling that will stand you in good stead.'

'You'll have to wait,' Caroline leaned across in front of Archie and hissed at her. 'Won't you?'

Fleur could practically see the ice in Caroline's eyes. She didn't want to believe this woman had given birth to her. Had Emma told her it was all lies and that she, Emma, was truly her ma then she would have believed her.

Fleur's blood ran colder in her veins than it had when she'd seen Paolo just now. She wondered if she would be able to see him if she leaned over the edge of the box. She doubted if Paolo would have been able to afford a box. His pa didn't pay him very much.

The only thing stopping Fleur from yelling, 'Help, I've been locked in!' was the fact the usherette had said she'd come back in the interval. But when would that be? And there was a film about to start which she'd been wanting to see for ages. Delia was going to be so jealous when she told her she'd seen it because films took forever to make it to Vancouver.

The credits began to roll and Fleur sat in her seat, as far away from Archie as it was possible to get without falling off the seat.

The film was good. One of the actors – Fleur couldn't remember his name now – reminded Fleur of her pa, his dark hair, his moustache, his handsome face, although her pa had been a lot taller. The box of chocolates was waved in front of her to take one, but when she refused for the third time she wasn't offered again. But she was happy enough to lose herself in the story for a while although she was aware that a bottle of something was being shared and that Archie and Caroline were leaned in very close to one another. Kissing? She didn't want to look.

The interval arrived more quickly than Fleur had expected it to.

There was a knock on the door and Archie got up to answer it.

Should she leave now? Say she wanted to go to the Ladies and then find a telephone and ring her ma? Should she? She'd half expected Archie to put an arm around her – or worse, touch her on the knee – but he hadn't. And she *was* enjoying the film.

'Chocolate ices all round,' Archie said, pocketing the key again and with three chocolate covered ice creams in silver paper in the other hand.

'Thank you,' Fleur said. She unwrapped her ice cream and licked at it. 'Better than Signor Cascarini's Italian ice cream.'

'Is it?' Caroline said, lightly. 'You won't be breaking your heart not to have to work there any more, then, will you?'

'How ... how ...' Fleur stared, horrified at Caroline. 'I knew it. You *have* been spying on me?' She glared at Archie.

'We had to know you can cut the mustard as the saying has it in the looks department, if you're to make it in films.'

The ice cream seemed to have turned to ash on Fleur's tongue. She was seeing things more clearly now.

'You don't want me for myself because I'm your daughter do you, Caroline? You only want to make money out of me, both of you! Well, I'm going. Now. Give me that key, please, Archie.'

Fleur jumped to her feet, but Archie gripped her wrist, yanked her back towards him. Fleur pulled with all her might and Archie lost his grip on her. She crashed into the edge of the balcony, looking down. A sea of faces looked up towards her at the noise. *Should she scream? Would anyone do anything if she did? Perhaps Paolo would rush to her rescue?* It was then that she noticed two policemen walking up and down the aisles.

'Help!' she screamed at them. 'Help me, please! I'm being kept here against my will!'

'Bloody hell!' Archie said, jumping up. He grabbed Fleur and put a hand over her mouth, his nails digging into her cheeks, dragging her back into the box. 'You little fool!'

'Leave her!' Caroline hissed. 'Let's get out of here!'

'Bloody hell! Women!'

Archie took his hand from Fleur's mouth but she was too terrified now to scream again. She was pushed to the floor, and Archie kicked out at her before both he and Caroline made for the door.

She felt sick. And faint.

'Ma! Ma! Ma, I'm sorry. I love you,' Fleur said, curling herself up into a ball. Everything her ma had told her about Caroline dumping her on the table in the bakery was true. Caroline had done it then, and she'd done it again now.

'Well, well, well, what have we got here?'

Fleur looked up. A policeman was standing over her, arms folded across his chest.

'I'm Fleur.'

'And I'm not your ma. You're under arrest.'

Chapter Seventeen

August was busy for Matthew in the garage. Mercifully busy in a way – a thought he didn't like himself much for because it meant he had little time to drive down to Torquay to see Stella. He'd had six car sales in just over a week and most of those customers had wanted him to teach them how to drive as well. Extra car sales meant more repairs than he and William could reasonably handle so he'd taken on another mechanic, Cecil, who'd come back broken in body from the war, if not in spirit. Now, more than a few operations on, Cecil's bones had mended and he'd put on muscle again, and he'd got his strength back. He'd been so grateful for a job that Matthew thought for a moment Cecil was going to pay *him* for the pleasure of working. As Cecil himself had said, if he could mend a lorry or a weapon under gunfire then he could cope with anything. So far, he was proving to be a good mechanic.

Poor Stella seemed to be taking an age to get well. The last time he'd seen her she'd had a bit more colour in her face and had become quite animated talking about all the things she and her dressmaker had planned. He hoped she hadn't spent too much on materials and all the other things needed to make clothes. If she had, then he'd reimburse her, although he had a feeling she wouldn't want that.

Stella hadn't mentioned the necklace – Emma's amethyst necklace – that had become entangled in his fingers on his last visit, and which he'd blatantly lied about, saying it had been his mother's. He had a feeling she hadn't believed a word of it but wasn't going to question his explanation. She'd spoken animatedly – or as animatedly as a sick woman could – about a headdress that apparently Stella and her dressmaker had agreed would look better on a woman her age than a veil. Matthew hoped he'd nodded in the right places as Stella talked excitedly on. But he'd been careful to be non-committal about the wedding. He would have to tell her very soon that there wasn't going to be a wedding – not his to Stella anyway.

He picked up the letter he'd received that morning from Emma. Definitely his Emma.

... I should be most grateful if you could bank the cheque I left at your office almost three months ago now. Even if you don't, I like to keep up to date with my finances. While my cheque remains uncleared I'm unable to do that. I have tried to reach you on the telephone on a number of occasions but you are almost never there, hence the need for me to write to you ...

He would telephone her now. No, he could do better than that. He'd waited long enough to see Emma. He'd go to her house now.

Matthew called William into the office and told him he was in charge again and then jumped in his car and headed for Paignton, and Romer Lodge.

And Emma.

Matthew drove through the gateway of Romer Lodge, his eyes searching for the car he'd sold Emma, but it wasn't there as far as he could see. The garage doors were wide open and it was just blackness inside.

A man came running up steps from a sunken garden to the left of the house. A gardener by the look of him. He had a long-handled hoe in his hands and a concerned expression on his face. A face that was vaguely familiar to Matthew, but then he'd seen a few thousand people in his lifetime, hadn't he? And in all sorts of places.

'What's your business?' the gardener asked as Matthew opened the door of his car and stepped out onto gravel that was neatly raked and totally weed-free. Emma employed good staff, that much was obvious. The gardener placed the rake between himself and Matthew, feet planted firmly on the ground about a foot apart.

Challenging. Good. At least Emma had someone on her side.

'I've come to see Emma Jago. Is she in?'

'Not at the moment. I'm waitin' fer 'er to come back before I go 'ome.'

Matthew didn't think he was doing any such thing, but he had to give the man ten out of ten for quick thinking and loyalty.

'Then we'll wait together. Matthew Caunter.' He offered the gardener his hand.

'Tom,' the gardener said, shaking it firmly. 'Emma and my wife, Ruby, are best friends. 'Er gave me this job. Emma, that is.'

Tom's eyes were huge round pools of darkness and Matthew thought he saw the sheen of tears in them. How gaunt this man was, and yet how proud he sounded mentioning his wife's name. And Emma's. Matthew had a feeling he knew who he was now. He remembered Emma's friend, Ruby. He'd seen her a time or two when both women had worked at Nase Head House and Matthew had been there visiting the owner, and his friend from school days, Rupert Smythe.

'You were a gardener up at Nase Head House before the war, am I right?'

'You are.' Tom's eyelashes flickered, and he lowered his eyelids, hung his head, as though he didn't want Matthew to see what horrors he was remembering behind those eyes.

'Emma's daughter – is she at home?'

He rather hoped she wouldn't be because he wanted this first meeting with Emma to be just them alone. Who knew how it would go? He didn't think he'd be able to bear it if Emma told him to go away, but in his heart he didn't think she would. Not if she still felt about him the way she had when last they'd met. When she'd asked him to kiss her. If only he had …

'No. 'Er went to see the Italian lad 'er's sweet on. 'Er 'elps out in 'is father's ice cream parlour. Paul, or whatever the fancy Italian name is fer it. All dressed up 'er was in a fancy frock. Blue it were, like a field full of cornflowers. Women and their frocks, eh?'

'Indeed,' Matthew said. The thought of Stella and the wedding dress that he guessed was all that was spurring her on to get well making him feel distinctly uncomfortable.

'Are you a friend of Emma's then?' Tom asked. His hands were still firmly clasped around the handle of the hoe and he hadn't budged an inch. 'Only the name Caunter rings a bell.'

'I am.'

And I'd like to be more than that.

''Ere,' Tom said. 'I'm placin' you now. You was up to Nase Head House fer Smythe's wedding. Best man and that. I saw you dancin' …'

Yes, best leave it at that, Matthew thought, as Tom's voice trailed away. He'd seen him dancing with Emma, as had most of the room in all probability. Seen him holding her so close it had been almost indecent, and especially as she was Seth's wife – or so everyone thought at the time.

'In that case,' Tom went on, ''ow about a cup of tea while we wait for the women to come 'ome? I've got free run of the kitchen – well, the 'ole 'ouse really if I wants it, only I don't take advantage.' Tom turned and leaned his hoe up against a shrub that had purplish blue flowers on it, a bit like roses, only Matthew knew they weren't that. 'I don't know what's keepin' 'em. Emma were visitin' a friend, she told me when 'er went out. Women do prattle on a bit when they get goin', don't they?'

Matthew couldn't imagine Emma, his sharp-thinking,

fiery Emma, 'prattling'. But it wouldn't hurt to agree with Tom, would it?

'It's been known!'

Tom laughed. 'Come on, I'll get the kettle on.'

Matthew slammed shut his car door and followed Tom around the side of the house and in the back door.

Tom bustled about in the kitchen, boiling the kettle and bringing cups and saucers, tea strainer, milk and sugar and a full teapot to the table. They sat in easy companionship until the tea had brewed and Tom had poured it into the cups, putting the milk in first.

'Did you fight, Tom?' Matthew asked. 'In the Great War, I mean.'

Tom set the teapot on the table, blinked, closed his eyes as though trying to shut out some ghastly scene and Matthew regretted asking the question. Tom reached for his own cup, drained it of tea even though it was still very hot, his eyes still closed. Then he slowly opened them and Matthew could see they were full of tears.

'I'm sorry. I shouldn't have asked,' Matthew said. 'I didn't fight. I wasn't called up, and I didn't enlist. And I wasn't a conchie either.' God, but he was babbling now. Emotional women he was used to and could cope with, but he'd never met a man who looked so wretched after one short question before.

Tom smiled then, a rather lopsided and watery smile, but a smile.

'I 'spect, what with you 'avin' done the spyin' job you did before the war that you were too useful to send down a stinkin' 'ell-'ole of a trench, clearin' latrines, puttin' a bullet through a man to put 'im out of 'is misery.'

Tom's words were spoken with the deepest sadness Matthew had ever encountered – man or woman. But they'd been said without malice or accusation that Matthew had escaped all the things Tom had not.

'Yes,' Matthew said. 'That was exactly it.'

More or less.

'An' I dare say you saw things that come to you in nightmares sometimes, too.'

'That, too,' Matthew said. He picked up his cup. The tea was lukewarm now and he drank it down in one, put the cup back on the saucer.

'Well, all I can say,' Tom said, 'is that although it's a tragedy 'er's a widow now, even though it weren't a war as made 'er so, if it weren't fer Emma comin' back to England when 'er did, and bein' so generous with 'er money fer my kiddies, and a few other things you probably don't want to know about, and givin' me this job, I'd 'ave been another victim of that bloody war.' Tom thumped the table, making the now empty cups rattle on their saucers. 'More tea while we wait?'

'No, thanks,' Matthew replied. He tried quickly to think of something else to say. Change the subject. Lighten the mood. 'Fleur must be what, fifteen or sixteen now? Dark like her father or—?'

'Why do you ask?'

Tom looked suspicious all of a sudden and Matthew wondered just how much he knew about Fleur and who her birth mother was. Tom's wife, Ruby, and Emma had always been the best of friends and he couldn't think that Ruby didn't know – or if she didn't hadn't suspected that while Seth was Fleur's father, Emma most certainly wasn't her mother.

Matthew shrugged. 'Just curious. She was a toddler when I last saw her. Just wondering how she's turned out.'

'Beautiful's the word you need. Dark, like 'er pa. Same darkish skin, 'air like a raven's wing with the rain on it.' Tom laughed, and Matthew got the feeling he hadn't laughed in a long while. ''Ere's me comin' over all poetic.'

'So, when is she expected back?' Matthew prompted.

Tom shrugged. 'I 'eard 'er telling Emma she was stoppin' to tea or summat after she'd been workin' in the ice cream parlour. So not fer a while yet. Although why 'er wants to sit around with old man Cascarini and 'is mother-in-law is a mystery to me.'

'And Mr Cascarini's wife?' Sometimes Matthew couldn't help himself, weedling information out of people the way a pin gets a cockle out of its shell.

'Ain't got no wife no more. 'Er were killed by a bomb up to London so Emma told my Ruby. Old man Cascarini – Eduardo – is sweet on Emma I think. Only she ain't so keen. Been to the theatre together a time or two they 'ave, and out to dinner, so Ruby said, but it was only because Emma was asked and didn't like to 'urt 'is feelings seein' as 'ow 'e's still grievin'. Come to think of it, 'er 'asn't mentioned 'im in a while. 'E's not been 'ere neither to my knowledge.'

Unknowingly, Tom was providing Matthew with more information than he had dared hoped for. Emma didn't have another man in her life now she was a widow.

'Gawd, but I'm gettin' worried about Emma now,' Tom said when Matthew returned to the kitchen. 'I said I'd wait until 'er were back before goin' 'ome but I expected 'er 'ere before now. Oh! That's 'er comin' in in 'er car now. She'll come in the front door, I 'spect. Come on, I'll let 'er know you're 'ere and then I'll 'ave to go. If it'll be all right with Emma, you know ...'

Matthew knew exactly what it was Tom meant – that it would be all right for Emma and him to be alone in the house. He guessed Emma would have seen his car parked down the bottom of the drive and would wonder who had called on her. 'Tom! Tom! Are you here?' Emma's voice rang out, loud and clear, in the hallway. 'Only there's a strange car in the drive. Ah, there you are,' she said, sounding relieved as Tom stepped out into the hall.

'Just going,' Tom said.

From his vantage point, through the crack in the opened door, Matthew could see Emma taking off a hat and plonking it down unceremoniously on the hallstand. She had her back to him and he could see she'd cut her hair! Her glorious, glorious, mahogany hair was now ... a glorious, glorious, mahogany bob. And she had legs. Rather shapely legs and slim ankles above quite high-heeled shoes. He'd never seen Emma in anything but a skirt or a dress that covered her ankles before. How times change! And not quite as skinny as she'd been when he'd last seen her, worn out with worry that Miles was going to get to her and Seth, snatch Fleur, maybe kill to get the baby. Emma had a lovely wholesomeness to her now. Womanly.

Tom looked back over his shoulder towards the kitchen. He beckoned Matthew forward.

'Whose is the car, Tom?' Emma asked. 'Have you asked him, or her, to wait in the sitting room?'

'I think you'll know whose it is,' Tom said. 'The gentleman what's come to see you, Emma. 'E were Smythe's best man. I saw 'im at the weddin' dance. You an' 'im, dancin' like.'

'Really? Matthew, you mean? Here?'

'Yes. 'Im. Us 'ad plenty to talk about while us waited for yer, me and Mr Caunter. So it'll be all right if I leave you, won't it?'

Matthew stepped into full view then. He thought his face might crack with the wideness of his grin when Emma looked at him – but he was only mirroring her grin anyway.

'Perfectly all right, Tom,' Emma said. She opened the front door for Tom, as though she couldn't get rid of him fast enough.

'Same time in the mornin', then,' Tom said. 'Good day to you, Mr Caunter.'

And then he was gone.

'He took his time going!' Emma laughed, throwing herself at Matthew. 'I thought he was going to give me chapter and verse about what it was you'd been talking about!' She linked her hands behind the back of his neck. 'I can't believe you're here. The living, breathing Matthew and not the one I've dreamed about so many, many times. Pinch me so I know I'm not dreaming.'

'I wouldn't dare!' Matthew said.

'Oh, but it's so good to see you,' Emma said, leaning into him. She touched the side of his face, and then his neck, and then she ran a finger over his lips.

'And me, you,' Matthew said, hoarsely.

'You'll have to hold me up,' Emma said. 'I've gone weak at the knees.'

Matthew put his arms around her back, holding her as though she was an open, and very precious book, and then pulled her towards him.

'I can't tell you how many times I've dreamed of this moment. I've got so much to tell you, Matthew. But first ...'

And then Emma kissed him. Her lips warm and soft and just a little bit moist against his. She sighed from somewhere deep inside her and her lips parted slightly so that he felt the exhalation of her breath go from her mouth into his.

What else could he do but kiss her back? And keep kissing her until he knew that his lips would be raw around the edges and no doubt Emma's would as well.

Emma ran the palm of her hand up and down the front of his shirt and then she slid two fingers in between the buttons.

'Just checking it's really you,' she said, laughing, breaking off the kiss, but with her fingers still inside his shirt. 'Do you remember, way back in 1909, when I was your housekeeper and I washed one of your shirts and you got so cross with me for going into your room when you'd forbidden me to do so?'

'You can wash my shirts any time you like now,' Matthew said. 'And the door to my room is open.'

'No secrets to keep from me any more? Like the little issue of you telling me you couldn't read and write and then I found, when I was looking for washing because it was a windy and sunny day, when I went in your room that you *could* read because you had at least half a dozen books on your bed, and that you write very well.'

'Nothing like that,' Matthew said.

Which was the truth.

'Good,' Emma said, as she pressed her body close to his, leaving him in no doubt about what it was she wanted of him. 'I have every intention of making up for lost time.'

'Go easy on me, Em,' he said. 'I'm an old man now.'

'I don't believe it for a minute,' Emma said. 'That was the least whiskery, old man's kiss I've ever had in my life and ... oh my God, Matthew, I don't know I've ever felt like I do at this moment in my entire life.'

'Or me,' Matthew said.

He wanted – no needed – to make love to Emma, and he knew she felt the same. Her breasts were pressed hard against him and he could feel her nipples, stiff and erect, through the fabric of her dress.

'If I didn't think we'd be rudely interrupted by Fleur, then I'd—'

'Oh, we won't be,' Emma said. 'She's gone to see her friend Paolo. She said she was going to help in his father's ice cream parlour and that he was going to pay her. And that she's been invited to stop and eat with them. I told her to telephone me when she wants me to go and fetch her.'

So, what Tom had told him was correct. But it had been best to check.

'If I didn't know you better,' Matthew said, kissing her forehead, her nose, her lips – just the briefest of touches this time, to check he wasn't dreaming. 'I'd say you'd planned to have Fleur out of the way so we could ...'

'Could what? Play Ludo? Scrape the wallpaper off the

hall wall?' Emma jerked her head back a little, studying him.

Matthew laughed. Still the same Emma, making jokes to relieve the tension. Her eyes though were alight with her need of him, weren't they?

'It's what I've dreamed of,' Emma said more seriously. 'Night after night, over the years, even when I was with ...'

Matthew knew exactly what it was she meant – when she'd been with Seth, in his bed and in his arms probably. He hoped she'd been happy in the years between then and now, but now didn't seem to be the moment to ask.

'And trouble seems to be courting me again,' Emma said, her face serious.

'Is it something you can fix if I leave you now to go and fix it?'

Emma shook her head. 'I wish I could but I can't – not at this very second I can't. And you're here and I don't think I want to let you out of my sight for a moment. If we could turn back the clock, Matthew, how do you think our lives might have been?'

'Well, we could wind it back a little. I seem to remember you asking me down on Crystal Cove back in ... 1912 –'

'1913,' Emma corrected him. 'I asked you to kiss me one more time before we had to part and–'

'I refused to because I knew one kiss would never be enough and so did you, I think. Well, I stand corrected. I think I made the biggest mistake of my life that day.'

'Well, that's a first. Matthew Caunter admitting he was wrong.' Emma wrinkled her nose at him deliciously.

'So, if you have somewhere more comfortable than this tiled floor to do it on, I will rectify my error.'

How long would it take him to make love to Emma? All night wouldn't be long enough, he knew that. He wanted to make love to her slowly, gently, to begin with – that had always been his plan. But his body – and hers – was telling him that sort of lovemaking would have to wait for another time. Now, all the time they had was a little window – a couple of hours at best – before Emma had to go and pick up Fleur. And their bodies were aching for one another. And he had no intention of wasting another second until he could do something about it.

He scooped Emma up into his arms and she wound her arms around his neck, kissed him just below the earlobe. His turn to sigh with pleasure.

'Be gentle with me,' Emma said, laughing.

'The hell I will.' Matthew laughed back as Emma pointed in the direction she wanted him to take her.

Up the stairs, into her room ... back where they belonged, the both of them.

Chapter Eighteen

Matthew's lovemaking was every bit as wonderful as Emma had always dreamed it would be. He'd taken her to another plane somewhere and she'd screamed out with delight.

But now they were sitting up against the headboard, Matthew's arm around her and with her head leaning against his shoulder. Both were totally naked.

'I should have asked you, before we did that,' Emma said, 'if you were a free man, as in not married.'

'Stable doors and the closing of same and bolting horses springs to mind,' Matthew said. 'But if makes you breathe a little easier, I'm not married.'

'Well, I can't be sure I would have said "no" even if you were,' Emma replied.

'You always were impulsive,' Matthew said, stroking Emma's arm with a middle finger – such an innocent and guileless gentle gesture but one that was making her want him all over again. 'And thank God for that. But that took the biscuit.'

'What did?'

'You, throwing yourself at me, dragging me upstairs to bed.'

'You carried me, if you remember.'

'Ah, but you led the way – in more ways than one.'

'I know,' Emma said, nestling into him even further. They'd have to get up very soon but for now she would snuggle, breathe him in, taste him on her lips a little longer. 'It's just that, well, I've been a good wife – or at least I think I was – and I've been the mother to Fleur that Seth wanted me to be and I'm still doing that, and I've built up businesses only to have them taken from me by various means, and along the way I lost who I was. And then I saw you and I knew … and it was as though the years between had never been. I saw it in your eyes. I could see you felt the same way about me as I do about you and I … well, I lost all caution, all control, and I knew if it was only the once that we could make love then it would be worth being a wanton hussy for.'

Matthew groaned beside her.

'Too poetic for you?' she asked.

Matthew's finger ceased its rhythmic massage of her forearm. He jiggled his shoulders.

'Don't tell me my thinking was all wrong,' she said, anxious now.

'Not wrong at all,' Matthew said. 'Just getting a bit …'

'Uncomfortable? I'm no lightweight these days.'

'And there's not a spare ounce of flesh on you either,' Matthew said. 'I barely had anything to hold on to when you were getting your wicked way with me.'

'Hmm,' Emma said. She wasn't convinced. Something she'd said or done had brought him up sharp about something. Well, she wasn't going to spoil the moment by giving him the Spanish Inquisition about it.

'Oh,' Matthew said, leaning away from her a little and picking up her copy of *Pride and Prejudice* from the bedside table, the one he'd seen her throw across the back garden of Shingle Cottage way back in 1909 – almost eighteen long years ago now. The one he'd stopped up all night in the sitting room to mend for her while she slept in his bed, exhausted through illness and grief and loneliness. 'I see you've kept this on your travels.'

'Of course,' she said. 'My mama bought it for me and you mended it. The title's been very apt over the years – I had more pride than it's probably ladylike to have, and there was enough prejudice against Seth because of his criminal father and brothers to sink a whole fleet of their fishing boats. So, I always took it as hand luggage. I couldn't risk it being lost in transit by some careless baggage-handler, could I?'

'I should think not. I worked my fingers to the bone all night mending that for you.'

'And talking of night,' Emma said. 'Look at that sky out there.'

'It'll mean I'll have to drag my eyes away from you but ...'

'Flattery will get you everywhere,' Emma said, turning her face up to him and kissing his chin. 'I'll tell you. It's going to be a beautiful sunset. The sky's all stripy – darkish grey, which I expect will go indigo later, and raspberry, like one of Signor Cascarini's ice cream raspberry ripple sundaes. I'll tell you about him some time.'

Matthew yawned theatrically, and then he laughed. 'Tom, bless his heart, told me more than you probably wanted him to about Signor Cascarini. How he's sweet on you ...'

'I should never have encouraged him.'

'And I hope you didn't encourage him in the way you've just encouraged me?'

'Of *course* not!' Emma said, mock-outraged. 'What do you take me for?'

'A very sexy, beautiful, adorable strumpet at the moment.'

'Guilty as charged,' Emma said. 'And if it wasn't for the fact I really will need to go and fetch Fleur soon, I'd show you just how much of a strumpet I can be.'

'Ah ...' Matthew said.

'That was a very loaded "ah" if I may say so.'

'Was it?'

'Oh God, Matthew,' Emma said, sitting up straighter in the bed, removing her head from Matthew's shoulder to look at him, face to face. She knew that tone of voice. He had another agenda. 'I was right in my thinking just now when you stiffened after I said all that poetic stuff about being a good wife and a good stepmother to Fleur, wasn't I? What is it?'

'I love you, Emma, and that's the truth. Whether or not you will love me —'

'Matthew! Tell me! Please.'

She was frightened now. She'd been this man's housekeeper for months and months back when she'd been barely sixteen years old and she'd learned to read his moods. Learned that often what he didn't say was more important than what he did. And she knew beyond doubt when he was hiding something from her, and that when he thought he was hiding it from her for her own good. He'd got her to safety at Nase Head House – when he knew Reuben Jago and his sons Carter and Miles, Seth's father and brothers, would harm her if they could – on the pretext of taking her to dine and showing her how to read a menu and to drink champagne, hadn't he?

'We'll dress first,' Matthew said. He slid out of bed and handed Emma the clothes she'd thrown in her haste all over the floor.

'Yes,' Emma said. 'Fleur should be telephoning me soon. It's getting dark. Actually, I expected her to call before now. I —'

'You're worried about something?' Matthew said. 'That Fleur will take a dim view of her mother being made love to?'

'No. Not that.' She put her head in her hands. 'I don't know what I was thinking coming up here, thinking only of my own pleasure when Fleur could be in danger out there?'

She didn't trust Caroline further than she could throw her. There was an uneasy feeling in the pit of her stomach that there had been someone waiting outside in a car for Caroline the afternoon of Fleur's birthday. Were they being spied on? Had Fleur been spied on?

Emma shivered and Matthew put his hand in the small of her back and smoothed it, comfortingly, up and down.

'What sort of danger, Emma? You can tell me, you know you can.'

So she did. Almost word for word the conversations she'd had with Caroline. The words came tumbling out like water from an overflowing stream going over rocks. And there wasn't any relief in the telling, not even to Matthew.

'First things first,' Matthew said. 'We'll dress – much as I'd like a repeat performance or two of what we've just been doing so splendidly – and then you telephone Signor Cascarini and ask to speak to Fleur. It will put your mind at rest if nothing else.'

Emma's breath caught in her throat. 'What if she's not there? What ...' Matthew knew something, didn't he? The way he was looking at her – an uncomfortable mix of desire and fear and anger. 'What do you know that I don't?'

'Only what you've just told me. But I know Caroline of old—'

'You do?'

Matthew laughed, a little uneasily, Emma thought.

'Thank goodness you've never lost your habit of questioning everything a man says! But I don't mean I know her in the way you're probably thinking. I saw her in court, lying through her teeth but there was nothing that could be pinned on her, only Miles. But she's dangerous, Emma, and we both know it.' Matthew began pulling on his underthings, stepped into his trousers, stuffed his arms into the sleeves of his shirt.

Emma followed suit. She'd never dressed so quickly in her life.

'Name, miss,' the policeman said.

'I've already told you,' Fleur replied. 'In the cinema.' She glanced across the cell-like room to the woman police constable standing ramrod straight in the corner, with her arms behind her back. *Tell him I've already told him,* Fleur's eyes pleaded, but she was met with a blank stare.

'Tell me again. Terrible memory.'

Fleur sighed. Her head was beginning to ache. Were Caroline and Archie in the police station? Not that she wanted to see them but they were responsible for her being here, weren't they? What time was it? Should she ask this constable sitting across the table from her, looking bored out of his mind. Pushing back the sleeve of her jacket, Fleur gasped.

'My watch! My beautiful watch that Ma bought me for my birthday! It's gone. What have you done with it?'

'Look, miss, I don't know what your game is but I'm beginning to make a guess at it. Watch missing you say? A likely story. Name?'

'Fleur Jago. However many times you ask me, you'll get the same answer. It's the truth.'

'Address?'

'Romer Lodge. Cleveland Road. Paignton.'

Fleur was frightened now. Really frightened. How had she lost her watch?

'Father's name?' the constable asked.

'He's dead,' Fleur said, a lump in her throat. However many times she had to tell someone her pa was dead it still hurt.

'And what was he called before he died?'

Not an ounce of sympathy. But then, why should she expect him to have sympathy for her? The man probably dealt with the dregs of society; people like Archie, and – yes, she had to admit it – Caroline, every day. How could she ever have been duped by her? Why wasn't she here now protecting her if she was her mother as she claimed to be?

'Seth Jago,' Fleur said, swallowing back tears.

'Jago, you say. Now that name rings a bell.' There was the twitch of a smile at the corner of his lips and Fleur might have imagined it but she thought she saw the hardness in his eyes soften a little. 'Sit with the prisoner, Heatley, will you?' he said to the woman police constable. 'I think I need a word with the sarge.'

Prisoner? What am I guilty of?

'And make a note of anything she says,' the constable said as he left the room, slamming shut the heavy door behind him.

'Will do,' the woman police constable said.

And there's going to be nothing to write down, Fleur thought, because I'm saying nothing until my ma gets here.

Chapter Nineteen

'She's not there,' Emma said to Matthew, her hand shook holding the telephone receiver out in front of her as though it might bite. Or poison her in some way.

Eduardo, delighted as he was that she had telephoned him, had sounded genuinely puzzled as to why she thought Fleur was working in his ice cream parlour. Emma had asked if Paolo was there and been told he wasn't. Eduardo had no idea where he was, he'd said. 'Is Tuesday. He have half day on Tuesday. No work in afternoon. He too old to ask every step of his day, *si*?'

Why had Fleur lied to her? Again. Where was she? And with whom? Had it been Caroline on the telephone yesterday and not Paolo as Fleur had claimed? Goodness, she'd like to wring the little madam's neck for lying to her! No, she wouldn't – all she wanted was to see her, hold her, tell her that although she was cross she loved her dearly and would die for her. She nearly had once, back in 1912, when Margaret Phipps had beaten Emma black and blue in the churchyard of St Mary's and left her for dead, taking baby Fleur who'd been missing for a whole day almost before Seth's friend, Olly Underwood, had found her in a cardboard box in the back garden of Shingle Cottage, plonked on top of the compost heap.

'History is repeating itself,' Emma said to Matthew, her hand over the mouthpiece of the telephone.

'Emma? You there?' Eduardo's voice shouted in her ear, so loud that Matthew heard, the loudness of it making him start.

'Let me speak to him,' Matthew said.

'He's Italian. He's hard to understand sometimes,' Emma

whispered. She handed Matthew the telephone. It was good to have someone share this terrible moment.

Emma listened as Matthew asked simple questions. What time did Paolo go out? When was he expected back? Had Eduardo been at the ice cream parlour all day? Was his mother-in-law there?

'Thank you, Signor Cascarini,' Matthew said. 'I'll say goodbye now. I have other telephone calls to make.'

Emma clutched his arm. 'Matthew, there are things I have to tell you before you telephone anyone. About Caroline. What else she said.'

She tried to pull him away from the telephone and walk across the hall to the sitting room but her legs were more wobbly than half-set junket. Her breathing was rapid and shallow.

Stay focused. Getting Fleur back safely is paramount. I'd never have spent the afternoon in bed with Matthew if I'd known she was in danger. It felt bittersweet now – their reunion, their loving – to be shocked back into reality with this.

Matthew must have sensed her physical distress because he half led, half carried her into the sitting room and gently eased her onto a couch. He sat down beside her, taking both hands in his.

'Tell,' he said. 'As quickly as you can.'

'The day after Fleur's birthday tea, Caroline came back. She told me – but not Fleur – that Seth wasn't her pa, but that Miles was. And that Fleur wasn't born on the 16th of July, but on the 22nd September. The birth certificate she left for Seth was – is, I suppose – a forgery. I begged her not to tell Fleur any of that. She promised she wouldn't as long as I let her meet Fleur, and …'

And I've just realised that if that is true then it might not have been me who was unable to have babies in our marriage, but Seth.

256

'And?' Matthew prompted.

'And that's about the sum of it,' Emma said. She couldn't waste time thinking about babies and the lack of them now – it didn't matter. The only thing that mattered was finding Fleur.

And fast.

And it seemed Matthew was thinking along the very same lines because he leapt from the couch and ran into the hall. Within seconds she heard him speaking to someone, although she couldn't hear the exact words – it was just a jumble of sound, fighting to be heard against the blood rushing past her ears with her fear.

If she hadn't come back to England – to Devon – then none of this would be happening. Fleur would be in Vancouver and probably out enjoying a trip to the shops with her friends. Or at college doing a course of some sort. But whichever – she would be safe.

Oh, Seth, I am so sorry. I haven't looked after her as I should. And I was making love to Matthew, throwing myself at him, and all thoughts of Fleur banished from my mind while I did. What sort of a woman have I become?

More telephone calls followed. Emma heard Matthew say 'Thank you. Goodbye' a couple of times. The clock on the mantelpiece ticked slowly on – it seemed to echo in the room. Every second was precious. Critical for Fleur.

She heard Matthew return the telephone to the cradle. And then she heard it ring again.

'I'll answer it,' Matthew called to her.

More low mumbling from Matthew. She heard him say her name. And then Seth's. Just the names.

'She's in custody,' Matthew said, coming back into the sitting room. He had a big grin on his face.

How could he find something like that amusing?

'In custody? Where?'

'Torquay police station.'

'Why?'

'It seems there was some sort of brouhaha at the Odeon cinema. Fleur was in a box—'

'A box? With Paolo? Eduardo said Paolo had gone out. Perhaps—'

'Stop making up imaginary scenarios, Emma,' Matthew said, gently enough, but, to Emma, it sounded like a telling off. *How would he feel if it were his son who had gone missing?*

'Not with Paolo,' Matthew said. 'From the description the usherette was able to give the police I'm pretty certain Fleur was with Caroline—'

'Oh my God!' Emma's hand flew to her mouth. 'I might have known. I'll get my bag and a jacket and I'll go there and—'

'And it seems Fleur and Caroline weren't alone,' Matthew interrupted, ignoring her suggestion. 'There was a man with them.'

'Tell me this is a dream,' Emma said. 'A man? Who?'

'Darling Emma, if you'd just let me finish—'

'Go on,' Emma said, and then couldn't help but laugh that she'd interrupted him yet again, but relief was flooding through her now that Fleur was at least safe if she was in custody. Safe from harm being done to her by Caroline and the mysterious man.

'It's not a new situation. The cloakrooms were ransacked. Jewellery taken from jacket collars, money stolen. More than a dozen men have reported their wallets taken from their inside pockets in the foyer. Watches have been slipped from wrists without the wearers noticing.'

'Not Fleur?' Emma said. 'Please tell me Fleur had no part in that?'

'She says not—'

'And I believe her,' Emma said.

Just so you know. I am not going to let Fleur be tarred

with the same brush as her late grandfather and uncles. And – it seems – her birth mother.

'That's my girl,' Matthew said. 'As feisty and fiery as ever.' He kissed the tip of Emma's nose and while it was a lovely gesture she wished he hadn't done it because it was giving her all sorts of mixed feelings.

'I'm too old to change now,' Emma said. 'But I *do* believe her.'

'Of course you believe her. As I do. But as Caroline and this man managed to escape, they can't question them. Yet.'

'But they'll find them?'

'Oh, they'll find them, or my name's not Matthew Caunter.'

Yes, if anyone could find them it would be Matthew. And then a thought occurred to her – had he known all along that Caroline was around?

'Did you know she was back?' Emma asked. 'Caroline, I mean.'

'No.'

'I don't know that I can believe you. I can't believe you haven't lost the knack of seeing things that people shouldn't be doing, that they're trying to hide.'

'I find it sad you have such a low opinion of me, Emma. Don't you think I'd have protected you from all this had I known? Didn't I put my own life at risk once before to protect you and Seth, and Fleur when she was a baby? Didn't I show you just how much you meant to me then, and again just now?' Matthew pointed up at the ceiling and her bedroom overhead.

'Yes. You know all that's true. But you were so calm talking to the police. Detached. As if you were waiting to make such a call or be told such news.'

'Darling, Emma,' Matthew said. 'Forever questioning things. That was the old me, the surveillance officer of old taking over. Do you think I would have been any good at

259

my job if I let my emotions show? I had to keep a cool demeanour at all times.'

Darling. He called me darling. A second time.

'Of course,' Emma said. 'I shouldn't have questioned you. I think it's fear making me say things I oughtn't. And I know that Fleur will be frightened. All alone. It's dark now. She—'

'She's safe and that's all that matters for the moment. No harm can come to her having a cup of tea in Torquay police station, now can it?'

'I hope not,' Emma said.

'And Caroline probably has a lot of stuff – not all of it legally come by I'd bet my life-savings on – back at her mother's place and she will no doubt be going back there to collect it. And she'll have a welcome party when she does. And so, while we wait for the police to telephone again to tell me when we can go and collect Fleur, you can bring me up to date on what it is you've been doing all these years since we last saw one another. Still making delectable crab tarts?'

'I am. But not in a business sense. I'll make you one if you'd like one though.'

'I would. So, if you're not cooking what are you doing that enables you to afford a lovely house like this?'

'Seth left me well-provided for, although I'd have preferred it if he hadn't died.'

'I'm sorry,' Matthew said. 'There's a trite comment I could make to that, but I won't.'

That he wouldn't have come back into my life, he means. And we wouldn't have spent the last two hours making wonderful love.

'No. Don't. I loved Seth. He loved me. We had a good marriage. He'll always be in my heart.'

'I'd expect nothing less of you, Emma. Seth was a good man. But I can't imagine you sitting idly all day looking at magazines, listening to the wireless, taking tea with friends.'

'How well you know me!'

'So, what are you doing now in this beautiful house to keep boredom at bay?'

'Sewing,' Emma said. How wonderful it was to be talking of nicer things, of things that had a future. 'Couture dresses. Wedding dresses. Come into my atelier and I'll show you.'

Emma, feeling a little stronger in the legs now, walked ahead of Matthew and pushed open the door to her atelier. How she loved the unique smell of it – new fabric had a smell all its own which Emma found impossible to describe, but she'd know it anywhere. Three dresses – part completed – were wrapped in cheap cotton sheeting, to protect them from dust and fading, hung from the picture rail. They looked, Emma thought, like ghosts – if she believed in the existence of ghosts, which she didn't. No, more like a depiction of angels on Christmas cards – all they needed was a halo of tinsel to complete the look.

Stella's wedding dress was on the mannequin in the corner. *Would Stella be well enough by February to wear it?* At the hospital earlier, Stella had sounded sad when she'd told Emma that her fiancé hadn't visited her for a few days. 'I expect he's busy,' she'd said, not looking at Emma as she spoke, and Emma had got the feeling she didn't believe that he was, not really. It had been on the tip of Emma's tongue to ask her fiancé's name, but she had decided to let Stella have the pleasure of using the word for as long as she could. But the writing, as the saying has it, was more than likely on the wall and both Emma and Stella had known it.

'It all looks very organised in here,' Matthew said, tapping the accounts book on the table.

'There's only me to organise things,' Emma said. 'Although there are people who need a lesson in organisation.' She reached for the book, opened it, flipped through the pages until she found the entry for the cheque – still unpresented as far as she knew – she'd sent Exe Motors.

'Such as?' Matthew said.

'Whoever it is who owns Exe Motors. I bought a car from them weeks ago now – Eduardo Cascarini drove me to Exeter because he said he used that garage for his ice cream vans and could recommend them – and my cheque is yet to be presented. How Exe Motors can run a business with such slack practices I have no idea. I've even written to them but have yet to receive a reply. But I suppose, in the scheme of things, and what is happening with Fleur right now, it's hardly life-threatening, is it?'

'I'm glad you see it that way,' Matthew said, grinning at her.

Emma couldn't stop herself grinning back. However big a shock it had been to discover that Fleur had lied to her, had been in some sort of fracas at a cinema and was now in Torquay police station, it was still wonderful to have Matthew with his red-gold hair and his green eyes and his oh-so-kissable lips smiling down at her.

But still she couldn't help teasing. 'I expect it's a man who runs it. One who needs a woman to be his secretary to run things more efficiently for him.'

'Do you now?' Matthew said. 'And is it your opinion that men need women to organise their lives?'

'Well, we are rather better at things like running homes, and looking after children and, in my case, running a business.'

'*I* have a business. A garage business. In Exeter. I could use a secretary.'

Emma felt her eyes widen and her mouth go round with surprise. Stella? Stella had a fiancé who owned a garage. It couldn't be Matthew who was Stella's fiancé, could it? She'd asked if he was a free man as she was now a free woman and he'd said he had been. And there had to be more than one garage business in Exeter, didn't there?

'That's taken the wind out of your sails.' Matthew laughed. 'And close your mouth – you're in danger of catching flies. No, better still – I'll close it for you.'

262

He enveloped Emma in a gentle hug and kissed her lips and she knew when she was beaten.

'I think ...' Emma said, reluctantly pulling away because they didn't have time to follow up where that kiss was leading, did they? Someone from Torquay police station would telephone soon and then she'd need to go and collect Fleur. 'You have probably got more to tell me about what's been going in your life since we last met than I have to tell you what's been going on in mine.'

'Sharp as ever,' Matthew replied.

'I've got lots of pins and needles here to keep me so!' Emma picked up a tin of pins and rattled it at him. 'But now you know that I sew and I've not left my past behind me completely with Caroline turning up and causing trouble, and I know now that you run a garage business of some sort, what else do you have to tell me? You haven't married again, have you? I did ask you if you were free ...'

Not that she thought for a moment that he had. Would he have been so ready to get into her bed and love her with his body and his heart as he had done, if that were the case?

'And I am. Is that a proposal?'

'Certainly not!' Emma said, mock-outraged. 'I expect a proposal to be done in the right and proper way, on one bended knee and promising undying love.'

'I don't doubt it,' Matthew said, but the teasing had gone from his voice and a little bit of spark had vanished from his eyes.

And Emma knew there was ... something ... something he wasn't divulging. And she also knew it was always best not to ask anything of Matthew she knew in her heart he didn't want to tell her. Leopards rarely changed their spots. He'd said he ran a garage business that he needed a secretary for, but might that be a cover for something else? Emma was afraid to ask.

'You're certainly very good at what you do,' Matthew said, pointing to Stella's wedding dress.

Changing the subject.

'Thank you,' Emma said. 'I ought to have covered that up as well before I went out. It's a wedding dress.' She unfolded a clean length of cotton sheeting and shook out the creases.

'I guessed it might be.'

'It's not for me, if that's what you were thinking. Oh, I know Eduardo has thought along those lines but I certainly haven't. No, this is for a friend – well, that's how I think about her now, although she began as a client. I visited her in the hospital this afternoon. Stella – she's called Stella.'

'Stella?' Matthew said.

'You know her?'

Please, please, tell me you're not Stella's mysterious fiancé who runs a garage in Exeter? I don't think I could bear it if you're Stella's fiancé – the man she loves so much and is expecting to spend her future with. And I don't think I'll ever forgive myself for making love to a friend's fiancé if you are.

But before Matthew could answer the telephone began to ring and he raced off to answer it.

He was back in seconds.

'We can go to her now. Come on.'

Within minutes they were in Matthew's car and heading for Torquay.

Emma was itching to ask if Matthew knew Stella because she was his fiancée, and if his business was called Exe Motors, but was afraid to. She didn't want that to be true. She would leave it to Matthew to clarify matters.

Sometimes it was best not to know things, wasn't it?

'Does *he* have to stay?' Fleur said.

Her ma had turned up at the police station with a man.

A man Fleur had had no idea her ma even knew. Certainly she'd not seen him at the Grand Hotel when they'd been staying there, and neither had he been to Romer Lodge before, to her knowledge.

'This is my friend, Matthew,' her ma had said. 'Matthew Caunter.' Fleur instantly recognised the name. Caroline had told her that her ma and ... this man ... had been lovers.

And he was here again now. Sitting in the chair opposite her ma's in the sitting room of Romer Lodge with the ankle of his right leg balanced on the knee of his left. Relaxed. As though he had no intention of leaving soon. If ever.

How could she? At the police station Matthew had gone off to another room – cell? – somewhere to talk to a senior police officer leaving Fleur and her ma in the cell she'd been in for hours. She'd been cold and tired and frightened. And angry. It hadn't been a nice feeling to learn that the woman who had turned up claiming to be her birth mother was a confidence trickster. Or that her ma had arrived with a previous lover. *How had she kept him so secret?* How many times had her ma seen him since she'd been back in England? Or had she been seeing him in Canada too? Behind her pa's back?

While she'd been expecting her ma to bawl her out for lying to her – not being at the ice cream parlour when she'd said she would be – she had done nothing of the sort. She'd hugged Fleur and kissed her and told her she believed all the things she'd told the police about the afternoon's incident. And she'd told her she loved her over and over.

Perhaps she'd said all that because the policewoman had been standing in the corner, arms still folded across her chest, eyes everywhere like a hawk's.

'His name is Matthew, Fleur,' her ma said now, looking – Fleur thought – rather soppily at the man and not at her. 'Matthew Caunter. I introduced you in the police station. And yes, he is staying. For now.'

'I knew Emma a long time ago,' Matthew said. 'Before you were born—'

'She's not my ma. Not really.'

'I think you'll find she very much is your ma. But whoever gave birth to you, Fleur,' Matthew said, 'doesn't alter the fact I *did* know Emma before you were born. And Seth. I met him a time or two. I worked for his pa.'

'So you're a smuggler, too!' Fleur snapped.

At the police station – before they'd left – a sergeant had sat down with them all in an office and told Fleur that her grandfather, Reuben, had died in police custody, put there for smuggling. Her ma had just told her the same thing, but she hadn't believed her. But Fleur had wanted to know if it was true what Caroline had said – that her uncle Miles had been hanged – and the sergeant had confirmed that it was. And, it seemed that Miles's brother, Carter, had also been hanged. Both for murder. What sort of blood did she have in her?

'No,' Matthew said. 'I'm not, and never was, a smuggler. I worked for His Majesty's Customs, now His Majesty's Customs and Excise. I suppose you could say I was, in those days, a sort of spy.'

'A *spy*? You came back to England, Ma, to rekindle your friendship with a spy?'

'I didn't come back to England to rekindle anything, Fleur,' her ma said. 'I didn't know Matthew was here until this afternoon.'

Fleur saw her ma glance at Matthew briefly before looking away again. And she saw a flush pink her ma's neck. What had they been doing all afternoon while she'd been in police custody? What?

'Excuse me,' Fleur said, 'but you came waltzing into the police station, arm in arm, with a *spy*.'

'Surveillance,' Matthew said, quickly, casting a worried look at Emma. 'That would be a better word for what I did.'

Fleur shrugged. She didn't know what – or who – to believe. She knew what surveillance meant and it was one and the same as spying really, wasn't it?

'Did Pa know about this ... friendship?'

'Yes,' her ma and Matthew said at the same time.

Well, that was a surprise – that neither had hesitated in their response.

'Pa's only been dead two years, Ma,' Fleur said. She knew she was making it sound as though she was blaming her pa for being dead, which in a way she did because if he hadn't played the hero and jumped into a freezing sea and lost his arm and then got gangrene for his pains, he'd be alive now and none of this would be happening.

'I know,' Emma said, her voice low. Sad even. 'And he's not coming back.'

'But you don't miss him enough not to rekindle a friendship so soon ...'

'That's enough, Fleur,' Matthew said, standing up.

'You can't tell me things like that,' Fleur said. 'You're not my pa.'

'Indeed, I'm not,' Matthew said. 'Emma has been beside herself worrying about you—'

'I don't know why,' Fleur interrupted, pretty certain she was going to get a telling off in some way for doing it, but she didn't care. What did this man know! 'She's not my ma.'

'Isn't she? Isn't she the one who washed you, dressed you, fed you, nursed you when you were sick? Isn't she the one who I'm pretty certain sat up in the night with you at times? Isn't she the one who helped you learn your lessons? Isn't she the one who has started up a business so you can live comfortably in a lovely home in a very beautiful part of the country? Isn't she the one who risked her life defending you from a kidnapper before you were potty-trained? And got beaten black and blue for her efforts? Well, Fleur, that's all true, *n'est-ce pas?*'

267

With every sentence he spoke Matthew's eyes seem to darken, his body become stiffer. She was on the wrong side of him and she didn't like it one bit. She could believe now that he would have pursued a murderer until he was caught.

He'd even thrown in a French phrase to let her know he knew all about her.

Fleur struggled for something to say. And then she looked at her ma, who was sitting, hands clasped in her lap, legs crossed neatly at the ankle, back straight as a ballerina's. And she was silently crying. Tears were running down her cheeks and she was doing nothing to wipe them away. But Fleur knew she had caused those tears by her outburst and that everything Matthew had said was true.

She went to her ma and knelt down on the floor, put her head on her knee the way she'd done countless times over the years when she, herself, had been sad.

'I'm sad, too, Ma,' she said. 'And frightened.'

'Frightened? There's no need to be. You're safe now.'

'I don't mean that,' Fleur said. She was more frightened than sad really but tears wouldn't come. She wished they would – tears could heal, but could they heal all this?

'What, then? Tell me.'

Fleur took a deep breath. 'My world turned upside down on my birthday when Caroline showed up and I don't know how to make it get the right way up again. She mesmerised me with talk of Hollywood and films and I thought I ought to be dazzled because she was my real mother and she'd brought me into the world. She drinks. In the daytime. In the cinema she was drinking. They both were. And I know I've been sharp with you, and very rude at times since we came to England, and I've lied and lied to you when I ought not to have done. Now I've been alone with Caroline and know her true colours, I'm frightened I'm more like her than I want to be.'

'Oh, darling. I'm sorry you've had to go through all this. It's not what your pa and I wanted for you.'

'I want to be more like you, Ma.'

Fleur felt her ma's hand on her head, felt her run that hand down to the nape of her neck and massage it gently, the way she'd done so many times and which Fleur had always taken for granted. *Would Caroline ever have done that?* Fleur doubted it.

Mumbling into her ma's knees she told her about seeing Paolo with another girl in the cinema. 'I nearly turned tail and came back home but I didn't. I wish I had now,' Fleur finished.

'Paolo would still have been seeing someone else behind your back. I'm sorry you had to find out that way,' her ma said.

'Yes, but all that stuff in the cinema and the police station afterwards wouldn't have happened.'

'We can only learn from our mistakes,' her ma said. 'I know finding Matthew here has been a shock to you – and possibly not such a big a shock as it was to me – but thank goodness he was. Thank goodness he knew what authorities to contact, who to speak to, to make things happen when I discovered you weren't with Paolo.'

And by those words Fleur could tell her ma really liked Matthew and that he was going to stick around.

She yawned.

'Bath and then bed?' her ma said, gently lifting Fleur's head from her knees. 'Both of us, I think.'

'I'm going to write a letter to Paolo first,' Fleur said. 'Tell him I saw him at the cinema with *that* girl, and that's the last I want to see of him. It won't take much paper. I could get it all on the back of a postage stamp.'

'That's my girl,' her ma said.

'And that's my cue,' Matthew said.

Fleur got to her knees, but her ma stayed where she was.

Matthew walked over to her, leaned over and kissed her ma on the cheek, and then – for good measure – on the top of her head.

'I'll telephone you in the morning, Emma,' he said. 'Hopefully, by then, Caroline and her accomplice will have been apprehended.' He turned his gaze from her ma and looked at Fleur. 'I'm glad you're safe. For everyone's sake. I'll see myself out.'

Chapter Twenty

'Well, Emma, you stirred up a hornet's nest coming back.' Matthew was talking to no one but himself as he filed paperwork in his office, but just saying her name brought her sharply into focus in his mind.

Although he had telephoned Emma every day to check that she was well, he hadn't seen her for over a week now – and that by design.

Both Emma and Fleur needed time alone, he knew that. They needed space to get used to the new situation. Caroline and her man friend had been apprehended. The police – tipped off by Matthew who had given them Caroline's late mother's address – had lain in wait. At two o clock in the morning, they'd crept up through the back garden by lamplight and got the surprise of their lives to find themselves surrounded by police. Both were now in custody. What happened to them Matthew didn't care, but he realised that whatever sentence they were given they would be released sometime. And that 'sometime' could again be dangerous for Emma. And for Fleur.

He couldn't imagine what it must have been like for Fleur finding out that Emma wasn't her mother – well, not the one who had given birth to her but she'd done the mothering all the same. And then for Fleur to discover exactly what sort of person the woman who had given birth to her really was must have hurt her to the core.

Court case? Matthew slapped a hand to his forehead. Why hadn't he thought of that? Fleur was still a minor and it was highly unlikely she'd be asked to take the witness box and give evidence against Caroline and her man friend. That Fleur's watch had been stolen by one of them was good and bad in equal measure – bad that she had lost the watch Emma had so recently given her for her birthday, but good that it had been found in Caroline's possession when she'd been searched by the police.

He picked up the cheque Emma had left, weeks ago now, in payment for the car she'd bought from him. He would pay it into his account today. He knew now that the Emma Jago who had signed the cheque was indeed *his* Emma. He'd found her and he had no reason to hang onto her cheque, unpresented. She might see it as charity if he didn't bank the cheque, gifting her the car, and he could just see Emma's look of outrage if that were the case.

He would bank the cheque and then he would go and visit Stella. With a pang of regret – or was it disgust at his treatment of her – he realised that while he'd telephoned Emma every day it had been days now since he'd telephoned the hospital asking after Stella.

He wasn't liking himself one little bit at that moment.

And Stella was going to like him even less, wasn't she?

Matthew arrived at the hospital to find Stella sitting on a chair beside her bed. She was dressed in her own clothes – although even from the doorway he could see they were loose on her skinny frame – and not in a hospital gown and lying on the bed, looking frail. She had a little more colour in her cheeks since the last time he'd seen her, though, and he was glad of that. And she hadn't realised he was there yet.

A bowl piled high with fruit was on the bedside table on the other side of the bed. Untouched. He was glad he hadn't brought her fruit now, although it was obvious someone had. There was a little pile of magazines beside the fruit bowl. Walking closer he saw that the magazine on the top was a copy of *Vogue*. A lady's magazine. Fashion. Trousseau clothes and wedding dresses sprang to mind and he gulped back sadness for Stella that she'd been so excited, so happy, planning both those things and now …

'Matthew,' Stella said, turning at the sound of his footfalls.

Her eyes, Matthew thought, looked sad – as though she already knew what it was he had come to say. How could she not have guessed? She was an intelligent woman, trained to observe people as well as treat their physical ailments.

Matthew resisted going into apologetic mode – he'd been busy; he wanted to give her time to heal. All of those things were true, of course, but he knew Stella wouldn't want to hear them.

'It's good to see you sitting out,' Matthew said.

'It's good to be here,' Stella said. She kept her hands clasped together in her lap.

To kiss her, or not? Would it seem cruel to be kissed and then told their relationship was over? He remembered how he had felt when his wife – ex-wife now – Annie had told him she was leaving him. He decided not to kiss her, and neither did Stella tilt her head to one side, offering him her cheek.

'Doctor Taylor says I should be ready to return to my duties in another week.'

'Good, good,' Matthew said. She had something to look forward to now at least.

A nurse appeared in Stella's private ward then and offered to fetch a chair for Matthew. Both Matthew and Stella were silent while the chair was brought from the corridor outside and placed so he could sit opposite Stella, but on the same side of the bed.

Was this how Judas felt? Matthew wondered as he sat down.

'I've been lucky, Matthew,' Stella said. 'Very lucky to have survived this.'

'I wouldn't call it lucky to have been as ill as you have,' Matthew said.

'I would,' Stella said. 'Had I not gone down with

influenza and reacted very badly to it, I'd never have known I had a growth in my womb that shouldn't have been there. Doctor Taylor told me I'm lucky it was found when it was. I could have done without the blood poisoning I contracted afterwards, though.' She gave him a wan smile.

'But you pulled through. I'm glad you have.'

'Everything that's happened lately might be for the best,' Stella said. 'In the long run.'

And then Matthew noticed she was no longer wearing his engagement ring. And Stella saw him noticing. She unclasped her hands and placed them, palms down, on her knees.

'No ring,' Matthew said. He knew he was stating the obvious.

'No ring,' Stella said, with the shadow of a smile. 'It became very loose on me anyway.'

The 'anyway' hung there in the air between them ... there was another agenda here and all Matthew could do was wait until it unfolded. Stella had asked *him* to marry *her* and if he was reading between the lines correctly she was about to tell him she no longer wanted to.

'I'm sorry,' Matthew said.

'For?' Stella asked.

'That it hasn't worked out between us. We both know that, don't we?'

There – he'd been the one to start the unravelling of the end of their relationship; he'd prevented Stella from having to say what, to her, were probably unpalatable words. He'd pulled back one small crumb of self-respect here, at least.

Stella nodded, lips pressed together.

'I'd guessed. Long before today,' she said. 'When you didn't visit, I guessed. I can't imagine I wouldn't have visited you, daily, had it been you lying in a hospital bed close to death, as I was in the beginning.' Stella was looking directly into his eyes, unblinking, as she spoke.

Matthew was startled. Was the worm turning? Was he about to be on the receiving end of a litany of his own shortcomings? He had enough of them, for God's sake. He'd behaved like a cad over this. Stella – dear, sweet Stella – hadn't deserved that. But Emma had turned his mind. His heart.

'I met someone,' Matthew said. 'After you became ill, not before. Someone I knew many years ago. Someone I let go from my life when I ought not to have done. My head ruled my heart then—'

'But it was the other way around when you met her again.' It was not a question.

'It was after we became engaged—' Matthew began.

But Stella interrupted him. 'Well, thank goodness for that!' she said. 'Because I don't have you down as totally heartless.'

'No, no,' Matthew said. *More than he deserved.*

'Your ring's on the bedside table,' Stella said. 'You can fetch it.'

'No. You keep it. As you said yourself at the time it's not a traditional engagement ring, so you can wear it—'

'I can not!' Stella interrupted again. 'It would only eternally remind me of what might have been. And of what now isn't going to be. Because, you see, all this ...' Stella unclasped her hands and waved them about, over her body, over the bed, around the room, '... has had a purpose in a way. An incredibly painful purpose at times, but sometimes the things we have to bear the most can be the most worthwhile in the end. Don't you think?'

Yes. The pain of having to walk away from Emma back in 1913 had been almost unbearable. But now she was back. And this wonderful woman in front of him was setting him free to be with her. But he could hardly say all that, could he?

'I think, if I'm honest with myself,' Stella said, 'I always knew there was a part of you that would never be mine. Am I right?'

'You know you are,' Matthew said.

Stella stood up slowly and walked past Matthew, around the end of her bed, and along the other side. She took her ring from its resting place and leaned an arm out across the bed towards Matthew.

'Palm out,' she said.

All this was going against his instincts – the woman always kept the ring if things didn't work out, didn't she? But he'd hurt Stella enough. He wasn't going to stick another knife in by refusing to do as she asked.

'There,' she said, as she dropped the ring – cold and hard – into his palm. 'Do with it what you wish. I did love you, you know. I loved you very much.'

'But not now?'

He had to ask, even though he prayed she wouldn't ask him the same thing, because what could he say? *I don't think I did ever love you, not really? It was more affection than love? A fear of growing into old age with no one by my side?*

'No. Not now. For all the reasons I just gave you. And also,' Stella said, 'because I've been offered the chance to train as a midwife. And I wouldn't be able to do that as a married woman.'

Stella had looked almost triumphant saying that.

'So good has come from bad?' Matthew said.

'That's one way of putting it,' Stella said. 'I've already accepted the invitation from the hospital board. All I have to do now is see the dressmaker who had all but finished making my wedding dress. I won't be wearing it now. Not ever, I don't think. But perhaps she'll be able to alter it into something else – a cocktail dress perhaps. She said she'd be here today so ...'

And, as if on cue, Emma appeared in the doorway.

'Please, please,' Emma said, walking on into the room, 'will one of you tell me this isn't what I think it is.'

Chapter Twenty-One

'Don't say a word!' Emma hissed.

She was walking as fast as she could down Shiphay Road, back to her car. Matthew was so close behind her she could feel his breath on her neck.

'It's more than one word I want to say,' Matthew said. 'And slow down for heaven's sake, I'm older than you are.'

Emma twisted her head to look at him but didn't slow, or stop. 'Well, don't expect me to give you mouth to mouth if you have a heart attack.'

Matthew laughed.

'And it's not in the least bit funny.'

Emma saw a gap in the traffic and ran across the road. Matthew wasn't quite as quick.

'Wait!' he yelled.

Emma began to run now. She could see her car. She glanced back over her shoulder to see that Matthew still hadn't crossed the road. Good. If she was quick to crank her car over she could be in and away in seconds. On she ran. But she could hear Matthew calling her, and hear his feet pounding the pavement. Getting closer. He was a lot taller than she was and with longer legs.

One more road to cross and ... could she make it before that coal lorry drove past? She stood teetering on the kerb for a moment or two then stepped into the road, only to feel herself being yanked backwards painfully by her shoulder.

'You idiot!' Matthew said, as he pulled her to him and the lorry shot in front of them.

'Let me go!'

'No. Never. I've waited half a lifetime for you and I'm not letting you go now.'

'But you could let Stella go? As though she is less to you than a bit of rotting fish that's no use to man nor beast?'

'You know that's not how I see Stella.' Matthew loosened his grip on Emma a little, but tucked her hand through his arm, holding onto it with his spare hand. 'We need to talk.'

'I have nothing to say to you.'

'That's fine. I'll do the talking. You can do the listening. You'll know how much I love you if you do.'

Matthew began to steer her across the now clear road. In front of the isolation wing of the hospital he steered them to the left.

'My car's that way,' Emma said. She wanted to struggle from his grasp but she didn't have the strength.

'I know. You bought it from my garage, Exe Motors. My mechanic, William, sold it to you. I hope it's giving good service.'

There was no answer to that, so Emma didn't provide one. She still couldn't quite believe the coincidence that she'd been making a wedding dress for Stella, Matthew's fiancée. Ex-fiancée now. Stella had told them both, dry eyed and without even a hint of anger in her voice, how she'd guessed it was Emma Matthew was carrying in his heart when she saw the amethyst necklace that had fallen from his pocket – the very same necklace Emma had drawn onto Stella's wedding dress design.

'Where are you taking me?'

Matthew steered her right, and into a small park Emma hadn't known was there. A few yards or so and they came to a bench.

'This will do,' Matthew said.

It most certainly would. For what I have to say to you.

Matthew took a handkerchief from the pocket of his trousers and wiped the seat, then gestured for Emma to sit down.

Strangely, the gesture touched Emma more than she could ever have dreamed it would. She swallowed.

Do not show any emotion.

'I'm disappointed in you,' Emma said, when they were both seated. She shuffled a few inches away from Matthew along the seat, so they weren't touching as they had been when they'd sat down. 'I didn't want to believe that the Stella who's wedding dress you saw in my atelier was the same Stella who was so full of love for her fiancé who, I have to tell you, she never named. And I didn't want to believe that that same fiancé who owned Exe Motors, and from whom I was recommended to buy a car, was you. And I didn't want to believe that Stella's rather cold-hearted fiancé, who rarely visited when she was so ill, was you. Had I *known* any of that I'd never have let you make love to me.'

'Well, well,' Matthew said. 'For the woman who said just moments ago that she had nothing to say to me, that was rather a lot.'

'And there's more. I gave you every opportunity to tell me all of that before now. Before we all discovered what we did just now. I know Stella had told her fiancé that she'd found someone to make her wedding dress. And that wedding dress was on a mannequin in my atelier and you saw it. I saw the way your eyes widened, just a little, when I said the name Stella. You should have told me then.'

'Making sure Fleur was unharmed was more important, in my opinion.'

'And in mine. Don't split hairs. You know what I meant.'

Matthew leaned towards her, chin thrust out. 'See that?' he said, pointing to it. 'I'm taking everything you say there. I'm not proud of myself. But I'm only human. And I love you. I know now that if you never, ever, want to see me again – and I would understand completely and respect you for it – then the time we spent together in your bed will still be the best use of my time I have ever made. It was as though I'd been waiting all my life for the physical and the emotional aspects of love to come together in one place, at the same time. And they did. With you. And if that was the last time I'm ever to feel a woman's lips on mine, a woman's body against my skin, then so be it. But I cannot walk away from you. Even if you won't speak to me or see me then I still won't walk away. You know, and I know, that Caroline is mad and dangerous and won't be in prison for ever. I am going to stick around and make sure you are safe.'

'And Fleur?' Emma said.

And what have I told him by those two small words? That I want him to stick around? That I'll speak to him, meet him? Let him make love to me again? Do I want all that? Do I?

'It goes without saying,' Matthew said.

'I can't ask that of you,' Emma said.

'You're *not* asking. I'm *telling*. There's a difference. I owe you that much.'

'You owe me nothing.'

'Oh, yes, I do. Without you I'd never have known what it is like for two people to become one. As we did. You do understand what I'm saying?'

Yes. Oh, yes.

'Maybe, but it's not making me feel any better about myself,' Emma said. 'That I took the fiancé of a friend into my bed, I mean. Even though I didn't know he was at the time.'

'I can't make that better for you,' Matthew said. 'I didn't know you and Stella had met then.'

'Would it have made any difference to you if you had?'

'That's an unfair question.'

He means no it wouldn't have made a scrap of difference. To him. I might have seen it differently. No, not might ... would.

'I'll need time, Matthew, to think about all this,' Emma said.

'But preferably not the fourteen years I had to wait the last time I said goodbye to you.' Matthew laughed. And then before Emma could protest he cupped her chin in his hand and kissed her. Long and slow and deep and Emma did nothing to stop him. A dove cooed softly in a tree above them. Doves mate for life. Emma remembered reading that somewhere once. But Matthew was right. They had become one when they'd made love and they were becoming one now. It was as though she was powerless to resist him.

Almost.

'Not fourteen years,' Emma said, pulling away from him. 'But I still need time.'

Matthew stood and pulled her to her feet. 'Well, aren't you the lucky one, because that's something I've got plenty of.' He pulled her hand through the crook of his arm again and they set off down the path, back to the road. 'You know where to find me.'

Without speaking, Matthew found the crank and turned over the engine of Emma's car for her.

'*Au revoir*,' Emma said, her heart full of love and yet heavy with such an ache she wondered if it would ever go, as Matthew helped her into her car, placed the crank in the footwell, then shut the door for her and she drove away.

There was no one else Emma wanted to see now except Ruby. Not tomorrow or the day after, but now. Fleur was more than likely still painting. Since the drama with Caroline, Fleur had been reluctant to leave the house. Emma had taken Fleur to Axworthy's to buy cartridge paper and paints, and a small easel, and when she'd left earlier to visit Stella, Fleur had said she was starting a new painting – a view from her bedroom window down over the tops of the trees to the harbour. Tom said he'd wait until Emma got back before going home. *Keeping Fleur safe*. She knew he would honour that promise.

Driving far too fast, Emma hurtled in her Clyno down New Road, glancing swiftly to the right and then the left before crossing into Fore Street.

At the hospital she'd mustered as much dignity as she could as Matthew had taken the bull by the horns and told her that yes, he had been engaged to Stella, but was no more. Stella – bless her dear, kind heart – had jumped in and said she had asked Matthew to marry her in the first place, had now realised it had been a mistake to do so, and was releasing him.

But Emma hadn't stopped long. Just long enough to tell Stella, with tears in her eyes, that she would be in touch. Guilt that she had made love to Stella's fiancé had almost overwhelmed Emma at the time. And it was still doing that now, despite everything Matthew had said to her in that little park – would she ever be able to hear a dove coo and not remember that time? Ripples of ice seemed to be running up and down Emma's spine and yet her hands were clammy on the steering wheel. And it had started to rain, making vision difficult, as the wiper swished inefficiently over the windscreen. The rain suited her mood.

The ripple of ice rippling up Emma's spine spread over her shoulders and she shivered to try and shake it off. But it wouldn't go. Her jaw was clenched tight and she wondered if it would ever unclench.

Emma had a hunch that whatever it was Matthew had told Stella before she'd arrived it wasn't that he and Emma had made love. Well, she wasn't going to be the one to tell her, was she?

Emma drew to a halt outside Shingle Cottage and yanked on the handbrake. Not bothering to lock the car she ran up the path and rammed on the door.

No answer. She peered in the letterbox. From that angle she could see along the hallway into the kitchen, and could see that the back door was open. Emma had never, ever in her life entered anyone's home without being asked in but technically Shingle Cottage was hers. So she turned the handle and to her huge relief the door opened.

'Ruby?' she called, her voice a blancmange wobble. She swallowed. What Ruby had been through with Tom being so mentally ill for such a long time, and what she'd had to do to earn money to feed her family was a much bigger concern than the one facing Emma, she knew. But it was all relative, wasn't it?

No children came rushing out to see who had just walked into their house and Emma sent up a silent prayer they weren't in the garden when she stepped out onto the back path to look for Ruby. She hoped she'd be able to say what she had to quickly because as good and reliable as Tom was he'd want to get back to Ruby and the family before the children's bedtime, wouldn't he? But she *had* to talk to Ruby first. Needed to.

'Bleedin' 'ell, Em, you tryin' to give me an 'eart attack, or summat?'

Ruby shook mud from a bunch of beetroot she'd just pulled and dropped them into a wooden box by her feet. She wiped her muddy hands down the sides of her apron.

'You're all muddy,' Emma said. 'It's raining.'

'Drizzlin',' Ruby said. 'And beetroots fer supper don't pull theirselves out of the ground, now do they? What's wrong, Em? Aw gawd, it's not that bleedin' Mrs Prentiss up to 'er old tricks again? I can't bring meself to call 'er a Jago, same as you, even though 'er is. 'Ere, Fleur ain't 'urt is 'er?'

'No,' Emma said, her mouth bone dry with nerves, so dry she thought her skin might crack. 'Tom's—'

'Tom told me what you told 'im about 'er being arrested, and what 'appened to Fleur but, oh gawd, 'er 'asn't escaped, 'as 'er?'

'Not that I know of. I left Fleur painting and Tom said

he'd stay ...' The rest of Emma's sentence stuck in her throat. She just couldn't get the words out.

'Come 'ere,' Ruby said and opened her arms wide.

Emma rushed towards Ruby and threw herself into her friends arms. She'd never felt more in need of another human's touch as she did now. Not even after her parents and her brother, Johnnie, had died had she felt like this. And after Seth had died there had been a numbness but she'd known, even in that darkest moment, that her life would go on.

Only now she thought it might have ended. Matthew had said she knew where to find him which was tantamount to saying he'd be happy to be found. But did he deserve to be found? Did she deserve to have the sort of love she knew she had for Matthew?

'I've done a terrible thing, Ruby,' she said as Ruby enveloped her in her arms, and started crooning to her as she would one of her own children. 'I've done the worst possible thing any woman can do to another woman.'

'I don't believe it,' Ruby said, hugging Emma hard now. 'No one could 'ave been worse than me, eh? And I've come good – wi' your 'elp. So—'

'You don't understand,' Emma said with a loud sob.

'I understand we're standin' 'ere like a pair of fools gettin' soaked. An' I never will know what it is you've done if you don't tell me, an' even I know it'd be best if you don't do the tellin' 'ere where there might be ears.'

She released Emma from the hug, but put an arm around her shoulder and began to lead her down the path and back to the house.

'The beetroots,' Emma said.

'The rain'll wash 'em off a bit.'

'The children?'

'The little bleeders are at their grandmother's. 'Er misses that they're not there so much now I'm on the straight an' narrow, so they've gone up to tea with 'er. 'Er'll spoil 'em rotten, but it looks as though fate 'as dealt us a good 'and today, Em, don't it?'

They'd reached the kitchen now and Ruby gentled Emma through the doorway and closed the door.

'Tea first with a drop of somethin' in it,' Ruby said. 'And none of your protestantations.'

'Protestations,' Emma said.

'That an' all,' Ruby said. 'You'll live. I know it ain't protestantations and I only said it to test you. The true bossy Emma is still in there, ain't she?'

'I hope so,' Emma said.

Emma's heart rate was beginning to return to normal now. She found a handkerchief in her handbag and mopped her damp lashes. She ran a hand through her hair because Ruby had been smoothing it and ruffling it as she'd comforted.

'Well, there you are then.'

While they waited for the water to come to the boil on the hob Emma told Ruby about Stella. And how Matthew had been engaged to her – had been until a few short hours ago.

'Tom told me Matthew was back. 'Ow he looked really pleased to see you.'

'That's as maybe. But it doesn't alter the fact I made love to another woman's man, Ruby,' Emma said.

'But you didn't know they were engaged then, you daft lummox. You can't blame yourself for that.'

'But I do. And I was totally indecent. The second I set eyes on Matthew after all the years that have gone by since I last saw him, I couldn't get him into my bed fast enough.'

'Sounds like true love and passion if you ask me.'

Was she asking? But Ruby was entitled to her opinion and Emma knew if you told friends intimate things then you must expect for them to have their own views.

'Men are weak in that direction, Em.'

'What direction?'

'The bedroom door direction. An' any other bleedin' direction. An' don't I know it!'

'But Matthew?' Emma said. 'I never expected that of him.'

Ruby sighed. 'You are a little wet behind the ears, me darlin',' she said. 'An' I love you for it. Matthew, as 'andsome and as excitin' as 'e is, is no different in the genitals department, now is 'e?'

Emma gulped. Well, he was better endowed than Seth had ever been. *Oh!* Guilt sat heavily over her heart that she was even making the comparison. She'd loved Seth dearly and would forever be grateful for the love he'd given her and the comfortable life he'd left her with, but for all his attributes Seth had never taken Emma to the heights of ecstasy she'd experienced with Matthew. And not once but ... they'd lost count, hadn't they? But she could hardly tell Ruby that, could she?

'Oh, I get it,' Ruby said with a grin when Emma was slow to respond. ''E's a big man, is that it?'

Emma nodded. Her body began to tingle with the memory of how Matthew had made her feel.

But was she ever going to let him make her feel like that again?

'And you ain't goin' to tell me,' Ruby said, her voice more serious now as she tipped a measure of brandy into Emma's tea. 'Get that down you.'

'In a minute. It's a bit hot.' Emma twisted her hands over and over in her lap. Never in her life before had she felt so not in control of a situation. 'And while Matthew and I were making love, Fleur was in Torquay police station. She—'

'I knows that you daft bugger. About Fleur being arrested an' that. Not the bit about you and Matthew being in bed, of course. You told Tom and 'e told me, like you told 'im to.'

Yes, she had told Tom, but a condensed version of it.

'Fleur wasn't at the Cascarini's ice cream parlour with Paolo as she'd told me she would be,' Emma went on. It was easier speaking about Fleur than it was herself and she knew that was why she was telling Ruby things she already knew. 'She'd gone to meet Caroline—'

'Gawd, but I'd swing for 'er,' Ruby interrupted.

'Me, too,' Emma said.

'Were it of 'er own free will that 'er went to see 'er mother?' Ruby asked, and somehow the use of the word 'mother' stung Emma more than she thought it would.

'Yes. But Caroline was there with a man and it seems they went on a big pick-pocketing spree. They'd hired a box to watch a film with Louise Brooks in it. Fleur couldn't resist. She models herself on Louise Brooks at the moment.'

'Where are the buggers now, then?' Ruby asked.

'Matthew had the good grace to telephone me and tell me they've been taken into custody. The man – an American citizen – is going to be deported. He's some sort of failed film director, so Matthew found out from somewhere. His last film was a flop.'

'An' they thought they could make a film star out of your beautiful daughter and make their fortunes, I 'spect.'

'Something like that.'

Emma told Ruby about all the clothes Caroline had given Fleur and the film magazines. Things to whet her appetite for Hollywood.

'You should've told me before,' Ruby said. 'I'd 'ave seen straight through the schemin' minx. You ain't been over much.'

'I know. I'm sorry.'

'Forgiven,' Ruby said. 'You'm 'ere now. An' we got to work out 'ow to get you out of this fix, ain't we? But at least Mrs P is out of the way. Maybe 'er'll be deported an' all?'

'Not unless she's become an American citizen, I shouldn't think. But I don't know what's going to happen to Caroline, and I care even less.'

And I'm not going to get in touch with Matthew to find out.

'That's my girl!'

'Fleur was going to be Stella's bridesmaid,' Emma said, purposefully steering the conversation back to the reason she was there. 'I cut out the fabric for her dress only last week. Fleur's going to be so disappointed when I tell her.'

'Fleur's young. She'll get over the disappointment of not bein' a bridesmaid, especially if you turns that frock into summat she can wear some other place. Am I right?'

'Yes,' Emma said. 'It might cheer her up.'

Emma told Ruby how Fleur had seen Paolo with someone else at the cinema and how it was all over between them.

'Well, things ain't so sweet in the Jago 'ousehold right now, are they?' Ruby said. 'An' I'm the sorrier for it. Trouble seems to scent you out the way a dog follows its nose to the butcher's shop, don't it?'

'It would seem so,' Emma said. 'I'm beginning to regret coming back to England now.'

Or am I? Would I ever have seen Matthew again if I hadn't? Would I ever have known the passion that he made me feel?

'You talk a load of old rubbish sometimes, Emma Jago,' Ruby said. '*I* don't regret you comin' back one little bit. You was the savin' of me, and I'll do anythin' to 'elp you. Anythin'.'

'I know.'

The difference in Ruby between April and now was just astonishing and Emma knew she'd been instrumental in that change.

And I'd never have made love to Matthew had I not come back. And I'd have been the poorer for that, wouldn't I?

'Hmm, Emma Jago,' Ruby said, tilting her head to one side, studying her friend. 'I know you. You only regrets what 'appened to Fleur and not what 'appened between you and Matthew Caunter which ...' Ruby held up her hand to stop Emma interrupting, '... which I ain't goin' to ask the details of. I 'onestly don't see what the problem for you now is, Em. Matthew's a free man again. Fleur's back 'ome safe and sound. Caroline's locked up somewhere and likely to stay that way, so—'

'So, I'm going back home now,' Emma said.

Everything Ruby was saying was true. And she was grateful to her dear friend for listening, but all the same, it wasn't a nice feeling having her life laid out before her for scrutiny. She would make her own decisions, however sensible Ruby's might be at the moment.

'Said too much, 'ave I?' Ruby asked. She didn't sound as though she was the least put out.

'Possibly not enough,' Emma said, struggling to smile.

'Well, you always was stubborn, Em, and that ain't goin' to change. But if I says one last thing to you and you never wants to speak to me again, it's this – don't let love pass you by if that's what Matthew Caunter is offerin' you, besides the other.'

'Oh, Ruby ...' Emma said, and dissolved into tears again.

Whatever was the matter with her? She hadn't cried as much as this in her life before however sad she'd been at the time.

'I'd like to make a transatlantic phone call,' Fleur said.

Fleur crossed her fingers behind her back that there would be a quick connection. Tom kept downing tools to come into the house. Checking on her. No doubt he'd been told to report back to her ma about what she was doing. Well, so far there had been nothing to report. She'd painted until she thought her hand would drop off from holding the brush so long. Then she'd written to her friend, Delia. She thought about going to the post office to get a stamp for it but changed her mind. Her ma had told her Caroline had been arrested but she didn't want to run the risk of seeing her in town if she'd been let out on bail. 'I'm just popping over to Torquay, to the hospital, to see Stella,' her ma had said. Hmm ... she was being a jolly long time doing it. But she'd be there a bit longer with any luck.

'Number to call, please,' the operator said, dragging Fleur back to the present.

Fleur didn't have to look it up. It was etched into her mind. When she'd lived on Vancouver Island she'd telephoned Delia every night after school even though they'd been talking almost all the day, and at weekends to arrange to meet up, to go and see a film. And she'd telephoned her a few times, without her ma's knowledge, recently, too.

'Vancouver 278,' she said. 'Gethin is the name.'

'Hold the line,' the operator said, his voice clipped and business-like.

'Hurry up,' Fleur said under her breath. She had tried to work out what time it would be over in Vancouver but could never do it with any accuracy, not when there were so many time zones across Canada anyway. But she knew it would be morning. Delia and her ma were always up early. Mrs Gethin baked fresh bread every morning. And then she'd make a pie or two for pudding, and would more than likely get a big pot of stew on the go as well. How she missed Mrs Gethin's home-baked bread. And the pies. Her ma didn't make pies, only fancy French upside down apple tarts. *Tarte Tatin.*

Well, I'm sick of tarte Tatin. And I'm sick of England. I want to go back to Canada and I want to be able to put flowers on my pa's grave. I want to be as far away from Caroline as possible – so far she won't be able to find me.

Fleur sent up a silent prayer that Mrs Gethin's offer to give her board and lodging still stood. The house was big enough, she knew that. Delia was going to college to study art. Fleur was good at art, although not quite as good as her pa had been. But she was getting better and better though. She was pleased with how the painting she'd started today was shaping up. Maybe she'd see if she could join the same course as Delia. It would be better than being here, doing nothing except hold pins for her ma while she put bits of fabric together to make clothes for other people to wear, although she'd enjoyed designing dresses in secret. Something to think about for the future perhaps – dress designing.

And then Fleur remembered the bridesmaid's dress her ma was making for her to wear at Stella Martin's wedding. Well, with luck, she wouldn't be wearing it, although she felt a bit mean letting Stella Martin down because she seemed nice enough.

All she had to do now, while she waited to be connected to either Delia or her ma, was work out how she could persuade her own ma to go back to Canada. It wasn't going to be easy. But she'd try.

'Your call is connected.'

At last!

'Delia? Delia?' Fleur squealed into the mouthpiece. 'Wait 'til you hear what I've got to tell you.'

Chapter Twenty-Two

'I'm afraid I can't let you in,' Tom said.

Matthew thought he looked genuinely sorry that he couldn't.

'But Emma is in?'

'She is. She's doin' her sewin'. Busier by the day she is with that, what with women comin' in for fittin's, whatever they might be. They draws the curtains in the room what Emma does 'er sewing in so I can't see. There's one in there now.'

'And Fleur?'

'She's in there an 'all. Becomin' a fine little painter 'er is. Like her pa before 'er.'

'It would be nice to see them both.'

'I still can't let you in.'

'Did Emma tell you not to let me cross her threshold, or words to that effect?'

'I think you know the answer to that, sir,' Tom said.

'You don't have to "sir" me. You're my equal.'

'That's kind of you, s—' Tom stopped himself from saying what obviously automatically tripped off his tongue.

'It's me who isn't you're equal really,' Matthew said. 'You fought in a war, I didn't. I respect you for that.'

Keep Tom talking. Even though there's a nip in the air now that autumn has well and truly arrived.

'Leaves are coming down already,' Matthew said. 'Soon be bonfire night.'

'And don't I know it,' Tom said. 'The leaves comin' down, I mean. I had to put the sides on the barrow to get 'em all in when I raked 'em off the lawn yesterday. The chestnut leaves are as big as breakfast plates this year.'

'Telegraph Hill was covered in them,' Matthew said.

'Where's that to?' Tom asked.

'Halfway between here and Exeter. Haldon Forest way.'

Tom laughed. 'I've never 'eard of that either!'

Matthew wondered how a man could go to war – travel across the country to get on a ship to go and fight, yet not know what was less than twenty miles from his own front door. But there were many like Tom.

And while Tom was standing here by the gate, a pair of clippers in his hand, talking to Matthew he couldn't be gardening, and with luck Emma would come out of the house soon wondering why he wasn't. And he would see her. With his own eyes and not inside his head. Feel her in his heart.

She was a stubborn little minx and was refusing to take his phone calls apart from the one when he'd told her that the man Caroline had been with – Archibald Seymour – was to be deported, and that Caroline was in custody still awaiting trial and sentence. All right, she'd made it clear after the shock of finding him at Stella's bedside that the ball would be in her court and she'd contact him if she wanted to, but well ... he wasn't as patient as he'd thought he was. It was eating him up inside not seeing her. So he'd rung – every day – just to check she was well. Almost always now, when he rang, it was Fleur who answered and said she was sorry but her mother wasn't available – she was with a client, or out, or 'indisposed' whatever that last implied. Certainly not like some Victorian woman having the vapours. Emma was made of stronger stuff than that.

As was Stella, he had been surprised to find. Although he didn't know why he was surprised given the job she did. Stella had written to him, thanking him for the lovely times they'd had together and said that she'd do her best to forget the not so lovely times. *Finding out that her fiancé had been cheating on her was what she meant.*

'Do you think, sometimes,' Matthew asked Tom now, 'how good it would be if we could unwind our lives a little, take out the niggly knots that get into them by our own volition or by others, and then wind them up again?'

'The war for a start,' Tom said. 'I can't think there was a man in it – exceptin' maybe a few blood 'ungry generals and the like – who wouldn't want to do that. Sometimes, I think them as died, 'ad the better deal.'

Tom jerked his head, breaking the eye contact he'd had with Matthew all the way through this conversation so far. It was as though Tom didn't want Matthew to see the pain that was still there at times behind his eyes.

Ouch! I've hit a raw nerve here, Matthew thought. The last thing he'd meant to do was upset Tom in any way. He was grateful to the man, for goodness sake – glad that he was at Romer Lodge, day in and day out, keeping an eye on Emma. But how much longer could he be gardening every day with autumn already here, and winter just around the corner? Who knew what Caroline Prentiss – no Jago now – was capable of? When Emma had told him that Caroline said that Seth wasn't Fleur's father and that Miles was, and Fleur's birth date wasn't the 16th of July, but the 22nd of September, he'd made some enquiries. He'd discovered that while Miles had been in custody there had been those not averse to a few crisp five pound notes and a handful of sovereigns pressed into their hands to let Miles and Caroline alone in a room for as long as it took. But, of course, that wasn't going to prove anything, certainly not that Miles was Fleur's father and not Seth as it said on the birth certificate that Caroline now claimed was a forgery. There were ways he could find out if the birth certificate was bona fide or not, but he would have to get his hands on it first. He didn't think for a second that Emma would part with it.

'An' I've fast discovered,' Tom went on, his voice firmer

294

now, 'that it's often the wives and the children of them as was injured, either in their bodies or their minds, who suffered the most. My Ruby …'

But Tom couldn't go on. He made a strangled sobbing sound and seemed to shrink into himself, knees bent a little.

'Your Ruby,' Matthew said quickly, 'is the best friend Emma could have, I know that. Back when they were both working at Nase Head House, Ruby was loyal to Emma against all comers. Now wasn't she?'

Tom nodded. He still wasn't making eye contact again with Matthew but he was standing straighter.

'I expect, given the job you've done with the surveillance and that, that you know what my Ruby 'ad to do to earn a crust to feed our children when I couldn't because I was more 'elpless than a newborn. Back with my mother, for God's sake, doin' every last thing for me.'

Yes, Matthew had more than an inkling as to what it was Ruby had done. Shingle Cottage, where he'd once lived himself, belonged to Emma, he knew that, so he'd made it his duty to go past now and again when he was in the area, checking that it hadn't fallen into disrepair in her absence. And on the off chance she'd come back and would be there. A throwaway remark from a man coming out of the front gate had left Matthew in no doubt about what Ruby had been doing. Matthew laid a hand on Tom's shoulder. 'None of us knows what we would do, and how, if our backs were truly against the wall. And we shouldn't judge, as I'm not judging you, or Ruby. A man has to walk in another man's shoes to truly know how it feels to wear the things.'

'You'm right,' Tom said. 'An' I'd better get back to work or Emma will be out 'ere, 'ands on 'ips, shakin' that pretty little 'ead of 'ers, askin' why I'm slackin'.'

Which is just what I hoped.

'An' thanks for listenin',' Tom said. 'It 'elps sometimes to talk about things, man to man. Many of the lads I went to war with from around 'ere didn't come back and that's a fact.'

And you're lonely. You miss going down the Blue Anchor, or whichever pub it is you used to frequent, now there's no one to go there with.

'Glad to have been of help,' Matthew said, although he couldn't for the life of him recall when he'd ever felt the need to talk things through, man to man. But he was glad that he had helped Tom – he could see that he had by the way the man's eyes had more spark in them now. And the fact that there was a smile back on his face.

'I'll be off then,' Matthew said. He was feeling better about himself for listening to Tom while he offloaded his worries – less selfish, thinking only about his own needs and wants in coming here. He could wait a bit longer to see Emma.

He held out his hand for Tom to shake and the two men gripped hands, before Tom turned and walked back down the drive and into the garden.

He felt lighter in heart to learn that Emma was well and busy, making a life for herself. And her daughter.

But I'll be sticking around. For as long as it takes. Emma might not need me at this moment but as sure as eggs are eggs, I need her! And he'd be sticking around closer, geographically, than he could ever have imagined until an hour or so ago when he'd spotted a garage business for sale just a few streets away from Romer Lodge. No time like the present. He'd call in and see about buying it right now.

'You're joking, Mr Caunter,' William said. 'Or is it April Fool's Day?'

'Neither of those things, Will,' he said. 'I've been thinking of expanding the business for some time. And it just so happens a premises over in Paignton – in Roundham Road, just behind the harbour area – has come on the market and it's just the right size and the right sort of venue for me to open another branch of my business. So ...'

'... you're leaving me in charge here?'

'Unless you want me to get a manager in, pay him twice what I pay you, and you take orders from him, unlike the way I *ask* you to do things.'

William laughed. 'I might be cabbage-looking but I ain't green. Or I wasn't when I looked in the shaving mirror this morning!'

'Good. So we'll start with the books, shall we? Ledgers. Accounts. How to deal with the licensing authorities. I ...'

Matthew halted. It hadn't occurred to him to ask if William was literate. There'd been no reason to before because he didn't need to be able to read and write to change a tyre or put oil in a vehicle, or replace a carburettor. But he was good with customers, knowing the right thing to say, and with the right vocabulary.

'You're an open book at the moment, boss,' William said. 'You're wondering if I can read and write and do all those things you've just mentioned, aren't you? Well, I'll put you out of your misery – I can. I had to leave school to earn money to keep ma and the family together after pa died, but I was good enough at my lessons before that.'

Open book? What did William mean by that? he wondered. Best not to ask.

'Good,' Matthew said. 'I'm pleased to hear it. So I take it you're willing to accept the level of responsibility I'll be giving you?'

'I am. And I'll do my best by you. I'm hoping, though, that you employ someone to do what I've been doing seeing as I'll be doing, more or less, what you've been doing up to now? Cecil won't be able to do the work of two men.'

'Of course,' Matthew said, delighted to find that William was forward planning already. 'We'll get an advert in the

Western Morning News tomorrow. The sooner I can start interviewing men, testing their skills, the better.'

'Which will leave you free for your other agenda over to Paignton.'

And just what did William mean by that? He wasn't going to ask. Perhaps he wasn't the only one good at surveillance and William knew someone who'd seen him going to Romer Lodge looking for Emma, or at the hospital when Stella was there.

'Ha!' William said, when Matthew was slow to move the conversation on. 'Am I right that there's a little lady in the picture over to Paignton who you wants to be closer to? And am I—'

'Overstepping the boundaries of our friendship, yes I think you are,' Matthew said, but he couldn't help the corners of his mouth twitching up in the beginnings of a smile. Yes, of course the man was right!

'An' it isn't Miss Martin either, is it?'

'No,' Matthew said. 'I know I'm a bit late in the day telling you this but Miss Martin and I won't be getting married after all.'

'She's a nice woman,' William said. 'The few times I saw her, she was always smiling and chatted to me, like I was a friend because I work for you.'

'Well, you'll be working *with* me now, Will,' Matthew said, steering the conversation back the way he wanted it to go. 'I shall expect you to turn in a profit, keep the place running as I would if I was here every day. Which I won't be because there's a small cottage attached to the premises in Paignton. It will be perfectly suitable for bachelor living.'

'So, you'm selling your house here, is that it?'

Was he? Wasn't he? Matthew hadn't thought that far yet but obviously William had. He had to have somewhere halfway decent for his son, Harry, should he choose to come to England to stay and the fisherman's cottage in Paignton was hardly big enough for one, never mind two.

'No,' he said quickly. And he was thinking even more quickly. Once he'd won Emma over again – as he was sure he would eventually – then who knew what direction or where their life together would lead them? Emma might like city living. There might be better scope for her dressmaking business in Exeter. He would keep the house. 'I won't be selling the house just yet. But it will need to be lived in. So, how do you feel about renting it, keeping it aired?'

'Ooooh, I don't know, boss,' William said. 'If this new venture over to Paignton goes belly-up like a beached seal, how do I know you won't want me out of it in a hurry?'

'I like your thinking,' Matthew said, full of admiration for the way William seemed to be already taking charge of things. *He'll run the business as well as I do, I'm sure of that now.* 'But to put your mind at rest I'll get a tenant's agreement drawn up, and we'll sign it. Not that there will be a need because the house is big enough for both of us should I need to come back.'

Too big, with five bedrooms.

'An' are there to be any considerations as to who I can and who I can't have come to stop?' William asked.

'The whole chorus of the Folies Bergère if you want them to,' Matthew said with a laugh. 'As long as you keep the place clean and don't wreck the furniture! There's something on your agenda as well, am I right?'

William jiggled his shoulders and looked down towards the floor. 'Eve Benjafield. We want to get married but we can't just yet because she's nursing her sick pa. But she gets the odd night's rest when her sister, Doris, takes a turn, so—'

'Well, she's welcome to spend that night with you in my property,' interrupted Matthew, saving William's blushes.

So that was that all sorted. A good day's work although he

was yet to sell a vehicle. But a middle-aged couple, looking very well-heeled, had just walked onto the forecourt. The man was peering into the window of a Model T that was for sale.

'Possible sale has just walked in, Will,' Matthew said. 'Off you go and do your stuff. Oh, and ...' Matthew reached in the breast pocket of his jacket and took out his wallet, fingered out four £5 notes. He held the money out towards William. 'Buy yourself a suit. With a waistcoat. I've got a fob watch you can have.'

'Really, boss?' William said with a wide grin, taking the money and stuffing it in the pocket of his trousers. 'Thanks. You must be in love that's all I can say.'

'Customer!' Matthew said, and there was a lump in his throat as he said it. How good it felt to be helping someone else make something of their lives. 'Go.'

'I'm already gone, boss,' William said, hurrying towards the door.

Matthew took the calendar off the wall. He wrote 'Made William a partner' against the day's date. He'd already ringed Emma's birthday – 29th September. It was just a few days away now. A bunch of roses to remind her he was still around, and still thinking of her, wouldn't go amiss, would it?

Chapter Twenty-Three

'Ma,' Fleur said. 'I'm covered in boils and there's a rash on my backside.'

'That's nice.'

'There! I knew you weren't listening!'

'What?' Emma said. 'What *are* you talking about?'

'You'd know if you listened properly. But you've not been listening to me for weeks now, have you? I've said all sorts of rubbish and all you say is, "That's nice". A moment ago I told you I'm covered in boils and I've got a rash on my backside.'

Boils? A rash?

'You haven't?'

'Of course I haven't. Ma, what's wrong? There's something troubling you, I know it.'

Emma's hand began to shake. She could barely concentrate on the sewing job she was doing – hand-stitching the hem of a silk nightdress for a client. Of course something was troubling her. She was pregnant. Only seven weeks but she'd never been more sure of anything in her life. Pregnant with Matthew's child. With all her heart she didn't want it to be true but perhaps Caroline had been telling the truth, and that Seth wasn't Fleur's father. If he had been, then he and Emma would have had a child together, wouldn't they? Given the thousands of times they'd tried to make that happen they would have done. But they hadn't. It had to have been Seth who was infertile, not her, didn't it?

Although she didn't show at all at the moment she knew the time would come when she couldn't hide the fact that she was carrying a child. For a month now she'd been alternating between total joy and total dread. Joy that her long-held dream to hold her own flesh and blood in her arms now had a chance of becoming a reality, and dread that she had somehow to tell Fleur. It was a mercy she hadn't been afflicted with morning sickness as she knew so many women were. At least she hadn't been bringing her guts up morning, noon, and night – if she had then Fleur might have asked what was wrong before now.

'There's nothing troubling me, Fleur,' Emma lied. 'I'm burning the midnight oil with my sewing, that's all. It's taking off at last, as you know. Every day the telephone rings with someone else wanting to come and talk about their requirements. And Mrs Passmore over in Croy Lodge could keep me busy all on her own!'

'With an invalid husband what else is there to do but look nice?' Fleur said.

What indeed. But Mrs Passmore was a good client as well as being a decent, if very chatty, woman. Would Mrs Passmore still be a client once she knew Emma was with child? Would she?

'She's forever on the telephone asking if I've finished this or that.'

'Yes,' Fleur said. 'And Mr Caunter rings most days and you won't talk to him. Why not? I thought you liked him. He kissed you goodbye that night when you brought me back from the police station and you didn't look as though you hated it!'

'I didn't hate it,' Emma said.

'What's happened between you?'

I can't say. Not yet.

'Sometimes people turn out to be not what you thought they were. The way Paolo turned out to be quite different from how you thought he was.'

'Paolo!' Fleur said. 'I wish you hadn't brought *his* name up! I was beginning to forget him.'

But I'll never forget Matthew. Now more than ever.

'Sorry,' Emma said. 'I didn't mean to open old wounds. But you understand my meaning?'

'I suppose,' Fleur said. 'But all I can say is that although I didn't like Mr Caunter coming in and taking over in the police station, I'm glad he did now. He was very kind back when—'

'I know when he was very kind,' Emma said

But Matthew Caunter wasn't kind when he made love to me when he was engaged to the lovely Stella Martin.

Stella's wedding dress was still hanging from a rail in the corner of her atelier, covered in a length of cotton sheeting – a shroud for the death of Stella's dream of marrying Matthew. Having it there was haunting Emma, but she couldn't move it because Stella might be back any day to collect it. Or have it altered. Or sell it.

'Tom talks to him,' Fleur said. 'I saw them. Down by the New Pier Inn.'

'The New Pier Inn?' Emma said, alarmed. That was practically at the bottom of her garden! Was Matthew spying on her? Again.

Fleur shrugged.

'When?' Emma asked.

'Last week? Yesterday? I can't remember now. But it seems to me that little bit of information has struck a raw nerve, Ma. I wish you'd tell me what's wrong. Before I go.'

'Go? Go where?'

'Back to Canada, I hope.'

Fleur waved the letter she had in her hand at Emma. And now Emma was thinking about it, she'd seen Fleur with that same envelope in her hands for days now – seen her reading and re-reading the letter – and she hadn't thought to ask who it was from.

'You've had a letter from Delia?'

'I have. But this isn't it. This is from Vancouver College. They've got a place for me to study art if I want to take it up, I—'

'Oh, that's nice,' Emma said. And when Fleur looked at

her crossly she realised what it was she had just said, and what she could have been accused of. But not this time. This time she really was listening. 'Your pa would be so pleased to know you're taking after him.'

Perhaps she'd got it all wrong? If Fleur was artistic, as Seth had been, then he could be her father after all, couldn't he? Might it have been that she and Seth simply weren't the right mix for making babies? Did anyone really know how they were made?

'You're not going to bawl me out for going behind your back organising all this? I mean, I telephoned Delia's ma at least three times. Her offer to let me lodge with her still stands. It's only a tram ride to the college from the Gethin house and Delia will be on the course, too.'

'That's nice,' Emma said again. And then she laughed. 'Goodness, I can see Miss Walton's outraged face at my use of that banal little word. "Emma Le Goff! Nice? Nice? Why use that futile little word when there are so many other better ones in the dictionary to convey your pleasure?" Miss Walton will be turning in her grave listening to me!'

'Miss who?'

'Miss Walton. My English teacher when I was at school in Brixham. She hated lazy speech.'

Emma felt a tiny twinge of guilt that she was making jokes barely a second after Fleur had told her of her plans – plans made behind her back she was expecting to be told off for. But she was being presented with time and space to work out what to do about the baby and that was what she needed. She wouldn't have to tell Fleur about the baby just yet if she was in Canada, would she?

'So I can go? Back to Canada?'

There were a jumble of emotions inside Emma at that moment. Her thoughts skittered from one thing to the other the way a chained dog skitters when let off the leash. But one thought was clear – she would never be able to give her baby up for adoption. However much she might be frowned upon for having a child out of wedlock, she wouldn't give up her child. But she would face all that when the time came. She could move somewhere else and spread the story that her husband had died before she gave birth. But she wasn't going to make any plans now because she'd made plans before and had to change them.

But nothing and nobody was going to part her from this child. Not ever.

'It means I won't be able to be Stella Martin's bridesmaid in February,' Fleur continued, but Emma thought she didn't look in the least upset that she wouldn't be.

'Stella Martin won't be getting married now,' Emma told her.

And please, please, don't ask me why not?

'Well, that's all right then. It's a woman's prerogative to change her mind, isn't it?'

How swiftly and concisely Fleur had bundled up all the emotions that had gone into the untangling of Stella's engagement.

'Yes, yes,' Emma said. 'So the saying has it.'

'So I can go? Back to Canada?' Fleur asked again. 'I'd prefer it if you came, too, but I don't think you want to, do you? Not now you're friends with Ruby again and you've started the dressmaking business.'

'I can't,' Emma said.

'But, can I? Go back to Canada I mean. I really, really want to.'

'Can we talk about it?' Emma said. 'When I've finished this bit of sewing, or my reputation will be in as many tatters as this hem is at the moment.'

'But soon?'

'Yes, Fleur, very soon.'

Fleur had never expected it to be that easy – telling her ma she wanted to go back to Canada. Of course, she'd had to tell her that she'd made some long distance telephone calls to Mrs Gethin, and Delia, and that the plan had been in her head a long time. Almost as soon as she'd arrived in England, if truth were told, and she was honest with herself. But her ma hadn't made a fuss or gone on and on about the cost of the telephone calls or anything.

And now Fleur was packing. Her ma had got Tom to bring the old tin trunks they'd brought with them from Canada from the loft and Fleur was slowly filling them up. But not too slowly because her package was booked and her ma had found a companion – a minister's wife – to travel with her.

Mrs Passmore just happened to mention when she came for a fitting that she had a sister about to go to Canada to join her husband who was running a mission there. She was sailing from Liverpool to Halifax, and from there she was going across Canada on the train.

And so it had all been arranged. One week to go and Fleur would be off. On the last boat before they stopped sailing for the winter because the sea would be too rough, or iced up. She couldn't wait. She didn't even mind the thought of the very cold winter she knew was coming – she'd lived through thirteen such winters so she was used to it.

'Ah, I thought this is where you might be,' her ma said. She stood in the doorway with a coat draped over one arm and a pile of winceyette floral nightdresses she'd been making for Fleur in her hands. 'All finished. This lot should keep you warm enough.'

'Thanks, Ma,' Fleur said. 'I'll take care of them because I know for a fact Mrs Gethin can't even thread a needle!'

Excitement was bubbling up inside Fleur now.

'I'm going to miss you,' her ma said. 'But I wouldn't dream of stopping you.'

'But you don't want to come back?'

'No,' her ma said. 'Not yet anyway. But I'll come over to visit you just as soon as I can.'

'In the spring?' Fleur said. 'Or early summer. I'll be off college in the summer.'

'I'll try,' her ma said. She looked down at her feet as she spoke, and Fleur thought it might be because she was fighting back tears that she was leaving. 'Mrs Bailey told me her son and daughter-in-law might be going over for a visit next year some time. So it might be possible to travel with them.'

'I like Mrs Bailey,' Fleur said. 'She's good fun for her age.'

'For her age?' Her ma laughed, but the laugh didn't reach her eyes as her ma's laughs usually did, Fleur noticed. 'She's only a few years older than I am and I'm hardly old. I'm ...'

But her ma didn't finish the sentence. She walked on into the room and placed the pile of nightdresses on Fleur's bed, found a hanger and hung the coat up on a knob of the wardrobe.

'These things won't get packed with me standing in the doorway, will they?' she said.

Fleur didn't think there was an answer to that so she didn't give one. Instead she went to her dressing table and picked up the photograph of her pa. A head and shoulder study that gave no indication of what a big bear of a man he was, but in it he was smiling and Fleur could remember him telling her he'd had to hold the pose for so long he thought his jaw might have to stay that way.

'I'm going to take this,' Fleur said. 'And one of you. There's hardly any of you and pa together, only your wedding photograph and there's only one of those, isn't there?'

Her ma looked up sharply at her then.

'I wouldn't take it even if you said I could, Ma,' Fleur said quickly. 'You and pa look so happy in that photograph.'

'We were,' her ma said. 'Very, very happy. But I could get

it copied if you'd really like one. Although I don't know if it would be done in time. Don't forget Ruby and the children are coming over this afternoon to say goodbye to you.'

'I haven't forgotten. But it's not goodbye, it's *au revoir*. That's what you always say, isn't it?'

'It is. It sounds less final, I always think.'

'And I'll be back, I'm sure of it. If not to live permanently, then to visit. Or there might be art opportunities in London for me, once I've got all my certificates.'

Fleur began to wish now she'd gone to London while she was here. There were so many wonderful old buildings in London. And art galleries and museums. Well, none of that was going anywhere, was it? She could see it all some other time.

'Seth would have been so proud,' her ma said. 'As I am, of course. It's a brave thing to go to another country on your own.'

'I won't be on my own. Mrs Bailey will help the journey time pass quickly, I'm sure of it. And once I'm there it'll be like old times sitting up most of the night chatting to Delia.'

'And talking of chatting,' her ma said, 'I've got some pastries in the oven for tea this afternoon. And I've some little cakes to make and ice for the children. Oh, and did I say I've hired a gramophone from Harris & Osborne and bought some dance records so we can make it a proper party? There'll be dancing on the boat going over and this will give you chance to practise your Charleston.'

'Oh, Ma,' Fleur said. She swallowed back a sob.

The last party she'd had, when Caroline had turned up, was still too fresh in her mind for comfort. Not that she'd be turning up unannounced this time because she was in prison somewhere. Fleur shivered involuntarily. She didn't want to see *that* woman again as long as she lived, and going to Canada was a way of avoiding doing so, even though that wasn't her main aim in going.

And Paolo and his pa and his grandmother had been there as well. They'd all brought her lovely presents. She had them packed in her trunk to take to Canada, even the little leather purse with the Italian coin in it that Paolo had bought her. She hadn't seen him since the incident at the cinema, and she didn't want to either. He hadn't replied to her letter but she hadn't expected him to. But she wouldn't forget him. He'd been her first, and only friend in England and he'd been a lot of fun before he became a stereotypical Italian who couldn't keep his eyes – or his hands – off the girls. While Fleur had been tempted to let him make love to her, she was glad she hadn't now. She'd have been just another notch on the proverbial bedpost, wouldn't she? Before he found a good Italian wife.

'You haven't invited Signor Cascarini and ...' No, Fleur couldn't even say his name.

'Of course I haven't,' her ma said. 'While it might have been nice for Eduardo to come and say *au revoir* to you, I'm not so insensitive that I don't understand you wouldn't want his son there. So I haven't invited either of them.'

'Oh, Ma,' Fleur said again. She was going to miss her so much but staying here would stifle both of them. Fleur had a feeling the only reason she was refusing to take Matthew Caunter's telephone calls was because she was worried Fleur might not like the fact he was replacing her pa in her ma's affections.

I've only been here a bare six months and yet I feel I've aged six years in experience, Fleur thought. Of course she wouldn't mind her ma loving someone else, and being loved in return – she just didn't want to be around to see all the billing and cooing that was all. But why wouldn't her ma take Mr Caunter's telephone calls? What was all that about? Couldn't she see he adored her?

'Can I smell burning?' her ma asked.

Fleur sniffed the air.

'Not yet,' she said, laughing. 'I've got something for you. I haven't forgotten it's your birthday, you know.'

Fleur lifted her pillow from the bed and brought out the painting she'd done of her ma. A portrait, sideways on, of Emma bent over a piece of sewing. Fleur had peeped in through the crack in the door and done a pencil sketch. The light had been low and making her ma's hair glow, pinking her cheeks. It had been a race against time to turn it into a watercolour, painting it in her room, hiding it in her wardrobe when she went out so her ma wouldn't find it.

'You painted this?' her ma said.

Fleur pretended to look for someone in the room. 'Seems I must have seeing as there's no one else here.'

'Well, it's wonderful. I adore it. I shall treasure it always. And one day I'll tell you how very special it is to me. Thank you so much. And now I really can smell burning.'

And her ma ran from the room, clutching the painting to her – *so I won't see her tears. And so she won't see mine*, Fleur thought. She grabbed a pillow from the bed and held it over her eyes until the tears stopped.

And what did her ma mean by '*And one day I'll tell you how very special it is to me*'?

Emma was pleased she'd thought to invite Mrs Bailey to join them for Fleur's leaving party because Mrs Bailey turned up with her son and daughter-in-law – Adam and Rebecca. More people would mean less time to focus on Fleur and the fact she would be leaving soon.

Emma's hallstand was filling up with her guests' coats. Over in one corner of her large hall Tom was running a hand through young Thomas's hair in an attempt to tidy it. Ruby had rushed off to the kitchen to keep on eye on things there while Emma greeted her guests.

'I should have telephoned you to ask first, Mrs Jago,' Mrs Bailey said, 'but, well, I won't be seeing Adam and

Rebecca for a little while – almost a year to be precise – and they called in unexpectedly to see me so I thought I'd bring them along. I hope you don't mind me doing so, it will be give me another hour or two in their company before I set sail.'

'Not at all. I'm delighted to meet them,' she said, extending a hand first to Adam and then Rebecca. They were both around Emma's age and her heart lifted just a little that as she was about to say *au revoir* to Fleur, two new people were about to come into her orbit, as it were. Two people with whom she – and her baby – might be able to travel to Canada next year.

'Rumour has it you're a seamstress!' Rebecca said, laughing.

The exclamation mark on the end of her sentence seemed to dance between them in the air, like a sword in a highland fling. She was a small woman, barely five feet tall, with the most beautiful auburn curls. Her skin was whiter than alabaster and her deep green eyes – the same shade as holly leaves, Emma thought – smiled their pleasure at meeting Emma and that she was a seamstress.

'Seamstress, dressmaker, fashion designer,' Fleur joined the conversation. 'My ma can make *anything*.'

'So Mrs Passmore told me,' Rebecca said grinning.

'What my daughter-in-law is trying to say,' Mrs Bailey said, 'is that she's rather hoping you will be able to make her some clothes to, well … disguise.' With a huge grin on her face she tapped her tummy to indicate that Rebecca was expecting a baby.

Well, that makes two of us. Although why a happily married woman wanted to disguise the fact she was expecting a baby was beyond Emma. But thinking about it now, she'd hardly ever seen a pregnant woman in the town, or walking along the promenade. Where did they go when they were expecting? Was she expected to go wherever that place was? Did they get someone else to go to Dey's the grocer for them until their babies were born? Had she been in the position Rebecca was in then she would want to proudly carry her precious load before her for all to see. But she wasn't. But she was good at making clothes to disguise a person's deformity – be it a hunchback or a short leg or a withered arm. Or a baby.

Stop it! You're making pregnancy sound like an affliction. Something to be lived with, not embraced and enjoyed. And Fleur has given me the most beautiful painting of me carrying my child.

And if she made something for Rebecca then she could make the same thing for herself at the same time, couldn't she?

'I'll be delighted to,' Emma said.

And she'd worry about how she was going to get her food shopping done, and her sewing supplies fetched from Beares and Rossiters at a later date. She hadn't even begun to show yet, thank goodness. Or have her pregnancy confirmed by a doctor, but she knew. She *felt* different. And with winter coming on she could go out as the light began to fade and perhaps no one would notice her bump in the darkness.

'Gosh, could you?' Rebecca said. 'If you tell me how many *miles* of fabric I'll need then I'll go to Beares on Monday and choose something. I'm not four months yet and already I'm the size of a baby elephant.'

'Just as well I adore baby elephants, then,' her husband said, putting his arm around her.

Emma didn't think she'd be able to stand there a second longer, witnessing such love, such joint joy at the thought of the coming baby, knowing that she had no intention whatsoever of telling Matthew he was about to become a father again, albeit with an almost twenty year gap between his children. She couldn't imagine he'd be thrilled at the thought.

'I'll just go and see how Ruby's getting on in the kitchen,' Emma said. 'If you'll excuse me.'

'Of course,' Mrs Bailey said. 'Fleur and I can get to know one another a little better before we depart on our exciting journey.'

It was a much shorter journey for Emma to the kitchen where she found Ruby stuffing something into her mouth.

'Caught you!' Emma said. 'You're no better than you were when you were eighteen years old up at Nase Head House, forever stealing bits in the kitchen.'

Ruby looked mock crestfallen. She carried on chewing. Swallowed. She wiped the corners of her mouth with the back of her hand.

'Go on, Mrs Bossy Boots,' Ruby said, 'tell me off for doin' that an' all.'

Emma wagged a finger playfully at Ruby and shook her head in a there's-nothing-to-be-done-with-you-and-your-bad-manners way.

'The truth is, Em, I ain't 'ad a crab tart like this since you last made 'em for Mr Smythe's weddin'. And this little one 'ere just 'appened to be a bit broken around the edges.'

'Flattery will get you everywhere,' Emma said and laughed.

She'd made far more than she knew would be needed for her guests, and that with the intention of giving Ruby some to take home for the children for the following day.

'Talkin' of Mr Smythe's weddin' an' who was there an' crab tarts—' Ruby began.

'Don't!' Emma said. 'I know where this conversation is heading. And I don't know that I want to continue with it. We need to get these tartlets off the cooling racks and onto serving plates. Then there are the sandwiches to put together. I've done the fillings. They're in the meat safe outside the window.'

Emma pointed to the place on the north side of the house

where the meat safe overhung the garden – a good place to keep things cool, even in summer.

'I'll do 'em,' Ruby said. 'You go an' see to your guests. An' while you're out there doin' that tell my Alice I wants 'er in 'ere givin' me an 'and with things.'

'Thanks, Ruby,' Emma said, impulsively giving her friend a quick hug. 'I'll go in a minute. Thank goodness I've got you.'

Let Ruby read into that what she would.

'You're not regrettin' comin' back 'ere, then, now Fleur's about to fly the nest back to Canada?'

How could Emma answer that? She'd yet to tell Ruby she was expecting Matthew's child. And that it would be best if Fleur didn't know that just yet.

'Hmm,' Ruby said, when Emma was rather slow to answer, 'it seems to me that were one of they pregnant pauses you reads about in romantic books.'

Emma flinched. Of course she knew pregnant pause and a pregnant woman were not the same thing but it was the use of the word – she was only just getting used to it as applied to herself.

'Was it?' Emma said, knowing her voice was higher-pitched than usual.

'Yeah, an' you knows it. An' I knows you. There's another agenda 'ere and I think I knows what it is. You needs to go and see that Matthew Caunter and tell 'im somethin' 'e needs to know. An' you needs to do it sooner rather than later. An' the reason you ain't made an almighty 'oo-'a about Fleur goin' back to Canada is because she won't see things you don't want 'er to see. Not yet, anyway. Am I right?' Ruby returned the hug Emma had given her just moments ago. 'Don't answer that because I knows I'm right. An' I've got a mini mountain of sandwiches to make. But your secret's safe with me. Well, until such times as it won't be secret no more. Oh ...' Ruby's flow of words dried up as a car's tyres scrunched on the gravel outside. She turned round and peered out of the window that overlooked the end of the drive. 'Ireland's delivery van. An' a bloke in a peaked cap 'as just got out and is walkin' this way, 'alf 'idden by an 'uge bunch of roses.'

Ruby began to walk to the back door. Tradesmen's entrance. 'It ain't Fleur's birthday so—'

'I'll go,' Emma said, reaching out an arm to stop her.

'Oh, lawks!' Ruby said, slapping a hand to her forehead. 'Michaelmas. It's your birthday today, ain't it? And I forgot.'

'You being here is the only present I need, really it is.'

But Emma would bet every penny she had in the Devon and Exeter Savings Bank that Matthew Caunter hadn't forgotten. And that the flowers were from him.

He cared. He still cared. *But would he think, if she contacted him now, that it was only because she wanted him to support her? And his child?*

Chapter Twenty-Four

AUTUMN 1927

'Give my love to Mrs Gethin and Delia,' Emma said.

She and Fleur stood in the hallway of Romer Lodge their arms wound tightly around one another. Mrs Bailey had left them alone to say their final goodbyes and was sitting in a taxi on the driveway. But there was plenty of time yet. The train wouldn't be leaving Paignton station for a good half-hour and it was only a five-minute drive to get there. Neither Fleur nor Emma had wanted to say their goodbyes in a public place with everyone looking on.

'No, I won't,' Fleur said. 'Because I'm keeping it all for myself until I see you again. And I don't know that I want to go now.'

'Oh, Fleur, you say the nicest things and you'll have me dripping all over you in a minute. But you are going and it will do you good. I'm proud of you.'

'And me of you, Ma. The way you've built up a business after being snubbed by so many of the neighbours for not having a husband and being a *dangerous*, loose cannon of a woman.'

'Predatory, Fleur. I think they thought I would be a predatory woman, after their husbands, but that's not how I am.'

'No,' Fleur said, releasing herself from Emma's hold and stepping back a little so she could look Emma in the eye.' But you're a stubborn one, and a blinkered one.'

'Blinkered?' Emma said. She knew there was no point in arguing about being stubborn or not because she knew she could be that at times.

'Blinkered,' Fleur repeated. 'Now then, Ma, I want you to make me a promise. Say you will.'

'I need to know what it is first before I can do that. And there's a train waiting ...'

'I know. So here it is – what I want you to promise me. As soon as you hear the steam train chuffing out of the station I want you to pick up the telephone and call Mr Caunter. His number's on the pad by the telephone.'

'I know.' Emma had seen it there, ringed round in blue ink by Fleur a million times.

'I hope you wrote and thanked him for the roses for your birthday.' Fleur wagged a finger playfully at her.

Emma hadn't been able to prevent Fleur seeing the card attached to the flowers because she'd come into the kitchen to ask if she could help just as Emma had taken delivery of them.

'Of course I did. I know my manners. Tom hand-delivered it.'

'Huh,' Fleur said. 'A man who spends that much money on such a big bunch of roses deserves to be thanked face to face, I think, or at least spoken to. Why don't you telephone him? Now that I'll be out of the picture and you'll be free to, well, you know, put someone in Pa's place ...'

'No one could ever take your pa's place, Fleur,' Emma said. 'And that's the truth.'

'But you'll ring Mr Caunter?'

Emma sucked in her cheeks to stop herself from crying. She might not have given birth to Fleur but Fleur had certainly picked up Emma's stubborn streak, the way she wouldn't let an idea go once she got it between her teeth.

'I'll think about it,' Emma said. 'But I'm not going to talk about it with you a second longer.' She reached for Fleur again and hugged her to her. 'Be safe. Be happy. Never, ever, forget how much I love you. Write often. Or telephone and reverse the charges. I love you, Fleur, possibly more than you will ever know.'

'*Au revoir,* Ma' Fleur croaked into Emma's neck, her tears hot and sliding down Emma's skin now. '*Je t'aimes aussi.*'

And the fact Fleur's last words to Emma were in French – the language she had sung to her in as a baby, and which she'd taught her as soon as Fleur could speak – would stay with her forever. Fleur was truly her daughter even though Emma hadn't given birth to her.

She stood in the doorway of Romer Lodge waving and forcing a smile on her face, the tears coursing down her cheeks, long after the taxi with Fleur and Mrs Bailey in it disappeared.

Emma stood there until she heard the steam train's whistle. She turned then and went back into the house. She knew as she climbed to the tower room that had been Fleur's bedroom – her sanctuary after Caroline had turned up in her life – that she would be able to see the train going along the line, skirting the shore, towards Torquay. Something solid seemed to have lodged in Emma's chest that she knew only hard work would shift.

As the train disappeared into the tunnel under the road, Emma kissed the tips of her fingers and blew in the same direction.

And then she ran down the stairs to her atelier.

She had work to do.

The next morning Emma was woken by someone knocking on her front door. What time was it? She'd fallen into a deep sleep the night before because she'd stopped up long into the night sewing. Her sleep had been dreamless – or at least she didn't remember any dreams as she often did.

Wrapping her robe around her and jabbing her feet into a pair of embroidered slippers that had been a present from Fleur, and after putting a brush quickly through her hair, Emma ran down the stairs.

Still with the chain across, she opened the door a crack.

Mrs Passmore.

'I thought you might be needing a bit of company,' Mrs Passmore said, 'seeing as your lovely girl is on a boat by now and ... oh, here's me come to comfort you and it's me who needs comforting. I'm going to miss my sister so, I really am, even though she's a bit holier-than-thou sometimes what with her being a vicar's wife. And ...' Mrs Passmore dabbed at her eyes with a handkerchief.

'You'd better come in,' Emma said. She took the chain off the door and opened it just wide enough to let the not insubstantial form of Mrs Passmore in. 'Go through to the sitting room. I'll just go and make myself more presentable. Five minutes.'

Still dabbing her eyes Mrs Passmore did as she was asked.

Back in her room, Emma was shocked to find it was almost ten o'clock. Thank goodness it was a Sunday and Tom wasn't here to see she'd overslept. She had never, ever in her life before stayed in bed that long. Perhaps it was the child she was carrying making her more tired. Emma had always had boundless energy and she didn't know that she liked the thought of turning into a sleepyhead.

But she took less than the five minutes she'd told Mrs Passmore she would to get changed.

'I'll put the kettle on,' Emma said, peering around the sitting room door. 'And then I'll be with you. And then I'll light a fire in the grate.'

She turned to go but was surprised to find Mrs Passmore following her.

'No need to heat that big room just because I've turned up unannounced. Goodness, but my mother would turn in her grave to know I've called on a neighbour without giving her twenty-four hours notice! What my mother would think of women getting the vote, never mind as young as twenty-one years old, as I see might be going to happen before too long, I don't know. We can drink our tea in your kitchen.'

Emma pulled out a kitchen chair for Mrs Passmore to sit down.

'It was very kind of your sister to accompany Fleur,' Emma said. 'It's a long journey.'

'For both of them,' Mrs Passmore said. 'And trust me Margot will get as much, if not more, from the companionship as Fleur will. And Fleur will put a stop to Margot's flirtatious ways.'

Flirtatious ways? Emma didn't have Margot Bailey down as a flirt. A vicar's wife and all!

'I can see I've shocked you,' Mrs Passmore said. 'But my sister played the field before she settled down with the good reverend. I have to say I was a little concerned that she was going all that way on a ship full of handsome sailors all by herself so I was more than relieved when you mentioned your concerns about how Fleur was going to have a safe, chaperoned passage. Fortuitous, don't you think, how things have turned out?'

Fortuitous? A good word. It was fortuitous that Emma had no morning sickness, but did it follow that it was also fortuitous that she was pregnant and unmarried? She could almost hear dear old Beattie Drew saying, 'You're not the first, lovie, an' you certainly won't be the last. Worse things 'appen at sea.'

Emma swallowed back her emotions.

'Oh, dear,' Mrs Passmore said. 'Me and my ramblings. I've upset you now.'

'You haven't. Not one bit. As you say, fortuitous indeed,' Emma said.

She found some biscuits in a tin in the larder and put some on a plate for Mrs Passmore, knowing the dear lady wouldn't refuse a biscuit whatever the hour. Emma was forever letting clothes out, taking them in again, as

Mrs Passmore failed, or succeeded, with her latest eating regime.

'And how is Mr Passmore this morning?' Emma asked.

'As fine and dandy as a bedridden man can be. Maria is sitting with him. I left her reading the newspaper to him. Tip number one, Mrs Jago, never, ever engage staff who can't read.'

'My friend, Ruby, couldn't read until she was in her twenties,' Emma said, suddenly feeling protective of those less fortunate. 'But she learned so she could read the letters I wrote her when I lived in Canada, and so she could write back. Her husband, Tom, taught her.'

'Ah, yes. Tom. Your gardener.'

'He's not my gardener. He's a friend,' Emma said. 'A friend who happens to help me out by doing the heavy gardening I can't do.'

And certainly won't be able to as this pregnancy progresses.

'Goodness, how times change,' Mrs Passmore said. 'Best not let Mrs Grant hear you say that.'

'I have no intention of it,' Emma said. Mrs Grant had snubbed Emma's invitation to drinks once and she certainly wasn't going to get another invite.

Emma knew she'd gone on the defensive all of a sudden and it troubled her because Mrs Passmore had been a very good client, standing firm in front of less understanding neighbours who didn't like a loose cannon of a widow in their midst. But that, Emma realised now, was because Emma was hardly going to be a threat to Mrs Passmore's bedridden husband, was she?

'Could we get back to, er, Tom?' Mrs Passmore said. 'Does he drive?'

'A bicycle,' Emma said. 'I bought it for him so he could get here more easily from Brixham.'

'I meant a car, dear. Does he drive a car?'

'Not that I know of. Why do you ask?'

'Because the good doctor – Doctor Grenier over in Bishop's Place although he makes home calls, of course, for me and Mr Passmore – has recommended that my husband get some sea air. And that he gets it a bit closer than a little breeze coming in the bedroom window. My husband can walk a little – a few steps to get in and out of a car shouldn't be too much of a problem, but he can't stand for long. So … I was wondering, if I were to buy a car, do you think Tom would drive it for me? A couple of trips out a week to start with? Maybe over to Torquay with a little stroll along the promenade? Or down to Dartmouth and along the quay?'

'I'll put it to him. There's less to do in the garden now that winter is on its way and I'm fast running out of things for Tom to do in the house.'

And he needs the money, Emma thought, but didn't add.

'I knew the first time I met you, Mrs Jago, that we were like minds,' Mrs Passmore said. 'I'm glad I came over this morning and suggested this. You need something to think about now that your daughter has sailed away and this might be the thing. Teaching Tom to drive, I mean.'

Something to think about? If only you knew. I've got a growing baby inside me to think about.

'Yes,' Emma said, her mind in a daze now. As kind as Mrs Passmore was she was something of a steamroller in her approach and Emma knew she was in danger of having her life taken over by the well-meaning woman if she wasn't careful. 'I'm sure I could teach Tom to drive if that's what he wants. But I shall have to ask him first. But tell me, Doctor Grenier – do you recommend him?'

Emma knew she would have to go to a doctor soon to get her pregnancy confirmed, not that she wasn't sure she was pregnant but she would have to do the right thing by her child.

'Once you get past the foreign accent he speaks with, I'm sure you'll get on fine.'

'Accent?'

'Foreign. He can't pronounce the "th" sound. He says "z". Or sometimes "s". But I've got used to it. Although sometimes I've found myself mimicking him without realising I was doing it. So embarrassing!' Mrs Passmore gave a girlish sort of laugh.

'He's French?' Emma said.

Grenier was the French for attic, although Mrs Passmore hadn't pronounced it that way.

'He is. Makes a strange sort of noise in his throat when he pronounces his "r"s as well, but he's a good doctor for all that.'

Emma laughed. 'I'm half French myself so I'm sure Doctor Grenier and I will get on fine.'

And the sooner I see him the better.

'Well, that's all settled,' Mrs Passmore said.

Not quite. I've yet to ask Tom if he wants to learn to drive but thinking about it now, Emma could see it was a good idea. How soon would it be before she couldn't get behind the wheel of her Clyno and would need Tom to fetch things from the shop for her?

'More tea?' Emma asked.

'I've kept you long enough,' Mrs Passmore said. 'So, no, thank you. But there is one more thing? Can you tell me where you bought your car? I would only buy such a thing on recommendation.'

Oh! Emma hadn't been expecting that.

'Only I see there's a garage opened up on Roundham Road. Bay Motors. Run by a chap called Caunter so it says on the sign over the door. Do you know him?'

Oh, yes, I know him. And rather better than you think I might.

'I'll let you have his number,' Emma said.

Chapter Twenty-Five

Eventually Emma could put it off no longer – she had to go and register with a doctor. After her conversation with Mrs Passmore in her kitchen she waited another six weeks before doing so. Winter was well and truly on its way now the clocks had gone back an hour.

Doctor Grenier confirmed what Emma knew. She was with child. As she knew the date – and even the precise time, give or take half an hour – that her child had been conceived she was sure of her due date. Late May. The good doctor told Emma he could hear the heartbeat. He also chided her, gently, for leaving it so long before coming to see him. Emma had felt it move inside her, as though she had trapped wind that couldn't find an exit. The doctor laughed when she told him so.

'*Zut, alors,*' he said, clapping a hand to his forehead. 'Never have I heard an expression like zat to describe it.'

Emma answered him in French which made the good doctor's eyebrows shoot up almost to his hairline. And for the rest of the time Emma was in the surgery they spoke only French. How good it felt, how natural.

Just as Emma was leaving the doctor reverted to English. 'And is your husband thrilled at the prospect of becoming a father?'

'My husband,' Emma said, 'is dead.'

Best to tell the truth. And who better to tell it to than a doctor who had signed the Hippocratic oath?

'Ah.' The doctor steepled his fingers. 'Posthumous. I'm sorry.'

'Not at all,' Emma said. 'Seth died two and a half years ago now. In Canada. But this …' Emma placed her hand on the soft bulge of her stomach '… isn't a problem. I will be keeping the child. It's all I've ever wanted – to have a child of my own, and now ...'

Emma hadn't expected to well with tears because she'd rehearsed this speech all the way to the surgery, but now the words were out of her mouth it felt different somehow.

'Then I will do my utmost to see you are safely delivered of your child.'

And then, in a gesture Emma was certain wasn't in the Hippocratic oath, the doctor leaned towards her and kissed her on both cheeks in the French fashion. '*Bonne chance, madame.*'

I don't need luck, Emma thought, as she left the surgery. *I feel like the luckiest woman alive.*

There were a few loose ends of her life to tie up but when she'd done that, well ... life was there for the taking again, she was sure of it.

Fleur wrote often and seemed happily settled. She was enjoying her course. She had plans to come back for a visit in the summer. With Delia.

So that left just two people with whom Emma needed to make her peace.

Stella.

And Matthew.

In that order.

November was drawing to a close. Tom had a bonfire most days now, putting the garden to bed for the winter, so he said. Emma was kept busy making warm winter clothes – dresses and coats – for her clients. She bought a fur hat in Bobby's in Torquay but so far it hadn't been cold enough to wear it. Certainly it was nothing like as cold here as it had been back in Canada at this time of year. She hoped Fleur was warm enough, and she sent money often so that she could buy gloves and scarves and warm woollen cardigans should she need them.

She adapted a Butterick pattern for herself, moving the single button of the jacket higher so that the fabric below it fell in neat folds, minimising the visual effect of her bump. Rebecca Bailey had placed an order for three dresses and a coat but while she might have noticed the soft mound of Emma's baby she didn't comment on it.

Yes, she was busy but at the back of Emma's mind was the visit from Stella she knew would come. She'd been dreading it and knew Stella would call on her one day – later if not sooner. Stella's shrouded wedding dress was still hanging in Emma's atelier, waiting for her to collect it or tell Emma how she might like it altered for evening wear. Emma knew that Stella was well enough now to continue nursing. She'd told her so in a very short note, letting Emma know she would pay for the dress she'd had made. She'd begun her training to be a sister. And there was the possibility to train as a midwife at a later date.

A midwife? I'll be in need of the care of one of those soon.

Much had happened these past weeks. Fleur had written and telephoned Emma more than Emma had ever dared hoped she would, but Fleur seemed to be settled and happy and enjoying her course.

Mrs Passmore had bought a car and Emma had taught Tom to drive it. And so now, twice a week, Tom drove Mr Passmore out somewhere. Sometimes they were gone all day – as far as Dartmoor with often lunch at a pub in Princetown to sustain them for the return journey.

All Emma could do now was sit tight, keep well, give some serious consideration to what she was going to tell Fleur about the baby she was carrying.

Keep her head above water, as the saying had it.

December passed slowly, oh so slowly for Emma. And then, almost before she knew it, it was Christmas. Emma spent the day with Ruby and her family in Shingle Cottage and it had seemed almost like old times to Emma to be there, everyone squashed up together in the small space. But somehow it was her time spent there with Matthew Caunter that had been uppermost in her mind.

'You're goin' to 'ave to tell 'im,' Ruby had said, when Emma had told her about her baby and who the father was, not that Ruby hadn't guessed. 'Or someone else will.'

'Don't you dare!' Emma had said.

'What an' risk my life at your fair 'ands,' Ruby had joked.

But Emma had left Ruby's with the promise she *would* tell Matthew. It was finding the right time to do it that was the problem. And that time hadn't presented itself yet.

The ring of the doorbell startled Emma from her thoughts. Matthew? Her heart fluttered at the thought. So far she'd managed to avoid seeing him at his premises in Roundham Road by not driving that way, even though she had to drive the long way around to get to Romer Lodge. She took a deep breath and walked into the hall.

No, not Matthew. It was Stella. She could tell Stella's tall form, and the slimness of her, through the stained glass of the front door.

'Oh,' Stella said as Emma opened the door to let her in.

'Oh, indeed,' Emma said. There was no hiding her bump now, and the way it made her waddle a bit when she walked. 'Come in. If you still want to.'

There was no need to tell Stella that Matthew was the father of her child. She ached to see him. She wished now she'd let her heart rule her head that afternoon in the park in Shiphay when she'd told Matthew she needed time, and he said he had plenty of it. But pride wouldn't let her go to see him, or telephone him, or answer his telephone calls.

But she had a feeling he was still looking out for her. Sometimes she got that feeling, when she was walking along the promenade taking her daily exercise, or standing in the queue in the Post Office that she was being watched. But when she turned around there was never anyone there that she knew, or anyone looking at her at all in fact. But it wasn't an uncomfortable feeling – it made her feel safe somehow.

'I do,' Stella said.

Emma stepped aside to let her in. 'Atelier or sitting room?'

If they went into the atelier then Emma would be in control, could make suggestions about how to alter Stella's wedding dress. But if they went into the sitting room, well … who knew which way the conversation would go?

'Sitting room, I think,' Stella answered. 'Lead the way.'

'I'm so glad you're well again,' Emma said, having to say something. And it was the truth – she *was* pleased to see Stella looking so well. And to see that Stella had put on a little weight – she was less gaunt than she had been the last time Emma had seen her.

'I'm fine,' Stella said. 'But less about me, more about you. Have you seen a doctor?'

'Yes. Doctor Grenier. He's French.'

Stella laughed. 'It doesn't matter what nationality he is. Delivering women scream in every language!'

Emma couldn't help but giggle. 'That isn't really boosting my confidence!'

And how easily we seem to be slipping back into our old, yet blossoming, friendship.

'No,' Stella said, looking more serious again now. 'What are you? Six months?'

'It's due at the end of May.'

And we don't need to do the mathematics, do we? We both know Matthew and I made this child together when he was engaged to you and when you were lying close to death.

'Does Matthew know?'

There. His name had been mentioned and Emma had taken the coward's way out and let Stella say it.

'I haven't told him, no.'

'But you think someone else might have done?'

'I don't know. Before Fleur went back to Canada he rang almost daily. Fleur always took those calls and every day I refused to speak to him. I don't know that I'll ever be able to forgive him for ... for being with me when you were so ill in the hospital.'

'Forgive him,' Stella said. 'I have. That's not an order, of course.' Stella laughed easily enough.

Forgive him?

'I've forgiven him, in my heart, for this,' Emma said, cradling her unborn child in her arms. 'It's a dream come true.'

'Good. Did he leave messages?'

'Sometimes. He told Fleur that the man with Caroline had been deported, and that Caroline was in custody. I was never far from the telephone and often overheard.

Fleur always gave me a withering look and said, "My mother is indisposed."'

Stella laughed. 'Girls that age are good at withering looks,' she said. 'Does Fleur know? About the baby, I mean.'

'Not yet.' Emma ran the palm of her hand over her bump and the baby stretched at the touch. 'I don't know how to tell her.'

'And does Matthew still telephone you?'

'Yes. Most days. I think he does it just to make sure I'm here. I have to answer the telephone myself now, of course, and I have to answer it in case it's a client. Or Fleur. But I always answer it in a disguised voice and if it's Matthew, then I pretend to be the maid and say "The mistress isn't in". I haven't got a maid.'

'Then you're a silly goose,' Stella said. 'Not to be

without a maid, I don't mean that, but that you haven't told Matthew. Although I can't think for a minute that he doesn't know. Not after all the surveillance work he did when he was younger.'

'No,' Emma said. 'That thought occurred to me.'

'Tell me about when you first met Matthew,' Stella said, her voice gentle and encouraging. 'Before you went to Canada. Were you lovers then?'

'No! I was underage when I first became Matthew's housekeeper. And then, just before I left for Canada with Seth I saw him again. Babies didn't happen for Seth and me, well ...'

Emma knew she ought to be offering Stella tea, or a glass of sherry, or some sort of welcoming drink but instead she told Stella about her time with Matthew – a time that had never left her heart, not really.

'And it was only the once,' she finished, wrapping her arms over her growing child. 'With Matthew. To make him. Or her.'

'It's all it takes sometimes,' Stella said, smiling so benignly at Emma that Emma felt forgiven for stealing Stella's fiancé away, however unknowingly. 'But I hope you don't think I've overstepped the mark, asking you such private things?'

'I'm glad you have. I wanted to tell you but I didn't know how. I valued the friendship we'd begun and then I went and ruined it.'

'You haven't ruined anything. The threads of our friendship might have been frayed a little by what's happened but they haven't broken I don't think. Do you?'

'No. I'm a seamstress. I'm good at repairing things.'

'Then put in a stitch or two to repair things with Matthew. And that is an order!'

'Yes, sister!' Emma said.

'Joking apart,' Stella said, 'he loves you. I knew in an

instant that day in the hospital when you turned up and found him sitting there. His eyes couldn't leave you.'

There was little emotion showing on Stella's face and Emma guessed that that was merely the medical professional in her, but that deep down, inside, she had to feel hurt by it all. How could she not?

'Who else knows?' Stella asked. 'Apart from Doctor Grenier, and now me?'

'My friend, Ruby, knows. And her husband, Tom. I think my neighbour, Mrs Passmore, has guessed but she never comments when she comes for fittings. New clients assume I've got a husband around somewhere and I choose not to elaborate. So ...' Emma threw her arms wide and shrugged.

'So, you're in a pickle.'

'I've been in worse ones.'

'You don't have to wear sackcloth and ashes for ever, Emma,' Stella told her. 'I don't hold a grudge against you, or why would I be here?' Stella held up a hand to indicate she hadn't finished what she wanted to say. 'No, don't answer that. And pickles leave a sour taste in the mouth. Are you understanding me?'

Blimey – I've met my match in Stella Martin, haven't I? And this is a lecture I've been needing. I've been feeling monumentally sorry for myself, haven't I?

'Yes. I *will* tell Matthew, but not yet.'

'And I'm going to have to take your word for it?'

'You are. But I am more grateful to you than you will ever know over this. I've been hating myself for what I did to another woman—'

'Stop! It takes two. I know that with impunity now I'm on my midwifery course.' Stella said it as a joke but Emma didn't find it funny. 'And you wouldn't have succumbed to what I know are Matthew's not inconsiderable charms had you known he was engaged to me at the time.'

'Well, of course I wouldn't have,' Emma said.

'There we are then. You're absolved of all blame. But if you'll take my advice, once you've finished breastfeeding, you'll make Matthew do the night shift.' Again there was jokiness in Stella's voice and yet it was heartbreaking for Emma to hear it.

'You're a saint, you know that,' Emma said.

'Not entirely,' Stella said with a grin. 'There's this doctor at the hospital. He —'

'Don't tell me!' Emma said. He was married. She knew it. Probably with a wife who was an invalid or a stewed prune as the saying had it in Devon for a wife who was frigid. But Emma didn't want to know.

'He's probably all the things you're thinking of him.' Stella laughed. 'He's seen me at my worst. Matthew met him that day when I was taken so ill. But he's good for me, and I love him, and he loves me ... despite everything.'

'What's his name?'

Had I asked what your fiancé was called when first we'd met this scenario wouldn't be happening, would it?

'Simon Taylor. And I think you've guessed it! He's married. His wife is a Catholic and won't even think about divorce. But all is not lost. This way, I can remain a nurse, get further qualifications and I'll be giving and receiving love as I do it. And he wants to take me dancing at the Imperial Hotel in Torquay. So, that dress ... lead me to it. It seems a long time since I've seen it. I'm thinking perhaps you could alter it into something for me to do the Charleston in. A bit of fringing, perhaps? Life goes on.'

Indeed it does. God, but it was good to have Stella back in her life.

Matthew next. A man who telephoned so regularly wasn't thinking of abandoning her, was he? *And after what Stella has just told me about the way he looked at me ... oh yes, Matthew next.* But only when she was ready.

Chapter Twenty-Six

Emma gave birth to a daughter – a little earlier than expected – on Sunday, April 15th at 2.37 a.m. in the cottage hospital in Paignton.

'*The child that is born on the Sabbath day, is bonnie and blithe and good and gay,*' the sister midwife quoted. 'And I don't know when I've been at an easier birth than that, Mrs Jago.'

'Nor me.' Emma laughed. 'For which something tells me I must be grateful.'

Ruby had told her all sorts of horror stories about pain and discomfort and how your baby can embarrass you before he or she is born in all sorts of ways but none of it applied to Emma.

'She's a good weight,' the midwife said. She had Emma's daughter in a cotton sling suspended from a chain on top of which was a measure. 'Six pounds, twelve ounces. Ten fingers, ten toes. Heartbeat's good and strong and ...' The baby yelled then, long and loud. 'And a good set of lungs on her. And the longest legs I think I've ever seen on a newborn.'

The midwife finished her weighing, wrapped the baby in a gauze cloth, then a cotton blanket, and handed her to Emma. A nurse in the room bustled about clearing away the waxed paper that had been on the delivery bed and tipping away jugs of water that hadn't been used.

'It's a changing world she's been born into,' the midwife said. 'Did you see in the newspapers that two Frenchmen have flown around the world?'

'No,' Emma said. 'I was a bit too occupied to be reading

newspapers. I hadn't got a thing ready for little miss here, and she caught me by surprise.'

But if men had flown around the world it wouldn't be long before aeroplanes were going back and forth across the Atlantic and she would be on one of them, with her baby, to visit Fleur just as soon as she could.

'That's daughters for you,' the midwife said, taking a thermometer from her breast pocket and giving it a shake. 'Temperature.' She held it out towards Emma, and Emma accepted it in the corner of her cheek, holding it under her tongue. And while she waited the required time for there to be a reading, Emma gazed at her daughter. What else was there to do? Could there be anything better to do at that moment?

'Amazingly perfect,' the midwife said. 'I only hope life for you and this little one goes on as well as it has started. Doctor Grenier tells me you are, er, alone with this child.'

'For the moment. But alone isn't lonely, sister. I have friends. Good friends.'

Who don't judge me, she could have added, but didn't. Yes, a few of her clients had stopped their custom once they'd discovered Emma was a widow and pregnant, but there would be new ones coming along before too long, she was sure of it.

'Good. We all need those.'

The midwife left Emma and her daughter alone then – another mother had gone into labour and her services were required. Two nurses came in after a few moments and helped her into a wheelchair and a porter came and wheeled Emma, her baby in her arms, back to a side ward. A private room.

'A nurse'll be along shortly to help you into bed,' the porter said.

'I'm fine here,' Emma told him. 'But can you tell me where there's a public telephone? In the hospital, I mean.'

'In the corridor outside matron's office. I can wheel you there if you like. You might have to wait for someone to wheel you back though.'

'I'll be able to wait,' Emma said. She was starting to get tired now. Her labour hadn't been as long as the doctor had told her it might be, given her age and the fact it was her first child, but she'd still gone the night without sleep. 'Wheel me away.'

Emma had to wait for the church bells to stop ringing before she could make herself heard. She telephoned Ruby first, glad now that she'd gone to the expense of having a telephone installed in Shingle Cottage for Ruby and Tom. The whoops and squeals of delight on the other end of the telephone could, Emma was sure of it, be heard all over the hospital. Ruby promised to visit as soon as she could.

'But not today,' Ruby said. 'There's a certain person who needs to see you first. An' if you don't telephone 'im, I will, you stubborn bugger.'

'Ruby!' Emma said, laughing.

'Careful. You'll burst your stitches.'

'I haven't got any.'

'Then you're a stubborn, *lucky*, bugger.' Ruby laughed. 'An' I'm puttin' down this telephone to free the line so you can make that call.'

Emma replaced the receiver, waited a few moments, then picked it up again. No need to have Matthew's number written down. She dialled.

'You took your time making that telephone call,' Matthew said, a huge smile on his face, making him look so much younger than a man who was well into his forties. Emma never had known his exact age, not that it mattered. 'You left Romer Lodge at ten o'clock last evening. By taxi. And it's now ...'

Matthew looked at his watch and Emma took advantage.

'It was a textbook birth, actually,' Emma said, suddenly not tired, and not minding Matthew's teasing at all. 'But don't tell me. You've been spying on me.'

'I prefer to call it protection. And for the record you've cost me a fortune in telephone calls. "*I'm so sorry, Mrs Jago isn't available at the moment.*"' Matthew mimicked the voice Emma had used every time she answered the telephone.

'Mrs Jago can pay you back. And she's available now,' Emma said, softly.

'Not that I mind the cost of a few hundred telephone calls,' Matthew said, which made Emma think he hadn't heard her. 'Not now I've taken the one I wanted to hear. I don't think I've ever driven as fast before.'

'Well, you certainly didn't waste any time getting here,' Emma said, a huge grin on her face she knew would be there for hours, if not days. Years even. Goodness, but it was wonderful to be able to look at him. It was as though the time since she'd last seen him was no more than the puff off a dandelion clock. 'Indecent haste, I'd call it. Who did you have to charm to let you in?'

Matthew tapped the side of his nose.

'Once a surveillance officer, always a surveillance officer, eh?' Emma grinned at him.

'Once an independent little firebrand, always an independent little firebrand, eh?'

'Touché,' Emma said. 'Meet your daughter.'

She held out the baby towards Matthew, but he didn't take his daughter from her. Emma shivered a little. Was Matthew going to say he wanted her, but not the baby?

'I'm keeping her. I know it's not the done thing, but I'm keeping her. She's got your legs. Sister midwife Brumfield said so.'

'Did she now? I don't remember a sister midwife Brumfield seeing my legs.'

Matthew leaned over the top of the baby in Emma's arms and kissed her gently on the lips.

'Oh, you!' Emma said. 'I meant that she said the baby's legs are long. Your legs are long. Don't you want to hold your daughter?'

'I'd rather hold you first. It's been too long.'

'I know. But I was cross with you.'

'I know. A term of penal servitude isn't as long as I've had to wait for you not to be cross with me any more. Just as well I'm a patient man.'

'Hah!' Emma said. 'You weren't the afternoon we made her.'

She kissed the top of her now sleeping daughter's head. How good it was to have Matthew in the same room as her and to have slipped back into their easy banter.

'You started it if I remember rightly.'

Oh, yes, I remember. A thought crossed Emma's mind – how soon would they be able to make love again, given she'd just given birth? And was that a normal sort of thought to be having?

'The best afternoon's work I ever did,' Emma said.

'I'll drink to that,' Matthew said. 'We both will when I get you out of here. I'll stop off at Tolchard's on the way home and buy some champagne.'

Champagne. Emma had first drunk champagne with Matthew back in 1909 when she'd been just fifteen years old. And now it was as though the years in between then and now had never been and she was going to be drinking champagne again with him very soon.

'They won't let me out for days.'

'They will if I tell them I'm engaging nurses and the very best medical care money can buy to look after you.'

'I can—'

'Stop!' Matthew held up a hand. 'We mustn't argue in front of our daughter.'

Emma laughed. 'She's asleep. Not that I want to argue with you.'

'She?' Matthew said. 'Hasn't she got a name yet?'

'Rachel,' Emma said. 'I'd like to call her Rachel. After my mother. And I'd like for her to have Jago as a second Christian name, so that when she grows up and marries she'll still have Jago as a name. For Fleur's sake as much as anything. If you don't object, that is.'

'Why would I object? Seth Jago loved you and cared for you when I couldn't and he made a wonderful job of it, so it's only fitting. Besides, you could call her Cherry Blossom Boot Polish for all I care as long as she has Caunter for a surname.'

'Cherry Blossom Boot Polish? Have you been at the champagne already?' Emma laughed. 'And is that a proposal?'

Matthew dropped down onto one knee. He leaned forward, putting his arms around Emma and their baby.

'Emma, darling, will you do me the honour of becoming my wife?'

Gosh, Matthew was full of surprises. She hadn't expected for a second that he would respond to her cheeky remark quite so quickly. But there was only one answer, wasn't there?

'I will.'

They sealed their union with the gentlest of kisses.

'How soon will you be fit enough to stand in front of a registrar?' Matthew asked. 'How soon can you rustle up a pretty frock to marry me in?'

'I'd stand in front of the registrar tomorrow as long as you held onto my arm, propped me—'

'Try and stop me!' Matthew interrupted.

'I might need a week or so for the dress. It would be nice if Fleur could be here for the wedding but crossing the Atlantic this time of year probably isn't a good idea. I haven't told her about Rachel Jago yet—'

'Rachel Jago Caunter,' Matthew said. 'And Harry is going to get a shock when he realises his old man can still get —'

'Matthew!' Emma said. She put her hands over the baby's ears. 'You're going to have to watch what you say from now on.'

'I love you. I love you. I love you,' Matthew said. 'Is that allowed?'

'Pardon?' Emma laughed, feigning deafness.

'I love you!' Matthew shouted. 'And I don't care if matron hears that and comes running to tell me to pipe down, and brings the hospital board with her.'

Emma reached a hand out to Matthew and pressed a forefinger to his lips. 'And I love you.'

There, she'd said it. What had been in her heart for a long time was out there now dancing in the air between them, hovering over their baby daughter – a bridge, protecting her, keeping her safe.

Keeping them all safe. For ever.

'But before we go anywhere …'

Matthew put his hand in his pocket and pulled out something he was holding tightly in his fist. Slowly he unfolded his fingers to reveal Emma's amethyst necklace, the one that had been her mother's.

'You've kept it safe for me all these years,' Emma said.

'Do you remember what you said when you left it in my keeping?'

'That one day I hope to find you again. And when that day comes, you can – if you're a free man and I'm a free woman – put it around my neck for me.'

Emma knew, word for word, what she had said.

'And it's amen to all that,' Matthew said.

He walked to stand behind Emma's chair and placed the chain with the amethyst on it around her neck and did up the clasp.

'I'll never part with it,' Emma said. 'Or with you.'

Epilogue

28th APRIL 1928

What a difference a year makes.

When Emma telephoned Fleur to tell her about Rachel's arrival, Fleur had whooped with delight and promised to come back in June when the weather would be warmer and the seas calmer. She had, she said, guessed – a woman's intuition, so she'd said.

Matthew's son, Harry, had taken the news with disbelief, but it had rapidly turned to delight. He, too, promised to visit as soon as he could.

Matthew did as he'd said he would, and engaged a nurse to live in at Romer Lodge until Emma was back to full strength. Emma had countered that that wouldn't be long – she was as strong as a horse.

'Well, thank goodness you don't look like one!' Matthew had laughed.

So, on April 28th, Emma and Matthew married, by special licence, at the registry office in Totnes. Ruby was Emma's witness and William was Matthew's. Just the four of them standing in front of the registrar. Afterwards, Tom joined them, along with William's fiancée, Eve Benjafield, and with two-week old baby Rachel in a wicker basket, they all went to the Royal Seven Stars for lunch.

'To my beautiful wife,' Matthew said, raising his glass of champagne high over his head. 'Who, of course, has to respond with a toast of her own and say, "To my handsome husband".'

'Who's that then?' Emma said, with a giggle, happy almost beyond belief.

Everybody laughed. They chinked glasses.

'To absent friends,' Ruby said, looking at Emma ... possibly, Emma thought, thinking of Stella Martin. 'And to absent family.'

To Seth. Emma lifted her glass in a silent toast to Seth.

'To absent friends,' Matthew said. His eyes met Emma's. *He knows who I'm thinking about, doesn't he? I'll never be able to keep anything secret from him, not that I'll want to.* 'And to Fleur and Harry. And to the memory of Seth.'

'To Seth,' Emma said.

They all clinked glasses again, and everyone started talking at once.

'And to our darling daughter,' Emma whispered to herself. She sipped at the champagne. 'And to all that life will bring her.'

It might not be a smooth ride, but Emma hoped with all her heart it would be. Rachel might have been born into wealth but wealth could be lost in a heartbeat, Emma knew that.

But there was one thing her daughter was never going to go short of.

Love.

About the Author

Linda Mitchelmore

Linda has lived in Devon all her life, where the wonderful
scenery and history give her endless ideas for novels
and short stories. Linda has 300 short stories published
worldwide and has also won, or been short-listed,
in many short-story writing competitions.
In 2004 she was awarded The Katie Fforde Bursary
by the Romantic Novelists' Association. In 2011
she won the Short Story Radio Romance Prize.

Married to Roger for over 40 years, they have two
grown-up children and two grandchildren. As well as
her writing, Linda loves gardening, walking, cycling and
riding pillion on her husband's vintage motorbikes.

Emma and her Daughter is Linda's third
novel in the Emma series and sequel to
Emma – There's No Turning Back.

Follow Linda –
on Facebook: https://www.facebook.com/linda.mitchelmore
and Twitter: https://twitter.com/lindamitchelmor

More Choc Lit

From Linda Mitchelmore

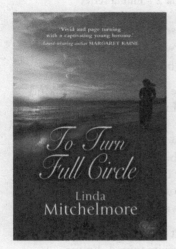

To Turn Full Circle

Book 1 – Emma series

Life in Devon in 1909 is hard and unforgiving, especially for young Emma Le Goff, whose mother and brother die in curious circumstances, leaving her totally alone in the world. While she grieves, her callous landlord Reuben Jago claims her home and belongings.

His son Seth is deeply attracted to Emma and sympathises with her desperate need to find out what really happened, but all his attempts to help only incur his father's wrath.

When mysterious fisherman Matthew Caunter comes to Emma's rescue, Seth is jealous at what he sees and seeks solace in another woman. However, he finds that forgetting Emma is not as easy as he hoped.

Matthew is kind and charismatic, but handsome Seth is never far from Emma's mind. Whatever twists and turns her life takes, it seems there is always something – or someone – missing.

Visit www.choc-lit.com for more details, or simply scan barcode using your mobile phone QR reader.

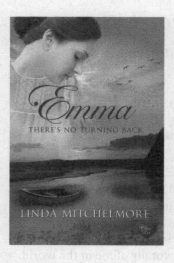

Emma – There's No Turning Back

Book 2 – Emma series

It isn't easy to look forward when the past is so close behind you

Life hasn't always been kind to Emma Le Goff. She has had her fair share of hardship and now finally, her life appears to be looking up. She and her childhood sweetheart, Seth Jago, are set to marry and both believe that an idyllic existence, free from heartache, awaits them.

However, when they discover that the past is more difficult to forget than they could have ever imagined, Emma continues to be haunted by the mysterious circumstances surrounding her family, and Seth is hounded by a jealous ex-lover set on revenge.

Seth plans for their escape to Canada, but when the charismatic Matthew Caunter returns to Devon, Emma finds herself uncertain of whether a move to Canada is really what she wants …

Visit www.choc-lit.com for more details, or simply scan barcode using your mobile phone QR reader.